Maybe We Can FAKE IT

Tammy Subia

AUTHOR'S NOTE

While the overall tone of this book is light, it does deal with topics that
may be potentially upsetting for some readers.
POTENTIAL SPOILERS AHEAD.

Loss of parents (off-page, in past)
Loss of best friend (off-page)
Discussion of possible homophobia

For anyone who cries at Luke's speech in the last episode of Gilmore Girls: A Year in the Life.

And for anyone who has read and supported Heartbreak Honey. It means everything to me. (Hope you enjoy the references.)

PROLOGUE

BRENDEN

I hate hospitals.

Hospitals smell like sick people, they have ugly fluorescent lights that highlight the sick people's sick faces, and people go into hospitals and don't come out. That's what happened to my parents less than a year ago, and now it's happening again. To my best friend.

I can't lose April too. I can't.

But I'm going to.

And knowing it ahead of time doesn't make it any easier.

Although I guess there's no easy way to lose people. Whether it's sudden like a car crash or slowly like with a terminal disease . . . the ending is the same.

The nurse at the desk points me toward the correct wing, and I steel myself before walking through the giant automatic doors. As much as I don't want to do this, I need to remember that this isn't about me. This is about April, and she wants to see me. I want to see her too, only I'm worried that I won't be able to hold it together in front of her.

Since hearing the news, the final verdict—*about a month to live*—I've cried so much that hopefully I'll have no tears left to spill in front of her.

Losing my parents at twenty years old was the worst thing to ever happen to me. But April was there for me through that. She's been there for me most of my life. When I came out in eighth grade, she was the one who got the bullies to back off me after she kneed Jeremy Mathers in the balls and made him cry. I finally managed to find my stride in high school, but then I was nervous about starting college and she was right there beside me, matching her class schedule up with mine.

Now I have to say goodbye.

I didn't get the chance to say goodbye to my parents. The paramedics were able to extract them both from the car, but they died shortly after reaching the hospital. And while I spent so many days after they were gone thinking up all the things I would've said to them if I'd had time, I can't think of one single thing I want to say to April now.

Except *please don't go.*

Today isn't the day for goodbye speeches, though. Today I just need to show up for her. The way she's done for me countless times in my life.

I reach the outside of room 403 and pause. Deep breath.

All right, I can do this.

I knock tentatively on the doorframe and hear a chorus of permission to enter.

Stepping into the room, my eyes scan everything—the sterile white walls, empty cabinets, beeping machines, wires and plastic tubing, April's parents sitting beside each other in two armchairs in the corner, the wriggling baby in Elise's lap—before I force myself to look at my best friend.

She's pale, lying propped up in the hospital bed in one of those ugly white gowns with a weird pattern. Her hair is dyed light pink, a change from the teal it was two weeks ago, the last time I saw her. It almost makes me laugh.

"Nice hair," I say, barely able to keep my voice from cracking.

She smiles. "What? You think just because I'm sick, that means I'll get boring?"

"No." I swallow around the lump in my throat. "You could never be boring."

A small sigh comes from her mom in the corner, and it's hard to say what that means. The Richardsons were always kind of strict. Or maybe not strict, exactly, but they liked conformity. And that clashed with April's deep-seated desire to be original. She used to get in trouble for things like dying her hair without permission, but she did it anyway. Now I'd wager her parents would happily let her do whatever she wanted if that would only stop this disease from taking her.

"Too bad I won't be able to convince you to get that tattoo with me," April says.

The tiny laugh that escapes me is pained. She's been on me about getting a tattoo since we both turned eighteen. I'm all for every person decorating their body however they choose, but needles terrify me, so I always told her there was no chance of that happening.

But you know what? I'd walk out of here, find the nearest tattoo shop, and get a full sleeve right now if that would be enough to save her.

"Brenden," Grant, her father, says, "why don't you take this chair? I've been sitting for days. My legs could use a stretch."

I murmur a thanks when he brings it over to me so I can sit by April's bed.

"Maybe you two should go get something to eat," April tells her parents.

"Oh, no, we're not hungry," Elise says.

"Mom." April fixes her with the best threatening stare I assume a person could pull off from a hospital bed. "I want to talk to my best friend alone."

Elise looks torn between giving her daughter whatever she wants and not letting her out of her sight for even a minute. Which is understandable. May is wriggling even harder in her lap now, trying desperately to stand up with her tiny fifteen-month-old legs.

Yes, April named her daughter May. She thought it was funny. And she said if she ever has another girl, she'll name her June.

Guess that's not going to happen.

She also chose the name May as a bit of an homage to this small town in New England that she and her parents used to go to every couple years when she was younger. While she's never had the greatest relationship with her parents and tends to avoid spending time with them if she can, she loved those vacations. The town must be some kind of magical place.

"Come on, Elise," Grant says, gesturing toward the door. "I can't remember the last time we ate."

Elise glances once more at April, frowns, and then stands, cradling May to her chest. She walks around the bed to meet her husband by the door, and May starts flapping her arms in my direction as they get closer, so I wave to her.

"Hey, sweet girl."

"*Bren.*"

Despite my mood coming in here, I grin. She can't really say my name yet, but damn if it doesn't melt my heart hearing her try.

When Elise takes her past me, she lets out a sharp cry and fusses more in her grandmother's arms, struggling to get down.

"Oh, no, *shhh*," Elise tries to soothe her.

"I can take her," I say, standing up. "I'm sure the two of you could use a break."

Elise's face pinches. She looks uneasy, despite the fact that I've been around May since the day she was born. Before then, I had no experience with babies. But neither did April. We figured it out together.

"I don't know," Elise says. "That's not . . ."

"*Mom.*"

Elise's eyes swing to April again before she relents and hands May over to me. I take her carefully, propping one arm under her butt and wrapping my other securely around her back. Elise still looks unhappy with this, but finally she steps back.

"We'll be right in the cafeteria if you need us," Grant says, reaching for his wife's arm.

Once they leave, I sit back down in the uncomfortable chair with May. She's quieted down now and is smiling at me. I stand her up with her tiny feet on my thighs, holding her under her armpits to keep her steady. God, I love this girl.

April watches me and her daughter together with a combination of fondness and sadness in her eyes.

Having a baby at nineteen certainly wasn't something April intended. College life had given her a first real taste of freedom, which kind of got the best of her—there was a lot of partying and random hookups. But that freedom didn't last long when she got pregnant and decided to keep her baby. Suddenly, she was dropping out of school and back home living with her parents (who surprisingly didn't disown her), ready to do whatever it took to raise May.

If you ask her, though, I bet she'll say she hasn't regretted her choice for even a minute. She loves May with everything she has.

And now . . .

Fuck.

Now she won't get to see her daughter grow up. And poor May won't even remember her.

These thoughts bring the tears I didn't think I had left to my eyes. I try to hold them back as May pouts at me, reaching out and poking my face with her stubby fingers. Sucking in a deep breath, I force a smile for her, and her eyes light up as she coos.

"I need to ask you something."

I shift my gaze to April. "Yeah?"

"I want you to be May's guardian."

"What does that mean?" I ask, distracted by May bouncing on my thighs.

"Brenden." April's serious tone yanks my focus back to her. "I'm asking if you'll adopt her and raise her once I'm gone."

Everything in the room goes still and silent. Or maybe the low beeping of the machines has been drowned out by the sudden whirring noise in my head. May stops bouncing, as if she's just as stunned by her mother's words as I am.

"You want . . ." I say. "Adopt . . . I . . ."

"I know it's a monumental thing to ask of you. It's way more than I have the right to. But . . ." She pauses, gestures vaguely at her own body in the bed, at the machines she's hooked up to, and lets out a small, humorless laugh. "But I'm dying. So I'm asking you anyway, because I need to."

At her bluntness, the ability to speak finally comes back to me. "But why me? What about your parents? That doesn't make any sense. Obviously, they'll raise her."

She glances down at her arm, drawing my attention to the bruising on the inside of her elbow. They must be sticking a lot of needles through there. Selfishly, I'm glad I haven't been here to witness it. "They could. But I don't want them to. I want you to do it."

"*Why?*" I ask again, a sharp tinge of desperation on the word. I'm twenty-one. I'm not ready to be a father.

"Because you love her."

My eyes swing back to May's perfect face. The blue eyes, the chubby cheeks. Of course I love her, but that doesn't mean I'd be the best parent for her. I have one more year of college, and then . . . Well, I don't know, really. My future has always felt like this entirely vague concept, something I didn't need to have all figured out ahead of time. I've always had this idealistic belief that I'd just somehow end up where I was supposed to.

"And she already loves you," April continues, making this totally crazy idea begin to sound slightly less crazy with every word. "Yes, I know my parents love her, and I know they'd keep her healthy and safe and provided for."

"They'd be able to provide for her better than I would," I say. "They'd know what they're doing."

She shakes her head. "Brenden, I *know* you're the right choice. She deserves more than just a roof over her head and food to eat. If she grows up to be anything like me, she's going to need someone who will understand her, who won't try to force her into some bullshit societal role she doesn't want. I want my daughter to grow up in a house filled with music and games and laughter. I want her to be healthy, but also to know that sometimes it's okay to have cookies for dinner."

I laugh despite how much I want to cry. This can't be happening. How is it fair that this little girl in my arms is going to grow up without ever really knowing her mother? How is it possible that I'm about to lose my best friend right after I lost my parents?

How am I supposed to survive in this world alone?

"I . . ."

"Please think about it," she says. "Sometimes you doubt yourself, but you're strong as hell. And I know May will be strong too if you teach her how."

To prove her point, May starts marching in place in tiny little steps atop my thighs. My need to hold tightly to her right now for my own comfort is overwhelming, but I resist the desire to crush her small body against me.

"What if I mess it up?" I ask, my voice breaking pathetically on the end.

April smiles at me, and for a moment, I imagine she's not sick. She's just my best friend, and we're talking about something silly, like whether that cute guy in my economics class was flirting with me or not. "As long as you love her," she assures me, "you can't mess it up."

My mind is racing with thoughts of what I'd need to do. If I could stay in school, do I have enough money from my parents' estate to hire a nanny, would I trust anyone else with May, is Philadelphia the safest place to raise a child . . . And under all this is the horrible thought that I'd be doing everything alone. Because April would be gone.

A choked sob escapes me, startling May. I gently hug her to my chest before she starts to cry, and I stare at April, struggling to hold back my own tears. "I don't want you to leave me."

"I know," she says softly.

And fuck, I'm a piece of shit, making this about me. It's not, it's not, it's not. She should be the one who gets to cry, not me.

But she's not crying. She looks calm, her eyes moving gently between her daughter's face and mine. And then she says, "I've had time to think about this. There's not much to do in this bed besides think. So if you need time too, I understand. But Brenden. I don't only want you to have May because I know she'll need you. I want you to have her because I know you'll need her. Once I'm gone, I don't want you to be alone."

Oh god. The fact that she's thinking about me at a time like this, that she's worrying about me when she's the one going through something terrible, is why I love her so damn much. It's why I don't know what I'll do or how I'll make it without her.

But then I look at the baby in my lap who has brought me so much joy since the day she was born. And with a sudden clarity, I realize what I'm seeing right in front of me.

My future.

"Okay," I say, and the floor feels solid beneath me for the first time since walking into this hospital room. "I'll be her father."

CHAPTER ONE

BRENDEN

TWELVE YEARS LATER

*D*aaaaad!"

I groan as I stumble down the stairs with half-open eyes, still buttoning my work shirt. Mornings aren't my strong suit.

"What?" I ask when I reach the kitchen.

My daughter turns to me with a mug of coffee clutched in both hands and raises her eyebrows like she's surprised to see me standing here. As if she didn't just yell for me like the damn house was on fire. "Nothing. I didn't hear you get up, so I wanted to make sure you weren't gonna be late for work."

Fixing her with a cold stare, I say, "I was up. I know how to set an alarm."

She holds my stare, unfazed. "You also know how to throw your phone across the room so hard it breaks, thereby turning off the alarm."

I open my mouth to argue, then snap it shut, because she's got me there. I did do that. But in my defense, it was only *one* time. Paying for a new phone taught me my lesson.

May smiles and extends her arms, holding the coffee out to me like a peace offering.

Taking it, I say, "Thanks, kid." As I step past her, I pause to press a kiss to the side of her head. "Do you want cereal or Toaster Strudels?"

"Did you remember to buy more of the raspberry ones?"

"Yup," I tell her, preening a little. See? Even though my thirteen-year-old daughter feels responsible for making sure I get up in the morning, I'm totally nailing this parenting thing.

"Then I'll have those, please," she says, as she goes over to pour herself another coffee from the pot. "And Dad?"

"Yeah?"

"You buttoned your shirt wrong."

Damn it.

After tossing a couple frozen pastries into the toaster, I fix my shirt. Then I grab a plate and wait for the strudels to pop up. When they do, I attempt to grab them, doing that hot potato routine where it takes a few times of dropping them back because they're too hot before I manage to get them out of the toaster. I've just finished spreading the icing on top when my phone rings.

I don't know who would be calling me this early unless there's something wrong at work. Setting May's plate on the table in front of her, I slide my phone out of my pocket and answer without checking the screen. "Hello?"

"Hi, Brenden!" replies a voice much too wide awake and chipper for this early in the morning.

I manage not to sigh. "Elise. It's good to hear from you."

That's a lie, but May's head perks up at her grandmother's name. I'm sure she's happy to hear from her, at least.

It's not that I dislike May's grandparents. My relationship with them is just . . . complicated. They were understandably upset when they found out April wanted me to adopt May. They even talked about fighting it, but ultimately, they gave up. Presumably because they knew they had no legal ground, since April made sure she got all the paperwork taken care of in time, and after my parents' deaths, I had enough financial means to support a child. I suspected they were also afraid that if they fought against me, I might keep May away from them entirely.

Even though they eventually accepted that I'd be May's father, they still make me a little anxious all these years later.

"How are you?" Elise asks. Followed immediately by, "How's May?"

I tell her I'm fine, then give her what she really cares about. "May's doing great! Her grades are excellent this year, like always. I think she's read her way through half of Mayweather's local library by now."

Glancing down, I catch May rolling her eyes at me, so I ruffle her wavy hair. I don't mention to her grandmother that I let her dye it lavender.

"We'll have to send her some gift cards," Elise says, and I try not to huff in annoyance. I may not be wealthy like her and her husband, but I can afford to buy my daughter books. "She has spring break coming up, doesn't she?"

"It starts tomorrow."

Elise hums. "Grant and I were hoping we could coordinate a visit, but unfortunately, he couldn't swing it in time with his work."

I let out the sharp breath I sucked in at hearing the word *visit*. The Richardsons know they're welcome to come up here from Philly, but they rarely do. They claim they don't like traveling, but they used to take vacations here when April was a kid, so that seems like an excuse. They probably just don't have the time to bother with the two of us, and that's sort of fine with me.

After April died and I adopted May, I ended up selling my parents' house and moving May to Mayweather. I'd never been here before, but I remembered how much April loved it here. And the idea of raising a child in the city felt daunting—the idea of raising a *child* felt daunting—so I picked this tiny town in Massachusetts, hoping this place would help me create a happy life for myself and May.

And it has. This town has given us so much.

But I'd be lying if I said that getting away from May's grandparents so they couldn't judge my every move wasn't a perk of the relocation.

"That's too bad," I say. "But May's here now, she hasn't left for school yet. Do you wanna talk to her?"

"Yes, of course! Thank you."

I eagerly pass my phone to May, who gives me a sympathetic smile. She loves her grandparents, and I'm glad for that. It's just different for me. They're not my family.

My only family is May. And that's more than enough.

"Hi, Grandma!" May says cheerily into the phone.

Slipping out of the kitchen with my coffee, I head out onto the front porch to give them some privacy. Not that May keeps any secrets from me.

Okay, so maybe I'm saving myself from overhearing how nice and easy their relationship is.

I plop down on the wicker loveseat, enjoying the fact that it's no longer freezing outside. It only took most of April for the spring temperatures to actually arrive. Finally, I can exhale without seeing my own breath. Hallelujah!

I lean back, bring my mug up to my mouth, and—*achoo!*—sneeze right into it. *Dammit.*

Every year, as I grit my teeth through frigid winters and pray for spring, I somehow manage to forget that my allergies act up during this season.

Frowning into my tainted coffee, I determine it not too gross, and take a sip. Because if there's one thing in this world I don't waste, it's coffee. If you cut me open, I'm pretty sure you'd find as much coffee running through my veins as blood.

A flapping noise comes from my left, and I turn my head in time to see an orange and white-speckled chicken land on the porch railing.

"Hey there, Delilah."

Cluck.

Sure, a person living in a normal town might be disturbed by a chicken appearing on their porch. But Mayweather is anything but normal, so I just go back to drinking my coffee.

Delilah belongs to my next-door neighbor Mitch. When May and I first moved to town, we hadn't been here more than a few hours before Mitch showed up knocking on my door to introduce himself. Being a hopeless people pleaser, I invited him in, not expecting a freaking chicken to follow him over the threshold and into my kitchen.

The kitchen was a disaster, with stuff all over the counters and unpacked boxes on the floor. But my coffee maker was set up, because *priorities*, and Mitch didn't hesitate to ask for a cup. After making it for him, I took a seat across from him at the small round table, and the chicken immediately flew into my lap.

"That's Delilah," he told me. "Or Delilah Doodle Doo. Delilah Doodle *Don't* when she's in trouble."

Very distracted—and mildly terrified—by the large bird in my lap, I unintentionally spilled my whole tragic backstory to Mitch when he asked where I'd come from.

I didn't move here wanting to be known as the twenty-one-year-old guy with the dead parents, dead best friend, and adopted child. Gossip spreads like wildfire in this town, though, and that's what I was.

But my life is pretty great now, so I try not to dwell on the past.

Mitch is nowhere in sight, but Delilah is typically super chill. She's been perched there watching me for about five minutes when I suddenly let out another loud sneeze, startling her. She gives a disgruntled squawk as she flies down into the grass, and then she promptly struts back to her own yard as if I've insulted her.

I quickly down the last of my coffee and get up to head inside for a tissue. But before I make it to the door—*Achoo! Achoo! Achoo!*

Ugh.

Well. Spring has definitely freaking sprung.

❀

MY DRIVE TO WORK is less than ten minutes, yet by the time I reach the Mayweather Inn's large, sprawling grounds on the edge of town, I've already completely drained my DEATH BEFORE DECAF coffee thermos. If the unexpected early morning phone call was any indication of things to come, I'm afraid this day might require something beyond my normally excessive amount of caffeine.

As soon as I head inside and approach the front desk, my theory already appears to be proving true. Because Danny, my assistant manager and right-hand guy, is scowling at the computer monitor while he crumples a piece of paper into a tight ball in his fist. Danny sort of has a resting grouch face anyway, unless he's in front of a customer. But this looks like a new level of *I want to burn this place to the ground.*

"Everything okay?" I ask cautiously.

"We're overbooked."

"No, we're not."

Danny turns his scowl from the computer to me, making me flinch. "So you're telling me I'm only imagining that this outdated, waste-of-space machine shows we have more reservations for the same date than we have rooms?"

"Hey, don't insult Cynthia!" I cry, reaching across the desk to pat the top of the computer affectionately. He's not wrong about her being outdated, but I like to think that if I treat her nicely and use enough words of encouragement, she might miraculously last me another year or so. Because buying another one is *not* something I want to think about right now. Running an inn is expensive. Who knew?

Danny isn't amused.

"Okay," I relent. "I'm not saying I don't believe you. I'm only saying we *can't* be overbooked, *pleasepleaseplease*, because I don't know what the hell I'm supposed to do if we are."

I've worked here since I first moved to Mayweather—I used to have Danny's job—but the inn's only been mine for almost a year now, and while I like to think I'm great at what I do, sometimes it feels like I'm just winging it.

There's always that fear in the back of my mind that I'm going to fail.

And then I might not be able to pay May's grandparents back the large sum of money they lent me to buy this place. Asking them for a loan was painful, but it was worth it for the chance at providing a better life for May.

Danny seems to take pity on me in my distress. He softens and lets out a sigh. "I've been trying to figure out all morning how this happened. I told you we need a newer computer that can run a better booking system."

He's not wrong, but fuck.

"I'll handle it," I tell him. But when I step behind the desk and see that he's talking about a date next week, right between the end of a large corporate retreat's visit and the start of Mayweather's spring festival, I already know I'll have to resort to something drastic to fix this. Like get the guests a room at another nearby inn for the night before moving them back here and comping part of their stay. That's seriously unprofessional, but luckily my sunny disposition and charm can get me a long way.

And tourists visit here for the small-town charm, after all.

Forty-five minutes and one headache later, everything's sorted, and I'm finally able to pop into the kitchen for more coffee. But the sight in there makes me pause.

Addison, my new head chef and culinary goddess, is crouched down, wringing her hands together as she peers into one of the ovens.

For the love of Drag Race, what now?

"Um. Everything okay in here?" I venture to ask.

"The oven's broken," she replies, not even bothering to glance my way.

"No, it's not," I say reflexively, then bite my lip. Is this déjà vu? A nightmare? Am I having a stroke?

Addison turns to me as she straightens up. Her shoulder-length brown hair is pulled back into a neat little ponytail, but her chef's coat is unbuttoned, and her Chainsmokers concert T-shirt has a stain on the chest. "I assure you, it is," she says dryly.

"Oh. Well. Okay. No big deal. We'll get it fixed."

No, no, noooo, please, no.

"In time for that big company's fancy thing?"

"Um, yeah, of course," I say. "I'll get someone to come out and take a look at it today. It'll be fine."

I might be lying my face off, but I can't show how stressed I am, because Addison's already been stressed for weeks over this corporate retreat and the festival. She's only been working for me for three months, after the previous chef who'd been here longer than me resigned. (And no, that's not a big deal to lose the head chef at an inn where the restaurant is a huge draw. *Nope, not at all.*) So these will be the biggest events she's had to cook for so far.

"Okay, but I have another problem." Picking up a stray dish towel, she starts balling it up like a marginally less hostile version of Danny.

"Which is?" I ask, even though I'm afraid of the answer.

"Randy and Ronny quit."

"*Excuse me?*" I squeak. Surely, this can't be happening. Not right now. I must have heard her wrong. Or I'm hoping that this is all part of some elaborate, three-weeks-late April Fool's joke my staff is playing on me.

All right, you got me, guys.

Addison nods solemnly. "Yup. They just sent me a text this morning saying they wouldn't be coming in tomorrow, because they got some crazy idea about something or other and they're moving to New Mexico. New Mexico!" She throws the towel onto the counter. "Don't they know how freaking hot it is there?"

"Woah." I hold up my hands in a placating gesture, like you would do to a bear approaching. Or maybe that's not what you're supposed to do with a bear, I don't know. I'm not a wilderness guy. "It's okay," I tell her.

It's really not, though.

Those irresponsible little shits. How many times have they been caught getting high in the walk-in and I let it slide? And now this is what I get?

"How am I supposed to get everything done in time when I'm down two staff members and one oven?" Addison asks, voice rising in pitch at the end. "This is going to be a disaster, and you'll blame me. And I don't wanna lose this job, because then I might have to crawl my ass back to my miserable, cheating ex-wife, and honestly, I'd rather chew off my own foot."

"Um." I don't know what to say to that. First of all, I'm not sure how chewing off her foot would help anything. And since Addison normally keeps to herself, we haven't gotten that close yet, despite my best efforts. So hearing her mention her ex throws me.

I've been determined to make her my friend though, because, not to toot my own horn, but I'm friends with basically everyone in Mayweather. I can tell you most people's birthdays, the names of their pets, and any serious allergies. The people in this town were here for me when I needed it most, willing to help a stranger take care of his small child, and I'll always be grateful.

Addison's renting a place right outside of Mayweather, but she works here, so she's a part of the town.

"None of this is your fault. I won't blame you," I assure her. "I promise I'll figure something out and everything will be fine."

She looks doubtful, so I try to give her a confident smile, but I'm faking it, for sure. *Fake it 'til you make it* has always kind of been my motto.

But what the heck am I going to do?

CHAPTER TWO

TRAVIS

As I scrape leftover food off a plate and into the trash, with the hum of diner patrons surrounding me, I take a moment to commiserate over the state of my life. Growing up, all I wanted to do was get out of this small, crazy-ass town. And that's what I did. I went to college in Boston, found a job after I graduated, and got an apartment. Yet somehow, I still ended up back here, serving what feels like endless turkey clubs and stacks of pancakes and cleaning up after all these fools.

But I made this choice.

Reed's Diner is a staple in town. My grandfather opened it and ran it until the day he died. And when I got that horrible phone call, I knew what I needed to do. My dad wasn't going to step up and run this place, since he has his own career. Not to mention, his culinary skills begin and end with spaghetti and a jar of Ragu.

A sense of family obligation is what brought me home. But honestly, my job managing a group of customer service reps for an online retail giant was boring as hell. I don't love having to deal with the public now, because customers can be majorly annoying sometimes, but I actually do enjoy cooking.

Most of my happiest memories took place in this diner with my grandfather teaching me how to do it. I was always closer with him than I was with my dad, and it would have killed me to let the diner go.

So here I am. I don't really hate my life. But I gave up things to come back here—mainly the freedom to be fully myself—and some days that weighs on me.

The bell on the door jingles, making me sigh. Today is just one of those days.

Getting into an argument with my produce supplier earlier over not bringing me enough heads of lettuce is probably what kickstarted my bad mood. I didn't realize until after I hung up on him that I'm the one who messed up placing the order. Then I felt like an ass, but I'm lousy at apologizing. I've known Connor Shaw since we were kids though, so I'll have to suck it up. Take him out for a beer or something.

When I come out from the back, I spot May Sanderson, with her unmistakable purple hair and giant backpack over her shoulders, grabbing a table. At least she has the common sense and decency to choose a clean one, which is more than I can say for some of the adults around here.

Seeing her lifts my mood. She's a cool kid—not something I say often. But mostly, the change in mood is because I assume her dad will be joining her.

Brenden moved to town with May the same year I moved back, but it took a while before I got to know him. I was busy figuring out how to run the diner, and he was busy getting his life set up here while taking care of a two-year-old all by himself. He can't cook to save his life though. So since the diner's prices are fairly cheap, we found ourselves interacting day after day, and over time, we became close.

We're not making each other BFF bracelets or anything. But my tendency to keep to myself was no match for his persistent friendliness, and he eventually wore me down. He probably knows me a hell of a lot better than most people by now.

And okay, fine. I'll never admit it to him because he would taunt me endlessly, but he's pretty much the bright spot in my days. Even when he's on my case about me refusing to participate in some town nonsense. Or when he calls me Grumptopus. Or when he begs me to serve him more coffee than it should be legal to consume.

I always enjoy his company.

May smiles when I approach her table. I swear she has her dad's smile, even though they're not biologically related. I ask if she needs two menus, despite the fact that she and Brenden likely know the menu better than I do.

"Yeah, Dad will be here in a minute," she says.

I turn to grab them for her, not letting her see how happy I am with that answer. "Orange soda?" I call out from behind the counter.

"Yes, please!"

I fill a glass from the fountain, and by the time I return with her soda and the menus, she's already got her backpack open and two textbooks spread out on the table. I carefully nudge one over so I can set the glass down. "Aren't you supposed to be on vacation?"

"Keeping tabs on my kid?" Brenden asks as he strolls in, bell jingling. He wraps his fingers loosely around my forearm and urges me to step to the side so he can sit down across from his daughter. The brief touch makes my skin tingle, but I ignore that. "I swear I know when she's supposed to go to school," he says. "I've got this."

He's teasing me, and I glance back down at May's table spread in case my cheeks turn pink. "I prefer to know when the schools are out so I can prepare to be invaded by a bunch of brats," I explain.

"*Hey!*" May complains.

"Not you."

"Today was the last day," she tells me. "But I want to make sure I get my assignments done early so I can enjoy the week off."

I shake my head because this girl is always doing schoolwork and studying. She's way too mature for her age. I like to give Brenden shit that she's more mature than him, which he never refutes.

"Coffee," Brenden says, abruptly cutting off the conversation. The desperate tinge to his voice makes me roll my eyes, and I refrain from giving him a lecture on manners.

"How many of these have you had today?" I ask when I serve him a cup. It's part of our routine, and he usually answers with something vague and absurd like, "More than one and less than ten."

This time though, he heaves a weary sigh and says, "I've lost count, but believe me, I needed all of them. Do you mind if we have some time before we order?"

I try not to be disappointed at the brush off. He is here as a customer, after all, and not to see me. But he's usually much chattier. He didn't even ask about my dad, which he's done every day since the stubborn idiot of a man fell off a ladder while doing his electrician work and fractured his hip.

Grabbing a rag, I begin wiping down the counter in an attempt to keep myself busy and avoid watching Brenden and May like a creeper. I can't help taking a few quick peeks at their table, though.

Brenden looks as good as ever, with his fitted dark gray slacks and a peach button-up—one of his typical work outfits. He looks more tired than usual though. A piece of his sandy brown hair falls out of place as he ducks his head to talk to May, and he doesn't bother swiping it back.

I refill a few customers' drinks and serve a couple meals. But the rush has already died down, so there isn't enough going on to keep me occupied, and my gaze keeps drifting back to Brenden. He and May are having a hushed conversation, with Brenden looking more stressed by the minute. May keeps patting his hand sympathetically.

Finally, I see him throw his arms over one of her books, thunking his head down on top of them, and I can't stop myself from going back over there.

"What's with you?" I ask.

"We're in crisis mode," May answers for him.

"We're not in crisis mode," Brenden disagrees, his voice muffled because he's talking to the table.

"You look like you're in crisis mode," I comment.

He lifts his head from his arms to give me a dirty look. "You're not helping."

I hold his eye contact, waiting him out. His blue eyes are missing their usual spark, and I experience a strong desire to do something to give it back to him. After a few moments, he starts to ramble about computer errors, broken ovens, and missing kitchen staff. His tone takes on a high-pitched, frantic quality the more he goes on, but I manage to follow along and determine that his most pressing problem, the one that's left him in this state, is the fact that his kitchen is unexpectedly short-staffed right when they have a large group due to arrive at the inn.

I frown in both concern and minor suspicion. "Did you come in here to ask me to help you out?"

He tries to glare at me again, but he comes off more like a snarky puppy, failing to make it threatening. "I came in here to drink coffee and eat a burger."

"And to ask for my help."

We have another short staring contest until he groans loudly and says, "Fine. I was considering asking for your help. But you don't have to! I know you have your own business to run."

He gestures around us, but the diner's almost empty by now, not quite illustrating his point. It gets packed for the typical mealtime hours though. Being one of only three sit-down restaurants in town will do that.

Shrugging, I tell him, "I can make it work." Truthfully, I'm not sure *how*, but I hate seeing him upset. It's rare, but it always gets to me. And my instinct is to help him whenever he needs anything, no matter how small or large the request is.

Our friendship began inside this diner, but it developed while hauling furniture for him in my truck bed, changing flat tires on his car, and blowing up thousands of balloons for May's birthday parties. These aren't services I'd be as quick to offer anyone else in town, but Brenden is . . . special.

"No, you really don't have to," he argues. "I'll figure something else out. I'll just have to help in the kitchen myself."

A sharp laugh punches out of me. Ignoring the eye daggers he aims my way, I say, "You can't cook. That's why you're always here."

His jaw drops. "How very dare you!" he says in mock offense. "I *can so* cook. Bagel bites and mozzarella sticks totally count as cooking."

"Nothing frozen counts."

"But I always get the cheese to that perfect gooeyness-without-melting-over quality!"

I do my best to look unimpressed, rather than charmed, but I think I fail. "Seriously, I don't mind helping. Benji can cover for me. He's always happy for more hours, and I trust him. I'll still have to pop back and forth to take care of some stuff, but it's doable."

Brenden looks up at me now, immense gratitude painted all over his face, and I know I'm making the right decision offering to help. Even if it's going to be a pain in the ass sorting everything out.

There's not much I wouldn't do for this man.

Luckily, I don't think he realizes that.

CHAPTER THREE

BRENDEN

In my office, leaning back in the cushy desk chair I splurged on for myself and flipping through some paperwork about the incoming retreat, I'm much less frazzled than I was two days ago. I'm actually starting to believe everything will work out fine.

Because Travis Reed is a godsend.

Asking him to help was my only option. But I hate being that person—the one who can't seem to handle things on his own. Who always goes running to a bigger and stronger man for help. Travis never seems to mind, but still.

My pride can't get in the way of keeping the inn running though. I love this place. But more than that, I love my daughter. I'll do anything necessary to ensure I can provide a stable life for her.

One of the last things I said to April was, *I promise May will grow up surrounded by love and joy and everything she could ever need.*

Thinking about April, even for a second, causes my eyes to well up with tears. *Fuck.* I blink them away and shake my thoughts clear, because I'm at work. Even in the privacy of my office, I need to stay the happy-go-lucky Brenden Sanderson everyone in this town expects me to be. I can't reveal all the sadness that hides under the surface. No one wants to be around that guy.

I grab my phone to play some music, hoping it'll cure my melancholy dip in mood. Skyler James is a perfect choice. May's a much bigger fan than I am—she was obsessed with Boys Will Be Boys when she was little—but there probably isn't a gay man on the planet who doesn't at least appreciate Skyler now. He's not exactly my type, but there's no denying the guy is gorgeous. I still can't believe he came out, or that all those theories about him and his ex-bandmate were actually true.

Score one for the gays! Or two, really, because Trevor Blue is also smoking hot.

After I finish going over some last details for the event, I remember I'm supposed to cover the desk for Danny's break. And then I'd like to pop into the kitchen to see how things are going today.

Travis already fixed the oven—it turned out not to be as broken as Addison thought. This saved me an unnecessary bill but agitated my chef. I get the sense she doesn't appreciate someone else showing her up in her own kitchen. I can't hold it against her for not figuring out what was wrong with it though. From what I learned when interviewing her, she owned a successful restaurant in Chicago for five years with her now ex-wife. But her role was mainly to handle the cooking while her ex took care of the business side of things, and that probably included dealing with appliance maintenance.

It's obvious Addison's grateful for Travis's help with the food prep, though. Now that she's less stressed, she's been excited to come up with even more new menu options for the corporate crowd. Lately, there's been a lot of food shoved in my face for me try, and you'll never find me complaining about that.

As I get up, my phone rings. Seeing Elise's name on the screen, I sink back into my chair and take a deep breath. She never calls this often.

"Hi, Elise," I answer faux cheerfully.

"Brenden!" she says by way of greeting. "I'm so glad to catch you again. We didn't get a chance to talk much the other day."

That's because you only really wanted to talk to May, I think a little bitterly.

We do the obligatory small talk thing for a minute. I ask how she and Grant are doing in Philly and how Grant's work is going before I'm tapped out. It's harder when we've already talked about May recently. She's our only common interest.

Then Elise asks me how things are going with the inn. And it may just be out of politeness, since I asked about her husband's work, but my hackles go up.

I tell her everything's running smoothly, business is steady as usual, my new chef is wonderful. The whole time I talk, though, I'm wondering if she's asking because she and Grant are expecting me to fail at running this place. They loaned me money, so they sort of have an investment in it being successful. But even if the place went under (*knock on wood*), I'd find another way to pay them back eventually. Being indebted to them isn't fun.

"It sounds like you're doing a great job," Elise says, and I breathe a sigh of relief, even though I have no idea if she really means that. "You've taken on so much, gaining ownership. I imagine the place keeps you constantly busy."

"Yeah, it's a lot," I admit. "But I love my job, and I'm good at it." Hopefully that doesn't sound too defensive.

"I know you are, dear."

Was that patronizing?

I take off my glasses for something to fidget with while I wait for whatever she's going to say next. It feels like there's a *but* coming.

"But I hope you still have enough time for May."

There it is.

"Of course I do." With one finger, I spin my glasses in half-circles on top of my desk. Maybe this is why I've scratched so many pairs over the years, but this conversation is filling me with a jittery, frantic energy. "She comes first. Always."

Elise hums in what sounds like agreement. But then—"You do a good job for a single parent. I only wish sometimes that May could have more than one parental figure in her life. She deserves that."

I accidentally fling my glasses off the desk, and they slide along the floor until they hit the wall. "I—I know," I manage to croak through my sudden panic. "She deserves everything."

And her grandparents don't think I can give her everything. They don't think I'm enough. This wasn't a call to check if I was failing at running the inn. It was to check if I was failing as a parent.

"It's just, with losing her mom . . ." Elise trails off sadly. "I only wish . . ."

"I'm seeing someone!" I blurt out, my mouth moving faster than my brain. "It's pretty serious. We practically live together."

Holy hell, stop talking.

Elise lets out a delighted, "*Oh!*" and I cringe. "That's wonderful! I can't wait to meet him."

"I'm sure you will next time you visit."

Or not. Because either she'll have forgotten I mentioned a boyfriend by whenever it is that she and Grant deign to come here, or we'll have conveniently just broken up. *What a shame.*

"This is perfect," she says. "Because I was actually calling to let you know Grant was able to move some work obligations around, so we're coming to see you in three days."

"Uh . . ."

"Sorry for the short notice," she goes on. "We didn't think we could swing it at first, but then everything sort of fell into place all at once. Isn't that great?"

Great isn't the word I'd use for it. There are many, many other adjectives I'd choose before that one, in fact. My mind rapidly cycles through them, with a couple of colorful cuss words thrown in too for good measure.

Besides the fact that their visits tend to put me a bit on edge, this is such a bad time with everything going on at the inn. I'm already on edge! Any *more* on edge, and I will go flying off the edge and crash to the floor.

Like my glasses. *Crap, where did they go?*

"Brenden?"

"Oh yeah, sounds great!" I lie, lie, lie. "May will be thrilled to see you." That last part, at least, is true.

"I can't wait to see her," Elise says. "And to meet this man of yours."

Oh. Shit.

Fucking shit on a cracker.

"He uh..." I start, but then I struggle to find a plausible excuse for why my imaginary boyfriend won't be able to meet them. He died? No, that doesn't make sense. *Oh!* He'll be out of town. That's a good one. "He'll be—"

"Hon, I'm so sorry, my oven beeped. I've got to take the roast out. We'll see you soon, okay?"

"Okay," I say dumbly. I might be in a state of shock.

After she hangs up, though, I snap out of it. Now I'm trying not to hyperventilate as I mentally run through ways I could possibly fix the mess I've just gotten myself into.

A throat clears, startling me out of wondering if fleeing the country with May and changing our names would be too extreme.

I look up to find Travis standing in the doorway of my office holding a plate of muffins and staring at me like I have three heads. Granted, he's a little blurry since I'm still missing my glasses, so it's possible I'm the one looking at him that way.

"Hi," I say, trying to smile like everything's normal and I'm not currently freaking the fuck out. I jump up and swipe my glasses off the floor.

I jam them on my face, then fall back into my desk chair. "Um. Are those for me?"

His gaze flicks to the plate in his hand. "I wanted you to choose the best flavor. Since when are you seeing someone who practically lives with you?"

"Um." Okay, so he's been standing there a lot longer than I realized. And there's a strange prickliness to his tone that I'm not used to. (I mean, prickly *is* kind of his baseline with everyone else, just not with me.) I don't even know how to begin explaining my dumbassery, but he's still standing there staring at me expectantly, so. I try.

His brow furrows when I tell him how I blurted out the nonsense about having a boyfriend because May's grandmother basically implied that I'm not enough for my daughter on my own.

"I'm sure she didn't say that."

I shrug uncomfortably. "Not in so many words, but yeah. I think she did. Then she said they're coming here. And they almost never come here, and I'm worried they want to check up on how the inn is doing, because they probably think I'm failing at this just like they think I'm failing as a parent, and oh fuck, they're gonna try to take May away from me, aren't they? That's why they're coming!"

"Breathe," Travis says. And I immediately suck in a huge gulp of air, but it still feels like I'm not getting enough oxygen to my brain. Has it always been so stuffy in this office? Why are there no windows to open? Who designed this place?

As I'm contemplating taking a sledgehammer to a wall—not that I'd know where to get a sledgehammer—Travis takes a couple long strides forward, and suddenly he's right in front of me, hovering over my desk in all his flannel-wearing glory.

He's still holding the plate, but he uses his free hand to reach out and grip my upper arm firmly. "Brenden. Get up."

I do as he says without thinking about it, then let him lead me out of my office, through the inn's common area with all the cozy armchairs, and out a back door to the wraparound porch. He doesn't let go of my arm the whole time, and I find myself staring at his long, thick fingers where they're curled around my very mediocre-sized muscle. He has sexy fingers. How have I never noticed that before?

They look a little rough, too. Because he does a lot with his hands. Cooking, fixing stuff, building things . . .

I don't know why my mind is wandering in this random direction. Maybe it's a trauma coping mechanism so that I don't have to think about what's going on. Shit, is it insensitive to call this trauma? It's not like the Richardsons are going to physically hurt me. I don't think. But if they wanted to, I guarantee they have the resources to hide the body.

"Sit," Travis instructs, pointing at one of the two chairs on either side of a tiny table. The whole porch has spaced out seating meant for the guests, but I've spent plenty of peaceful moments myself out here, enjoying the view of the grounds.

This moment isn't so peaceful, but again, I do what he tells me to, because having someone else be in charge for a minute feels good. He takes the other chair, setting the plate down on the table between us. When he pushes it closer to me with a pointed look, I reach for the nearer of the two muffins and pull off a chunk of the top to shove in my mouth. It tastes good, I guess, but I'm barely aware of what I'm eating. My mind is still spinning, and the only thing I can focus on that settles me a bit is Travis's deep brown eyes.

"Now," he says after I've finished chewing, "can you explain what's happening without losing it again?"

"I already told you, I'm an idiot loser who couldn't keep my mouth shut and lied about being in a relationship. So I guess now I have to find a fake boyfriend. That's what they do in movies, right?" I force a laugh, but it comes out manic. *Girrrl, get it together.*

Travis rolls his eyes. "Yes, that must be the only practical solution. Rather than simply telling them the truth."

He doesn't understand. And of course he doesn't. Since May and I moved to Mayweather, I haven't made it a habit to go around sharing the finer details about her adoption and the extended family dynamic.

But he's sitting here watching me internally freak out, and he's tilting his head like he *wants* to understand. Like he cares. And he's . . . Travis. I'm hesitant to call him my best friend, only because if I did, he'd probably scoff and stop speaking to me. He likes to pretend he's allergic to people, but he always manages to be there for me when I need him.

And something about his uncomplicated, steady presence helps tone down my energetic, sometimes over-the-top personality. Right now being a prime example.

It's also nice that he puts up with my antics though. Sometimes I like to be a pain in his ass just for the fun of it, to see how much he can take before I drive him crazy. Surprisingly, I've yet to find the threshold.

Because of all this, he's kind of my favorite person. Other than May, of course.

I press my finger into the edge of the muffin, watching it crumble and the sugar crystals fall off, while I gather my thoughts. I can trust him with this. "I can't tell them I lied about having a boyfriend. We don't have a terrible relationship, but we're not . . . close. If I say I lied to them, they'll think I'm being dishonest about other things too, and they'll question my ability to take care of May."

"You've been taking care of her almost her whole life," Travis points out.

Looking up at him, I find myself getting lost in his eyes again. He's such a good guy, despite the grumpy front. If only I could say I was dating someone like him, that might be enough to convince Elise and Grant I've got my shit together.

Okay, getting sidetracked.

"Do you know how May became my daughter?" I ask. I may not talk about it much, but I've known Travis a damn long time. It must have come up at least once, or he would have heard it around town.

"Her mom was your friend, right?" he says gently.

"Yeah. April was my best friend. She got pregnant really young, but she was so excited to be a mom. She swore she'd have the kind of relationship with her daughter that she never had with her own mom."

"She didn't get along with her parents?"

I shake my head. "Not really. Anyway, when she found out she was sick, she told me she wanted me to adopt May. She didn't want her parents raising her. And I didn't understand why she thought I could do a better job raising a kid at twenty-one than they could, but she said she knew I'd do an amazing job, and that . . ."

When I get choked up and can't go on, Travis waits. He nudges the muffin toward me again, so I break off another small piece and pop it in my mouth, still not really able to taste it.

"April told me that May was going to need me, but that wasn't the only reason she wanted me to take her. She knew I'd need May too. She didn't want me to be alone once she was gone."

After I spill that truth, I'm afraid to look at him. Because how pathetic is that?

May has turned into this awesome young person. She's smart and funny and kind. And she's totally self-sufficient. Most days she's the one making sure *I've* remembered to have dinner or do laundry.

April was right.

But I shouldn't need my daughter more than she needs me.

Something warm touches my forearm. Travis's hand. I'm sure it's supposed to be a gesture of comfort, but somehow the contact sizzles through me like an electrical current. Which is wrong on so many levels.

It's not like he's never touched me before, and I don't normally react like this. It must be because I'm feeling vulnerable right now. Maybe some wires got crossed in my brain, making sadness and horniness go hand-in-hand.

I don't want Travis like that. He's my friend.

And he's straight.

Not that I've ever seen him dating anyone. I would think he's a monk if it weren't for the fact that this town is full of nosy (but well-intentioned) people, and I've heard stories of how he "sneaks out of town to get his rocks off, thinking no one will find out."

I don't know why he doesn't date. He'd be excellent dating material.

"It's too bad you're straight," I say, letting something absurd fall out of my mouth without thinking for the second time in fifteen minutes.

He studies me, eyes a bit narrowed, like he really doesn't know what to make of me. Like he's torn between offense and confusion. And I remind myself that, *right*, he's not inside my head, so he couldn't follow my train of thought.

"If you weren't straight, I could ask you to be my fake boyfriend," I tell him, chuckling awkwardly.

Travis blinks at me. Once, twice. Then—"I'm not straight."

CHAPTER FOUR

TRAVIS

You're not . . . You . . . *What?*" Brenden stammers.

And what the hell is wrong with me? Did that really just come out of my mouth?

It's the truth, but still. He didn't need to know that. No one in this town knows about my sexuality. Especially my dad.

For a moment, I panic. But if there's one person in this town I trust not to blab things, it's Brenden.

"Are you serious?" he asks, when I say nothing to clarify for him.

I glance around us. Two little old ladies are playing a card game at another table, but they're too far away to overhear. A handful of workers are setting something up out on the lawn, also too far away and probably too busy to eavesdrop.

"Look, why don't we talk about this later?" I say, avoiding Brenden's curious eyes. They're a bright ocean blue, and I could easily sink into their depths if I'm not careful. "Somewhere more private?"

"But—"

"I've got to get back in the kitchen before Addison comes out to yell at me." I'm deflecting, but it's a fair concern. "I already pressed her buttons by suggesting a cherry-apricot muffin would be better than her strawberry rhubarb."

Brenden's gaze finally falls away from me as he looks down at the plate with the two muffins. The one I made, which he was eating, and Addison's, which remains untouched. "Is that what that was?" He actually picks up my muffin this time and takes a large bite out of it. The strangled moan he lets out a second later goes straight to my dick. "Damn, that's orgasmic."

Uh, yeah. Kind of got that impression.

My cheeks heat. I swear Brenden Sanderson is the only man on Earth who can make me blush. And he's not even doing it on purpose.

"Who knew you could get creative in a kitchen," he muses. "Why do you only serve blueberry and that nasty bran kind at the diner?"

"Because people go there for simple food. Like I've told you many times, lots of regulars eat the bran muffins. But people come here for a different experience. They want the fancy shit."

He laughs. "So eloquent."

I grunt in response, making him laugh some more. And I love that sound.

Then his expression turns serious, and he's staring at me again like he's trying to peer into my soul. Like he's remembering the bomb I just dropped on him.

I shift in my seat, scratching at the scuff on my jaw. It's a bit of a nervous tic, so I force myself to stop. "Anyway, uh . . . I meant it about being . . ." My words keep getting stuck, so I clear my throat. I'm a grown ass man. It shouldn't be so hard to say.

I'm gay.

It's not a new thing for me.

I flash back to my life in Boston, those years in college and right afterward when I was mostly out and living the life I wanted. Before I gave it all up to move back here.

This isn't the time or place for this conversation though.

One of the workers strolls up the porch steps and stops to ask Brenden a question, proving my point. After he walks away, Brenden turns back to me expectantly.

"We both need to get back to work," I remind him.

He smiles. "You don't technically work here."

"Tell that to Addison." I stand, grabbing the plate of muffins and handing it to him once he stands too. "And try her muffin."

Taking a small bite of it, he hums thoughtfully. "It's really good. Not as good as yours though." The little tease winks at me.

I have to tell my dick to calm down again. I usually have more self-control around him. All these years of friendship have gotten me used to his silly charm. Not immune. Just used to it.

He seems to hesitate in walking back inside, and I know I've left this giant weird thing hanging between us. He's normally a big talker. We can hold entire conversations where I say one word to his twenty. It says a lot more now, the fact that he's holding back.

Lowering my voice and wondering if I've lost my mind, I tell him, "Look, if you're really considering the, uh, the fake boyfriend thing— which I think is a terrible idea, by the way—then we can talk about it later."

His eyebrows shoot toward his hairline. "Tonight?"

"Sure. I'll come to your place?"

When he nods in agreement, I'm afraid I've already sealed my fate. *What am I getting myself into?*

As he leans in to give me a hug, I pat his back sort of awkwardly. "Thank you," he says, pulling back. Then—"*Achoo!*" He sneezes all over my chest and immediately looks mortified. "Oh god, I'm so sorry! I'm not sick, I swear! It's these fucking allergies. I'm so gross, I'm sorry!"

"It's okay," I assure him, though I'm afraid to look down at my shirt, because it probably *is* gross. "You're fine. You're human, you know."

"Nope. Not allowed to be." He laughs like it's a joke, but something in his tone makes me wonder if he actually believes that, at least a little.

I gesture toward the door to head inside, and he steps through, mumbling, "Freaking spring."

Making my way back to the inn's kitchen, I mentally prepare myself to do whatever Brenden asks of me. As if I don't already. Faking being his boyfriend may be in a wildly different league than helping out here or shoveling his driveway for him, but oh well.

Between his minor meltdown and his slightly red nose from the allergies, he was looking so miserable it made me want to wrap him up in a blanket and keep him protected at all costs.

I swear I don't have a savior complex or anything. For the most part, I keep my head down and worry about myself. If you let yourself get involved in other people's problems in this town, it could never end. But for some reason, I can't resist when it comes to Brenden.

If I stopped long enough to analyze it, I might have to admit my feelings for him go a lot deeper than friendship. Not that I've been pining for him all this time. Or if I have, it's only in the way you might pine after something that you know deep down couldn't be meant for you.

Brenden is all light and joy and openness, while I'm . . . closed off, hiding in the shadows with a hint of bitterness.

Addison huffs when I enter the kitchen, not bothering to hide her annoyance. The fact that I'm not an employee and am only here as a favor doesn't seem to matter.

I can't figure her out. She seems like she could be really cool. Or maybe *was* really cool, in another life. But she's guarded, always a little on edge, moves through the day like she's not sure how she found herself here.

Considering that's pretty much how I live *my* life, I should probably be able to understand her better.

She snaps some instructions at me, and I only cut her slack because I know she's under a lot of stress with this corporate thing coming up. I'd be stressed too if I had to cater to a huge group of corporate tools. I worked a corporate job—I know how those people can be.

But when she asks me to crush the strawberries so she can make a batch of muffins large enough for the retreat in a couple days, I can't help but reiterate my cherry-apricot suggestion that she ignored the first time.

"You remember I'm the head chef, right?" she says, ponytail swinging lightly as she turns to glare at me. "I think I know what I'm doing."

"Not saying you don't," I tell her. And then—although I don't know what makes me do it—I brag, "But Brenden liked my muffin better."

The way I metaphorically puff up my chest is immature, and really, why do I even care? This is her kitchen and her event to plan for. I have no real stake here. Except, secretly, I can't help but be proud about Brenden's intense praise for my baking skills.

And I can't help remembering the obscene noise he made. If I can get him to sound like that just with food, I wonder what noises I could have him making in another context . . .

Nope. I abruptly cut off that train of thought before it can get rolling.

"No way am I just going to take your word for it," Addison says.

What are we talking about?

Muffins. Right.

I'm about to drop it and let her go on thinking her unoriginal muffin choice is superior, but then Brenden chooses that moment to come strolling into the kitchen, looking much peppier than he did earlier. He heads right for the coffee machine and starts to pour himself a cup. Mid-pour, he glances up, notices me and Addison both staring at him, and freezes.

"Uh . . ." He shoots us a concerned look.

And since I've apparently turned into a gorilla, I literally puff up my chest this time as I say, "She doesn't believe you liked my muffin better. Will you tell her?"

"Oh, *well,* I . . ." His panicked eyes dart between me and Addison.

I immediately feel like a jerk for putting him in an awkward position.

Who I am to him, really? We're friends, sure. But Brenden has a hundred friends. Addison, on the other hand, is arguably the most important person to his business, after himself. He shouldn't piss her off.

Before I can find a way to take my words back, though, he starts babbling.

"I didn't say I liked it better! I may have said, 'Damn, that's orgasmic.'" He turns quickly to Addison. "But yours was orgasmic too! Plenty of orgasms to be had here! Oh god, shut up, shut up, shut up."

I can't help but laugh. "Are you aware we can still hear you?"

"Of course, I am! Only a crazy person would talk out loud to themselves and forget that people can hear them!" Face red, he spins on his heels and rushes out of the kitchen, half-full coffee cup in hand. "Anyway, gotta go! Lots of important things to do, running an inn and all that, ya know."

Right as he makes it to the doorway, Addison calls out, "Wait! You need to pick which muffin we should bake for the retreat!"

Backing up, he uses his ass to nudge the swinging door and says, "Why don't you go with both? They're both delicious. Both of your muffins bring all the boys to the yard! Bye!"

Addison cocks her head at me like, *What the hell was that?* But I just chuckle. Because *that* was Brenden Sanderson. Ridiculousness is part of his charm.

WHEN THE EVENING COMES, I show up at Brenden's house with two large pizzas from Ricci's. He's bought me plenty of pizza over the years as a thank you for things I've done for him, so I know all of his and May's favorite toppings.

What I don't know is whether I should even be here right now. Yes, I want to help him however I can. But this whole fake dating thing sounds like something out of a cheesy movie. People don't do this in real life, right?

And he'll be expecting me to explain what I told him earlier. About me being . . . *not* straight.

I'm not ashamed of who I am. I never have been. It's just something I've gotten used to not talking about.

Hiding. I've gotten used to hiding it.

And *that's* something I'm a little ashamed of. But it is what it is.

When I knock on the door, it takes a minute for it to open, and then May's standing there, hair up in a sloppy bun seemingly held together by the pen speared through it. She's peering down at the notebook she's holding, with a pencil between her teeth.

"Come on, you're on vacation," I say.

She jumps a little as she looks up at me. Like she forgot she answered the door and there would be a person on the other side of it. Taking the pencil out of her mouth, she eyes me curiously. "This is for extra credit. I didn't know you were coming over. Did something break?"

I jut my chin at the boxes I'm balancing on my hand. "I brought pizza. Are you hungry?"

She either doesn't notice that I didn't explain my reason for being here, or she doesn't actually care, because she says, "Heck, yeah!" Then she tosses her notebook on top of the pizza boxes and takes them from me, striding off toward the kitchen.

I step inside, shutting and locking the door behind me. Brenden never locks it, and while I know this town is one of the safest you'll find, I also know we live in a pretty messed up world. I've had this argument with him multiple times.

Brenden's in the kitchen, putting a few dishes away one-handed because his other hand is holding an oversized mug of coffee. "Oh, hi!" he says, a slightly anxious edge to his voice despite his warm smile. "I was just cleaning up a bit."

"You didn't have to clean up for me," I tell him.

"It wasn't really for you."

"Is he why you vacuumed?" May asks, setting the pizza boxes on the counter.

A flush creeps up Brenden's neck as he says, "Excuse me, don't act like this house is always a disaster. I vacuum all the time."

The reproachful look she gives him almost makes me laugh. "You wait for me to get so sick of the crumbs in the carpet that *I* vacuum."

He glares at her, then turns back to me. "She's lying. I absolutely vacuum. I'm a fully functioning adult who totally has his shit together."

"I know you are," I placate him, still fighting not to laugh. Why is he trying to impress me? We've grown close enough over the years that I know he can be a bit messy and forgetful sometimes. He's great at his job and being a parent—it's all the less important stuff that he's not as concerned about. And I don't judge him for that.

May is already opening up the first pizza box and reaching for a slice. The cheese stretches off the end as she picks it up, so she tears it with her fingers, and then she takes a large, extra cheesy bite.

Brenden hands her a plate and a few paper towels. "Hey, kid. Would you mind taking your pizza up to your room? Travis and I kind of need to talk about something."

She looks confused for a second, followed by minorly suspicious. But then she grabs two more slices and spins on her heels, strolling out of the kitchen.

Once Brenden and I are alone, my heart starts beating faster. Guess it's time to talk.

He passes me a plate and gestures to the round table in the corner of the room, in front of the window. I grab a couple slices of pizza before taking my plate over there. The magnolia tree in his backyard has bloomed, and focusing on the yellow flowers soothes my nerves a bit.

"So," he says, taking the chair closer to me, rather than opposite.

I appreciate the seating arrangement, because it makes it appear less like this will be an interrogation. But my god, is he really going to make me watch him drink coffee with pizza? I shouldn't be surprised, but I don't know if my stomach can take it, especially when it's already tied in knots.

He finds my gaze and holds it. "You don't have to explain yourself or your sexuality to me. But I'd be lying if I said your reveal earlier didn't shock and confuse me."

Slowly chewing a bite of pizza, I wonder what about it was so shocking. Granted, he had no way of knowing, but is it really that hard to believe I could be into men? Shit, I don't come off as grossly homophobic or something, do I?

It would kill me if he thought of me like that, though I assume he wouldn't be friends with me if he did. He should know I don't think there's anything wrong with him being gay. There's nothing wrong with him at all. I think he's kind of perfect.

Of course, he doesn't need to know that last part.

I wipe my fingers on a paper towel, stalling for a couple more seconds to figure out what I want to say. "I don't mind explaining," I tell him. "It's just a little strange to be talking about it with someone I'm not . . ."

Going to hook up with.

It's only relevant when I'm at a bar in some other town trying to get laid. Not that I do a ton of that. But I'm certainly not celibate.

Brenden's earnest eyes bore into me. "Are you . . ."

"I'm gay."

"Oh." He nods a few times like he's processing. "But nobody around here knows?"

"No."

"Your dad?"

"*No,*" I say with more emphasis, and understanding slowly dawns on his face.

Folding my paper towel, I use it to sop up some of the grease on my pizza. If I ate like Brenden does every day, I'd need to go running a lot more than a couple times a week. He must have great genes to be able to eat nothing but garbage and not exercise and still stay slim. The men in my family have a history of high cholesterol. It eventually killed my grandfather, and my dad's doctor is constantly harassing him about getting his under better control, so I try to watch myself. Lord knows I can't control my dad, but I can at least take care of my own health.

I realize I'm stalling, and Brenden's letting me, not pushing me like he usually does. I almost wish he *would* push, because it might make it easier if he just forced this all out of me, rather than letting me get around to it on my own.

"I figured out who I was when I was in high school," I tell him, still fussing with my food. "Back then, there was only one out gay kid in town. Andrew Rowland."

"Oh, Andrew's awesome," he interrupts. "I go to trivia with him in Stoneridge sometimes."

"Yeah, he's cool. But . . ."

His face falls in concern. "Did he get bullied?"

"No. It was almost the opposite. Everyone treated him like some sort of celebrity. Like they wanted him to be the poster boy for how progressive Mayweather was becoming." I shake my head, remembering how ludicrous it seemed.

Frowning, Brenden sips his coffee. "But things *have* progressed here. Drew is far from the only queer person in town anymore. They wouldn't make a big deal like that if you came out now."

"I know, but it's not . . ." I trail off, scratching at my jaw. "That's not the only reason I haven't."

He's watching me closely, and I can tell it's taking all his self-control not to blurt out the question. This isn't easy for me to talk about, but I've kept it inside for so long, that suddenly I almost *want* to tell him. It's just that he knows my dad, obviously, and I sort of feel like I'm about to betray the man somehow. This will probably change Brenden's view of him.

"My dad wasn't one of the people celebrating that Andrew was gay. He'd roll his eyes whenever they wrote something about him in the paper. 'Queer Teen Makes National Honors' Society' and stuff like that."

To my surprise, Brenden lets out a short laugh. "Are you telling me you *didn't* roll your eyes at that?"

Yeah, he's got me there, but that's not the point.

"Sure, I did. But you need to understand, it was a lot for me to deal with back then. I realized I was probably gay, because checking out the girls in their cheerleader uniforms did absolutely nothing for me, but one glimpse of Ryan Hansen's thighs in the locker room had me running away to hide my erection. The idea of being gay didn't bother me. I just didn't want to become another spectacle for this crazy town. Then I started noticing my dad's attitude toward queerness. It wasn't exactly the ideal environment for coming out. And, of course, I hadn't actually *done* anything with a guy yet, so a part of me was still questioning myself."

When I finish this little speech, my words seem to linger in the brief silence that follows. I consider me and Brenden close, but I realize my idea of closeness is probably different than most people's. I've never shared things this personal with him before.

Picking at the crust of his pizza, he finally says, "I understand questioning yourself. And even once you know, it shouldn't be a requirement for anyone to come out. But I want to say something about your dad."

He hesitates here, looking at me with imploring eyes and waiting for my nod before he continues. "I've been as out as can be from the day I moved to town, and your dad has never been anything but nice and friendly to me. It doesn't seem like he treats me any differently than he treats anyone else."

It's true. My dad thinks he's great. Honestly, sometimes I think he gets along with Brenden better than he gets along with me.

"I'm not saying he's completely homophobic or anything." At least, I can hope not. "But what if it's different for him when it's his own son?"

He nudges my forearm with his elbow. "I think there might be only one way to find out."

But is it worth it?

"You don't get it," I tell him. "It wasn't only the stuff with Andrew. My dad loves watching sports, right? So when I was younger, I used to like watching them with him. But eventually, I started to notice how he'd get all macho and aggressive about it. When he'd get angry because his team was losing, he'd say all this shit. I don't remember everything now, but there was one time I heard him refer to some guys that weren't playing so hot as a bunch of . . . well, you know."

Brenden winces. "Yikes."

"Yeah. Yikes. So."

"So . . .?" he prompts.

So I kept my mouth shut, because I was scared of hearing my dad call me a slur.

When I don't voice my thought out loud, he elbows me gently again. "Hey, it's okay. I'm glad you're trusting me with all this, and I hope you know I'm here to listen to anything you want to say. But you can also tell me to stop prying. You don't owe me anything."

That's the thing though. I *don't* feel like I owe the truth about my sexuality to anyone. But something about Brenden makes me want to open up to him. Want to try, at least. It's just difficult for me, since I'm so used to not opening up to anyone.

When you spend so long shoving things down inside you, it can take a lot of strength to yank them back up.

He waits a moment as I try to gather that strength, and when all I can give him is a probably hopeless look, he smiles sympathetically. Then he downs the rest of his coffee, pushes his mug to the side, and stands. "I forgot to offer you a drink."

Going to the fridge, he bends over to reach into it, and I might deserve a medal for not staring at his ass. When he straightens and spins back around, he's clutching two beer bottles by the necks between his slender fingers. He sets them on the counter while he rummages through a drawer, and I see the labels. Sam Adams Cold Snap.

He's not much of a beer drinker, so it's a surprise he even has any in his house, but the fact that he has *this* means he must have gone to a liquor store outside of town. Because the only place to buy beer in Mayweather is the grocery store, and they don't often stock seasonal varieties of anything, unless it's pumpkin spice crap in the fall.

I can't help but wonder if he went out and bought this specifically for me, though I shouldn't read too much into the idea. He's always friendly and accommodating. That's the entire basis of his career, isn't it?

He finally finds a bottle opener, then struggles to pop the cap off the first bottle. I almost get up to help, but I remain in my seat, because I know he's capable. He looks proud of himself when he gets it, and then he does the second one more easily.

Returning to the table with a beer in each hand, he passes one to me, and I thank him as he sits back down.

"So you never came out to your dad," he states, succinctly summing up my story.

I take a long pull from my beer before responding. "Nope. Maybe that makes me a coward, but it didn't seem worth it, taking the risk of losing him if he reacted badly. I held it in until I went off to college in Boston, and once I was there, I got the chance to explore my preferences. Then I graduated, got a good job in the city, and didn't plan to move back home. I dated a few guys, but none of my relationships ever got serious enough that I needed to bring them here and introduce them. So it just . . . never came up."

And then I moved back here to run the diner, knowing I'd have to sacrifice that piece of myself. Though, at the time, sex and dating were the last things on my mind. I was upset about losing my grandfather and focused on not tanking the business he put his whole life into. It wasn't until quite a few years later that putting myself back in the closet started to feel like a sacrifice. But by then, it seemed almost too late to come out to my dad.

Or I was still just a coward.

Still *am*.

Brenden's waiting for more, so I tell him, "It's not some tragedy. Sometimes I still wonder how my dad would take it, if he'd surprise me. But it doesn't matter, because I'm not interested in dating anyone anyway. And he doesn't need to know who I have sex with if it's just sex."

His cheeks darken again. I didn't say anything scandalous, but I know I've never talked about my sex life with him before. Whereas he doesn't hold back in either gushing or whining to me about the guys he dates.

His relationships never manage to last long though. Right when he seems to be getting serious with someone, it falls apart. And I can't for the life of me figure out why. I mean, who wouldn't want to be with this man?

Since nobody seems to appreciate him the way he should be appreciated, maybe he'd be better off giving up on dating and simply enjoying the hookup thing like I do.

As soon as that thought crosses my mind, I almost growl. I don't want to picture a bunch of random, undeserving men getting their hands all over him.

He pushes his empty plate away, making me realize I've barely touched my pizza. But I'm not hungry. "There's nothing wrong with that," he says. "The uh, sex thing. But also not wanting to come out. Like I said, there's no rule that you have to." He pauses, twirling the edge of his beer bottle on the table. "For what it's worth, though, I don't think a crappy, ignorant comment your dad made that long ago necessarily has any bearing on how he would feel or what he would say now. If you did tell him."

"Believe me, I've considered that. But I'm pretty comfortable with my life. And what he doesn't know about me can't hurt him." And what I don't know about *him* can't hurt *me*. The last thing I want is confirmation that he's not the kind of guy I hope he is.

Brenden reaches out and wraps his hand over mine where I've got my bottle in an iron grip. *Okay, this is new.* His warm touch encourages my muscles to loosen.

"I'm not judging your choice. And I know you don't normally do feelings and stuff, so I'm gonna drop it. But you said we could talk about you pretending to be my boyfriend, and I don't see how that's possible if you're in the closet."

When I make the mistake of gazing down at his hand, he takes it away.

"If you don't want your dad to know you're gay, then this is risky," he continues. "I know he's out of town right now, and we'd only be pretending in front of May's grandparents, but still. What if someone else here finds out? You know how quickly Mayweather rumors spread. There's no way people wouldn't tell your dad."

He's right. But I don't see how anyone would find out. It's not like I plan to make out with him in the middle of the town gazebo. Shit, I wouldn't do something like that even if I *was* out. Public displays are absolutely not my thing.

And yet, the thought of making out with Brenden sends a flash of heat through me. But I shake it off and attempt to think this through.

My dad's out of town. He's stuck on crutches for weeks because of his accident. It would've been difficult for me to take care of him and keep a constant eye on him to make sure he doesn't do anything stupid when I work so much. Plus his bedroom is on the second floor of his house, and I live in the tiny apartment above the diner. So the easiest solution was for him to go stay with my aunt who's retired and lives in a one-story house forty-five minutes away.

Honestly, that distance is the only reason I'm even letting myself consider going along with Brenden's plan.

"We'd have to be careful," I warn him. "But if we only need to act like a couple around them and May, it should be okay."

His eyes fly wide. "Oh my god. May! Just slap me and call me stupid."

"Huh?"

"I'm such an idiot! I need another piece of pizza."

I have no idea how that's going to help anything. But I offer him my untouched slice, which he doesn't hesitate to take, even though there's plenty left in the boxes on the counter. "Why are you an idiot?"

"I've been so busy freaking out, I didn't stop to consider how May factors into this. I'd obviously have to tell her what we're doing. She'll think I've lost my mind!"

"*I* think you may have lost your mind," I say. Because I'm willing to help him with this plan if it's what he really wants to do, but that doesn't mean I think it's a particularly *good* plan.

He squints his eyes like he's trying to glare, but it gives off more of a disgruntled puppy vibe than a threatening one. Then he sighs and picks at the pizza, pulling off some of the cheese. "I probably have. But I dunno. It's like . . . I wonder if maybe they're right? Maybe I am doing a shitty job here. Am I the worst parent in the world because I'm considering asking my kid to lie to her grandparents for me?"

The anguished look he gives me breaks my heart.

How can he even think he's a shitty parent? I've seen the way he's raised May all these years. Every kid deserves parents that dedicated to them. If one day May has something important to tell her dad about herself, I'm sure *she* won't be scared to do it.

"You're doing the best job a parent could," I tell him. "You and May have an incredible relationship. Just talk to her. She'll either agree to go along with this, or she'll tell you she's not comfortable with it. And if she says that, then I know you won't do it, because you always put her first."

He takes a bite and chews slowly. As I watch him, taking in his features—the black-framed glasses, his defined jawline, his perfectly sculpted eyebrows, plump bottom lip glistening with grease and just about begging to be bit—it hits me that even though this is probably a bad idea, I almost *want* to do it. Some crazy, selfish part of me wants to know what it would feel like, pretending to be his boyfriend.

I bet it would feel good.

Even if it could never be real, because Brenden has a playful energy that would only get zapped out if he was foolish enough to fall for a guy like me.

When his tongue darts out to swipe at the grease on his lip, my eyes track the movement hungrily. "All right," he finally says. "I'm gonna ask her."

Well, okay then. I expect him to get up and do it right now, but he doesn't. Instead we both stay here, finishing our beers.

This day has been a lot. While I'm not used to sharing my feelings with someone, what I *am* used to is pushing the idea of coming out to my dad to the back of my mind. I haven't even considered it in so long. I don't particularly want to consider it now, but Brenden's quiet presence feels like a safe space, so my mind begins to wander.

It's true my dad doesn't seem to have a problem with any of the queer people in town. And it's been so long since I heard him use the f-slur, that sometimes I almost question my memory and the stuff I heard from him back when I was young.

But then again, there's also the fact that he's constantly hounding me, asking when I'm going to find someone and get married. Never mind that my mom left him—and me—when I was little, and he's been bitter about it for the last twenty-five years. Even though he never bothered to try again, he still pushes all that heteronormative crap on me. At least he hasn't talked about wanting grandkids.

I haven't been in a relationship in so long, and I haven't missed it. But if I had the option to date someone here without hiding it, do I think that's something I might want at some point?

I don't really know.

All I know is that if I end up pretending to date Brenden for a week, my dad can't find out about it. Maybe I *could* come out to him someday, but I'm not ready to make the decision now. And there's no point in coming out for a fake relationship anyway.

CHAPTER FIVE

BRENDEN

Looking up from my phone, where I've been busy triple and quadruple-checking that everything is ready to go for tomorrow morning's events at the inn, I realize that May has already scarfed down half of her burger and fries while I was too distracted to even order anything. Day one of the corporate retreat went off without a hitch, but that hasn't stopped me from sending check-in texts to Danny and Addison every fifteen minutes since I left. I'm not sure I'll sleep tonight, because I'll be dreading some sort of emergency call from the night staff.

Maybe I should go sleep there. There are no available rooms, but my desk chair is comfortable enough.

Yeah, no. Sleeping hunched over my desk would definitely fuck up my back.

I just need to relax and . . . focus on the other thing I'm stressed about.

Elise and Grant are coming tomorrow evening, and I've barely had time to prepare for them because of the retreat. And I haven't talked to May because I'm a big fat pile of chicken shit, so I haven't been able to tell Travis whether or not we're actually doing this, and—

"Dad?"

"What?" I croak.

"You looked weird. Are you breathing?"

"I think so." I am now, at least. Forcing a smile, I ask May, "Are you excited to see your grandparents?"

She sucks down some of her orange soda, then nods. "Yeah, it'll be fun."

Nope. Not the word I'd use.

"How are you?" she asks. "I know sometimes you get uneasy around them."

Damn, she's too perceptive and knows me too well. "I'll be fine," I lie. This would be the perfect transition into asking her to do the biggest, most absurd favor I'll hopefully ever have to ask of my daughter. Instead, I steal a fry off her plate and jam it into my mouth.

"Get your own food," she complains.

I pout at her. "Travis is busy now."

Most Saturday nights, there's another server helping him. But tonight he only has Sullivan in the back cooking, and he's handling everything else alone. I take a glance around the packed diner to locate him. It's the middle of the dinner rush, and he's been running around since we got here. I know this because I was sneaking occasional peeks at him while I was on my phone.

Ever since he came out to me, I've been looking at him differently. Which might sound messed up, but I don't mean it in a bad way. Obviously. It's just that I've never looked at him as more than a friend before. Even though I love talking to him and teasing him and letting him give me shit for my unhealthy habits. I love how he complains about all the town events but participates in little things when I ask him to. I love the way he pays attention to May, and cares about her, and is always there whenever she needs anything. And, of course, whenever I need anything.

But I've always assumed he was straight, and I make it a point not to fall for straight guys. Now that I know the truth, though?

I don't know.

Yes, I'm aware that just because we're both into men, that doesn't mean we have to be into each other. But damn, Travis is hot.

I subtly track him as he hustles between serving plates, refilling drinks, cashing people out, and hopping on the grill when Sullivan gets backed up. He's removed his flannel shirt at some point during all the running around, leaving him in only a tight black T-shirt. If I said I didn't appreciate how this provides a glorious view of his bulging arm muscles, then I'd be a lying liar who lies.

He should be happy—because a steady stream of customers means more money—but it looks like he's barely managing not to frown as he serves people. He probably reached his peopling capacity for the day about thirty plates ago.

"Flag him down," May insists. "You know he'll come over for you."

"No, that's rude. I can wait."

She bites into a fry and lets the end dangle out of her mouth, taunting me with it. "I told you to order when I did."

"I can wait," I say again. And it would've sounded believable if my traitorous stomach didn't choose the next moment to let out a loud rumble.

May snorts. "You look like you're two seconds away from eating your own hand."

Right as I'm coming up with a witty retort, a giant plate of food is slammed down in front of me. "Wha—" I look up to find Travis hovering beside me. "I didn't order anything."

"You need to eat. Stop worrying about work."

"I wasn't wo—"

"Yes, you were," May interrupts me.

I scowl. It's true, but I was also worrying about Elise and Grant coming tomorrow. And what I'm going to say to May about the fake dating thing. I'm a multifaceted worrier.

When I look up at Travis again, he's smiling at me. A real one, not his obligatory customer service one. I know the difference. "Just eat, okay?"

A sudden swell of emotions rushes through me. "Thank you."

With a simple nod, he walks away.

As I dig into the juicy burger—the man even put mayonnaise on the bun for me so I wouldn't have to do it myself—I get lost for a moment in a memory. Back when I first moved to town, I wasn't in the best place financially. I was able to use the money from selling my parents' house to buy my house here. But because I needed more and more stuff for May as she rapidly grew, and I didn't have the best job yet, I had to be careful.

Since I suck at cooking, I did come to the diner for meals more often than I should have, but a lot of times I'd let May order whatever she wanted for breakfast, then order something cheap like toast for myself. One day, when Travis dropped off our food, he set down May's plate of pancakes and set an omelet in front of me.

When I told him I hadn't ordered it, he grumbled, "Made it by accident. Don't wanna let it go to waste." Then he walked off before I could even thank him.

I was pretty sure the accident thing was a total lie. And after that, I considered us friends.

Travis was doing things to help me out even way back then. Now he's offered to do a huge, crazy thing for me in pretending to be my boyfriend. Knowing I'm running out of time if I'm going to make it happen, I look at May and steel myself for this conversation.

As she's wiping her hands with a napkin, she looks up and makes a face. "Why are you staring at me?"

"Because . . . I love you?"

She rolls her eyes. "Sure, okay, but what's the real reason?"

I glance around to make sure no one nearby looks particularly nosy today. Betty Harlowe is notorious for spreading information she wasn't even told directly, but there's a few tables between ours and hers, and she currently seems very invested in the slice of cherry pie she's eating. Plus with the din of everyone in here talking at once, it's pretty hard to overhear anyone unless you're really trying.

Still, this is probably the worst place to talk about this, so I say, "Is it okay if we get out of here, and then we can talk about something on the way home?"

"You're making me nervous. What's wrong?"

"No, nothing. You don't need to be nervous." Shit, I suck. "Are you almost done eating?"

She tucks a wavy strand of lavender hair behind her ear and says, "I'm fine. Let's go."

Looking for Travis, I spot him as he's coming out of the kitchen with a tray of clean coffee mugs. He moves behind the counter to put them away, and I jump up and go over there to catch him.

"Hey, can I grab a box and pay?"

"You need to eat that food," he says, his back to me as he slides the tray into place on top of another one beside the coffee machine.

"I will, I promise. I just need to get out of here so I can talk to May before I lose my nerve."

He turns and gives me a searching look, then recognition dawns in his eyes. "You're going to ask her about . . . the thing?"

I shift my weight nervously, pulling my wallet out of my pocket. "Mm-hmm. I'm sorry I waited 'til the last minute, I've just been caught up with work and—"

"It's fine." Reaching below the counter, he grabs a Styrofoam takeout container and shoves it at me. "Go. Talk to her. Let me know what you guys decide."

"So you're still cool with . . ."

"Yeah. Whatever you need."

Smiling, I hand over my card. He rings me up, and when I go to sign the receipt, I notice the amount is way too small. He didn't charge me for the burger he made me. I want to protest, but he's already rushed away to take care of another customer, so all I can do is leave a hefty tip instead.

By the time I get back to our table, May's burger is completely gone. I hastily dump my food into the box along with her leftover fries, and then we head out. As we cut across the path through the town green to walk home, I pop the box open and start munching on fries.

"Dad." May nudges me in the side.

I finish chewing and brace myself. My time's up. I either have this incredibly awkward conversation with my daughter, or I have an even more incredibly awkward conversation with her grandparents when I explain that I completely lied about being in a relationship. Only one of those options has me talking to someone who I know loves me.

"This has to stay between us," I tell her.

"Is there a celebrity staying at the inn?" she asks excitedly. "Oh my god, please tell me it's Skyler James!"

"What? No."

Her face falls. "Damn."

Shaking my head, I say, "Anyway, this is something that nobody else in town knows, and it needs to stay that way, but . . . Travis is gay."

"Okay. That's none of my business, so why are you telling me?" she asks. Then, eyes growing wide, she grips my forearm. "Oh my god, you guys are dating!"

"Yes," I say, relieved she gets it. Oh, wait. *No.* "No, we're not dating. Why would you think that?"

She cocks her head at me. "Um. Because you guys are kind of obsessed with each other?"

"*What?* We are not!"

"Sure . . . Then if this isn't about the two of you, why do I need to know about Travis's sexuality? He's a private person."

God, she's too mature. And yeah, I guess I didn't need to start with that. I stuff another emotional support French fry in my mouth while I recalibrate. Then as we walk past some of the small businesses on the other side of the square—the general store, the salon—I spill everything.

I mean, not *everything*. I don't explain my fear that her grandparents might try to swoop in and take her away from me. She doesn't need to know about that.

But she knows how off-kilter they can make me feel sometimes. So when I explain how I accidentally told Elise I had a boyfriend, that's probably why she's kind enough to try to hold back her laughter.

"It's fine, you're allowed to laugh at me," I tell her. "I'm a mess! I don't know what happened. I just blurted it out, and now they're expecting to meet my imaginary boyfriend."

"So tell them the truth."

I cringe. "Right. Yes. See, I *could* tell them the truth, except it feels like I really can't. I don't want them to not trust me or think I'm a bad parent. It's hard to explain, but your grandmother really liked the idea that I had someone else around to help take care of you."

May frowns. "I don't need anyone else."

"I know," I say automatically. Although maybe I'm wrong and Elise is right. If that's the truth, I really don't want to face it. "But I think it would be best if we just go along with this and make her happy."

"How the heck are we supposed to go along with it?" she asks. "You can't just pull a boyfriend out of thin air." She abruptly stops walking and stares at me, mouth hanging open for a second. "Tell me you did not ask Travis to pretend to be your boyfriend."

I pick at the corner of the Styrofoam. "Um. Well."

"Dad! You can't do that to him."

"To him?" I only thought she might be upset about me lying to her grandparents. What am I doing to Travis? "He said he wants to help me."

She rolls her eyes in perfect thirteen-year-old-girl fashion. "Of course he wants to help you, because he—" Cutting herself off, she pauses, then says, "All right."

"All right?" I question. "As in you're okay with this? Because you don't have to be! I know how much it sucks asking you to go along with this in front of your grandparents, but it'll only be for their short visit, and then I swear after they leave, I'll tell them we broke up."

I feel guilty for not specifying when I'll tell them. I'm thinking maybe in four years—when May's close enough to eighteen that they won't bother trying to take her from me.

May sighs. "Stop stressing, please. I hate the idea of lying to them, but it's not going to hurt them. If this will make their visit easier for you, then it's fine. You do so much for me. I can do this one thing for you."

I didn't think it was possible for me to love my daughter more than I already do, but for this, I just might. Because this is hardly the first thing she's done for me. She does so much for me, apparently without even realizing it.

I hold the box out so she can grab some fries. "Have I ever told you that you're the best daughter in the world?"

"Many times."

"Well, you are," I say as we start walking again. "You know what? I should get you that pony you always wanted."

She laughs because she's never actually asked for a pony. She grew up happily playing with Delilah. "I'm a little past the pony stage now."

"You're really sure about this?" I double-check, joking aside. "I promise I'll never ask you to do anything this insane ever again."

"Somehow I doubt that. But yes, I'll do it." Hopping off the curb, she peers up at me. "Can I make a suggestion though?"

"What?"

"After grandma and grandpa leave, you should probably look into therapy."

I gape at her, unsure if she's joking. Her face is telling me it's one of those things you joke about but also sort of mean. And well. That's fair, I suppose.

"I love you, kid."

"Love you too," she says, coming closer to snag another fry.

Passing her the box, I take out my phone and text Travis. The plan is on. Tomorrow.

AS PREDICTED, I didn't sleep well last night, too preoccupied with worries about the inn and the Richardsons arriving today. I'm on my third cup of coffee already, but it's not doing much to help me keep my eyes open. Although when I see Mr. Bennington—the businessman in charge of the retreat—approaching me from across the lobby, I manage to fake some perkiness.

I need to stay on my game, because the inn could use more events like this. They're stressful and meticulous to plan, but they bring in the money.

"Mr. Sanderson," he says when he reaches me at the front desk. Even though I've told him multiple times that I don't mind everyone calling me Brenden.

"Mr. Bennington," I reply, because he has *not* told me to call him by his first name.

"Do you have the projector screen set up in the ballroom?"

"I do," I assure him. It was touch-and-go there for a minute, because I'm not the most tech-savvy person. But he doesn't need to know that.

He nods his head once. "Excellent. And you'll have a table set with coffee and pastries?"

"Yes! I think everyone will enjoy the selection we have for you today."

This gets me a small smile. "My team have all been raving about the food here. Compliments to the chef."

My pleased grin is hard to hide. Addison will be relieved and proud to hear that. But Travis deserves some of the credit too. He's been here almost as constantly as she has. Honestly, I have no idea how he's keeping the diner running at the same time, but he hasn't complained once. Hasn't given me any indication that he needs to be anywhere else.

Mr. Bennington, on the other hand, clearly has no desire to spend any more time in my presence than necessary. With a final nod, he turns and marches away. I try not to take it personally.

Refocusing on the task in front of me, I finish double-checking reservations for next week, because I can't afford another error in the booking system. Everything looks good, which is a relief.

I'm about to pop into the kitchen to see if Addison and Travis need anything (not that I could truly offer much help to them, considering my lack of cooking proficiency) when the inn's main doors open, letting in a nice spring breeze. I turn on instinct to greet the guests—only to face Elise and Grant strolling in, luggage in tow. A *lot* of luggage.

"Hello, dear!" Elise greets me warmly.

I freeze, taking a beat too long to respond. "Hi. Uh. What are you doing here?"

Her smile falls, and it sort of knocks my brain-to-mouth filter back into place.

"Sorry. I mean, I thought you were getting in this evening." I rush forward to help them with their bags. "I was going to pick you up from the airport."

The closest airport to Mayweather is almost two hours away, but I intended to use that time to mentally prepare myself for this. For them. I've been so focused on what to do about the lie I told, that I haven't stopped to process the fact that they'll be *here*, in my town, in my *house*. For an undetermined amount of time.

Elise leans in to give me a hug and a kiss on the cheek. "It's okay, we wanted to rent a car. And we were able to get an earlier flight, so we thought we'd surprise you!"

Color me surprised.

Grant moves in to hug me as well, though it's really more of a quick, one-armed pat on the back. "I told her it'd be better if we gave you a heads up."

"Don't worry, it's totally fine," I lie through my smiling teeth.

"Do you mind showing us to our room?" he asks. "I'm a bit tired from the flight and the drive. We can rest for a while and let you carry on with whatever work you're doing."

The way he says "work" grates on me just a tad. Like he doesn't necessarily equate what I do here—running this whole damn inn—with what he traditionally considers work.

Then the first part of what he said hits me.

Oh, crap, I didn't even tell them they wouldn't be staying here like they normally do.

"So . . ." I start nervously. "I don't actually have a room for you here. I'm fully booked. If I'd known you were getting in now, I would've had you meet me at the house."

This situation, having them stay with me and May, is less than ideal. For me, and surely for them. But with the corporate retreat not leaving until tomorrow evening, and MayFest next weekend, there's no way I can give them a room here. Tourists come early for the festival.

Surprisingly, Elise looks delighted at this news, her face lighting up like I offered her a free upgrade from coach to first class. Not that she'd ever fly coach. "Well, that's no problem at all. We'll get to spend more time with you and May this way!"

Yeah. More time with me, May, and my fake boyfriend.

When I came up with the brilliant idea of faking a relationship, I imagined Travis wouldn't need to spend that much time around Elise and Grant. Maybe we'd all share a meal or two, just so they could meet him. Easy-peasy-someone-squeeze-me.

But I forgot to take into account the fact that they'll be staying at my house instead of the inn. They'll be there all the time. All. The. Time. And they might expect Travis to be around a lot too. Since my dumb ass told Elise that my boyfriend and I practically live together.

Travis and I haven't even had time to work out the details of this mess

I've created.

Jesus, maybe I *should* look into May's suggestion of therapy. That's an issue for another day though. After I survive this visit.

"I can head over there with you two now and get you set up," I tell them. "I only need a minute to make sure I'm covered here."

Before they can reply, Travis comes barreling around the corner from the kitchen and almost slams into me. He grips my shoulder to steady himself. "Sorry. Can I have the key to the linen closet? We need more rags. A lot more rags."

"Everything okay?" I ask.

He grimaces. "It's fine. We just need to come up with another dessert that can be made quickly for the dinner service."

I pinch the bridge of my nose. I don't want to know.

Travis notices the Richardsons, who are watching this interaction as if it's a show, and he grimaces again. "Sorry, I didn't realize you were with guests."

"Oh, we're not guests," Elise offers. "We're—"

She cuts herself off, leaving the sentence hanging uncomfortably. Because how do you define what they are to me? They're the grandparents of my daughter. But technically, to me, they're nothing. They're not . . . family.

I attempt to turn my grimace into a smile and tell Travis, "This is Elise and Grant, May's grandparents." My eyes send him a quick apology, because this wasn't how I pictured the introductions going.

He blanches and glances down at the not-so-white-anymore apron he's wearing. It looks like a crime scene, covered in splotches of dark red. "Nice to meet you," he says. "I'm Travis." His eyes flit to me questioningly, and at my subtle nod, he lowers his voice and adds, "Brenden's boyfriend."

The lobby's mostly empty, but I understand the caution. If someone local overheard, it would spread like wildfire through Mayweather and reach his dad out of town by the end of the day. And I'd *hate* myself for getting him outed.

"Oh!" Elise says. "We've heard about you. Hello! It's wonderful to meet you."

Grant's expression darkens. "Your boyfriend is your employee?" he asks me.

"No! He's not." Do they really think so little of me to think I'd date an employee? "He owns the diner in town. He's only helping me out in the kitchen for a bit with a couple big events."

"I see," Grant says curtly. Admitting that I need my boyfriend to help me run my business probably doesn't make me look much better in his eyes.

I hold back my groan of frustration. All of this could've been avoided if they had arrived when they were supposed to.

"I actually need to be there for the dinner rush tonight," Travis informs me. "I don't have any coverage, but Addison said she'll be fine here once all the prep work is done."

"Yeah, of course."

"Does that mean we won't get to see you tonight to meet you properly?" Elise asks Travis.

"Oh, I—" His gaze shoots to me, looking for the right answer. But damned if I know it.

"Whenever you're finished at work is fine," Elise goes on. "I'm sure we'll all be up late catching up."

When I give Travis another nod—because we might as well get this circus act started—he agrees he'll stop by after the rush is over. "It shouldn't be too late. I can probably sneak out by eight."

"Excellent!" The gleam in Elise's eyes is mildly frightening. "I can't wait to get to know you."

Travis ducks his head shyly—which is *not* a characteristic I usually associate with him. "There's not much to know."

"Nonsense. If you're a part of Brenden and my granddaughter's lives,

I need to know all about you."

At Travis's clearly panicked look, I jump in. "You will. But why don't we let him get back to the kitchen now, and we can head over to the house."

Elise and Grant agree, and I grab Travis the key to the linen closet before I go. As I'm telling him I'll see him later, I sense both of them watching us, so I graze my fingers over the back of his hand in what I hope comes off as a familiar gesture.

The zap of electricity that shoots through my fingers and up my arm at the contact is definitely new though. Somehow I manage to play it cool as a cucumber, but Travis, not quite so much. And I can't tell if his expression this time is because he's worried about the touching in public, or if it's something else. Did he feel the electricity too?

"I've got to . . ." he starts, scratching at his facial hair. "Dessert. Kitchen."

"Right," I say, letting him go.

Tonight will be interesting.

CHAPTER SIX

TRAVIS

Tonight is going to be a disaster. What were we thinking? We can't pull this off. Not with the way I almost lost it at the slightest physical contact from Brenden earlier. I wasn't even thinking about the fact that we were at the inn and someone from town could've seen us. All I could think was . . .

Woah.

I already knew his touch did things to me that it shouldn't. But for years, I've been able to ignore the effect he has on me, because I know he's only ever meant his touches to be friendly. Patting my back as a thank you, gripping my arm when he's excited, occasionally poking at the corner of my mouth when I'm frowning too hard—those things I can handle. One graze of a fingertip, though, and it felt like my insides melted.

My brain knows the intimate touch was only him pretending we're together. But now I need to pretend too, and I hope my dick and heart also get the memo that that's all it is. *Pretend.*

Stepping onto Brenden's porch, I hesitate before knocking. Maybe May's grandparents expect me to have a key. But that's irrelevant anyway, because I'm sure Brenden left the door unlocked like always. Should I go right in as if I'm here all the time? Can't hurt, I guess.

Okay, it's showtime. Turn on boyfriend mode.

My boyfriend mode is pretty rusty, considering I haven't been anyone's boyfriend in over a decade, but I can do this. For Brenden.

I reach for the doorknob, and my assumption about it being unlocked is proven correct. As soon as I step inside the house, though, Brenden comes flying over and grabs my wrist in a surprisingly strong grip, making me question if I did the right thing.

"Please save me," he hisses dramatically in my ear.

"What?"

"They're already unhappy with me because they don't like my tea selection."

I cock my head at him. "You drink tea?"

"No, of course not!" he whispers-yells, as if I've offended his love for coffee. "But I know they do, so I bought a box for them, and apparently my choice is like a sacrilege or something. They went on about how if they drink caffeinated tea in the evening, they won't be able to sleep, and yadda yadda." His grip on me tightens as he continues to rant in a hushed voice. "You'd think they were British for how much it matters to them. I thought all tea was the same!"

"Seriously?"

"No, I guess not," he admits. Then he starts yanking on me in an attempt to drag me in past the foyer. "I don't care. Just come on so they can focus on you instead of me."

Can't say I love the sound of that, but I did know it was coming. And the distress on his face is kicking my protective instincts toward him into overdrive. So if he needs me to be a distraction, that's what I'll be. But first.

I wrap my hand—the one with my wrist not locked in his death grip—around the nape of his neck, brushing my thumb over the short hair there. "Try to relax."

See? I'm boyfriending already.

And apparently thinking in nonsensical Brenden-speak.

"They've got me so on edge," he says, but he leans his head into my touch. He's still in his work outfit—a pale yellow button-up and fitted black slacks that hug his small round ass perfectly. Not that I looked.

Okay, I looked earlier while he was flitting around the inn like a sexy bumblebee. But I won't look again.

"They've visited before, haven't they?" I ask.

"Yeah, but they've always stayed at the inn, so I didn't have to worry about things like providing them with adequate tea. And May was cool with sleeping on the couch so they could stay in her room, but I'm wondering if I should've given them mine instead. Because her full-sized bed is a major downgrade for them, I'm sure. Granted, my queen probably is too, but at least it's slightly better. Except I'm too old to sleep on a couch for more than one night at a time. My body will get all stiff and creaky."

I'm tempted to remind him I'm a year older than him, but instead, I search for something encouraging to say as I continue rubbing his nape.

"That feels good," he practically purrs, finally loosening his hold on my other wrist. Then he lets it go to slide his hand slowly up my forearm.

Trying not to hear his words in a filthier context, and reminding myself why I'm here, I release him and gently nudge his hand away. "We should go before they come looking for us. But it's going to be fine. I'm here for you."

When standing up straight, Brenden's only an inch or two shorter than my six-foot-one. But right now he's slouching, which makes him seem smaller. I can't tell if it's because he still feels defeated, or because I actually helped relax him. Either way, he has to look up to meet my eyes. It feels like he can see all the way into my soul, and I'm worried about what he might find there.

"I know you are," he says softly. "Thank you."

He straightens himself up, then takes my hand in a much more casual hold and begins to lead me toward the kitchen. "Uh, is this okay?" he asks, squeezing my hand once. "We didn't have time to discuss—"

"It's fine," I assure him. While this is certainly new for us, holding his hand is something I could easily get used to. *But I shouldn't.*

In the kitchen, May and her grandparents are sitting at the round table with mugs in front of them. I notice May's is filled with coffee, despite it being eight thirty at night. *Like father, like daughter.* I almost smile but can't, because that's such a terrible habit. At least she's still on school vacation.

Brenden releases my hand as he goes over to the empty chair, the one with another mug of coffee in front of it. Instead of sitting down, though, he glances at me, unsure. So I walk over to join him, and then we both stand there awkwardly as I exchange do-over introductions with Elise and Grant.

With that out of the way, May jumps up and tells me to take her seat. Before I can decline the offer, she grabs her coffee and scoots closer to her grandmother, resting her butt against the windowsill. Brenden sits down and tugs me toward the vacated seat.

For a few moments, nobody says anything, and the tension in Brenden's body seems to have returned already. He's white-knuckling the handle of his coffee mug.

"Would you like some tea?" Elise asks me, politely breaking the silence. "I'm afraid there's no decaf."

Brenden's jaw twitches, so I slide my hand onto his thigh under the table and give it a reassuring squeeze. "No thank you, I'm fine."

"Would you prefer coffee?" Grant asks. "There's a pot on. Although I don't understand how these two"—he gestures between Brenden and May—"can drink it at this time of night."

"We like to live on the edge," May jokes.

Elise tuts her disapproval. "Honestly, Brenden, I'm not sure May should be drinking coffee at all at her age, and especially not at night."

Brenden pales a little. "Well, um, I . . ."

Seeing him like this, with his confidence zapped, kills me. I subtly rub his thigh with my thumb, because I realize he might actually need me here for support as much as for playing a role. Or is this just a part of playing the role? Boyfriends are supposed to be supportive.

Either way, it seems to work. He takes a breath to compose himself, then says, "I respect your concerns. But I've raised May to make her own decisions, and I promise you she's healthy and responsible."

"I think there are worse things a teenager could be drinking," I add. Because while I may pretty much agree with May's grandmother, I don't like her questioning Brenden's parenting decisions.

"I suppose there are," Grant says.

Brenden's hand lands on top of mine under the table and squeezes. I'm pretty sure that means *thank you*. He leaves his hand there after that, keeping mine trapped on his thigh. And I can't say I mind it.

"Although, she's barely a teenager," Elise argues.

"Grandma, I don't even have school tomorrow," May says, giving the woman an angelic smile. "Don't worry."

"I know, sweetie," Elise tells her. "I was only stating my opinion."

May waits until Elise takes her eyes off her before she has another sip of her coffee. Then she glances worriedly between Elise and Brenden. I'm pretty sure she loves her grandparents, but it's clear to me whose side she'd take if it came down to it. I've never seen a closer relationship between a child and parent.

Brenden leans toward me to ask, "Do you want a beer?"

"I'm fine," I tell him. While a beer might usually ease my nerves in a situation like this, seeing him so nervous has oddly been enough to keep me calm. I want to be a steadying presence for him.

"Anyway," Grant says, "we were asking Brenden about the two of you, but he so eloquently told us to *hold off on the interrogation* until you got here."

"I didn't say it like that," Brenden mumbles.

May snorts. "You totally did."

He shrugs sheepishly. "I think I was joking."

"So how did you two get together?" Elise asks, zeroing her attention in on me. "Brenden said you own the diner in town, so you must have known each other for a while before you started dating."

"Right, well . . ." I look to Brenden for help.

"Yeah, um . . ." he says not so helpfully.

As we both flounder for an answer, I realize with horror that Brenden didn't leave us any time to actually prepare for this. We should've come up with a story. We can't just say, "Hey, we're boyfriends," and expect that to be enough.

"Dad and I eat at the diner all the time, so they've known each other for years and were friends first," May smoothly jumps in. "They'd bicker over silly stuff, though it was obviously their way of flirting. I could tell they liked each other, but both of them were too chicken to do anything about it." She shoots a challenging look our way, as if daring us to contradict her.

Even though we definitely don't flirt, I'm keeping my mouth shut. Hopefully, she knows where she's going with this. If she can come up with a cover story for us, then she can say whatever she wants.

Brenden must be thinking the same thing, because he says nothing too. Though it looks like he's fighting hard to keep his face neutral.

May turns back to her grandparents. "So one day, I told Travis my dad was lonely and that I wanted to set him up with someone, and I asked if he had any suggestions. He got all grumpy and told me to leave him out of it. But I kept pushing until he admitted his feelings, and then I told him if he didn't hurry up and ask Dad on a date, I'd find someone else who would."

Well, shit, kid. Thanks for making me sound kind of pathetic.

Considering how easily that came to her, I'm worried she might actually believe some of what she said. She's a smart girl. I'm good at hiding my feelings, but is it possible she sees right through me?

No. She's just covering for us and likely messing with us at the same time. She doesn't know.

Brenden's still silent. I have no idea what he's thinking, but one of us needs to say something.

I clear my throat. *All right, I'm up.* It feels like I'm back in school and forgot to study for a test. "Guess I just needed that push," I say. "And it helped to know May approved of me dating her dad."

"Obviously, I do," May says, giving me a smile that looks very genuine before turning to her grandparents again. "Travis has been around the whole time I was growing up. He's come to my birthday parties. He's always been there for me and Dad, even before they started dating. I know he'll never hurt either of us."

Her eyes meet mine again, and her faith in me gets me a little choked up. Even though the whole thing about me and Brenden being together is fake, it sounds like she means this part. And she's right. I'd never hurt them.

That's why I've never let my feelings for Brenden slip. Because he deserves more than a grumpy closeted guy with hermit tendencies.

"Isn't that sweet," Elise says, reaching out across the table to pat my forearm. "I do appreciate knowing there's someone here taking care of these two."

Brenden's back goes ramrod straight.

"I'm happy to be here for anything they need," I tell her as I squeeze Brenden's thigh lightly. "But there's nothing for you to worry about. Brenden is more than capable of taking care of May and himself. I don't know anyone else who can handle as much as he does. He built a life here for the two of them, all on his own. Gave her a home and everything she needs while working his way up in his career to get where he is now. He and May have an incredibly close relationship, and everyone in town loves both of them."

Brenden exhales loudly, like he was holding his breath. Then, very slowly, his palm slides along the back of my hand until he laces his fingers with mine.

"Well, we did help him out significantly with purchasing the inn," Grant says, "but I'm sure you're right about everything else."

Brenden tenses again. "I hope you know how much I appreciate the two of you offering me a loan."

"Yes, we know, hon," Elise tells him.

"But it's still his good sense for business and hospitality that's keeping the place so successful," I remind everyone. Maybe I shouldn't be causing waves here, but I want to make sure May's grandparents know how smart and capable Brenden is. I want to make sure *he* knows it too.

"The inn's always been a lovely place," Elise says. "We're excited to see what it's like now that it's yours."

"It's, uh . . ." Brenden starts. "Things are going great. It can be stressful, because something constantly comes up that I have to figure out and adapt to. But I love the work, and the guests are always happy."

Elise idly taps one manicured nail against her mug. "I'm sure they are. I hope we can still have some meals there, even if it's not where we're staying."

"Yes, absolutely!"

I can tell by Brenden's face that he's relieved she wants to eat at the inn. Because he certainly has no business cooking for them.

"And we'll have to eat at your place too," Grant adds, turning toward me.

Brenden hastily shakes his head. "No, you don't have to do that. It's not your kind of restaurant."

"Maybe not exactly," Elise admits. "But we'd still like to see it."

"Of course, you should stop in," I say, giving Brenden's fingers a squeeze to let him know it's okay.

It's going to be tricky, navigating how to keep them believing we're a couple while not letting anyone else in town catch on to us. The diner is like gossip central, so we'll need to be careful. But we can do it. I promised him we'd do this.

This handholding is already messing with my head though. We should've talked about touching and boundaries. If I'm doing this, I want to make it believable, but I don't want to do anything that would make Brenden uncomfortable. And I didn't really prepare myself for the way acting affectionate with him would make *me* feel.

But it doesn't matter. Right now, he seems perfectly content to keep our hands together on top of his thigh. I think the contact is keeping him from spiraling. So I'll hold his hand and try to tamp down the warmth that's sneaking up my chest.

After everyone has finished their drinks, Brenden gets up, his fingers slipping out of my hold, and collects the mugs to bring them to the sink. May steals his seat as her grandparents turn all their focus on me. They ask about my life (boring), why I chose owning a restaurant (not entirely a choice), and my family (a dad who doesn't really know me).

I don't say this about my dad, of course. And when I mention that he also lives in town, Elise and Grant insist they need to meet him. But I apologize, letting them know about his injury and how he's staying with his sister for at least another few weeks until he recovers. No chance of that meeting happening, *thank fuck*.

The conversation still makes me squirm a little though. Not necessarily the questions, but the utterly bland impression I must be giving them. Brenden clearly seeks their approval of him and his life choices. I don't want them to think *I'm* a bad choice. Even if this isn't real.

I find myself standing and drifting over toward Brenden when I run out of things to say. He's at the sink washing dishes, so I step up behind him and place a hand on his hip, hoping the move doesn't startle him. It needs to look natural. His jump is so tiny, I'm sure everyone else missed it, then he quickly settles into my touch.

Stepping closer, I rest my chin on his shoulder. And I swear I'm doing this for him. To sell this thing. I'm not doing it because I like how it feels. "Need any help?"

He shakes his head, his cheek briefly brushing mine. "Almost done."

We stay like that a minute while he finishes up, and when he turns to reach for a dish towel, I grab it for him. It's a slight disappointment that I have to step away to do it.

Then Elise says, "Well, it's getting late. I think we'll head up to bed. Travis, you're staying right?"

I'm hit with a flash of panic.

"Don't let us get in the way of whatever it is you two would normally be doing," she adds.

"*Eww,*" May says.

"Hush," Brenden tells her, face flaming. He glances nervously at me, and we attempt to have a silent conversation.

Finally, I nod, because it seems like the only option. "Yeah. I was gonna stay."

Brenden's face is a strange mix of relieved and worried now, and I can't say I'm not experiencing a mix of emotions myself. Of course Elise and Grant would assume that I spend some nights here, but I kind of figured that the respectful thing for a boyfriend to do would be to stay at home and give them space for their visit.

Brenden and I didn't talk about the possibility of me actually sleeping here. We didn't talk enough about anything. *Damn it.* We'll need to work out all the details of this ridiculous plan tonight. In his bedroom.

Fuck.

Me.

CHAPTER SEVEN

BRENDEN

Well.

Here we are.

Elise and Grant are in May's room for the night, and May is all set up downstairs on the couch. And somehow Travis and I have found ourselves standing in my bedroom, facing each other on opposite sides of a bed that I forgot to make this morning.

"Uh . . ." I scratch at an itch on the inside of my elbow.

"I'm sorry," Travis says, his gaze flicking rapidly from me to the bed, then back to me again. "I didn't know if you wanted me to stay since they expected me to, or if I was supposed to make up an excuse to leave."

"Don't be sorry," I tell him. "We should've had a plan for this. But I don't mind you staying. Unless it'll be uncomfortable for you."

I grimace at my own words. Of course this would be uncomfortable for him. He'd obviously rather be at home sleeping in his own bed than here sharing mine with me. This is really pushing the boundaries of our friendship.

It's true that I got us into this situation, but I'd hate myself if I ruined our friendship for the sake of saving face with two people whose opinions of me will never be that high anyway.

"Maybe we can sneak you out?" I offer half-heartedly, glancing at the window then scratching myself again. "This is all my fault, I'm so sorry."

"Don't apologize." He comes around to my side of the bed and takes me by the forearm. "I signed up for this. I'll do whatever you need me to do to make it work. And I'm not sneaking out the window like we're in high school."

I can't drag my eyes away from where he's holding on to me. That itch is gone. "I'm sorry I'm such a mess."

His grip tightens, and my eyes jolt up to meet his. "What did I say about apologizing?"

I figure it's a rhetorical question, but he continues to stare at me imploringly until I swallow the lump in my throat and answer him. "You said don't. But—"

"Nope," he cuts me off. "Stop." He moves to sit on the edge of the bed, tugging me gently so I sit beside him. "You're not a mess. Lying to May's grandparents about having a boyfriend probably wasn't the best thing to do, but for whatever reason, you feel like you can't tell them the truth now. So we're doing this."

He pauses and squeezes my arm. "Personally, I think if you gave them the chance, they'd accept you for who you are, and they'd realize that being in a relationship doesn't make you somehow a better person. But you asked me to be your fake boyfriend, so I promise I'm going to do a good job at it. If you want me to stay the night, I can stay the night."

When he lets go of me, I immediately mourn the loss of contact. It's as if I'm suddenly touch-starved or something. Which is weird. I'm not usually like this. May's always been available for cuddles whenever I need them.

But Travis's touch is different. It's solid, steady. Like him.

It makes me feel like I can be solid too.

"If you're sure you don't mind, then you should probably stay so they don't suspect anything," I concede. "We should go over the details of what faking this relationship is actually going to look like anyway, and what we're each comfortable with doing. And then I can sleep on the floor."

"You're not sleeping on the floor," he argues, angling himself toward me so his knee presses slightly into my thigh. "I'll sleep on the floor."

"You're my guest. I can't let you do that."

His smile is teasing. "I'm not your guest. I'm your boyfriend, remember?"

"Fake," I remind him.

He shrugs.

"Is it . . ." I clear my throat. "Is it maybe okay for fake boyfriends to share a bed?"

There's a flash of something I can't identify in his eyes, and I'm about to backtrack, but then he says, "Yeah. I'm good with that if you are. I don't think either of our backs would do well with sleeping on the floor."

I laugh. "Well, if I woke up and could barely walk tomorrow morning, that might help to sell this relationship."

He makes a strangled, choking sound, and my face heats. What in the world possessed me to make a joke like that? We joke around all the time, but it's always about innocent stuff, never about sex. Never about gay sex. With each other.

I kind of want to roll over and face plant myself into the comforter to hide. But then suddenly, Travis is laughing so hard he clutches his stomach. I slap a hand over his mouth, though now I'm laughing a little too. "*Shhh.* They're right down the hall."

"Sorry," he says, getting a hold of himself. "I'm sorry."

His voice is muffled, which makes me realize I'm still covering his mouth. *Oops.* Removing my hand, I tuck it safely under my thigh. But the ghost of his lips remains on my palm.

No.

Nope.

Not huh. Not happening.

I really don't know how my brain got so scrambled, but it needs to unscramble fast, because Travis is my friend. There's no way I should be imagining what his lips would feel like on the rest of my skin.

And yet . . .

"So we agree we can share?" His voice jolts me out of whatever nonsense was going on in my head, and he pats the bed beside his hip.

"Oh yeah, totally," I say, hoping he can't hear how nervous this idea makes me. Because there's no reason to be nervous, right? "It's big enough. It's not like we'll have to cuddle."

He cocks his head, amusement dancing in his eyes. And *seriously*, what is wrong with my mouth tonight?

"Let's pretend I didn't say that. Or maybe anything I've said since we stepped into this room."

"But it's fun to see you flustered," he says.

My eyebrows shoot up my forehead. Is he flirting with me? We don't flirt. We give each other shit. I smile at him, and he grouches at me. That's our thing.

Or is this pretend flirting? Because we're pretend boyfriends, so maybe he's just staying in character. We really need to talk about this.

"Right," I say. "So sleeping arrangements are settled, I guess. Good."

He gestures at his jeans. "I didn't exactly bring anything to change into. Do you have some sweats I can borrow?"

I glance down at where his thick thighs are resting on the edge of the bed. Then I picture him squeezing into a pair of my pants, and a sudden heat creeps up the back of my neck. I could really use a drink of water. "I'm not sure anything I have will fit you."

As his eyes sweep over me, from my head down to my feet, it feels like he's noticing my body for the very first time. I resist the urge to cover myself, not even sure which part I should cover. My legs, my skinny arms, my relatively flat but soft stomach.

I'm not ashamed of my body, and the guys I've dated haven't seemed to have any complaints. But I'm not defined like Travis. He's rugged and muscular, all hard edges, whereas I'm just . . . me. Not small enough to be considered a twink, and yet when other queer men look at me, I'm pretty sure nothing about me screams "top" to them.

There's been more than a few guys who were surprised—and not pleasantly—to find that I liked to do it both ways.

"You're probably right." Travis stands. Now he's the one looking self-conscious. "I can just sleep like this. It's fine."

"No, that isn't fine. Sleeping in jeans is the worst." God, this poor man was only trying to help me out. And now here he is, stuck at my house, forced to share a bed with me, and even willing to be in physical discomfort while he does it. "You can, uh . . . just take them off."

The corner of his mouth quirks up like he wants to smirk, but I cut him off before he can say anything.

"Don't tease me!"

"I'm sorry," he says, his fingers reaching out to graze briefly across my arm, leaving tingles in their wake. "This whole thing is a little . . . unexpected. But I think you being nervous and awkward is helping me stay grounded."

"Gee, you're welcome."

His face becomes unbearably soft. Unbearable in the sense that I don't see this softness from him often, and it's making me want to lean closer to him. To climb into his lap and let him hold me.

Resisting this newfound urge is painful, but I'm strong.

"What I mean is," he says slowly, "I don't want this whole thing to make anything weird between us. When we're done being a fake couple, we have to go back to being you and me, right? Pretending we're together is bound to be a little awkward. So if we can joke about it, I think that's a good thing."

"I know," I agree. "I'd never want things to be weird between us either."

I couldn't imagine losing Travis's friendship. The bantering, the easy company. Not to mention, May and I would probably starve.

He tugs at the material of his jeans. "So do we talk first or get comfortable first?"

"Might as well get comfortable and get used to sharing this bed."

His rich brown eyes study me a moment. Then he turns away, clears his throat, and says, "Yeah, okay."

We both get up, and I point him toward the ensuite bathroom, letting him know there should be a new toothbrush under the sink he can use. Hopefully.

While he's in there, I open my dresser drawer and gather my sleepwear. A pair of thin navy blue drawstring pajama pants and a plain white T-shirt that's a bit baggy on me. I don't normally wear a shirt to bed, except sometimes in the winter, because I feel like I'm being strangled. But there's no way I can get into bed shirtless with Travis. Nope. No way.

When he emerges from the bathroom still fully dressed in his flannel and jeans, I experience a pang of disappointment. Not that I expected him to strip down and walk out to show me. But I wouldn't exactly have been *opposed* to that.

He gazes at me questioningly. "Your turn?"

I snap myself out of it. "Right, thanks. I'll just be a sec." Stepping past him, I avoid eye contact.

As I change and brush my teeth in the bathroom, I give myself a silent but stern talking to.

Stop it. Travis is your friend. Nothing's going to happen. It doesn't matter that you're dying to know what he looks like under his clothes. Stop imagining what those strong thighs would feel like if he had his legs wrapped around your waist, squeezing you with them while you fucked him.

Unsure whether that little talk helped or made things worse, I take a deep breath and step out of the bathroom. Travis is sitting up in my bed, shoulders propped against the headboard, the covers pulled up to his waist. He's removed his flannel, leaving him in a black undershirt that hugs his pecs and biceps. Suddenly, I wish I had x-ray vision, because I assume he's removed his jeans too.

I can almost sense him actively *not* looking at me as I move around the room, dropping my dirty clothes in the laundry basket and plugging in my phone by the nightstand. Then there's nothing left for me to do but get in bed.

In bed.

With Travis.

No big deal, right?

Carefully, I lift the covers just enough for me to slip under. I match his position, leaning against the headboard, but angle myself toward him so we can talk. When I stretch my legs out, my foot grazes against the bare skin of his calf. He stiffens, and I jerk it back.

My queen bed has never seemed so small before. There's plenty of room for me to spread out like a starfish when I'm alone. But I'm not alone now, *nope, no siree.* Travis isn't a small guy, and the lack of space between us is apparent.

"So . . . we were gonna talk," I say, somewhat idiotically.

"Yeah. I want to make sure you're okay with me touching you like I did downstairs. I was trying to play the boyfriend role and went with what felt natural. Plus you were upset, and it seemed like I was able to help you calm down. But if you need us to have clearer boundaries, we can set them now."

What he's saying makes sense, and talking about this is the mature, smart thing to do. But all I can think about is how good it felt when he put his hand on my thigh under the table earlier when I was stressed. He's always been there for me as my friend, but no one would call him a touchy-feely guy. His touch in those moments offered me a whole new level of comfort. And I'm afraid I liked it way too much.

Because like he said, he was only playing a role.

"Brenden?"

"Oh. Uh." *Focus. What was he asking?*

"Do you have any boundaries as far as physical contact that you want to discuss?"

I shake my head. "Right. No. At least, I don't think so. I need this to look believable between us, because if Elise and Grant find out I lied and did something this crazy . . ."

Remembering exactly why we're doing this whole thing makes me shudder. It's way too late to call it off.

Travis shifts so he can face me easier, and his knee presses into my thigh again. "We'll make it believable. So you're okay with hugging, holding hands, light touches?"

"Yes," I answer quickly. Probably a little *too* okay with it.

"And what about . . ." He hesitates, and for the first time in this conversation, he seems to be the one who's nervous.

"About what?" I prompt.

"What about kissing?"

My whole body goes tense, shocked at even hearing the word "kissing" coming out of Travis's mouth in regards to me.

Wow, I really threw both of us into this mess without thinking it through at all, didn't I?

"We don't have to," he says. "I'm sure they won't think it's weird if we don't kiss in front of them."

"No, we should!" That comes out sounding a bit too eager, and I blush. "I mean, we can. If it seems appropriate. I don't think we need to be making out in front of them or anything, but yeah. A simple hello or goodbye kiss occasionally will help sell it."

His knee nudges into my thigh a little harder, but I don't know if it's on purpose. "I think so too. So if it feels right, we'll just go for it. We need to look like we're fully comfortable with each other, and then they won't question anything."

I've always been fully comfortable with Travis. Until now. When we're sitting here talking about things like holding hands and kissing. Now my mind is shooting off in all different directions. Up until recently, I didn't even know he swung this way. Can I picture him kissing a guy?

I go tense with the realization that yes, in fact, I *can*. And the guy I'm picturing him kissing looks an awful lot like me.

I shift a little, trying to ward off the effect that sudden mental image has on me. But I'm not very successful, and before I can stop myself, I blurt out, "Maybe we should practice."

Whoopsie.

Travis blinks at me a few times, and I resist the urge to shout out, *Haha, just kidding!*

Because even though I might have said it for entirely unscrupulous reasons, it's not a terrible idea. If we kiss for the first time in front of May's grandparents, who knows how awkward it will look. We should get used to it first.

"We can do that," he finally says.

Which makes the reality of the situation set in. If he and I kiss, there's no going back after it. Not that I think one kiss will make me fall in love with him or anything. But it would be foolish to assume that nothing will be different.

I just have to hope our friendship can survive this.

"Okay," I say.

"Okay," he repeats. "Uh." He scoots closer to me, and I find myself holding my breath. "So I'll just . . ."

He leans in, bringing one hand up like he's going to cup my face, but then he lets it fall down to rest on my shoulder instead. Using that connection, he gently guides me forward until our lips meet.

It's soft, hesitant, brief. The barest of grazes before he pulls back. But I felt it.

Sweet lord, I *felt* it.

And I want to feel it again.

So without stopping to consider what that means, I lean in this time and press my mouth to his. He exhales sharply, like I took him by surprise, but then he kisses me back, moving his lips gently against mine. His fingers curl tightly around my shoulder for a second, then his hand drifts down my biceps before it falls away. But he's still kissing me.

The kiss probably only lasts about ten seconds, but when we stop, my head is spinning like I lacked oxygen for much longer than that.

Travis gives me one deep, imploring look, making me wish I had answers to whatever silent questions he's asking. But I'm afraid I don't. My mind is offline. Then he moves away from me, back to his side of the bed, and I reboot, managing not to follow him there even though my body wants to.

"Well," he says finally. "I think that went okay."

Okay? I want to ask. Because that was a hell of a lot better than okay. But I keep my lips pressed firmly shut, trying not to linger on the memory of the way they felt against his. Of all the tiny sparks.

I did theater in high school, and one time I had to kiss this girl that I didn't particularly like, because she was kind of a snob. Our director had us practice countless times to make it look real. And although we eventually got it and it looked natural, it still felt nothing but practical. We were just doing our jobs.

That's what this was supposed to be.

So why did it feel so much *more* than practical?

"Brenden, are you okay? Did that make you uncomfortable?"

I almost laugh, because the only place it made me uncomfortable was in my pants. Thankfully, my pajamas leave enough room for things to . . . *happen* without it being painful. But the last thing I want is for Travis to realize I got hard simply from ten seconds of kissing him.

If he knew, then he'd be the one uncomfortable with this situation, and he might want to back out. That can't happen, so I need to get myself under control and remember this is nothing more than him doing me a huge favor.

"I'm fine," I lie. "I think we got the hang of it, right? We don't need to practice again."

There's still a concerned look on his face, but he says, "Right. I think we're good."

"Ready to sleep?"

"Yeah."

"Great," I say, the exhaustion from this stressful day suddenly hitting me like a wrecking ball ridden by Miley Cyrus. "Thank you again for doing all this."

"Don't worry about it," he tells me.

But it's sort of impossible not to worry about how I'm having all these new feelings for my friend.

Lust. It's only lust, I tell myself. Nothing more.

And lust, I can handle. It's only natural when you get all up close and personal with a smoking hot guy. But I'm a father, and I have to be responsible. I can control my libido. It doesn't have to control me. It's possible to be lusting after Travis but still want us to remain friends.

I'll get over it. Lust always fades.

I scoot myself down the bed until I'm lying on my back, and the mattress shifts as Travis does the same next to me. "Goodnight," I say, rolling onto my side and facing away from him to put a bit more space between us. Not that I actually *want* the space. But I need it.

"Goodnight," he replies.

Then we're both quiet. I'm holding my body so rigidly, keeping myself from spreading out the way I normally would. Despite how tired I am, it takes me a long time to fall asleep. And before I do, I recall the totally-out-of-left-field story May made up for her grandparents about me and Travis.

How the heck did she come up with that? She made it sound like he was pining away for me all these years.

Like there'd be a chance in hell of that.

But luckily, Elise and Grant have no way of knowing how crazy and unrealistic the story was.

CHAPTER EIGHT

TRAVIS

I wake before the sun rises and before my alarm. My body's used to this because of all the mornings I need to get up super early to open the diner. Like today. The alarm will probably sound any minute, so I need to turn it off before it wakes Brenden. I start to move, but then freeze, realizing something.

Brenden.

He went to sleep last night with as much distance between us as this bed allowed. As if I have cooties. He was practically falling off the mattress.

Now, obviously having migrated my direction during the night, he's so close I can smell his shampoo. Which wouldn't be a big deal, if it weren't for these two facts: I'm hard, and his ass is pressed right against my erection.

Taking a deep breath, I roll the other way, careful not to disturb him, and reach for my phone on the nightstand. I turn off the alarm just in time. My plan was to sneak out before anyone else is awake, open the diner, then sneak back in here to continue playing the boyfriend role.

There's no time to freak out about the compromising position we were in. But believe me, that doesn't mean I'll be forgetting about it.

In the dark, I find my clothes and get changed, tucking my dick away and willing it to soften. I spare only one more quick glance at Brenden's peacefully sleeping form. He was a ball of anxiety last night. I'm glad he seems to have gotten some good sleep.

I sneak downstairs as stealthily as my fairly large body will allow, mindful of the fact that May's asleep on the couch as I creep past her. Once I've made it out the front door and shut it quietly behind me, I hightail it to my truck and drive away.

As I unlock the diner and dash upstairs to my apartment to change, I mentally run through my checklist of opening tasks, even though the routine is entirely second nature after so many years. Maybe I'm just trying to distract myself from thinking of how I woke up practically cuddling Brenden.

Morning wood is natural, sure. But there was a moment there where I had to fight the urge to press farther into his ass, rather than roll away. That was before I came to my senses, of course.

I can't remember the last time I slept in a bed with someone else. Normally, I hook up and leave immediately afterward. So maybe my body only reacted because of the novelty of it.

But it's fine. I shut that shit down. I don't actually want to molest Brenden in his sleep.

What isn't as easy to shut down, though, is the memory of the way he kissed me last night. It was only supposed to be for practice, so I feel guilty for enjoying it, but I did. The moment his lips touched mine, it was like a tiny jolt of electricity, zapping me awake from some deep sleep I didn't even know I was under. But again, it was practice. Fake.

Fake boyfriend.

Back in the diner, I flip the chairs down off the tables and wipe all the surfaces, then I get the first pot of coffee brewing. That's when I take out my phone to call my dad. I've been checking in with him as often as I can.

Which is mostly due to my guilt about sending him away while he recovers instead of taking care of him myself. I know that wouldn't have been practical, but he's my dad.

Despite our relationship not actually being all that close if you really examine it, I love the stubborn bastard. He's the one who stuck around and raised me when my mom left.

I'm talking to him more often now that he's out of town than I did when he was right here and I could see him every day. But his fall kind of scared me. It forced me to confront the idea of losing him one day. Possibly one day soon.

"Travis!" he answers the phone in lieu of a hello, his voice managing to sound both gruff and happy to talk to me at the same time.

"Hey, Dad." I press the switch to grind the decaf beans, even though I won't brew a pot until someone asks for it. First thing in the morning is not the time people want decaf.

"What the heck is that noise?" he asks.

"Coffee beans," I tell him, rolling my eyes. It's not like he didn't grow up in this diner the same way I did.

He hums in understanding, then says, "You know Kristy is trying to get me to drink her fancy shit coffee with all these foofy flavors. I've told her that I'm a man and coffee should just be coffee, but she keeps trying to sneak them by me. Like I won't notice the taste of pecan and banana and whatever other weird shit they put in there."

I bristle at the "I'm a man" comment, grateful he can't see me my face. This is the kind of crap I didn't want to explain to Brenden. My dad's not a bad guy. I really believe that. But he's a product of the time in which he was raised, and he doesn't see anything wrong with letting comments like this about what it means to be a man or not tumble out of his mouth.

Should I correct him and keep trying to nudge him into this century? Probably.

But I think it's already clear I'm somewhat of a coward when it comes to him.

So I maintain the status quo. "You should be watching your caffeine intake anyway."

"Oh, fuck off with that," he says, and I laugh. At least I'm not afraid to harass him about his health.

I ask how he's doing besides the coffee situation, then listen as he tells me for about the hundredth time how he's bored out of his mind. You'd think a man who has worked hard all his life would be able to appreciate taking a break for a while, but he just wants to get back to work.

He could really use a hobby. Though I'm pretty sure he thinks hobbies are for girls.

"You'll be walking without crutches and able to come home soon," I assure him.

"Yeah, yeah. Not soon enough," he grumbles.

Silently, I disagree with him. Because if he were to come home now, that would end my ability to help out Brenden with the fake relationship.

I stiffen up like I'm about to get caught out. As if by even thinking about Brenden, my dad will be able to sense what I'm doing with him. But, of course, I know he's not a mind reader. And honestly, he's not even the most observant guy.

While I was living in Boston and sharing an apartment with Christian—my ex, and the longest relationship I've had—Dad never questioned anything. Didn't find it at all strange when we went on a trip to Cancun, just the two of us.

As he complains to me about something else, I'm distracted by the idea of coming out to him. Which is crazy. Keeping this part of myself from him has always been my reality, simple as that. It's something I came to terms with long ago, and until my talk with Brenden about it the other day, it wasn't taking up any space in my brain. Now it's hard to talk to him and not think about the *what if.*

What if I told him the truth?

Would he hate me? Would it ruin our relationship for whatever time we have left together?

I mean, he's not dying. It just seems like, since he's pushing sixty and I've gone this long without telling him, there might not be a point to doing it now. Maybe it would be harsh to force him to confront that I'm not who he thought I was all this time.

Or maybe, again, I'm nothing more than a coward.

IT'S STILL VERY EARLY when I sneak my way back into Brenden's house, carrying a bag of ingredients to make breakfast. After I got the diner set up and ready to go for the day, Benji arrived to cover for me, and I slipped out right as he was flipping the sign on the door from CLOSED to OPEN.

May's grandparents strike me as early risers, but I'm hoping they're still asleep. Although I guess it's not really suspicious if I left to open my business. Even if Brenden and I were really dating, that would still be something I needed to do. This whole lying thing just has me paranoid. I don't want to be the one who messes it up and gets us caught out.

As I open the unlocked door and close it behind me, I try to make as little noise as possible to avoid waking May. Of course, my big dumb ass has to go and whack my knee on a table as I'm crossing behind the couch, and I let out a curse before I can stop myself.

"*Shit!*"

There's some noise and movement from the couch, so I freeze, feeling stupidly like a teenager about to get caught sneaking in after curfew. Then May slowly emerges from a nest of blankets and sits up, peering at me while rubbing her eyes.

"Sorry," I say quietly. "Go back to sleep."

"I'm not like my dad," she tells me, with a sleepy smile. "Once I'm up, I'm up, but it's okay."

I set the bag on the floor and move around to the front of the couch. "I'm guessing Brenden has to be dragged kicking and screaming out of bed?"

"Sometimes. Usually when he needs to get up and do something he really doesn't wanna do."

I chuckle, because I can picture her forcing her dad to get up, even though it should be the other way around.

As she stands, I notice her pajama pants are printed with little pictures of books and coffee cups, which fits her perfectly. She immediately starts folding her bedding, so I jump in to help. When we're done, I tell her I need to put some things in the fridge, and she follows me into the kitchen.

It's no surprise that she heads straight for the coffee maker. While she starts a pot, I get to work setting out the things I'll need to make breakfast for everyone. We navigate around each other with ease, and that makes me happy in a way I didn't expect.

Over the years, I've spent plenty of time alone with Brenden, but me being alone with May is much rarer. I like that she seems perfectly comfortable having me here in her space with her.

"You don't have to cook us breakfast," she says, eyeing me as she stirs sugar into her coffee.

"I'm trying to make a good impression."

Her brow furrows thoughtfully. "But you don't need to try this hard. You're doing enough just by being here."

I shrug. "It's for Brenden."

After a few beats of silence, she says, "I dunno what my dad told you about my grandparents, but they're not that bad."

"I'm sure they're not. Your dad is just . . ."

"A mess?" she finishes for me, amusement dancing in her eyes.

"Something like that," I mutter fondly. He may be a mess sometimes, but he's also pretty incredible.

"I know I was too young to understand what things were like between them when he first adopted me," she says. "But I don't think he needs to be so worried about everything around them. They don't hate him."

As I begin preparing pancake batter, I tell her, "He worries because he loves you so much. He doesn't want anything to hurt your relationship with them. And I think it's a bit more complicated than just not wanting them to hate him."

"Eh. Sometimes I think adults *make* things more complicated than they need to be."

I stop what I'm doing and stare at her, processing her words. She's probably not wrong. Brenden certainly complicated his situation with Elise and Grant by lying to them about having a boyfriend. Thinking about the way we floundered like idiots last night, I remember how May jumped in to save us.

"Hey, thanks for last night. With that save and, uh . . ." A flush creeps up my neck. "The stuff you said about me."

She leans her back against the counter beside me, with her mug cradled in her hands, and offers me a sweet smile. "It wasn't hard to come up with a story. The two of you *do* banter an awful lot. If you guys were in a romcom, that would totally be construed as flirting." Before I can argue that Brenden and I don't flirt, she continues. "And what I said about you always being there for me and my dad wasn't a lie at all. I hope you know how much he appreciates everything you do for us. We both appreciate it."

Swallowing past the lump in my throat, I admit, "I like seeing both of you happy."

"My dad likes to pretend he's always happy, but I'm not a little kid anymore. I can see through him."

Okay, yeah. This girl is too perceptive.

"But when he's around you, he really seems the happiest," she adds. "So if . . . well, if you two actually did want to start something between you, I'd be cool with that. Just so you know."

Just so I . . .

Fuck.

Can she see through me as well as she can see through her dad?

It's nice to know she'd be okay with the idea of me and him dating. But hearing her suggest that something really could start between us only reminds me that my dad not knowing I'm gay isn't the only reason I've kept a leash on my feelings for Brenden. There's also the fact that he's a father. And despite having May's approval, I can't stand the idea of dating Brenden and ending up hurting him somehow, because I know that would hurt May too.

I could never do that to this girl who trusts me so much.

In a slightly pathetic attempt to change the subject, I ask her if she wants to help with breakfast.

She gives me a concerned look. "You know my cooking skills are on par with my dad's, right?"

I laugh. "I bet they are, but I happen to be a pretty good cook. I'm sure I could teach you some things." Like my grandfather taught me.

For a moment, she's quiet, peering down into her coffee. But then she lifts her head to meet my gaze, and a broad smile takes over her face. "I'd love that."

Despite being someone who's never been great with kids, or even liked them all that much, I find myself smiling back at her. Because yeah. I think I'd love it too.

CHAPTER NINE

BRENDEN

In the morning, I wake up alone in my bed. Which is exactly how I'm used to waking up, of course. But after a few groggy seconds, I remember that Travis slept here with me last night, and I try not to be annoyed at him for leaving without saying goodbye. Maybe I'm expecting too much from him, but if Elise and Grant didn't get to see him this morning, then what was the point of him staying the night? Other than to get me all confused and flustered and mildly horny.

Aw, crap on toast.

It suddenly dawns on me that maybe he left because I pushed it too far by kissing him last night. I probably freaked him out. (Even more than I freaked myself out with how much I *liked* kissing him.) He agreed to it, but I'm beginning to wonder if Travis would agree to anything I ask of him. That doesn't mean he was comfortable with it.

As I head downstairs, mentally planning my apology and assurances that he'll never have to suffer through kissing me again, I hear the familiar music of a Skyler James song. May must be playing it somewhere. Following the music, I find myself in the kitchen and then stop dead, taking in an entirely *unfamiliar* sight.

May is standing at the counter, lavender hair thrown up in a messy bun, swaying her hips and bopping her shoulders along to the upbeat song. This wouldn't be strange, were it not for the fact that while she's bopping, she's also using a wooden spoon to stir something inside a large mixing bowl. My daughter takes after me in that she doesn't cook, so I have no idea what she's doing.

But that's not even the strangest part.

Nope.

The strangest part is the sight of Travis Reed in my kitchen standing right beside May, chopping up vegetables on a cutting board. I could be mistaken, but I think I catch his shoulders getting in on the bopping action for a couple seconds too.

Does. Not. Compute.

May uses her free hand to reach for the mug of coffee next to her and takes a large gulp from it, which is pretty much the only thing that makes sense to me about this picture. As she sets the mug down, she notices me and smiles brightly. "Hey, Dad! Wanna help?"

"Help?"

"We're making breakfast."

"You don't know how to cook."

She rolls her eyes in a spectacularly dramatic fashion. "Well, okay, I'm just stirring the pancake batter like Travis told me to."

"Which is more than I'd trust you to do," Travis says to me, turning around. And I feel suddenly unsteady on my feet, because he's smiling. *Smiling.*

It's not that he never smiles. It's just . . . he doesn't smile *here*, in my kitchen first thing in the morning, standing beside my daughter while listening to pop music.

"I think I need a fainting couch," I unfortunately utter out loud.

"A what?" May asks.

Ugh, now I feel old. "Never mind. Is there coffee for me?"

That gets me another teenage girl eyeroll and a response of, "Duh, I didn't drink the whole pot."

"You act like that's an impossibility."

May might not be quite as addicted to caffeine as I am—thankfully—but she's working on it.

I squeeze past Travis to get to the coffee maker and pour myself a cup, then step back and eye the two of them again. "So is anyone going to tell me what's going on here?"

"I *did*," May insists.

"She really did," Travis adds.

Great, now they're ganging up on me.

Narrowing my eyes at him, I say, "You, hush." Then I shake my head. "Actually, no. Talk. Because there's no way I had all this stuff in my fridge."

"By 'stuff' do you mean the ingredients to make a proper meal?" he asks.

"Yes, exactly. I mean, what *is* this?" I go to pick up a handful of spinach leaves he's set to the side, but he swats my hand away. "I've never seen it before. Are you sure it's edible?"

"Please tell me you're joking."

I fight to keep a straight face.

He holds my eye contact for a few moments, then goes back to what he was doing before I interrupted. "I had to wake up super early to open the diner, so I grabbed all this from there because I figured, correctly, that you'd have nothing. I snuck back in before anyone else was awake."

Damn. Now I feel bad that he had to go to the diner but still came back here. He must be exhausted. Though I suppose he's used to the early hours. You wouldn't find me dead getting up that early for work. Or I guess you would, because if I had to do that, it would kill me.

After taking a much-needed gulp of coffee, I tell him, "You didn't have to cook for us."

"I think I've heard it's what boyfriends do," he says dryly. Then his face cracks into a smile. "Elise and Grant are having their tea and coffee out on the porch, but we can all eat together before I need to get back to work. You took today off, right?"

"Mmhmm," I confirm, leaning around him to ogle the food. "If you're making pancakes, what's with the veggies?"

Again, he swats my hand away as I go to snag a small piece of red pepper. That's what I get for wanting a vegetable. "I'm making omelets too. I knew you and May would be happy with pancakes, but I figured her grandparents might appreciate something healthier."

"You figured right."

"I also realized I didn't have a change of clothes," he says, "so I changed at home, and this way it'll look like I keep clothes here."

"Can I stop stirring now?" May whines. "I think I'm getting carpal tunnel."

Travis laughs. "You're as bad as your dad."

"Thank you," she says proudly, and I beam at her.

"Can I do anything?" I ask Travis. Though I'll admit, I'm relieved when he shakes his head.

Spinning around, he offers me a whole strip of pepper. "Just sit down and look pretty."

His eyes are playful, and I'm glad I'm getting the chance to see him this way. Less grumpy, more carefree.

I accept the veggie, giving him a shove for good measure, then munch on it while I sit and watch him cook. I watch him teach May how to pour the pancake batter and add the blueberries and when to flip them. He looks comfortable in my kitchen. I don't know how he knows his way around it so well, but it's like he's been cooking meals here for years.

It would be easy for me to start imagining that he really is my boyfriend.

And *that* is a very dangerous thing.

❀

WALKING THROUGH TOWN with May and her grandparents, I'm hyper-
aware of my phone in my pocket. Every time it jostles against my thigh, I
jump, thinking for a second that I'm getting a call. Then I reassure myself
that Danny and Addison have everything under control at the inn.

Today is the last day of the retreat, and I desperately want to be there,
but I figured Elise and Grant wouldn't appreciate me working on their
first day in town. At least the retreat schedule is pretty light today, as the
group will be leaving late afternoon.

Spending the day with Elise and Grant, though, poses another challenge for me, because I have to feed them. Normally, I would've just taken
them for lunch at the inn, but there's no way I'm going to distract Addison
and add to her workload by making her cook for us today.

When I explained how busy the inn would be, Elise immediately
jumped in with the suggestion of having lunch at the diner. And before I
could come up with a plausible reason to keep them away from there, May
enthusiastically agreed. The little traitor. I think she's enjoying seeing me
and Travis squirm as we navigate this fake relationship.

All I can do to minimize the potential damage that might come from
me and Travis having to put on a show in public—where other people in
town could witness it, and either find out about him or blow our cover—
is stall in getting there. I figure if we go for a very late lunch, during a typical lull, there shouldn't be too many other customers.

So I've made sure to take a meandering path around town on the way
to the diner, under the guise of giving a town tour. As if Elise and Grant
haven't been here before. And also, as if they even give a crap about Mayweather.

"Hi, Barbara!" I call out, pausing as we walk by the elderly woman's
pastel green house. Yes, I'm still stalling. But I also genuinely like her.

She's sitting on her porch in a rocking chair, but she stands (very slowly) to greet me. "Brenden, dear! How are you?"

"I'm great!" *Lie.* "How are you?"

"Oh, you know," she says, shrugging one bony shoulder. "Same old, same old. That's how it is when you get to be my age."

I wave my hand at her with a smile. "Nonsense. You've still got plenty of excitement in your life. Have you finished your cats in outer space puzzle?"

Grant chortles behind me, but I ignore him.

Barbara's face lights up. "Yes, a few days ago! Thanks for asking! I'm working on one with a bunch of cowboys now."

"Shirtless cowboys?" I ask, waggling my eyebrows playfully.

"You know it."

"You'll have to take a picture for me when you finish it," I tell her.

"I will," she says happily. "Thank you for stopping to chat! You're so sweet."

As we move on, Elise asks me, "Was that a friend of yours?"

"She's just someone I like to talk to."

May squeezes my forearm as she walks beside me. "Dad's friendly with everyone in town. Everyone loves him."

"I can see why," Elise says, and I can't help but preen a little. Though I'm not sure how sincere she's being.

When we reach the town square, I do a lap around it, rather than heading straight to Reed's. Most of the storefronts have flowerboxes outside, which are filled with spring blooms that add pops of color to the street. Several people stop us to say hello, and I introduce them all to May's grandparents. Elise does seem delighted at how friendly everyone is here, but Grant's face remains impassive the whole time.

Once we're standing in front of the diner, I know I can't stall any longer, so I turn to Elise and Grant. "All right, we're here. Just please, let's all remember that Travis is working. I don't want to bother him too much. We like to keep our private and professional lives separate."

That's totally bullshit. Because for one thing, we're not really dating, and for another, if we *were* dating, that would be pretty much impossible in a town like this. But Grant nods like he appreciates the concept.

Elise smiles. "I promise we won't embarrass you."

The comment makes me pause. It sounds like something a parent would say to a teenager. And it has me thinking painfully of my own parents, and of Elise and Grant with April, and . . . Well, it makes me wonder if there's any reality in which these two *could* see me like a son. But I shake all that off, because there's no use dwelling on people who are gone or things that are nearly impossible.

Hand on the door handle, I plaster on a smile and fake some confidence that this is all going to go fine. However, as soon as I step inside and lay eyes on Travis, I freeze, causing May to bump into my back.

"What the heck, Dad, move," she urges, shoving me forward.

I wave awkwardly at Travis, then lead my group to an empty table. Luckily, my stalling paid off, and there's only a scattering of other customers in here. May gives me a weird look as she takes a chair beside me, but I ignore it.

Because no, I don't know why I malfunctioned like that.

Travis is wearing the same thing he wore at my house this morning—his typical jeans, black tee, flannel shirt outfit that he wears practically every day. Yet for some reason, I was overwhelmed just now by the sight of his total hotness.

Maybe it's because I kissed him. Which, *yes, okay,* I'm still realizing was possibly not the best idea. But how was I supposed to know one innocent kiss was going to be so good that it would affect me like this?

While we were at my house, pretending to be a couple, we were sort of in this fantasy-type bubble. One where Travis wasn't exactly Travis, my friend, the grumpy guy who owns the diner. Now here inside Reed's, it's back to reality. And the reality is that I kissed my friend, and I really liked it.

Shit, I just hope I can be normal around him again once this charade is over.

"Hey," he greets us, coming over and passing out menus. "I'm glad you all stopped by."

When he sets his hand on the top of my chair, his knuckles brush against my upper back and I malfunction again, letting out a noise that sounds something like, "*Glumph.*"

He shoots me a concerned look, and May brings her hand up to her mouth, probably to cover an amused expression.

"Are you okay?" Grant asks.

I nod vigorously. "Yeah. Sorry. Had something in my throat."

Travis is still looking at me like he can't decide if I need the Heimlich or a mental wellness check. Guess Elise didn't need to worry about embarrassing me. Nope, I can do that just fine on my own, thank you.

"Hey, Grandma," May says, drawing everyone's attention from me. The sweet angel. I take back calling her a traitor. "There are a couple salads on the menu that I think you'd like. They're really good."

"How would you know?" I ask. "You don't eat salad."

"No, *you* don't eat salad. But I do sometimes, when you're not around asking if I want a burger."

Clutching a hand to my heart and laying on the theatrics, I tell her, "I'm so disappointed in you."

Elise and Grant look appalled at this, but before either of them can comment on how horrible of a parent I am, Travis jumps in with, "He's kidding."

"Yeah, totally kidding," I confirm. They really don't get my sense of humor.

"Anyway, can I grab everyone something to drink?" Travis offers, gracefully moving us all along. For which I'm so grateful, I could kiss him.

Or not kiss him. It's not like I *want* to kiss him. Whatever.

He's quick to get a cup of coffee in front of me, which helps me chill out somewhat, so that I make it through lunch without blowing the fake dating cover. Or blowing Travis's cover to anyone.

And I swear I don't think about blowing *Travis* at all.

Okay, maybe just once, when I turned my head to find him standing beside me with his crotch practically at mouth level.

I mean, seriously. I eat at these damn tables in this diner all the time, and I've never noticed this phenomenon before. If I didn't know any better, I'd think he was purposefully fucking with me. But no. Pretty sure I've fucked with myself by coming up with this hare-brained scheme.

How am I supposed to make it through Elise and Grant's trip pretending to date this man without doing something stupid and disastrous like throwing myself at him?

He's my friend, I remind myself firmly.

He's my friend, and I want him to stay my friend. I don't *want* him like that. This whole pretending thing is just making everything confusing. But it'll be fine. I'll get myself together.

At least, I'd better. And I'd better do it fast.

CHAPTER TEN

TRAVIS

Despite being the only bar in town, Roddy's is entirely empty other than me and the bartender, Roddy's nephew Tate. Guess it's a bit too early for this town to start drinking.

I left the diner right after Brenden and his group did, before the dinner rush could hit. As they left, Elise was thankfully discreet when she asked me if they'd be seeing me at the house tonight. In my haste to end the conversation before any of the diner's stragglers got curious about what was going on, though, I mumbled what I think was an affirmative. So I'll have to head over there later.

First, I'm meeting Connor for a beer. I invited him out as an apology for snapping at him on the phone the other day over my produce order that I messed up. I might be grumpy, but I try not to be a total asshole.

As I sip whatever IPA Tate poured me while I wait for Connor to arrive, my mind keeps drifting back to this morning. More specifically, to how I woke up this morning. In Brenden's bed. With my hard dick pressed right against his ass.

Despite how I've spent all day trying to lock that moment away in a vault and shove it toward the back of my mind . . . *well*. The lock must be faulty or something.

Luckily, before I get myself too worked up with the memory, the door opens, and Connor wanders in. He quickly spots me on my stool at one of the high-top tables against the wall. In the dimly lit room, he almost glows with his white T-shirt, blond hair, and pearly white smile as he heads my way.

He eyes my pint glass when I ask what I can grab for him. "I'll take whatever you're having. Thanks."

Tate is playing around on his phone as I approach the bar, so I have to clear my throat to get his attention. He apologizes, but I wave him off. When you only have two customers, you're not just going to stand there staring at them the whole time.

I bring the beer back over to Connor, and he asks how I've been. My answer doesn't take long, since my life never seems to change. Wake up, cook people food all day, clean up after them, go to sleep. The only interesting thing happening to me right now is the one thing I can't tell him about.

I've known Connor forever, and I'd trust him to keep Brenden's absurd fake dating scheme a secret if I asked. But explaining it would only tempt me to explain my very real feelings for Brenden. And Connor, like everyone else except Brenden, doesn't know I'm gay, so that would require a whole other conversation.

After my boring answer, I do the polite thing and ask how he's been too, but I immediately regret it. Everyone in town has heard about his divorce by now. How Emma left him and their son because she wanted to go off and find herself. Whatever the hell that means.

Other than cringing almost imperceptibly before telling me he's doing fine, he seems to be taking this oddly in stride. He talks about the farm for a while and mentions his son.

"How's Mason handling everything?" I ask, though from my own experience of being a kid whose mom left, I can pretty much already imagine.

He swipes at a bead of condensation on his glass before answering. "He's holding up. I mean, he's been better, for sure. Emma and I tried to explain to him why it was best for us to separate, but he's too young to truly understand the complexities of it. And even if he could understand why we got divorced, no kid deserves to be abandoned by their mom."

"Yeah, that's bullshit," I say without thinking. Then I apologize, because I didn't know Emma well enough to judge her actions.

"No, it's okay, it is bullshit," Connor agrees. "I get why she wasn't happy. I really do. We've both spent our whole lives simply going along with what everyone expected of us. And those expectations can weigh you down after a while. If she wanted to leave me, she had every right to. But leaving her son?" He sighs, rapping his knuckles lightly on the table. "It's a little harder to forgive her for that."

By the time we finish our beers, he's told me more than I needed to know about how he and Emma stopped having sex two years before they split. About how he wasn't happy in the marriage anymore but didn't think he could do anything about it. He felt too guilty at the idea of asking Emma to leave her home—the farmhouse he built on the edge of the property at Shaw Family Farm and Orchards. But he obviously couldn't leave it either.

The farm isn't just a job for him. It's his family's legacy, something he always wanted to be a part of. He took over most of the responsibilities of running it from his dad, letting his parents basically retire early, although they still help out.

So he was stuck between a rock and a hard place.

"Honestly, it was sort of a relief when she told me she wanted out," he admits. "And that makes me feel like shit."

"You shouldn't," I assure him. "You didn't do anything wrong. You were willing to stick it out while she wasn't."

"Yeah, but now everyone in town thinks she's the villain who broke my heart, when really, we were both looking for exit strategies. And in a way, now I'm free too."

I offer to grab us another round, needing to step away for a moment, because I'm not the best at emotional crap like this. I'm better at solving problems with clear solutions, not at having to navigate how someone feels. That's probably one of the reasons I've been okay with resigning myself to hookups outside of town, rather than trying to actually date anyone.

I consider Connor a simple guy (like me) and a pretty open person (unlike me), but our friendship's always been surface level. I guess I didn't realize how much more he kept inside him.

"I didn't mean to unload all this on you," he says when I come back and hand him his beer.

"It's fine," I tell him. "Sorry, I'm not the greatest sounding board though. I don't really know what to say."

"You don't need to say anything. I guess I just needed to get this stuff off my chest."

We're quiet for a minute, each sipping our beers, but it's not uncomfortable. I'm cool with not talking.

Except I find my mind drifting back to Brenden, and for fuck's sake, I need to stop going there. He knows I'm gay now, but that doesn't change anything, does it? I still don't date. I can't just grab him and say, *Hey, now that you know I like dick, you wanna let me on yours?*

Because that's obviously a terrible idea that could ruin our friendship.

Because May trusts me not to hurt her dad. And I don't *want* to hurt him.

Because if I fucked him, even one time, I'm pretty sure I'd never get over it. I'd never stop wanting more.

"Can I tell you one more thing?" Connor asks, and I nod, grateful for the reprieve from my own thoughts. "I think . . . I mean, I *know* that I . . . I've always been curious."

"About what?"

"Men."

A swig of beer goes down the wrong way, and I start coughing. "Excuse me?"

He shrugs. "I've been pretty sure since I was younger that I swing both ways. But I sort of held myself back, because of growing up on the farm and doing all the typical masculine stuff, you know? People assumed I was one way, and I didn't do anything to let them think otherwise. As a teen, I was just getting brave enough to maybe explore it, but then Emma and I got together, and there was no reason for me to think about it anymore. It didn't matter."

I realize I must be gaping at him when he frowns.

"Shit, sorry," he says. "You probably don't wanna hear about this."

"It's okay," I tell him quickly. Because even if I normally stay pretty closed off to people, he just had the guts to come out to me, and I don't want to make him regret it. "No judgement here, I swear. Definitely didn't see that one coming, that's all."

"I'm betting nobody will. If I decide to tell anyone else, that is."

"Do you think you're going to?"

He shrugs again. "We'll see. It's not like dating is the first thing on my mind right now. I need to make sure Mason is okay, and there's always the farm keeping me busy. But I can't say I haven't thought about the possibility of seeing if my attraction to men could amount to more. Now that I'm free to do . . . whatever."

"You don't have to make a big announcement, you know. If you meet someone and you want to see where things go, then you could just go for it. Let everyone else figure it out on their own."

He nods, but he has no idea how hypocritical it is for me to give him advice on coming out. Our situations are a bit different though. It's not the whole town I'm afraid to come out to—I don't give a crap what they think. It's my own damn father I'm worried about.

For Connor, I imagine the issue is that this town has seen him for so long as Emma's husband and Mason's dad. He's right that everyone assumes things about him, and who knows how people would react if he went out and shattered those assumptions? It wouldn't be another celebration like with Andrew in high school. This would just confuse everyone.

People in Mayweather like things to be how they expect them to be.

"But it's probably pointless to even be thinking about this," he says glumly. "It's not like there's a huge pool of queer men in town for me to potentially date." His eyes grow unfocused for a few seconds, like he's thinking about something (maybe someone?) and not sharing. Then he shakes his head as if clearing it. "I finally have the chance to explore my options, but there aren't many options here."

I'm here, I have the sudden urge to blurt out. *I'm here and I'm queer.*

I don't say that though. Of course not.

It's not like I actually want Connor to consider me as an option. He's hot, in that all-American, jacked-from-physical-labor kind of way, but he's not my type. It might help him to know, though, that there are more queer men around here than he thinks.

But I can't do it. All I do is take a long gulp of my beer, draining the glass, to swallow the words down.

Guess I'm more a product of this town than I'd like to admit. I'm good with things not changing. I'm good with easy and uncomplicated. This is why there's no point in letting myself entertain the idea of telling Brenden how I feel. I'm not going to come out to my dad, and I can't ask Brenden to be with me and hide it.

Maybe if I'm being honest with myself, it's more than just the fear of coming out or the fear of hurting Brenden and May that's holding me back. Being with Brenden would mean *being* with him. Letting someone truly in. Not being alone.

And being alone is all I've known how to do for the last ten years. I'm used to it. I'm used to quietly pining for Brenden and not having him. If by some miracle I actually got him, I'm not sure I'd know what to do with myself.

Some people are simply built to be alone.

❈

I DIDN'T SIGN UP for this kind of torture.

Well, maybe I did, but I don't deserve it. Despite my faults, I like to think I'm a decent person. All I wanted to do was help Brenden out. I never expected that agreeing to be his fake boyfriend would wind me up here. Facing my second night in a row of sharing a bed with him, hoping I don't pop a boner like the first time.

He looks unnecessarily adorable right now, in his pajama pants that hang low on his hips and are probably super soft. Not that I'll be finding out.

"You can put your clothes away in the dresser if you want," he says, gesturing to the duffle bag I'm holding. "I'll make some room."

"No, don't go through the trouble," I tell him. "I'll keep this out of the way." Crossing to the corner of the room by the ensuite, I set my bag on the floor and give it a little shove with my foot to tuck it away as much as possible. "Is that okay?"

I packed some clothes and toiletries before coming here and kept the bag in my truck. Then I snuck back out to grab it after Elise and Grant went to bed. Having my clothes here will help sell us as a couple, plus if I'm going to keep spending the night, I need deodorant and my own shampoo and all that shit.

Brenden's shampoo is fruity. And while it works for him, I'd rather not be walking around smelling like a strawberry or whatever.

"Yeah, it's fine there," he says. "I don't mind making room for you though."

Of course he doesn't. That's just how he is. But my clothes aren't that important to me. "Nah, don't worry. I'm gonna change and brush my teeth, and then we can . . ."

He looks both nervous and amused as I trail off. I have no idea how to finish that sentence. And then we can *what?* Get in bed with each other. That's the only thing left for us to do in this room.

So I squat down and rifle through my bag until I find what I need, then slip into the bathroom to do my business and try to get my head clear. Sleeping in sweatpants sucks, but as I tug the pair over my thighs, I remind myself that this provides an extra layer of protection in case my dick decides to misbehave again.

Not that it's going to.

Absolutely not.

I *will* have my body under control tonight.

With that likely false sense of confidence, I exit the bathroom to find Brenden sitting on top of the covers on his bed, back propped against a couple pillows, with one knee pulled up toward his chest. He actually looks a lot more relaxed now than he did last night. I don't know if it's because we've already made it through one night doing this, or because he's made it through his first full day of the grandparents' visit. Either way, relaxed is a good look on him.

Of course, he has no idea about the precarious position I found us in this morning. About my little—well, not so *little*—issue. And I'm sure as hell not about to tell him.

When I join him on the bed, he adjusts his position so that he's still propped up, but leaning on his side to face me, his knee now pointed my way. He gives me a soft smile. "Have I thanked you yet today?"

"For what?"

"Everything."

Giving him a smile of my own, I say, "You probably have."

"Good for me then," he replies with a little giggle.

I'd love to bottle up that sound and keep it forever. To have it for those nights alone in my apartment when the silence starts to sound too oppressive.

It's not often that happens. Built to be alone, remember? But occasionally, I do get sick of my own company. Those are usually the nights when I drive out of town looking for a hookup, but just hearing Brenden's laughter and getting to think about him could possibly be even better.

Realizing he's watching me with intrigue now, I adjust my weight nervously. I don't even want to know what my face must have been doing just then.

"What would you want in a boyfriend?" I ask, shifting the focus onto him.

He scrunches his face in confusion. "What do you mean?"

I think the meaning is obvious. But I'm only asking to get a better idea of how I should play this role for him, so I tell him as much. "Help me learn what you look for in a guy. What's important to you in a relationship? That way I can make sure to be that in front of May's grandparents."

His expression shifts to deep appreciation, and I don't know what to do with that. So I squirm some more as I wait for him to consider his answer. Maybe this was a stupid question. It doesn't matter, really, what he wants out of a relationship, because we're not actually dating. I'm sure I can continue to fake it just fine without this intimate knowledge.

Then he says, "The biggest thing for me is just having someone I know I can depend on."

And now I want to wrap him in a hug.

"I've done everything by myself for so long," he adds. "And I know I can handle it, but it would be nice if there was someone else I could lean on when things are hard."

I resist going in for the hug, because that would be weird, but I do inch out my hand and place it over his knee. "That makes sense."

He laughs humorlessly. "Does it? Or does it make me sound weak?"

"No," I say adamantly, giving him a squeeze. "You're the furthest thing from weak. I'm sure most people would like to have what you're describing."

"You do everything on your own too, though. And you don't seem like you need anyone else."

No, I don't think I *need* anyone. But like he said, the idea of having someone else to lean on sometimes does sound kind of nice. If it was the right someone. "I do have my dad," I say, which is true, for the most part.

"Yeah." He sighs. "I don't have family like that."

I could remind him he has May, but I understand that's not what he means. Almost without my permission, my thumb starts rubbing his knee over the thin material of his pajama pants. I was right—they are soft. And it might be my imagination, but it feels like he shifts just the tiniest bit closer to me as his eyes peer down at where I'm touching him.

"You have me," I tell him. Because even though that sounds like an embarrassingly cheesy line from a romance movie, I mean it. And it's important he knows it.

The achingly appreciative look is back on his face as he raises his eyes to meet mine. "I know I do, and I'm so grateful for that."

"I know you are."

"You have me too, you know," he says quietly. "I know you don't need me for anything, but . . . if you did, I'd be there."

Fuck. Why does it feel so good to hear him say that?

Since I'm not good at handling emotions, I awkwardly mumble my thanks. Then I ask what else he wants in a boyfriend, in the hopes of steering the conversation back to less vulnerable territory. Less vulnerable for me, at least.

And maybe he senses my need for levity, because he says, "Rock hard abs and at least eight inches." Then the little fucker winks at me.

I can't help it, I burst out laughing. He's never said something that obscene to me before. Luckily, the shock of it made it funny, rather than a turn on.

As I calm down, I tell him, "While I may be able to provide that, I don't think it's something I can display in front of Elise and Grant."

His blue eyes flash darker for a second, and I replay my own words.

Shit. Am I flirting?

Quickly, I move past the talk about dicks and add, "So how about something that helps me illustrate to them how much I care about you? As your fake boyfriend, I mean."

"Let's see . . ." He twists the extra material of his pillowcase between his fingers. "Is it super self-centered if I say I want a boyfriend who totally adores me?"

I adore you.

"Not at all," I reply, holding in my first thought. "You deserve that."

"It's just that I've always put all my focus on being a good dad for May. So if I'm going to give someone else part of my focus, I want to know that it's worth it. I need to know that they really *want* to be around." He nudges the back of my hand with his knuckle, and I realize I haven't taken it off his knee yet, so I reluctantly do that. "But don't worry, Elise and Grant don't seem suspicious about us. I think they'll buy this thing without you having to pretend to fawn over me. In fact, you doing that would probably be hilarious and just blow our cover, because fawning doesn't fit your whole Grumptopus vibe at all."

I pretend to be offended, though he's not exactly wrong. "Hey, I could fawn."

He gives me a look like he's fighting to keep a straight face, and then he laughs. "Sure. Right. I totally buy that."

"I could," I argue. Because now, inexplicably, I feel the need to prove it to him. To prove I could be the kind of boyfriend he wants. And actually, I'm pretty sure I fawn over him all the time in my head. It's just the doing it openly part that would likely be hard for me.

"Hmm," he says, tapping his finger against his chin, like maybe he's trying to picture it. Which, yes, I imagine isn't easy. Then he gets an evil glint in his eyes and says, "All right, so I expect a flash mob."

"A what now?" I say. Even though I do know what flash mobs are. Ridiculous, publicly humiliating spectacles.

He nods enthusiastically. "Yup. That's the level of fawning and adoring I'm talking about. I want a guy to be so into me that he needs to make sure everyone else knows it too."

I honestly can't tell how much he's fucking with me. Like I know he's joking around, but is there a part of him that really might want something like that? Maybe not a flash mob, necessarily, but big romantic gestures?

While I don't know if I'd be capable of giving that to him, I meant it when I said he deserves it. And that's just another reason I need to keep my feelings for him to myself. He deserves so much more than me.

"Okay," I say, resorting to my old buddy sarcasm. "One flash mob coming up."

"Good."

"What else are you looking for?"

He slides down a bit so he's closer to lying than sitting now, his cheek smushed adorably into his pillow. "Why don't you tell me what you want in a boyfriend?"

Bright blue eyes, endless smiles, and an obnoxious coffee addiction.

That's my immediate thought. But since I can't say it, and I honestly don't even know how else to answer, I fake a yawn and tell him, "We should probably get some sleep."

He gives me an assessing look, and I pray that he hasn't magically developed mindreading powers in the last thirty seconds. Then he smiles and agrees.

As he gets out of bed to hit the light switch, I fold down the covers so we can get under them, and I say another prayer that I don't wake up with morning wood again. At least he didn't kiss me this time, so I should be fine. I know I'm the one who asked him about kissing and agreed we could do it in front of Elise and Grant to sell this relationship, but after that first kiss, I realized it's a terrible idea. For me, at least.

I'm still willing to do it when we need to. I refuse to let him down. But I'm honestly not sure how much of it I'll be able to take without going crazy. Just that small taste I got last night was enough to make my desire for him—the desire that I've been able to tamp down for so long—come burning furiously up to the surface.

"Are you comfortable?" he whispers sweetly after he's settled in.

We're both sticking as far as possible to our own sides of the bed, but I can still feel his heat. Or maybe I'm only imagining it because I *want* to feel it. Either way, this isn't helping in my fight to keep my body under control.

"Yeah," I lie. "I'm good."

CHAPTER ELEVEN

BRENDEN

With the corporate retreat over, I can finally take a deep breath. Only one though. No time for more, because MayFest starts Saturday. Travis is helping Addison get the menus ready for the new influx of guests plus the booth we'll have at the festival. But then he'll be off the hook. I feel guilty that I've monopolized all his time for the past week, between him helping out here and pretending to be my boyfriend.

Speaking of pretending . . .

It's only been a couple days, but Travis has already been doing such a good job at acting like we're a couple that he's almost got *me* convinced. When I woke up with him in my bed this morning, I had a moment—just one—where I forgot that he was only there as a favor. But I can't do that again. I can't forget for even another moment that this is all fake.

Because it *is* fake. F.A.K.E.

My newfound lust for Travis, on the other hand? I'm afraid that's unfortunately very real.

But I'll survive that. I'm no stranger to being alone and horny. I've never been the kind of guy to go for a quick hookup. I prefer dating, actually getting to know someone first. It's been a while since I've gone out with anyone though. I got tired of meeting men who ended up disappointing me. There have been a few guys who didn't disappoint, who lasted a little while. But even with them, it never felt entirely right.

Last night when Travis asked me what I wanted in a boyfriend, it was nice getting to imagine my ideal relationship. In reality, though, I'm not expecting to ever have that.

It would take a special kind of man to truly fit into my life. To *want* to fit in. To accept a preteen daughter and a crazy work schedule, and not to mention, *me*. I've got a lot of great qualities, I know that. But I've also got some not-so-great ones. I can't cook, I hate cleaning, and I may be on top of things when it comes to my daughter and work, but when it comes to taking care of myself, I can be pretty scatterbrained. And I put on a good front, but underneath that, I'm hiding plenty of insecurities.

"Brenden, who picked out these tablecloths? I don't think they're the best quality linens." Elise runs a finger over the cloth as we sit at one of the inn's dining room tables, waiting for lunch to be served.

I fight both the urge to roll my eyes and the urge to cower under the criticism. It's not hard to figure out where some of my insecurities stem from.

"I think they go well with the rest of the room's décor," I say, defending my choice. Because it's *my* choice. It's my inn.

That they helped pay for.

"Surely you could find someone to make these for you in the same pattern but with better material. It's worth the extra expense."

"I'll look into it," I tell her, even though I have no intention of doing that.

I subtly check my phone for the time, wishing May were here. But unfortunately, she's back at school today, meaning it's up to me to entertain her grandparents on my own. I tried to convince her to take a few more days off, ready to write her a note feigning illness, but my little smartypants wasn't having it.

My excuse of having to work only gets me so far when Elise and Grant insist on coming here to have lunch with me.

Thankfully Addison appears before Elise can find something else to criticize, strolling out of the kitchen with three plates of food balanced on her arms. She could've sent out a server, but I know she's trying to make the best possible impression on these two for my sake. Even through her own panicked state over everything going on, she's already noticed how tense having them here makes me.

This morning when I lamented to her about how I'd have to take a break to eat with them, she actually stepped away from her food prep long enough to awkwardly give me a few pats on the back. So I think I'm wearing her down on the friendship front. Me being a mess has seemed to make her like me more. I'll take it as a win, I guess.

"This all looks wonderful," Elise says, taking in the fancy lunches Addison whipped up for us. I revel in the praise, even if it's more a compliment for my chef than for me.

Already digging into his food the moment Addison leaves the table, Grant asks, "Will we be seeing Travis again tonight?"

"Yes, you told him he needs to come for game and movie night, didn't you?" Elise says.

"He'll be there. He's looking forward to it."

That last part is a big fat lie, but he did promise to get coverage for the diner's dinner shift so he could make it.

Honestly, I didn't expect us to have to do so much to keep up this ruse. I expected that Elise and Grant would want to spend most of their visit alone with May. And with me too, I guess, since May and I are basically a package deal. I thought Travis would only need to pop in for a couple guest appearances. But they seem determined to get to know him and treat him as part of the family. Not that I'd actually call this weird thing the four of us have a family.

We eat in silence for a bit until Grant asks me, "So that event you had here went well?"

"Oh yeah," I tell him, spearing a baby carrot with my fork. Normally, I hate carrots, but Addison put some kind of glaze on these that made them deliciously sweet. If only all vegetables could come sweetened.

Grant watches me a few seconds, and when I don't elaborate, he says, "That's good. Would you like us to move into a room here now that it's over? We don't want to keep putting you out."

"Yes, we're sorry. We didn't realize we were coming at such a bad time," Elise adds. "But I am glad we'll be here to see this spring festival May's been telling me about."

It occurs to me now that they haven't given me an end date for their stay. It makes sense that they'd want to stay for the festival, but I assume they'll be leaving right after. They never like to slum it here for more than a week.

Unfortunately, because of the festival coming up, the inn is still booked solid this week. I mean, that's not unfortunate for the inn. Only for my mental state, since I can't move them here.

When I tell them as much, I make sure to hide my feelings about the situation.

Elise apologizes again, while also assuring me they're happy to stay at my house. "And we'll find things to do on our own," she adds. "We won't keep bothering you at work."

I'm not sure if she's intentionally using reverse psychology on me, but her implying that they're bothering me actually makes me feel bad, so I wind up saying, "Oh no, you're not bothering me. I can always make time to have lunch with you. I'm the boss, after all."

Elise looks happy, while I try not to cringe at my own words. This weekend can't come fast enough. I'm not going to let them ruin my fun at the festival with May. And then after it, they'll be gone, and my life can go back to normal. No more faking, no more sleepovers with Travis.

As I chew another carrot, the sweet taste turns almost bitter in my mouth. For a second, the thought of going back to my normal friendship with Travis disappoints me.

Only for a second, though.

✱

MAY IS TOO GOOD at board games. When she was a kid, I used to let her win. She was around eight when I realized I was no longer *letting* her win—she was just beating me at everything. You might say most board games are primarily about luck, but I don't know. It seems like she finds a way to outsmart me every time.

After winning two games of Clue, she asks if anyone wants to play Scrabble. Thankfully, Grant is happy to take her up on it so the rest of us can bow out. She really makes me look like a dummy when she kicks my ass at that one. I should stop letting her read so much.

Elise stays to watch, but Travis and I sneak off to the kitchen to take care of the cookies we're baking for the movie later. Well. The cookies *Travis* is baking. From scratch.

I might not cook, but May and I are big fans of sweets, so I do know how to pop some pre-packaged cookie dough in the oven. I even remembered to stop at the store to buy it. But when Travis saw, he scoffed and ran out to get ingredients to make his own cookies.

Show off.

I watch him as he takes the bowl of dough he mixed out of the refrigerator and finds the cookie sheet in the right cabinet on his first try. He looks particularly good today. His jeans seem tighter than usual. Or maybe they're not. Maybe now that I've let myself acknowledge how hot he is, my eyes are just more drawn to his ass.

God, the things I could do to that ass if he'd let me.

No.

Nope.

Not going there. As if that would ever happen.

Meanwhile, I'm over here looking like a bum in maroon lounge pants and an old Skyler James concert tee. May insisted we both get them when

I took her to his show years ago. I'm not that obsessed, I swear.

After he scoops out the cookie dough and sticks the sheet in the oven, we hang around here. He grabs himself a water bottle out of the fridge—and no, I didn't know I had those in there—while I get a pot of coffee going.

"You know drinking coffee in the evening really isn't good for your sleep," he says.

"It won't keep me up," I tell him, filling my mug. "My body's so used to it."

He raises an eyebrow at me. "That's not how bodies work. Even if you don't have trouble falling asleep, it's still in your system and it will affect the quality of sleep you get."

"Should I start calling you *Doctor* Grumptopus?" I tease.

He lets out a long-suffering sigh. "Fine, I'll keep my mouth shut and not worry about your health."

He's turned away from me, taking a seat at the table, so thankfully he doesn't catch the way I get stuck for a few moments, frozen in place, hand around my coffee mug. His words hit a strange place inside of me that I wasn't aware of. A place that might appreciate having somebody actually worry about me. Somebody besides my daughter.

Last night I told him I wanted a partner I could depend on. Maybe he's just playing the part. Worrying about my health kind of falls into that category, right?

I shake myself out of it and join him at the table. Quietly, I tell him, "In case I haven't said it enough, thank you. For doing all this."

He chuckles. "You've thanked me about a hundred times."

"Well, consider this one hundred and one."

Leaning in closer to me and keeping his voice down too, he says, "I'm still not sure I understand where your anxiety with the two of them comes from. They seem nice. Different than you, sure. But they obviously love you and May."

"They love May."

His eyes peer into mine, making me feel like he can see all the way inside me to the vulnerable squishy parts. "You don't think they love you?"

"I think . . ." Unable to articulate what I think, I take a sip of coffee instead. But he doesn't stop looking at me in that imploring way, so I have to continue. "They care about me in the sense that they know I'm raising and loving their granddaughter. I don't think they approve of a lot of my choices, though, and in the beginning, they wanted to fight me for custody. But April, May's mom, had all the paperwork done up legally, and I had the money to support a child from my parents' deaths, so they knew they didn't have enough of a case. They let it go and tried to be civil because they were probably afraid I'd cut them out of May's life entirely."

Travis reaches out and takes my free hand, the one not gripping my mug like a lifeline. "That sounds tough. But I don't think it means anything negative against you. I'm sure most grandparents in that position would've done the same thing. It's unusual for a mom to choose a non-relative to raise her child, but it shows how much your friend trusted you, how she knew you'd be everything May needed."

April knew I'd need May just as much as she needed me. And she was right.

I keep that thought to myself. Even if I've already shared it in a moment of weakness with him before, I don't need to remind him how pathetic I am. Instead I stare, transfixed, down at our hands.

Giving mine a squeeze, he says, "I'm sure now that you've all been in one another's lives for so long, they love you like family."

"But I'm *not* family," I whisper.

"I think they see you that way. Maybe you just don't realize it because you're too caught up in the assumptions you've made about them."

Yikes, that kind of makes me sound like a jerk.

I'm at a loss for how to respond. It's possible there could be some truth to what he's saying. But how would he know? He doesn't know them like I do. He hasn't experienced years of these awkward visits. Hasn't watched the way they criticize everything I do.

But he's been around a lot these last few days, and maybe it takes an outsider's perspective to see things clearly. Or maybe he's wrong. I don't know.

"Well, isn't this cozy?"

I jump at Elise's voice, tearing my hand from Travis's on instinct. Although, we're supposed to touch, so I don't know why I feel like I got caught doing something scandalous. "Sorry," I say.

"No need to apologize, hon," she replies. "I didn't mean to interrupt. It just gets boring watching those two play that game. They take it so seriously, both staring at their letters so hard I'm afraid they'll set the tiles on fire."

"May's obsessed with Scrabble," I tell her.

"She's so smart, I can see why."

A tiny burst of pride swells in me. As if I can really take any credit for May's brain. If anything, her intelligence comes from her mom and grandparents.

"Brenden's always been great about her education," Travis says. "He used to sit at the diner with her when she was a kid and help her with her homework. And he gets her all the books she asks for, which is a lot. He'll probably need to add an addition onto the house soon in order to fit them all."

Elise smiles. "It's wonderful that she's such a big reader. She gets that from her mom."

See?

The oven timer dings, and Travis says, "I'll get the cookies." But I jump up first, banging my knee on the table in the process of beating him there.

Trying not to wince at the pain, I hobble over to the oven as quickly as I can. My clumsy, unnecessary eagerness is embarrassing, but I just want to put an end to that conversation. I already know Elise and Grant think I'm unintelligent. They think that, because I run an inn for a living, it means I wasn't capable of doing anything more.

But I love what I do. I chose this. I may not be saving lives like a doctor, but I provide a service which makes people happy. The most important thing, though, is that I work hard so I can ensure May will have the opportunity to pursue whatever career she chooses, because she's capable of doing anything.

In my frazzled state, I open the oven door and reach inside with my bare hand. My fingers make contact with the hot metal cookie sheet before my brain catches up to me. "Shit!"

I yank my hand away, stumbling backward. I probably would've fallen on my ass, making an even bigger fool of myself, if it weren't for the solid body right behind me. Both of Travis's arms circle my waist and I sag in relief, letting him brace me for a second.

"Are you okay?" he asks, so close his breath tickles the side of my neck.

I try to tell him yes, but then the burning in my fingertips registers, and a tiny whimper escapes me instead.

"Come on." He keeps me in his hold as he steps over to the sink, forcing me to go with him. He turns on the tap, and his hands are gentle as they guide mine under the cold water.

His chest remains solidly pressed against my back as he takes care of me. I feel like a child. And who knew he had these nurturing instincts? I'm the parent here. I'm supposed to be the one who's good at this stuff.

I guess I am with May—just apparently not so much with myself.

"Now I understand why you don't cook," he says, his chuckle vibrating against me.

I'd turn around and shoot him a glare, if only I could move. He's not holding me *that* tightly. But I seem to be under some sort of spell that's made me lose control of my motor functions. I think I like being taken care of. Or maybe it's him specifically. Maybe I like Travis taking care of me.

He keeps my hands under the water longer than probably necessary. Until I murmur, "It's cold," and then he lets go of me to turn off the tap. But he doesn't step away.

I find myself leaning back simply to test if he'll hold me up. He does. One of his hands rests on my hip now, the other on the counter. I turn my head to look at him, and his face is so close.

Tilting my chin up, I press a soft kiss to his lips and whisper, "Thanks."

When he opens his mouth to reply, I realize what I just did. *Oh, crap.* I struggle to get away, but his fingers curl tighter into the material of my pants, preventing my escape.

We agreed that kissing is okay to sell the relationship, but we haven't done it since that practice one. And I didn't even do this for Elise's benefit. In fact, I completely forgot she was in the room.

I did it because it felt natural.

Craaaap.

Travis brings his free hand up to my face, thumb brushing along my jaw. Then he kisses my temple and says softly, right by my ear, "Any time."

When he releases me and takes a step back so I can move, I turn to find that Elise has removed the cookies from the oven and is now fixing herself a cup of tea, seemingly minding her own business. I grab a large plate and a spatula and begin plating up the cookies, trying to appear unaffected by what just happened.

"Are you okay, Brenden?" Elise asks.

It takes me a second to realize she's referring to how I burned myself. Not to how I kissed Travis, which was arguably even more stupid. "Yup, all good," I tell her.

"We should put some burn ointment on it," Travis suggests.

"Who the heck keeps burn ointment in their house?" I ask.

Elise *tsks*. "You should always keep a fully stocked first aid kit in the house, especially when you have children."

Great. She's found another way in which I'm a failure as a father.

Travis gives me an apologetic look. "I'm only used to having it around because burns happen all the time at the diner. Hazard of the business. I'll bring you some to keep here."

He's moved on from me kissing him like it wasn't at all weird. Maybe he's a better actor than I would've suspected.

"Should we go pick out a movie?" Elise asks. "Hopefully their game will be finished soon."

In agreement with her, I grab the cookies to bring into the living room. Before I can make it two steps, though, Travis swoops in and takes the plate from me. "For safety," he teases.

"I'm perfectly capable of carrying one plate," I insist, doing my best to look annoyed.

"I know you are, baby," he says patronizingly.

I want to continue this bantering, but my mind gets stuck on the word *baby*.

Then I notice Elise watching us with a smile on her face, and *ohhh*. Boyfriend. *Fake* boyfriend. *Duh*. He's only playing his role.

Of course. Obviously. Silly of me to forget.

Letting him carry the cookies, I backtrack to refill my coffee mug, then join everyone else in the living room. Travis is already sitting at one end of the couch, looking like he's squashed himself as far against the arm as he can, and Elise is at the other end. May and her grandfather must have finished their game, because Grant is now sitting in the armchair, and May is stretched out on the floor in between the couch and the coffee table.

I survey the room as if some more seating will magically appear.

"Come sit," Elise says, patting the empty space in the middle of the couch. "There's plenty of room."

There's not *plenty* of room. Enough room for me to fit, sure. But that would put me a lot closer to her than I'm comfortable with. My eyes flit between her and Travis, until Travis smiles at me and holds out his arm along the back of the couch like an invitation.

Not left with much choice, I go to him, carefully stepping over May's legs. I sit down so that I'm closer to him, leaving more space between me and Elise. He puts his arm around my shoulders as soon as I'm seated, and I let myself lean against him. His fingers start traveling up and down over my shirt sleeve in a very comforting way.

For someone who doesn't do relationships, he's really good at this.

His touch soothes my anxiety, and by the time the opening credits of the movie appear on the screen, I've sunk into him so much that I'd fall over if he decided to get up.

Turning his head toward me, he whispers in my ear, "How are your fingers?"

The question takes me a second to process, because being held by him honestly made me forget all about the burns. Now that I remember, they do hurt a little. Instead of admitting that, though, I just shrug in response.

He gives me an appraising look, like that wasn't a good enough answer. And then he reaches for my hand, brings it up to his mouth, and slowly presses a soft kiss to each burnt fingertip.

I'm holding my breath the entire time. Are Elise and Grant watching us? Is this all a show for them? Surely, it must be. But then why does it feel like it's really for me?

When he's done, he gives me my hand back. Although it doesn't feel like mine anymore. Pretty sure he owns it now.

Also pretty sure I need to get myself the fuck together. I've been friends with Travis for a decade without lusting after him. I can get through another week of this without jumping him.

Probably.

Maybe.

Hopefully.

CHAPTER TWELVE

TRAVIS

Y ou wanna change?" Brenden asks, holding out a pair of my sweat-pants that he grabbed from his dresser drawer. Apparently, he made room for my clothes and put them away for me, even though I assured him it wasn't necessary.

The gesture is sweet, but it's also made the line between real and fake look a bit blurrier. The more days we spend pretending to date, the more the line blurs. And that's how I end up doing silly things like kissing his fingertips because I want to, not because I'm trying to sell this.

It's been way too easy fitting myself into his life. Although maybe that shouldn't surprise me. We've fit so easily into each other's lives in a platonic way for years. I know what he likes and dislikes, his strengths and his weaknesses, how to make him happy with simple things. Is adding some handholding really all it takes to tip the appearance of our relation-ship from platonic over to romantic?

He shakes the sweats at me, snapping me out of my brief daze. "Sorry you had to stay up for the movie" he says when I take them from him. "You must be exhausted from all the jumping back and forth between the diner, the inn, and here."

"Yeah, I'm pretty much ready to crash."

Honestly, I almost dozed off a few times during the movie. But having Brenden's body tucked against mine kept me awake. It was comfortable in a way that could have lulled me to sleep—if it weren't for the fact that I wasn't willing to miss a moment of the closeness.

That should scare me. It *does* scare me. He is not mine to keep, and I need to remember that.

I go into the bathroom to change, and since Brenden was already wearing clothes he could sleep in, I find him lying in bed when I come back out. I set my folded jeans and flannel on top of his dresser before going over there. It looks like he's a little more in the middle of it than he should be. So far, we've both stayed as much on our respective sides as possible. That is, until we inevitably migrate closer in our sleep.

At least this morning when I woke up, Brenden was lying on his stomach about a foot away from me. Only his hand had crept closer, his fingers curled around my hipbone. That was less dangerous and awkward than waking up with his ass pressed against my dick.

Deciding it would be rude to ask him to move over in his own bed, I slide in and do my best to keep some semblance of space between us. But he immediately rolls on his side to face me, closing the distance, and he gives me a look like he's considering something.

Is it something about me?

Even though I have no idea what type of answers he's searching for on my face, I hold perfectly still, like that will make some kind of difference.

And then right when I'm about to break and ask him what he's thinking, he says, "I think we should kiss again."

My eyes grow wide.

"We only practiced once," he adds quickly. As if once wasn't enough to sear the feel of his lips into my brain. "And I kind of freaked out a little when it happened tonight in front of Elise. We need it to look more natural."

"Uh," I say, his proposition rendering me dumb. Somehow, it's even more surprising this time than the first time he said it. Maybe because it almost made sense the first time. To practice. But now?

We don't need more practice. When he kissed me tonight—because *he* kissed *me*, it didn't just "happen"—it certainly *felt* natural. At least until he flailed around trying to get away from me.

"I just think it would be helpful," he says. His face has shuttered his emotions, leaving me unable to read him. And I don't like that. He's usually so expressive. "We don't have to if you don't want to."

Oh, I *do* want to. That's the problem.

My whole reason for being here, though, is to help him out. So if he needs to kiss me more to get himself comfortable with it, then I can do that for him. I can keep my desire for him in check. I've been doing it for years.

I scratch at my jaw as I say, "All right, we can . . . Do you want . . ."

Ignoring my inability to finish a sentence, he scoots closer and practically flings himself at me. Even with his uncoordinated movements, our lips instantly come together like they're magnetized. And he seems to settle as soon as we're kissing.

His fingers curl into my shirt, and I can feel the warm press of them through the fabric. I'm on my back, and he's propped himself up so that his face is slightly above mine, allowing him the easiest control of the kiss.

And *fuck*, I'm fine with letting him control it. Because his mouth is hot and exploring, his tongue sneaking out to lick across the seam of my lips, urging me to part them for him. As soon as I do, that wicked tongue meets mine, and it sends sparks of want shooting up my spine.

One of my arms is trapped between our bodies, his chest pressed tightly against it. But I manage to roll myself onto my side to mirror him, and I use my free hand to cup the back of his head. He moans softly when my nails scratch along his scalp. And then he freezes, like he didn't mean for the sound to escape him. But it did, and I can't unhear it.

So I use my hold on his head to guide him back into kissing me. I shouldn't be doing this, but the flames are growing hotter, and it's like his tongue is both stoking the fire and putting it out at the same time.

I need him.

Need his tongue and his lips and his body against mine.

I kiss him like I want to devour him. Because I do.

It's not until he bites my lip gently, then pulls back a bit, that I come to my senses and relinquish my hold on him. His fingers remain tangled in my shirt. It feels like an act of possessiveness, though I'm sure it's not.

"That was . . . um." His blue eyes bore into me as he struggles for words. He doesn't look scared, but he looks . . . something.

I remind myself that he asked for this. I didn't do anything wrong. Not technically. But damn, he probably wasn't asking me to maul him. Although, to be fair, he kind of mauled me first.

He lets go of my shirt as he shifts backward, putting a bit of space between us. That seems to clear his head, and he nods decisively. "Right. So I think that was good. Believable, I mean. It was probably enough practice."

"Yeah," I agree, trying to calm my wildly racing heart.

"Well." He bites his lip, and I instantly think of the perfect, slight twinge of pain when he did it to mine. "I'll let you get to sleep now."

"Yeah," I say again, stupidly. Because what the hell else can I say?

I can't tell him how much kissing him affects me. How it feels like so much more than practice. How I *want* it to be more, and it's getting harder and harder to pretend that's not the case.

I've wanted Brenden Sanderson for so damn long. And I'm afraid getting this taste of him, this tease, has opened the floodgates for me. I'm not sure I can hold back my desire any longer. But I'll have to keep trying.

Because the last thing I want to do is ruin the relationship we have by pushing for something more, something that could never work anyway.

❀

I'M HAVING THE BEST DREAM, a warm body in front of me, my cock rutting against supple ass cheeks. My hips keep rocking, seeking more, seeking entrance. Someone moans. Was it me?

My eyes fly open.

The dream vanishes in an instant, and reality hits me so hard I gasp. Once again, my dick is trying its absolute best to press into Brenden's ass through the barriers of our pants.

My instinct, now that I'm awake and in control of myself, is to bolt. But before I move, I realize that something solid is resting on top of my ankle. His foot. Can I disentangle myself without waking him?

I hold as still as possible and try to steady my breathing, because *goddammit*, my dick is throbbing with the need to come. Any small twitch from Brenden's body might be enough to set me off.

"*Mmf.*" He lets out a tiny whimper in his sleep, and my dick jerks in response.

Fucking hell. If I don't do something fast, he's going to wake up to my rock-hard erection stabbing him in the ass.

Carefully, I slide my leg out from under his foot. I attempt to move away from him in this awkward, hips-first maneuver, but he lets out a louder whine this time and presses his ass back like his body is subconsciously seeking my heat. When his ass bumps into my cockhead, my sweatpants aren't enough of a barrier anymore to keep me from losing it. The orgasm is so close, I can taste it. And then—

"Travis?"

Fuck, shit, damn it.

"Sorry," I mutter as I roll quickly away, practically falling out of the bed. I run for the bathroom, slamming the door closed behind me. Somewhere in the back of my mind, I feel vaguely guilty for possibly waking other people up. But the situation is fucking dire.

There's no way I can will this thing to go down. I'm way too far gone for that. With one hand, I roughly shove my sweatpants past my knees, and with the other, I reach for the tap on the sink, turning the water on.

Brenden was probably disoriented when he woke up. There's a chance he didn't have time to register what was prodding him. Maybe he'll just think I ran off because I really needed to piss.

Feeling like such a creep, I wrap my hand around my dick and give it a long, firm stroke, finally offering myself some relief. I speed up on the next stroke, adding a twist of my wrist at the head, and I have to bite my lip to hold in a moan. Even with the water running, I'm worried about being too loud.

I need to be fast, so this doesn't look even more suspicious. Which shouldn't be a problem, considering how on edge I am already. But a sudden knock on the door makes me freeze, hand around the base of my dick.

"Can I come in?" a small voice asks.

"I'm, uh . . ." I clear my throat when my words come out too husky. "I'm not decent."

There's a long pause, in which I assume Brenden's walked away. But then he says, very clearly, "You didn't answer my question."

What the hell? Is he fucking serious?

A million thoughts fly through my mind in the span of only a few seconds. Thoughts like, *Absolutely not,* and, *He's my friend,* and, *We can't do this,* and, *It'll fuck everything up.*

But then my dick overrides my brain, and I croak out, "Um. Okay."

The doorknob turns slowly, then the door cracks open and Brenden's face appears in the gap. I'm just standing here frozen, slumped sideways against the sink with my hand still on my dick. I can't let go, because that will leave me even more exposed. As if it's possible to be any more exposed than this.

What if he somehow didn't know what I was doing in here? What if he thought I was hurt, and he was only concerned?

Well. If he didn't know before, he does now. And instead of fleeing, he opens the door all the way, steps inside the bathroom, then closes the door behind him, leaning his back against it. For a few long moments, we stare at each other. Despite the immense awkwardness of the situation, my need to come hasn't become any less urgent. My dick hasn't gotten the memo that we should both go into hiding immediately.

Brenden steps closer, and I hold my breath as he reaches out, slowly, slowly. But then his hand moves around me to turn off the tap. *Right. Yeah.*

My heart is pounding so hard, he must be able to hear it now. He steps back again, and I still haven't moved. When his eyes deliberately trail down my body, I almost moan. Gaze lifting back up to meet mine, he raises his eyebrows. Like a challenge.

Still not understanding what reality we're in, I begin to stroke myself again. He steps forward, and I go faster. Then he moves in even closer, the small space of the bathroom putting him right in front of me in only a couple steps. His hand comes to my hip, and I break at the contact.

All self-restraint lost, I grab the side of his face with my free hand and yank him to me, my lips crashing onto his. I kiss him hard as I jerk myself harder. He grabs my bare ass and squeezes, which is embarrassingly all it takes for me to shoot off like a rocket, my cum landing who-knows-where between us.

And then it's over.

Our kissing slows to a stop, and I reluctantly separate from him. I pull up my sweats, ignoring the sticky mess. Then my eyes drift downward, and I can't help but notice the erection that his thin pajama bottoms don't do much to conceal. I glance back up at him, words failing me.

I've obviously fallen into a parallel universe. That's the only explanation for all this.

And please, just let me stay here. I don't want to go back.

Brenden blushes, looking unbelievably shy now. Like somehow

watching me jerk off wasn't a big deal, but him getting turned on by it is. "Oh," he says quietly. "Um. Yeah."

I reach out for his waist, but he shakes his head.

"You don't have to."

"Do you want me to?" I ask him.

He gives me another deer-in-headlights look, and I almost apologize for offering. Apologize for all of this. But then he bites his lip and nods.

That's all I need. Surging forward, I back him against the door before dropping to my knees. His sharp intake of breath only spurs me on. I'm mindful of the way his cock is jutting straight out as I begin to lower his pajamas, but once they've safely cleared his erection, I quickly tug them down to his ankles.

His cock is thinner than mine but a bit longer, the pink head glistening with a drop of precum that begs to be licked. So I stick out my tongue and taste it. The slight flavor of salt hits me, and I dive in for more.

He lets out a groan as I wrap my lips around the head. I glide my mouth down over his length, stopping before I take him too far. I'm tempted to force myself to take him deeper until I'm gagging on him. Sloppy, choking blowjobs are great, but I don't want that for this first time. I want to savor him.

My mental faculties are returning, and I'm dimly aware that this will probably be the *last* time, because *what the hell are we doing?* But that's even more reason to go slow, to enjoy every delicious second of his cock in my mouth, and to make damn sure he enjoys it too.

I pull off him to lick a long stripe from his base all the way up to the tip, where I swirl my tongue around his head. I'm back down and tonguing at his balls when his legs start to tremble. Glancing up, I'm treated to the sight of him with his eyes glazed over and mouth fallen open. His hands are hovering around my head like he wants to grab it but isn't sure he's allowed.

"You can touch me," I assure him. "However you want."

As my mouth gets back to work, slowly sucking him down again, his fingers twist in my hair and tug, causing me to moan around him. That makes him moan too, but then I hear a *thunk*.

When I look up to check on him, he's got his head tilted all the way back against the door, baring his throat in a sexy way that makes me want to wrap my hand around it. If only I could reach.

"You okay?" I ask.

He uses his grip on my hair to guide me back to his cock, so I'll take that as a yes.

I suck him off in earnest now, unable to hold back any longer. I use my hand to gently cup his balls as I press the tip of my tongue to the spot right under his head. He lets out a string of curses as his knees buckle. So I move both hands to hold his hips, pressing them firmly into the door. Once he seems stable, I let go.

"You can fuck my mouth," I tell him.

"Can't. Legs . . . not working."

I give him a satisfied smirk before I resume sucking him like it's my job, using my lips and tongue for all they're worth.

Then he whimpers, "*So close.*"

Fighting back my gag reflex, I take almost all of him down and swallow around his head. He explodes in my mouth, his whole body shaking as he empties down my throat.

I don't pull off until he pushes weakly at my shoulder, and I know he must be getting sensitive. My joints creak a bit as I stand, and when he reaches out to hold on to me, I'm not sure if it's for my benefit or his.

His eyes have regained focus, but he avoids looking at me, even though his hand is still on my waist.

Everything we just did hangs in the air between us. How are we supposed to move on from this? How do I explain myself? Because it was my fault, right? My inability to control my body's reaction to him is what brought us here.

But he was the one who wanted to come into the bathroom. He had to have known what I was doing in here. And he essentially encouraged me to continue getting myself off in front of him.

Didn't he?

Shit, what if I read the whole situation wrong? What if he was actually disgusted at what he found and expected me to apologize, make my walk of shame out of the bathroom, out of his house, and out of his life?

Did I force something on him that he didn't want? That thought curls dread in my stomach. He trusted me. I was never supposed to do anything to hurt him. I'm such an asshole.

But no. It seemed like he wanted it. It seemed, for a few minutes there, like I could actually have more of him than what I thought I was allowed. Or maybe I only saw what I wanted to see. Maybe I was foolish to let myself believe the fantasy that he might want me the same way I want him.

"Stop freaking out."

My eyes finally find his, and I breathe a little easier. Because he's not looking at me with disgust or contempt. Not at all. He's giving me that soft Brenden look that I like to imagine is reserved only for me. I know he offers it to everyone though. I'm not special.

"Did I do something wrong?" he asks. And when my utter confusion keeps me from answering, he adds, "When you let me come in, I figured it was okay to . . . participate."

That makes me chuckle, despite the situation. "Don't worry. I thoroughly enjoyed your participation."

"That's not even the right word," he says. "I didn't really do anything for you. You did all the work on both of us."

"Trust me. You did a hell of a lot for me."

He did more than I can say. Just looking at him was enough of a turn on, watching him watch me. And I can't forget how it was *him* I was rutting against when I woke up. His soft, warm body that fueled my desire to an unmanageable level.

"So um . . ." He glances down at where he's still touching me and lets his hand fall away. I try not to regret the loss. "What now?"

"I don't know."

"I don't want this to make things weird between us."

"Me neither," I tell him.

"Maybe this could be . . ."

"Be what?" I ask, my heart racing when he trails off. Is he going to tell me he wants more with me? Is it not such a foolish fantasy?

He gazes at me hopefully. "Like a fringe benefit of the whole fake dating thing?"

My heart sinks like a stone. A fringe benefit. Not the start of something real. "Oh. Um. Yeah. I guess it could be. I don't see why not."

Other than the fact that being *friends with benefits* with him might kill me.

When he smiles, eyes bright, I know I'm a goner. That's it. I've accepted my fate. I'll never be able to say no to this man. And if he wants friends with benefits, then I'll make sure to give him the best damn benefits he's ever had.

My sense of self-preservation clearly went out the window days ago.

CHAPTER THIRTEEN

BRENDEN

It's just my freaking luck that when I finally manage an afternoon off from both the inn and May's grandparents, I've wound up stuck at home chickensitting.

Yes, you heard that right.

Chicken. Sitting.

Elise and Grant took off with their rental car, saying they wanted to explore the surrounding towns a bit and get to know the area better while they're here. Lord knows why. They visit so rarely, it shouldn't matter. But I suppose there are only so many times an outsider can wander Mayweather's tiny downtown without getting bored.

It's only knowing everyone in town and getting filled in on all the new gossip while we're out that keeps us locals satisfied.

All I wanted to do with my precious free time was put on some music, maybe have a few glasses of wine, and relax. I was even considering taking a bath. God knows I could use a way to destress after the last few days of trying to convince Elise and Grant that I'm an entirely capable, responsible parent. And that I'm in a relationship with a guy who's never actually seen me as more than a friend.

But then Mitch showed up asking if I could watch Delilah for a couple hours, because she's been depressed lately, and he didn't want to leave her outside in her coop. As if this was a super simple, casual request that made any kind of sense.

When I asked him if chickens could even get depressed, he assured me they could. Then he also admitted that he's hoping it's just depression, because otherwise the way she's been acting lately could mean she's dying. Which might sound melodramatic, but what you need to understand is that this chicken is old. She's got to go sometime. Probably sometime soon. And Mitch, though he comes off as a bit nuts, is sane enough to know this.

Of course, this isn't the first time he's been worried she might be dying. In fact, it's happened so many times now that it's become almost a joke around town. Still, the way Mitch's eyes watered when he told me this today tugged at my stupid heartstrings, so here I am.

Just please don't let her die on my watch.

Determined to still enjoy my time off—despite the fact that Delilah is lying in the corner of my living room on a freaking cat bed and watching every move I make with her beady little chicken eyes—I pour myself a glass of wine and get comfortable on the couch, one leg tucked up underneath me. This is a fairly cheap merlot, but it does the trick. I turn on Netflix, knowing I'll likely spend more time scrolling for something decent to watch than actually watching. Any activity that shuts off my brain is welcome at this point though.

I can't keep thinking about the dirty, early morning activities between me and Travis, or else I'll wind up needing to jerk off. And there's no way I'm doing that in front of a chicken. Seems like it could be a felony.

God, that was so hot though.

Last night when I asked Travis to practice kissing again, my motives weren't entirely pure. Yes, I really need Elise and Grant to believe we're a couple. But maybe even more so in that moment, I needed to know if it was a fluke or not. The way our first practice kiss rocked my world.

Turns out, it wasn't a fluke.

I went to sleep worrying about how my attraction to Travis was spiraling out of control. Then when I woke up to his hard dick pressed against my ass, my worry switched off, and all I could think was *more, more, more.*

It felt like maybe there was a chance he was attracted to me too. So I stepped into the bathroom with him, knowing full well what he was doing in there. It was probably crazy, but I couldn't waste the opportunity to shoot my shot. I know Travis well enough that I figured if he wasn't interested, he'd at least reject me nicely.

Seeing him with his hand wrapped around that thick, gorgeous cock made my mouth go dry. And then I got weirdly shy and nervous and didn't actually do anything. I just stood there watching him get himself off, and then I let him get me off too. *Selfish.*

Next time, I'll do better. Next time I'll show him what *I* can do.

"Ouch!"

A sharp pain on the top of my foot makes me drop the remote midscroll, but thankfully I keep hold of my wine glass. Looking down, I find Delilah standing right in front of the couch. Did she just beak me?

"What are you doing?" I ask stupidly. "Mitch said you'd lie on your bed and not move."

She squawks, then turns her head to side-eye me.

"Go back over there," I say, pointing.

At this, she flaps her wings threateningly.

"*Delilah*," I warn.

And then she flies up and lands on my lap, and suddenly it's all sharp claws and a flurry of feathers and red wine sloshing onto the couch.

"Shit!"

I jump up, dislodging the giant bird, who proceeds to squawk and flap her wings again.

Oh no.

Before I have any chance of stopping her, she flies off, knocking over a lamp on my end table. It smashes against the edge and breaks as it falls to the floor.

I scream out another curse as I lunge for the feathered menace, but I barely manage to graze a wing. She's squawking and hopping and flying all over the room now, both of us equally frantic.

At a loss for what to do, I call out, "Delilah Doodle *Don't*," in my sternest voice. Because that's what Mitch calls her when she's in trouble.

But it does absolutely nothing to deter her from destroying my house. If anything, it seems to make her more agitated.

I'm scurrying around now trying to catch her, but she just keeps hopping out of my reach. There are feathers on the floor, scratches up both of my arms, and wine soaking into my couch.

After forcing myself to calm down, I stand a few feet from her, giving her a chance to calm down as well. When she does, I take a step closer.

And she flies off again.

Well, fuck me, I guess. And fuck her too.

Running back to the couch, I grab my phone, looking around for something to wipe up the wine with at the same time but coming up blank. I pull up Travis's contact and call him, barely waiting for him to say hello before I launch into a nonsensical tirade about a depressed chicken on the loose and my broken lamp and the sad, sad state of my life.

He says, "What?" a few times. But I just keep babbling faster and faster, until he says, "*Brenden*," so commandingly that it makes me stop.

Wow, I wish that had worked for me on Delilah.

After he tells me he'll be right over, I hang up and allow myself to breathe the tiniest sigh of relief while keeping my eyes on the chicken. He probably didn't understand a word I was saying, but he obviously heard the distress in my voice. And he's coming to help.

Of course he is. Because that's what Travis does.

I feel slightly guilty for calling him, because he's already doing so much for me between the inn and the grandparents. But who else do you call when you've got a chicken emergency if not your fake boyfriend?

I try halfheartedly to capture Delilah a few more times while I wait for him, but we're in the middle of another standoff when I hear his truck pulling up the driveway. As soon as he opens the door, I launch myself into his arms.

"SOS! Save my ship! Or my house, or my skin, or something."

"What's going on?" he says, rubbing a hand up and down my back.

Reluctantly, I step away from him to point an accusing finger at Delilah. "That bird is *evil*."

His eyes widen as he spots her, then he takes in the sight of my living room before focusing back on me. "What the fuck. You really do have a loose chicken in here?"

"I told you I did! Did you think I was lying?"

"I . . . I thought you wanted . . ."

"Wanted what?" I ask.

Clearing his throat, he says, "I thought you might have been hallucinating."

I gesticulate to the entirely non-hallucinated chicken defensively. "You know Delilah is real."

He furrows his brow. "Yeah, but I didn't know you were crazy enough to volunteer to take care of her."

"I didn't *volunteer*," I argue. "But whatever. Can you help me?"

Dubiously, he asks, "What exactly do you want me to do?"

"Turn her into chicken tenders!" I yell spitefully.

He gives me a horrified look.

"I'm not serious, jeez! Don't hurt her. Just help me catch her!"

"And then what?"

"Then . . ." I try to come up with the next logical step, but I've got nothing. So I throw my arms up in exasperation. "I don't know. But please do *something!*"

I'm growing hysterical again. All I wanted to do was watch Netflix, for fuck's sake. What did I do to deserve a goddamn chicken running amok in my living room?

Travis steps closer and pulls me back into his arms. He guides my head to his shoulder, his fingers splayed through my hair, rubbing tiny circles over my scalp. I gratefully lean more of my weight against him. If humans could purr, I'd be doing that right now.

Screw the chicken. She can have the house. It's not that nice anyway.

Humming softly, Travis kisses the top of my head. Now *that's* nice.

Squawk.

He startles, releasing me. "Okay, we've got to do something about the bird."

"That's what I've been saying!"

He gives me a look that suggests I should shut up, so I do. Then he steps farther into the room and assesses the situation before taking control like I wanted him to. It takes a lot of stealth and coordination between the two of us, but eventually we manage to wrangle Delilah into Travis's arms.

She immediately stops trying to flap away. In fact, she appears perfectly content being held by him.

I know the feeling, girl.

"What now?" I ask.

Travis glances down at the chicken warily. "Let's go over to Mitch's yard and put her in her coop."

I frown. "I'm supposed to be watching her because she's depressed. Or possibly dying."

The exasperated look he gives me is probably fair.

"Fine," I say. "But we have to sit there with her."

The exasperation grows stronger.

"Well, *I* have to sit with her," I amend. "You will obviously be free to go on living your life. I'll just remain on sacred chicken duty by myself."

With an eye roll, he says, "I can stay with you."

I try not to smile too smugly.

After we successfully deposit Delilah in her coop, we drag two of Mitch's Adirondack chairs over to it so we can sit in front of her. I take a couple subtle peeks at Travis beside me, checking him out. He's relaxed back in the chair, jean-clad thighs splayed open in what looks like an engraved invitation to climb into his lap.

Forcing myself to look away before I get caught—or actually attempt to climb into his lap—I train my gaze on Delilah, watching her for any signs of distress. "I don't know why she freaked out on me," I tell Travis. "She hangs out in Mitch's house all the time and acts normal."

"There is nothing normal about that," he says.

Well. True.

As Delilah struts proudly around her coop, I think about my destroyed living room and lost relaxation, and I get a bit depressed.

"I hate my life."

"No, you don't."

I shake my head. "No. I don't. But seriously. How do I wind up in so many ridiculous situations?"

Travis assesses me a moment, then says, "It's because you're too nice."

"Since when is being nice a bad thing?"

"Not saying it is. Just that you get roped into helping people out with stuff because you want to please everybody."

Frowning, I consider that. He definitely pegged me correctly as a people pleaser. And true, I'll lend a hand where I can, but . . . "*You're* the one who always helps everyone."

He makes a face like he tasted something awful. "Absolutely not."

I laugh. "Are you kidding? You're helping me right now. With chicken-sitting *and* pretending to date me. Any time I need something, you're always there for me."

He mutters what sounds like, "For *you*," but before I can ask what that means, he's unfolding himself from the chair and standing up. "I'm gonna run back to your place and grab a beer. You want anything?"

"Uh." I hesitate, a little thrown off balance for some reason. "No thanks, I'm good."

"Be right back."

Geez, you'd think I offended him by saying he's a nice person. Maybe he just wants to uphold his reputation. I mean, I don't call him Grump-topus for nothing. But underneath the cranky-old-man attitude he gives off at the diner, he's got a huge heart. I can't be the only one who sees that.

When he returns with his beer, he deftly changes the subject, and I let him. Mitch comes home soon after and thanks us—not even bothering to ask why Delilah's in her coop instead of my house—and then we're free to go.

Standing in the war zone of my living room once again, I choke back a frustrated groan. This is going to be a pain in the ass to clean up. Before I can thank Travis for his help and send him on his way, he crouches down to pick up the pieces of the broken lamp.

"Oh, you don't have to—"

"I'll help you fix all this mess."

I bite the corner of my lip to keep from smiling. This isn't doing anything for his claim that he doesn't help people. But I'm not going to point that out.

Once everything's back to its relatively normal state, I expect him to head out. Instead, he goes to my kitchen and grabs himself another beer. He takes it over to the couch—that wine stain is *not* coming out—and slouches down in the middle, legs spread invitingly again. But he looks tired. Which is obviously my fault for numerous reasons.

I take a seat next to him, angling myself toward him so my knee presses into his thigh. "I know I've been saying this to you a lot lately, and it's prob-ably lost all meaning by now, but thank you. Seriously, I really appreciate what you did for me today. And for the past week. And, you know . . . *always.*"

He turns to get a good look at me. I wish I could know exactly what he's seeing. He probably thinks I'm a complete disaster by now.

He doesn't say anything, just gives me the tiniest smile and a nod. Then he puts his hand on my thigh and squeezes. When he leaves it there, I lightly trace the veins over the back of it with my finger. He still doesn't pull away, and it's like my pesky fingers have minds of their own, because they dance a path up his forearm and biceps and over his shoulder.

I reach the side of his neck, sweeping my thumb over his pulse point, and he lets out an audible exhale. Suddenly it's not only my fingers that are out of my control—it's my whole body. Without really making a conscious decision to do so, I swing my leg over both of his and find myself straddling his lap.

Well. Since I'm here.

Cupping his face with both hands, I lean down slowly until our mouths are only inches apart. "*Thank you*," I whisper one more time before my lips briefly graze his.

"Brenden," he says in a tone I can't decipher.

It makes me freeze with my hands still on him.

This morning we agreed to friends with benefits, didn't we? He seemed into the idea.

But what if our bathroom hookup wasn't what I thought it was? Like what if he just got caught up in the moment because I barged in on him while he was getting off? And then because I was rudely waving my erection at him, he felt like he had to get me off too.

It's possible he only agreed to my proposition in order to avoid an awkward conversation about how he doesn't really want me like that. Maybe he never intended to go through with it.

Oh crap, that would be embarrassing.

Before I can apologize and crawl off him, his lips fly to mine, pressing insistently, and then the only thought left in my head is, *Fuck, yes.*

My position makes me taller than him, which I take advantage of to control the kiss. I slow it down, savoring his lips and the feel of his facial hair under my palms. One of his hands lands on my waist. And I'm aware he's still got a beer in the other one, but I'm not willing to stop this long enough to do something about that.

But as soon as I sneak my tongue into his mouth, meeting his, he groans and wraps his arm tightly around my back. Then he holds me to him so that I don't topple off his lap while he leans over and sets the bottle on the end table. And that was such a good idea, because now both of his hands are on me, rucking up the bottom of my shirt until I can feel his fingers grazing the skin of my lower back.

I kiss him harder and rock my hips experimentally. This earns me another groan and his grip tightening on me, so I do it again. And again. My hands come down to explore the contours of his chest over his T-shirt, and his hands move down to grab my ass, pulling me flush against him and keeping me there.

No complaints from me.

That is, until I try removing his shirt but can't because there's no room. I whine until he lets me move back enough to get it off him. Then before he can pull me in again, I yank my own shirt off my head with zero finesse, almost knocking my glasses off, and throw it on the floor.

Travis sucks in a sharp breath, and I experience a moment of self-consciousness. I know my body isn't sculpted like his, but I didn't think it was that bad, *sheesh*.

But then I realize he's staring at my side with a look of awe on his face, not disgust. Ever so slowly, his fingers trail up my ribs, the touch so soft it tickles.

Oh.

"You have a tattoo," he says, not taking his eyes off the large piece of art that covers my side.

"I do."

"I didn't know."

I laugh softly at the way he sounds mesmerized. "Guess I don't run around town whipping my shirt off."

"Does it mean something?" he asks, using the tip of his index finger now to trace around the curved lines of the flowers.

Of course, it does.

I squirm slightly away from his touch, even though I love having his hands on me, and his eyes finally come back up to meet mine. His gaze is unsure now, concerned, like he's wondering if he did something wrong. But he didn't. He couldn't have known why I'd rather not talk about this while I'm trying to make out with him. Or *ever*, preferably.

"I'm sorry," he says.

His hands fall away from my body, but I quickly grab one and bring it back to my waist. "No, it's okay. It's just . . ."

Despite my fear of needles, I got the large and very painful tattoo a year after April died. After my first year of being May's father. Of course it means something. It's just something I don't normally talk about. But I feel safe with Travis.

Sliding his hand up to cover the top flower, I tell him, "This one's a daisy. It's the flower for the month of April. It's also a symbol of motherhood, and new beginnings, and rebirth." I move his hand down to the flower below. "And this is lily of the valley. It's the flower for the month of May."

He squeezes my side gently, his warm brown eyes full of understanding. "They're beautiful."

I nod, choking back the tears that threaten to come. He must recognize my need to not dwell on this topic, because he slides his other hand into my hair and pulls me into a deep, slow kiss. I let the pain of missing April melt away as I lose myself in his lips.

His forehead bumps into my glasses, knocking them askew, and he pulls back. When he reaches out for them, I expect him to fix them or quickly get rid of them so we can resume kissing.

Instead, he carefully removes them from my face and frowns at them. "These are so dirty."

"Who cares?" I reply. Because *come onnn.*

Ignoring me, he blows hot air on each of the lenses and grabs his shirt off the couch beside him to wipe them off. When he holds them back up for inspection, he frowns again. "How can you even see out of them?"

Huffing in frustration, I take the glasses from him and toss them with minimal care onto the table. "Problem solved."

He gives me a scolding look and opens his mouth like he's about to lecture me, but I grind roughly against him, which makes him let out another wonderful groan instead.

Now this is more like it. No more distractions.

We resume making out, and he's rougher now, nipping at my bottom lip a few times until I whimper. Then he sucks my lip into his mouth and licks across it, soothing the sting. Pulling my mouth away from his, I kiss along his sharp, scruffy jawline and down his neck. I suck hard on the skin there, and he thrusts his hips up once, then goes for the button on my jeans.

I helpfully lift my hips so he can get them down past my ass. But I have to climb off him in order to remove them completely, which sucks.

Resisting the urge to hop back on his lap immediately, I take the time to get his jeans off him too. And when I straddle him again, I decide my effort was totally worth it, because now there are only two thin pieces of cloth covering our hard cocks as we rut against each other.

His finger dips below the waistband of my briefs, skimming along the top of my ass cheeks, and it's all I can do not to beg him to fuck me right now. It's been a while, and Travis is all rough and muscular. I've had thoughts of topping him before, but in this particular moment, he's making me desperate to bottom.

I'm about to crawl off his lap, with the intention of lying down and pulling him on top of me, when the front door opens. Elise and Grant are talking to each other as they come inside, and the sound of their voices is like a bucket of ice water being dumped over my head, dousing my libido.

Scrambling off Travis and grabbing for my clothes, I almost fall off the couch. But he catches me. Then he quickly lets go like my skin is on fire, and he's reaching for his shirt right as the Richardsons step into view.

"Oh!" Elise's hand flies to her mouth.

"Oh my god, I'm so sorry!" I say, throwing my legs into my jeans and hopping until I've got them pulled up. How the hell did I forget about these two?

"No, it's—" Elise starts.

"We should've knocked," Grant talks over her.

"Not your fault," I tell him. *God, where's my damn shirt?*

My eyes land on Travis, widening when I realize he's got his shirt on but is sans-pants and still sporting a semi. He grabs a throw pillow and uses it to cover his groin. His face is bright red like I've never seen it before, and he looks entirely panicked.

Somehow his extreme embarrassment helps me calm down and refocus. I find my shirt and pull it over my head, then ask Elise and Grant if they could please give us a minute to get ourselves together. They oblige, quickly heading upstairs with their shopping bags.

Once we're alone, I hand Travis his jeans and take the throw pillow away from him. His erection has gone down now, and I can't help but experience a pang of disappointment at that.

"I messed up, I'm sorry," I tell him as he finishes getting dressed. "I shouldn't have gotten carried away down here."

He smiles shyly, his face still a bit red. It's not a look I've seen on him often. Or ever. "I think it's safe to say we both got carried away."

"Um." I don't want to push my luck, but I need to know . . . "To be continued later somewhere more private?"

Reaching for my hand, he tugs me closer and plants a chaste kiss on my lips. "Sounds good."

I grin. It does, doesn't it?

Friends with benefits was the best idea.

I'm still grinning even as I make the dreaded trek upstairs to let Elise and Grant know it's safe for them to come down. It's not until the four of us are all hovering awkwardly around the kitchen, making beverages and small talk, that I realize the indecent display they walked in on must have sold the fake relationship better than anything else so far.

Truthfully, though, that's just a bonus.

CHAPTER FOURTEEN

TRAVIS

People eat too much, I swear. My whole afternoon has been a nonstop parade of burgers and melts and clubs. Endless amounts of coleslaw, potato salad, fries, pickles. There are children starving all over the world, and everybody is just sitting here, stuffing their greedy faces.

As I serve a double bacon cheeseburger with fried onion straws to Sal the mailman, I can feel my own arteries clogging, and I have to stop myself from turning around and dumping the entire plate in the trash.

Okay. I guess you could say I'm in a mood.

A group of new moms was in here earlier with all their strollers and diaper bags and snotty, wiggly babies. That chaotic mess has been hard to recover from.

Probably the only thing that's prevented me from blowing up on a customer today is the flashes I keep having of last night in Brenden's room before we went to bed. Of Brenden with his fist wrapped around both of our cocks. Of our lengths gliding together, leaking and slick, until one after the other, we both spilled over his hand and onto our stomachs.

If I picture that scene for too long though, I'll wind up abandoning the diner and running for my apartment upstairs to take care of myself.

Hell, I shouldn't even be hooking up with him. It can only lead to problems. But my ability to say no to him—which wasn't high to begin with—has decreased drastically since we started this fake relationship. And when he's asking to get his hand on my dick? Well. What the fuck do you expect me to do?

Moving to the counter, I'm greeted with a giant pile of crumpled napkins that someone left all around their empty plate. I grumble internally about the wastefulness as I pick them up and toss them in the trash.

Then the bell on the door rings, and Evelyn Morris walks in, making her way right for me as quickly as her seventy-two-year-old legs can carry her. I brace myself for whatever it is she wants, because knowing her, it could be anything. Yelling at me for the hundredth time about how I don't serve grapefruit juice, asking me to clean out her rain gutters, or wanting to know why I won't be having a booth at the spring festival, even though I've never once had a booth at any of this town's crazy events.

"Travis Reed," she says, tone scolding. "Have you been keeping secrets from us?"

By "us" I'm assuming she means her and all the other busybodies in this town. And I wince, because, *yes,* I've been keeping secrets for a long-ass time. But I hope she's referring to something inane, rather than the biggest secret that I like to sleep with men. Or damn, she couldn't know about me and Brenden pretending to date, could she?

"What do you mean?" I hedge.

She wags her finger at me. "You know very well what I mean. I heard you've been spending quite a lot of time at a certain Brenden Sanderson's house lately. What's going on there?"

Crap.

"We're friends," I tell her, which is true enough. "He's just needed my help with some things around the house."

"Oh, but I still haven't gotten you to do my rain gutters. I see how it is."

I resist the urge to ask this woman why she feels entitled to my time just because she's known me since I was born.

"Anyway," she goes on, "are you sure it isn't more than that? Because Brenden is a lovely man, you know. And he's gay as can be."

"I'm not—Uh—We don't—"

Fucking hell, make a sentence.

Why is she bringing this up with me? She doesn't know I'm gay. She can't possibly know. Nobody knows but Brenden.

"Relax dear," she says, shaking her head. "I know you don't swing that way. I'm only saying . . ."

"What?" I ask, though I'm afraid to know.

She reaches out a veiny hand to pat my forearm. "People can change, can't they? You never know. Can't say I'd ever want to take a dick up the ass, but to each his own. And you've been alone for so long. Wouldn't you like to find someone? I'm only saying, it might be nice. Might be a good match."

My eyes have grown so wide I'm afraid they might fall out of my skull. Pretty sure I heard Ellie, the children's librarian, choking on her food at the dick-up-the-ass part.

Okay, I need to get myself together and shut this down before gossip leaks back to my dad.

"Mrs. Morris," I say, fighting to keep my voice even. "This isn't an appropriate conversation to have here while I'm working. Not sure where you got these ideas, but it's not really appropriate for you to ask me about my sex life at all."

"I'm not asking about your sex life, I'm asking about your dating life," she counters. As if the words *dick* and *ass* didn't come out of her mouth in a horrifying way that I'll never be able to forget.

"Either way, I don't think my personal life is any of your business."

"I only want to know you're happy, dear. We all want you to be happy. Especially your father. He'd be thrilled to see you finally settle down. He worries about you, you know."

He wants me to find a woman *and settle down,* I think bitterly. Pretty sure he wouldn't be thrilled if he found out I was dating Brenden.

Not that I really am. Or ever will be.

"I promise you, I'm happy," I tell her. And if the words feel forced . . .

"If you were happy, you wouldn't be such a grouch all the time."

Someone laughs at that, but I don't look to see who. I'd give anything for this not to be happening.

Gritting my teeth to avoid yelling at a senior citizen, I ask, "Mrs. Morris, would you like to order anything?"

She looks at me like I'm the crazy one, then says, "No dear, I already ate. Have a nice day." And with that, she turns and strides out, leaving behind a trail of her overly floral perfume.

In her absence, I risk a glance around the room. Most of the tables are filled with customers. Neighbors. Gossips. And everyone's eyes are on me.

"What are you all looking at?" I snap. "Eat your food or get out."

That does the trick. Everyone returns their focus to their plates and their dining companions, but I'm left reeling.

What the hell was that? I know everyone in this town is nosy, especially the older people who have nothing better to do than gossip all day. But since when has anyone besides my dad ever cared about whether or not I was dating anyone?

If it was just Mrs. Morris, I could brush it off. But I'm sure she left to find a group of her old lady friends to discuss this with, and soon they'll all be talking about me. And how did she even know about me being at Brenden's house so much anyway?

I guess I was foolish to think nobody would notice. Mitch has probably seen my truck and blabbed to a handful of people already.

Fuck.

He's friends with my dad.

Has he told him?

They're more just town friends than call-each-other-up-for-a-chat friends, so hopefully not.

The saving grace is that Mitch must not have noticed me parked at Brenden's overnight. Because that certainly would have warranted a phone call to my dad, and then my dad would've called me. And Mrs. Morris would have come in here with a whole lot more to say. Like more things about male body parts that would scar me for life.

It's strange, though. The way she suggested I could be with Brenden without having any idea about my sexuality. Is it really so simple for her? She didn't seem at all put off by the concept of me being with a man. Have I been wasting my energy hiding the truth of myself all these years?

No.

Because the opinions of a bunch of town gossips aren't really what I'm worried about. It's just my dad. My dad who has certainly never talked so openly and casually about men fucking each other. Like it's no big deal. Like it's not disgusting.

To be fair, he's never actually said he thinks it's disgusting. At least not to me. But that doesn't mean he'd be okay with his son being gay.

When are you going to man up and get married?

That's what he says to me. And it's easier to let him be disappointed by my lack of desire for a serious relationship than it is to disappoint him with the reality of who I'd marry if that was something I wanted.

Yeah. It's easier this way. So Brenden and I just need to be more careful about not getting caught during this whole scheme. I can start walking to his house. That way nobody will have anything to gossip about.

I KNOW I CHOSE cooking as a profession. But between the diner, the inn, and Brenden's kitchen, it's feeling like I'm doomed to spend my life chained to a stove. Cooking for Brenden and May, though, gives me a sense of satisfaction I don't get when I'm cooking for work, which makes the burnout worth it. This may be part of a show for May's grandparents, but I like knowing that she and Brenden are getting some nutrients in them for once. Lord knows how they survive on all the processed, packaged crap they eat all the time.

Since Brenden isn't home from work yet, he gets no say in what I'm making. I know he'll like it, but I'm prepared for at least one complaint about vegetables anyway.

Grant is in the living room reading a newspaper. He must have gone out of town to pick it up, since all you can find here is the Mayweather Gazette, which barely qualifies as a paper.

Elise asked if she could help me in the kitchen, though I politely declined, telling her to enjoy her time with May. She's been nothing but nice to me, but let's face it. I'm not a people person. I can only take so much small talk.

She and May are now in the backyard planting something. (I fear for the life of whatever it is if Brenden ends up in charge of tending to it after Elise leaves.) I've been watching them through the window as I cook, and it's clear how much Elise adores her granddaughter. It makes me wonder why she and Grant don't visit more often.

This family dynamic is none of my business, though, even if Brenden essentially dragged me into it.

As I chop broccoli, letting my alfredo sauce simmer, I have time to contemplate what I'm doing here. In Brenden's house. Playing his fake boyfriend. It's what I agreed to, and we seem to be doing a great job of making Elise and Grant buy it. But I'm starting to worry that I've set myself up for unnecessary pain.

I think I might be leaning into my role a little too much. And I'm definitely enjoying it too much. Just simply the permission to touch and kiss Brenden was enough to have me wishing this was real. Now that we've added orgasms into the mix . . .

It's too good. And it's getting harder and harder to imagine going back to my old life where I'm grumpy and alone all the time, and where he's just a friend I only sometimes see outside of the diner.

A commotion from the living room breaks me out of my thoughts. It sounds like Grant is arguing with someone. I turn off the burner before running out there to see what's going on.

Mitch is standing in the entryway, gesticulating wildly as Grant blocks him from coming farther into the house.

"What's wrong?" I ask them.

Without taking his off Mitch, Grant says, "This man just waltzed right into the house. When I asked him to explain himself, he questioned who *I* was. As if he has more right to be here than I do."

"I needed to borrow some sugar, and Brenden's car wasn't here, so I didn't think I'd be disturbing anyone," Mitch says, sounding exasperated. "I told this guy I live next door, but he doesn't believe me!" He pauses, then squints his eyes at me. "Wait. What the heck are *you* doing here if he's not home?"

I immediately move into damage control mode, stepping up to the two men and assuring Grant that Mitch does in fact live next door and is friends with Brenden, before grabbing Mitch by the elbow and tugging him toward the kitchen with me.

"I'm making dinner," I tell him. "Brenden will be home soon."

"But why?" he asks, and I purposefully step on his foot.

I assume Grant is following us, so without considering the ramifications of this, I explain as quickly and quietly as I can, "You need to pretend I'm dating Brenden, okay?"

"But—"

"Is this a normal thing around here, for people to come into other people's homes uninvited?" Grant asks. My gaze swings to where he's leaning against the doorframe with his arms crossed and a frown on his face.

"The front's always unlocked!" Mitch exclaims, clearly winding himself up again. But at least this takes his focus off me and why I'm here cooking dinner. "People are friendly around here! Unlike wherever it is *you* came from."

Grant's face pinches up so much he looks constipated.

"I'm so sorry," I say, hoping to pacify them both. "Grant, this is Mitch. He's a friend of Brenden's, and I'm sure Brenden wouldn't mind him coming in to borrow something. Mitch, this is May's grandfather. He and her grandmother are here visiting."

Mitch and Grant continue to eye each other distastefully. The differences between the men are highlighted by their clothing choices. While Grant is wearing slacks on his vacation, Mitch is sporting cutoff jean shorts and a T-shirt with a semi-vulgar beer advertisement.

"You said you needed sugar?" I ask Mitch, breaking the silence when it's obvious the two of them aren't going to exchange pleasantries.

"That's right," he tells me. "Half a cup will do."

I turn to get it for him. If he was after any other ingredient, I'd be doubtful about finding it in Brenden's kitchen, but sugar, I know he has an abundance of. There's a small ceramic jar shaped like a snail beside the coffee maker, and he keeps more in a cabinet. What he doesn't have, however, is a measuring cup (not a surprise), so I find a suitable Tupperware container for Mitch and eyeball the amount I pour.

"Thanks, man," he says when I hand it to him. Then his forehead scrunches up like he's thinking hard, and he adds, "I mean, thanks, *Brenden's boyfriend.*"

Holy fuck, I'm so ready for this day to end.

Luckily, Grant already thinks Mitch is a weirdo and doesn't look too confused by the ridiculous line. Still, I usher Mitch out of the kitchen before he can open his mouth again. Grant steps aside to let us through the doorway, and thankfully, he doesn't follow as I keep ushering Mitch all the way out the front door and onto the porch.

"Yo, what's the rush?" he gripes out as he stumbles. "I pretended good, didn't I?"

I close the door behind us a little too forcefully, then hiss at him, "Please tell me you'll keep quiet about this."

The last thing Brenden needs is for the entire town to hear about how I'm pretending to be his boyfriend, because then some idiot will end up blowing his cover in front of Elise and Grant.

And the last thing *I* need is for my dad to find out about this and start wondering if I'm actually . . . well, what I am.

"And what is it exactly that I'm supposed to be keeping quiet about?" Mitch asks. "Why the heck does that boring man think you're Brenden's boyfriend? You don't like dick." He gives me a frighteningly calculating look before adding, "Or *do* you?"

Jesus, these people. Does nobody have tact anymore?

"It's a long story," I tell him. "You can ask Brenden to explain it to you after May's grandparents leave."

I probably should have reaffirmed his belief that I'm straight, instead of ignoring that last question. But even though my heart's racing at the possibility of being found out, I don't think I have it in me to flat out lie about my sexuality.

Maybe a couple weeks ago, I could have. But now saying I'm not into men would be like saying what me and Brenden have done together wasn't real. The dating may be fake, but the attraction and orgasms are all too real.

Mitch looks like he wants to pry some more, and if he does, I might fold like a house of cards. Because at this point, my feelings for Brenden are almost overriding my common sense. But mercifully, right then, Elise and May appear from around the side of the house.

"Hey, Mitch," May greets him as she climbs the porch steps. "How's Delilah?"

Mitch lights up. "She's doing great! I think she was just going through a bit of a teenage angst phase, but she's back to herself now."

"That's good, I'm glad," May says, like the sweet girl she is. Acting like this man and his damn chicken are perfectly normal.

"Okay, I'll be out of everyone's hair," Mitch tells us. He waves the container of sugar in front of himself. "Just needed to borrow something, and *Brenden's boyfriend* here was nice enough to get it for me."

I almost groan but manage to hold it in. The way he calls me Brenden's boyfriend is so exaggerated again that he might as well have winked at me. And does he not understand the concept of borrowing something? I don't think he intends to bring the sugar back. But I'm not going to point that out to him, because I just need him gone.

May looks like she wants to laugh. Instead, she tells Mitch to have a nice day, and then says, "Come on, Grandma," leading Elise inside the house.

My alfredo sauce will be ruined if I take much longer getting back to it, but I need to give myself a minute out here to breathe. At least now I don't need to worry about Mitch spotting my truck overnight, because he knows what's going on. Sort of. But I'm seriously doubting his ability to keep this a secret.

As I'm standing alone on the porch, Brenden's car pulls into the driveway, and my heart does a flip inside my chest. Even though he's managed to bring chaos to my otherwise normal life, I can't deny that seeing his face still lifts my mood. Every damn time.

He gives me a questioning look as he gets out of the car and comes up the porch. "What are you doing out here?"

I quickly fill him in on Mitch barging in and how I had to tell him we were pretending to date.

His expression turns pained. "Oh god, he's gonna tell everyone, isn't he?"

"I don't know. Probably not on purpose, but maybe by accident." I'd like to assure him that Mitch will keep his mouth shut, but I can't lie.

He groans and steps closer, burying his face against my chest.

Wrapping an arm around him, I rub his back and tell him, "It'll be okay."

Because no matter what, I'll make sure everything's okay for him. And the trusting look in his eyes as he lifts his head to peer up at me tells me that he knows this.

My heart flips again, and I kiss the top of his head. "Let's go inside."

"What's for dinner?" he asks.

"I'm making shrimp and broccoli alfredo with garlic bread."

"No broccoli," he whines, pulling a face.

"Yes, broccoli, and you're going to eat it, not pick it out," I tell him sternly.

His sigh is extremely dramatic. And then he says, "Okay, daddy."

As he moves around me for the door, I pinch his ass, making him yelp and laugh in a way that lights up my soul.

During dinner, when he tries to sneak a piece of his broccoli onto my plate, I catch him and feed it to him off my own fork. He lets me, smiling sweetly before licking his lips in an entirely sinful way that promises me an interesting night once we're alone.

I'm not sure when all this flirting and casual affection with each other began to feel like second nature. But *fuck*, I'm in *so* much trouble here.

CHAPTER FIFTEEN

BRENDEN

MayFest starts tomorrow, and as much as I love every event May-weather puts on, a part of me can't wait for it to be over. Ever since I took ownership of the inn, I don't get to simply enjoy the festivities anymore. Most of the businesses in town participate, and I have to make sure everything runs smoothly with our booth. But I trust Addison and my other employees to handle things so I can spend at least some of the festival with May and her grandparents. And there's no way I'm missing out on doing the May Games with May. It's our tradition.

At least once the two-day event is over, a lot of my guests will be leaving, so I should finally have a room available here for Elise and Grant. That should reduce my stress level, which has been at a maximum high for the last couple weeks. Though I doubt they'll be staying much longer after the festival anyway.

Popping into the inn's kitchen to grab myself a cup of coffee—my third, actually, but who's counting—I find Addison busy topping a large tray of mango tarts with thin, curled fruit slices. The tarts look delectable, and I'm sure they're going to sell out quickly tomorrow, so I reach out to take one, but she smacks my hand away.

"Ow," I complain.

"Stay away from my desserts. I've been baking all morning."

"You know this is *my* inn, right?" I argue. "So technically, they're my desserts."

The challenging look she gives me is a bit scary. And this woman is adept at wielding a knife, so I do the smart thing.

Holding up my hands to show I'm harmless, I slowly back away from the tray. "Do I at least get coffee?"

She rolls her eyes and gets back to her work. "As if I could keep you away from the machine. You'd probably walk around carrying it with you all day if it wasn't so heavy and you didn't have noodle arms."

"Hey!" I protest. Though, really, I can't argue that.

"Travis is upstairs if you're looking for him," she says without turning to me.

I falter as I'm pouring coffee into my thermos. Why would she assume I'm looking for Travis? As if he's all I think about.

He's not.

Even if I can't get the feel of his hard cock in my hand out of my mind.

Wait a minute.

"Travis is upstairs? Why? What's he even doing here? I thought you didn't need his help anymore."

"I told him I don't, but he wanted to check in and make sure everything was good to go for tomorrow. And he was gonna help bring the booth over to the green and get it set up."

"He doesn't need to do that." There are people here who I actually pay to do these jobs. I don't want Travis to feel obligated to help with everything. He's already done so much.

Addison continues artfully placing mango slices as I come back over to her workstation with my coffee. "I let him know Leo and Paul were set to do it, but he said he doesn't trust either of them to do it right, and he'd feel better knowing it wasn't going to fall apart on us."

Despite his lack of faith in the staff I hired, a burst of happiness shoots through me at hearing how much Travis cares. Even when I don't ask him for help, he's still helping me. He might be all gruff and growly with people sometimes, but I think it's an act. If people knew just how good of a person he is, they'd walk all over him.

I need to be careful that *I'm* not doing that. I'll make sure to let him know things at the inn are covered and he doesn't need to worry about us anymore. Addison got in a bunch of applications, so she'll be able to hire more help once all this craziness is over.

"But wait. If he came to help with the booth, then why is he upstairs?"

Addison barely lifts one shoulder in a half-assed shrug, still laser-focused on her task. "He heard one of the cleaning staff mention a wobbly bed, and I assume he went to fix it."

"Oh geez."

That man, I swear.

Taking my coffee with me, I leave the kitchen and head upstairs to check the rooms. Most of the guest room doors are closed, but it doesn't take long to find the open one. And when I spot Travis, I damn near swallow my tongue. He's on the floor, ass up in the air, fiddling with one of the bed's legs.

And did I mention his hot, denim-clad ass is up in the air?

I shamelessly ogle him a few more moments, then step farther into the room, closing and locking the door behind me.

At the sound of that, his head swings my way. "Hey," he says. Then he goes back to fixing the bed like he doesn't know he's the most perfect man ever.

"You do not have to do this." I take a sip of coffee before setting the thermos on the dresser.

"It's no trouble," he replies. His ass is still pointed up, and I'm two seconds away from marching over to him and smacking it. That's not typically my thing, but man. I want to feel the muscle give and the heat of him under my palm. "There, that should do it."

When he stands, black shirt tight across his chest and eyes bright like he's happy to see me, I can't hold back any longer.

"You are the fucking best," I tell him, striding forward until I'm inches from him, and then stepping even closer so he's forced to step back. He knocks into the bed, and I waste no time in pushing him down onto it. His body bounces slightly on the mattress, but bless him, the bed doesn't wobble at all.

"What are you doing?" he asks, a mixture of confusion and amusement on his face.

With a mischievous smile, I jab one finger into his chest, encouraging him to lie down, and I straddle him as soon as he complies. My shoes are on the bed, which compromises the inn's standards of cleanliness. But running my hands up Travis's sides, I couldn't care less.

As I lean down to kiss him, he threads his fingers through my hair and pulls me in, so I'm not sure who ends up kissing whom. But it doesn't matter. I suck on his bottom lip, then pull back to nip at it before sucking on it again. Once I let go, he licks at my lips, and I open for him. His hand on the back of my head provides a gentle pressure that keeps my face close to his, and I've never minded anything less.

But soon I ache to get my mouth on him in other places. Places I've yet to explore. We've fooled around a couple times now—a fact which still blows my mind—but I haven't had a taste of his cock yet, and that needs to be remedied immediately.

I whine, which makes him release me, allowing me to pull back and move down to his neck. Tugging his shirt collar aside, I bite down on the place where his neck meets his shoulder. He groans and his hands come around my back, gripping me tightly.

Shuffling myself so I can get to his stomach, I ruck up his shirt and lick a line down his abs with the tip of my tongue. They flutter under the treatment, so I lick my way back up and then down again. Then I switch to using teeth, which earns me another, louder groan and his hand back in my hair.

I bite, and he tugs. And when he lets out a raspy, "*Fuck, baby,*" my dick twitches almost painfully in the confines of my slacks.

As I work on getting his jeans undone, desperate to free his cock, my mind keeps hearing *baby, baby, baby . . .*

It was a heat of the moment thing, I know that. But damn did it feel good hearing him say it to me. I wonder what else I can make him say if I try.

Once I've gotten the fly of his jeans open, I carefully climb off his lap and sink to my knees on the floor. I tug at the jeans, and he lifts his ass so I can slide them past it. Then he props himself up on his hands, staring down at me with glazed eyes as I pull the jeans all the way down to his ankles. His cock is tenting his boxers obscenely, threatening to poke through the slit.

Well. Can't threaten me with a good time.

"What are you doing?" he asks again, a little breathless.

I slide the boxers down to his knees, allowing his cock to spring free. "Isn't it obvious?"

"But are you sure? I mean. You're at work."

Yeah, I keep forgetting that part. Oh well. Now that I've got his thick cock in my face, glistening with precum, there's nothing short of guests waltzing into this room with their luggage in tow that will stop me from getting him off.

Instead of replying, I wrap one hand around him and take a little taste at the tip. *Mmm.*

When I slide his cockhead past my lips, he abandons holding himself up, and now he's lying down so I can't see his face. Even though I'd love to see his expressions as I take him apart, I can still tell how much he's enjoying it by the jerky movements of his hips and the little moans he tries to cut off.

Though it's possible I'm enjoying this even more. Honestly, I love giving head. Maybe it's part of being a people pleaser, but it's also such a powerful feeling. Being on your knees for someone but being able to drive them crazy, controlling when and how they get to come.

I'd like to take my time teasing him, wait until he's begging for it. *Would he beg? Fuck, that would be so hot.* But I remind myself of where we are. It's not like I can get fired, since I own the place, but still. Making this quick is probably a good idea.

I suck him down farther, and damn, he really is thick. I only get about half of him in before my mouth feels so fucking full. But I can do this. I know the things I'm good at, and this is one of them. Relaxing my throat, I take him in deeper, letting my tongue lick along the underside of his shaft as I go. He seems to like that, judging by the way his thighs tremble slightly and he scrunches up the blanket in his hands.

To speed things along, I cup his balls gently, rolling them in my palm, and then rub my finger along his taint. I'm tempted to dip lower, see if he'll let me play with his ass. I really can't gauge if he'd be into that. I picture him as a total top, but even tops like a finger or two sometimes, right? At least, I've known some that do. It's probably best, though, to save that question for another day and just achieve the goal I set out to accomplish here.

Making Travis come down my throat.

I move up and down his shaft in earnest now, swallowing around him when I have him all the way down, and swirling my tongue around the head when I come up. Over and over, faster and faster, until he chokes out, "Brenden, *fuck*, I'm gonna—"

That's all the warning I get before he unloads. And damn, it's a lot. But I manage to swallow it all, proud of myself for not leaving a cum stain on the blanket. Although I should change the bedding anyway, right?

Oh, hell.

Travis is still panting hard after his orgasm, while reality comes slamming back into me, and I think about what I've just done. I'm in a guest room. On my knees in my work pants on this hardwood floor with Travis's bare ass lying on the bed. I've *never* done something like this at work.

And yet, do I regret it?

Not even a little bit.

Travis spends a few more moments panting. Then he sits up and pulls his jeans back up, rebuttoning them with clumsy fingers.

I grin smugly, because I did that to him. *Me.* Little innocent Brenden Sanderson.

Ha. As if.

Standing, I brush off the knees of my pants. Thankfully, they're not dirty. Kudos to my cleaning staff.

"Can I help you with that?"

When I look at Travis, I find his gaze pointed down at my crotch. *Oh.* I had so much fun sucking him off that I didn't even think about myself, but yup. I'm hard as a rock.

I shake my head regretfully. "I'll be okay. This was . . . um . . . I should probably get back to work."

All of a sudden, I feel a bit awkward. In the heat of the moment, I was more than happy to take charge, but now standing here facing him, I wonder what he's thinking of me. How he feels. Because I . . .

I *really* liked doing that with him. And while this friends with benefits arrangement is convenient while we're already faking a relationship, I'm starting to think I'd like to keep doing this even after Elise and Grant leave.

But that's dumb.

Travis has never wanted me before in all the years I've known him, so how could I expect anything to have changed now?

Convenient. That's what this is for him. A way for him to get off while he's busy helping me out. With all the time he's spending with me, he obviously has no time to go looking for hookups elsewhere. But May's grandparents will be gone soon, and then he won't have to keep spending his nights at my house. He'll be free to get his rocks off wherever and with whomever he chooses.

It's silly to think that, when he has his options back, he might still choose me.

So I should just enjoy him while I've got him.

He clears his throat as he stands. "How about I return the favor tonight?"

I force a smile and say, "Sounds good," because I'm not turning that down.

But even if it's only an expression, I don't like to think of him getting me off as another favor he's doing for me. That feels kind of gross and wrong. Though the way he smiles at me now—warm and eager-looking—makes it seem like that's *not* how he sees it. I can only hope not.

"I need to change these linens before anyone checks in," I tell him, sending a guilty glance toward the rumpled bed.

He chuckles almost shyly. "Right. I'll let you get to it."

"Thanks for fixing the wobbly leg."

His laugh is fuller this time. "Pretty sure you already thanked me really fucking well."

That makes my face heat up, and I'm not sure how to respond. But he solves this by leaning in, not even hesitating about kissing me after I had his dick in my mouth. It's brief, though, and then he says, "See you later," before walking out of the room.

In his absence, I stare at the bed, kind of not believing that happened. What the heck has gotten into me?

No, not what. *Who.*

Travis fucking Reed. That's who.

He's gotten into my pants and into my head, and I'm not sure how easy it'll be to get him out again. But it sure would be nice if maybe, just maybe, I didn't have to.

CHAPTER SIXTEEN

TRAVIS

B renden Sanderson is going to be the death of me, I swear.

How the heck am I supposed to concentrate on setting up this booth for him when I keep remembering exactly how fantastic his warm mouth felt wrapped around my cock? It's a miracle I haven't hammered my finger instead of a nail yet.

Leo, one of Brenden's employees who came with me to help, luckily hasn't noticed my distracted state. He's not the most observant guy. Sure, he follows directions fine, but I think I was right not to trust him being in charge of this job.

We're not the only ones out here on the green getting things ready for the festival. People are bustling around everywhere. Some of them are holding shouted conversations with one another from opposite sides of the green while they work, which also isn't helping my concentration.

This is exactly the kind of town hoopla I usually like to avoid. But for Brenden, I can endure it.

My phone rings, and I pause what I'm doing to take it out of my pocket. I accept my dad's call right as Leo carelessly swings around a piece of plywood and almost knocks me in the head.

Ducking swiftly, I let out a curse rather than a greeting.

"Travis?" my dad says, sounding alarmed. "You okay?"

"Yeah, sorry, I'm fine." I send a pointed look Leo's way, and he grimaces apologetically before carrying on with what he was doing. "How are you?"

A vague, grumbling sound is the only answer I get to that question. Then Dad says, "I need you to do me a favor if you can."

"Sure. What's up?"

As he explains that one of his employees is on a job site and needs a part picked up and brought over to him, I continue directing Leo with hand gestures. We're just about done here, so I should have time to run the errand.

"No problem," I tell him.

"Thanks," Dad says. "Christ, I can't wait to get back to work. All this sitting around on my ass is killing me."

I understand where he's coming from, but thinking about his fall is still a bit scary for me. "You're resting, which is what you're supposed to do," I remind him. "Because falling off a ladder is what actually could've killed you. So when you do go back to work, you need to promise me you'll be more careful, okay?"

"Hey, who's the parent here?" he gripes.

"Dad. Please."

He heaves out a loud sigh. "Yeah, yeah, all right. I hear ya."

While listening to him complain about something else, I gather stuff up so me and Leo can leave. As I'm finishing, I spot Elise and Grant rounding the gazebo and strolling down the path that cuts through the middle of the green. Elise smiles and waves when she sees me.

I give her a wave in return, though the gesture feels unnatural. I don't make it a habit of waving to people I spot in town. If I did that, then I'd never get anything done, because every person would want to stop and gossip. I don't have the time for that or the interest.

But May's grandparents would likely be coming over to talk whether I waved or not, so I hastily tell my dad I need to go and promise to pick up that part for his employee. Can't have him overhearing anything incriminating Elise or Grant might say.

"Do you mind throwing this stuff in the back of my truck?" I ask Leo as they approach us. "I'll be right there to drive you back to the inn."

He takes everything without complaint, and I'm ashamed of my relief at getting rid of both him and my dad. I don't want anything to blow Brenden's cover, but really, I'm worried about my own secret just as much. And I guess it's a little ridiculous that I'm a grown ass man still afraid of what my dad might think of me if he found out I wasn't straight.

But I don't have the time to dwell on my issues, because Elise and Grant reach me right as Leo walks off the other direction.

"Travis, hi!" Elise greets me. "It's a gorgeous day, isn't it?"

"Sure is," I reply, offering her a smile.

Grant gestures to what's set up behind me. "Is this your booth? I thought Brenden said you refuse to have a booth at the festivals."

I frown, because while that's true, it kind of makes me sound like an ass, doesn't it? "I serve people all day long inside the diner," I explain somewhat defensively. "I'd rather not walk outside and have to do the same thing."

Elise laughs. "I suppose that's fair. So what's this then?"

"Oh, it's Brenden's. The booth for the inn is always a big draw. His chef, Addison, has been baking for days to prepare."

The way they're both smiling at me now is weird.

"You do a lot for him, don't you?" Grant asks.

Crap.

"No, I, uh . . ." That's exactly the kind of thing Brenden doesn't want them to think. He wants them to think he's capable of doing things on his own. Which he is.

"It's obvious you really care about him," Elise says.

Oh. Maybe my instinct to help him reveals more about my feelings for him than his capabilities.

"It's clear how much you care about May too," she goes on. "And May adores you. She speaks very highly of you. We're glad Brenden found such a good man."

Are my ears turning red? They feel hot. I'm not used to people singing my praises.

"I care about them both a lot," I admit, ducking my head. "But believe me, I'm lucky Brenden even looked my way. He's so ... warm. And charming. He could have anyone he wanted."

"And he wants *you*," Grant says. "So that says something about you."

Okay, my ears must be red. Probably my cheeks too.

But Brenden doesn't want me. Not in the way I want him to. He might want my body for now, but he doesn't want all of me. My anti-social tendencies and general attitude don't make good boyfriend material.

I've just been putting on a nice show for the grandparents.

"So what are you two up to today?" I ask, not so smoothly changing the subject. Both to save myself from further embarrassment, and before any of the town gossips walk by and overhear anything they shouldn't.

"We're simply wandering, looking for something to keep us occupied," Elise tells me. "We passed by the yoga studio, but I'm not sure that's for us. And the art supply store was doing ceramic painting. It's such a nice day, though. Seems a shame to spend it inside."

"Have you checked out Shaw Family Farms?"

She tilts her head questioningly.

"They always have stuff going on over there. You can pick your own fruit, and there's a small store where they sell all kinds of jams and things."

Elise turns to Grant. "That sounds familiar."

He nods. "We've been there before. But it's probably been at least twenty years."

That doesn't make sense. "You were here that long ago? Before Brenden and May moved to town?"

When Elise smiles, it's small, almost sad. "We used to come for family vacations with our daughter."

"With . . ." *Shit.* Now I remember Brenden once talking about why he chose to move to Mayweather. Because May's mom—his best friend—had told him how much she loved it here. "I'm so sorry. I guess I forgot, but Brenden did mention that before."

"No need to be sorry," Grant assures me. "I know we don't talk about our daughter much. Honestly, it's a little hard being here. We . . . Well, that's sort of why we don't usually stray too far from the inn or Brenden's house when we visit. This town brings back memories."

Hearing the tinge of pain in his voice causes a lump to form in my throat. Is *that* why they rarely come to visit? Brenden thinks it's because they don't care, but has he considered what being here is like for them?

"Let's not spoil the lovely day," Elise says, and this time her smile is a bit brighter. "We decided we wanted to explore more on this trip, see all that the town and the area has to offer."

"That sounds nice."

Grant clasps me on the shoulder. "You know, it took us a while to make the connection, but we remember your diner too. I'm sorry we can't say it was our top choice of restaurant in the area, but April loved the pancakes, so we had to go at least once each trip."

"Oh wow. Small world, I guess. Or small town, more like." I smile to myself, thinking of how May always gets pancakes when she comes in for breakfast. Like mother, like daughter.

As Grant releases my shoulder, Elise steps closer. "We remember your grandfather. He used to recognize us even if we only came in once every couple years. He was a people person, treated all the customers like they were family."

The lump in my throat is suddenly back and has grown to the size of a tennis ball, making it impossible for me to breathe. Out of the last three generations of Reed men, my grandfather was definitely the friendly one.

God, he would've loved Brenden. Too bad he never got to meet him.

Shit. I miss that old man.

Elise must see the tears welling up in my eyes, along with the panicked look on my face—because I don't cry, damn it, especially not in the middle of the town green—and she reaches out, loosely wrapping her fingers around my forearm.

A horn honks, and I stumble away from her touch. Whipping my head toward the sound, I spot Leo leaning out the window of my truck, giving me an impatient look.

"Sorry. I should go," I say.

"Right," Grant says. "We won't keep you any longer. I'm sure you're busy."

"But we'll see you tonight, right?" Elise asks. It doesn't sound like a demand. It sounds like she's genuinely hoping she will. Which, I hate to admit, actually feels kind of nice.

"Sure, of course," I tell her. After our goodbyes, I watch the two of them walk off for a moment before jogging over to my truck.

When I hop in, Leo asks, "What took you so long? Who were those people?"

Cranking the engine, I grasp for an explanation. "They're Brenden's, uh . . . They're May's grandparents."

"Ah, okay. I think I've heard something about them."

I turn on the radio, then set my eyes firmly on the road as I take off, hoping to discourage him from asking anything more. It's not my business to tell people about Brenden's family situation. Especially one of his employees. I know his relationship with Elise and Grant is complicated.

Though I can't help but wonder again if Brenden even knows their conflicted feelings about visiting Mayweather. Would it change anything between them if he knew how hard it was for them to come here? That they do it *despite that* for him and May? And is it my place to tell him these things?

If I were really his boyfriend—his partner—then maybe. But I'm not. We're just faking it.

So I should stay out of any emotional minefields and simply enjoy the perks of this fake relationship while I can.

❀

"WHO'S READY FOR MayFest tomorrow?" Brenden asks cheerfully, as he passes Elise a mug of chamomile tea. He's learned how to fix it perfectly to her taste.

I press myself farther into the arm on the opposite end of the couch to make room for him in the middle. He glances down at May, who is sprawled on the floor again with all her school stuff spread out on the coffee table. I probably should have scooted myself to the middle to make it easier for him. But I'm pretty glad I didn't when he sort of takes a dive across my lap to get into the open spot. I catch his leg to prevent him from kicking May in the head, and we're both chuckling by the time he gets settled.

He flushes when he notices Elise and Grant watching us with amusement. May hasn't even looked up from her homework, her concentration unwavering.

"The festival sounds delightful," Elise says, not commenting on Brenden's less than graceful moves.

Brenden grins. "Oh, it'll be absolutely delightful when May and I kick everyone's butts at the May Games! They're named for her, so obviously we always win."

At this, May's head snaps up, and he reaches down to ruffle her purple hair. A guilty expression crosses her face, but I don't think he notices in his excitement. "They're not named for me," she says. "They're named for the month. And the festival. And the town."

"And *you're* named for the town," he tells her. "Therefore, they're named for you."

She sets her pen down on her notebook and twists to face her dad better. "We don't always win."

He scowls. "All right, fine. We usually win. But we're not letting the O'Brien twins beat us this year. I don't care if they have freaky twin advantages. We're the dream team."

May's guilty look returns. "Um, Dad? About the games . . ."

"What?" he asks.

"I asked Grandma if she'd do them with me this year. Since we've never gotten to do anything like that together before."

Brenden's face falls, the brightness dimming like the sun sliding behind a cloud. But he recovers quickly, giving her a smile that *almost* looks real. "Oh. Well, sure. Of course you should do it with your grandmother, if that's what you want. That'll be fun for you guys! I'll get to just chill out and watch for once and cheer you on from the sidelines. That'll be fun. Super fun. Maybe I'll make an embarrassing sign to hold up."

I reach out and gently squeeze his thigh, hoping to calm him so he'll ease up on the babbling.

"Actually, I figured you'd want to compete with Travis," May says.

Woah there. Compete with who *now?*

My panicked eyes meet Brenden's. I'm planning to do the boyfriend thing and go to the festival with him. But my participation is not supposed to extend beyond watching and trying not to sneer at the madness.

He grimaces. "May, you know that's not Travis's thing."

When she glances at me, her guilty look has morphed into something else. Something a little more mischievous. "I know it's not normally his thing. But I'm sure he'd *love* to compete with you. Isn't that the kind of thing boyfriends do together?"

She smiles sweetly, but I see the calculation behind it. She knows exactly what she's doing—trapping us. Is it weird to be scared of a thirteen-year-old?

"We, um." Brenden kicks her subtly, out of her grandparents' view. "He . . . It's . . ."

"What's the matter?" Elise asks. "Are you two afraid you'll get beaten by a teenager and an old lady?"

Oh hell. They're in on this together.

"There's no way you'll beat us!" Brenden exclaims. Then he shoots me an apologetic look, because that sure sounded like an agreement that we'll be competing together.

I hold his gaze, wanting to be a good fake boyfriend, to give him whatever he wants. But come on. Those games are ridiculous. Do I really need to make a fool of myself to be a good boyfriend?

Fake.

A good fake boyfriend.

His mouth silently forms the word *please*, and I know I'm done for.

Huffing out a sigh, I say, "Fine. I'll throw a damn egg at you."

"*To* me," he corrects.

"Sure. That."

May claps, sounding positively delighted as she says, "See? This is going to be so much fun!"

When I shoot her a side-eyed look, she gives me another faux-innocent smile. I resist the urge to flip her off, because that's probably inappropriate.

It's clear that she planned this. Yeah, I believe she might have wanted to do the games with her grandmother. But I'm certain that forcing me and Brenden to do them together also factored in there. I'm just not sure the reason for it.

She probably thinks it'll be funny, since she knows how much I hate this kind of shit. I've lived in this town most of my life and managed to avoid it. But when my usual urge to give Brenden what he wants is compounded by the new urge to give his daughter what *she* wants . . .

I had no hope of resisting, did I?

"Fun," I say grudgingly.

She looks way too pleased with herself as she turns back to her homework.

Brenden leans over to give me a quick kiss. "Thank you."

All of my annoyance melts away instantly. I thread my fingers through his hair and pull him in for one more kiss. "You don't have to thank me. It's what boyfriends are for."

His eyes twinkle, like we're sharing a private joke, before he leans back out of my space.

A bit later, I'm still wondering what May's angle really is, when she stands up, yawning, and says, "Is anyone else tired? I think I'm ready for bed."

Brenden scoffs at her. "It's Friday night."

"But we should be well-rested for tomorrow, right?"

"I swear it's like you're thirteen-going-on-senior-citizen," he tells her, rolling his eyes.

Elise stands too. "Well, *I'm* certainly not thirteen, so I'm going to head upstairs."

One by one, May, Elise, and Grant leave the living room.

Brenden turns to me with a perplexed look on his face once we're alone. "I feel like I'm missing something. Are you tired?"

"Not really."

"You wanna watch something?"

Before I say yes, I get a better idea. A much better idea. Or possibly a much worse idea, if I think about how much it's going to suck later when the two of us go back to being just friends. So I won't let myself think about that. Not now.

"No," I tell him. "Let's go up to bed."

"But you just said you weren't tired."

"Exactly."

CHAPTER SEVENTEEN

BRENDEN

I almost trip up the stairs in my haste to get to my bedroom. Travis is laughing behind me, but I'm not slowing down. This is the first time he's been the one to initiate fooling around, and let me tell you, I am *here* for it.

You'd think having his dick in my mouth this afternoon would've been enough to keep me satiated for more than twenty-four hours. But apparently not. Plus if I recall correctly—and seriously, as if I could forget—he promised me a blowjob.

Travis barely gets the bedroom door closed behind us before I'm stripping off my shirt and pants, leaving them in a messy heap on the floor. He laughs again. "Eager much?"

"Nope. Not at all," I lie brazenly.

"Okay, good. Because I think I'm more tired than I thought. Maybe we should just get to sleep." He lets out a long yawn as he stretches his arms behind him.

My mouth hangs open for a moment before I force myself to shut it, attempting to hide my disappointment. I run my finger over the waist-band of my boxer-briefs awkwardly. "Oh. That's fine." When he cracks a smile, I suck in a breath. "Wait, are you fucking with me?"

"Of course I'm fucking with you."

"Well, that's just rude." I turn away from him, pretending to be offended.

He reaches for me before I can step away, his large hands wrapping around my upper arms and tugging me backward until my back hits his chest. "Let me make it up to you," he suggests, voice low and growly in my ear.

"Okay," I say. And I say it perfectly normally. I absolutely do not squeak it.

His idea of making it up to me starts with his teeth grazing their way down the side of my neck and along the top of my shoulder. When I sag into him, he splays a hand over my stomach. It's not exactly a dirty move, but the possessiveness of it sends a zing shooting up my spine.

He brushes his pinky down my happy trail and then dips it below my waistband. I press my ass into his front, hoping to encourage him to go farther. His other hand comes to the front of my hip, holding me tightly against him. I'm tenting my underwear now and rocking upward trying to get contact on my dick, but he's stubbornly refusing to grab it.

"You're a liar," I complain. "You're not making it up to me."

"Not yet," he says, sounding awfully smug.

"Then when? Because if you don't hurry up and get on with it, I'm going to take matters into my own hands."

To show him that by "matters" I mean myself, I reach for my dick. But before I can wrap my hand around it, he grabs my wrist and carefully maneuvers my arm behind my back, trapping it between our bodies. I whine and he lets go, his hand coming up to wrap loosely around my throat instead.

Despite being free to move my arm now, I don't. I don't move at all. His other hand is still pressed over my hip, and his fingers might as well be rope for how restrained I feel. And I mean that in a good way. A pretty fucking awesome way, actually. Because he has my body flush against his and he clearly wants to keep me here.

I suppose I'll survive a few more minutes without touching my dick. Maybe.

Thirty seconds, at least.

Even though he's not that much bigger than me, Travis maneuvers my body easily, like I'm his puppet. He brings both of my arms up over my head and settles my hands on the nape of his neck. I scratch my nails lightly through his hair as he continues to tease me with kisses to my neck and shoulders.

This time when I start a rocking motion, pushing my ass against him, he doesn't stop me. In fact, his grip on my hip tightens, but he uses it to guide my body back and forth. He uses his other hand to take turns playing with my nipples until they harden and I lose my rhythm.

I'm squirming more than rocking now. But I can feel his stiff length poking into my ass, so hopefully that means he's ready to end this torture and move on to the main event.

I don't even notice my hand has drifted out of his hair and down to my dick again. Travis notices though. And rather than grabbing my wrist this time, he responds with a hard bite to the top of my shoulder.

"Ow! Fucking hell," I cry. But even though it hurt, it also made my dick twitch in my hand. *Weird.*

"Too much?" he asks, licking over the spot he just attacked.

I whip my head fiercely side to side. If he wants to bite me, he can bite me. Hell, I'll let him do pretty much anything he wants at this point, as long as he puts my dick in his mouth before I explode. Because I'd like to explode *with* my dick in his mouth, thank you very much.

With no warning, he squats down a bit, securing one arm behind my thighs, and then scoops me up bridal-style like I weigh nothing. Wrapping my arms around his neck instinctually, I let him carry me the few steps to the bed. Which he proceeds to toss me onto.

Before I have a chance to complain—not that I really would, because damn, that was *hot*—he's on top of me, bracing his forearms on either side of my head, both caging me in and preventing all his weight from landing on me.

"Hi," I say, a little lust-drunk at this point and fighting a dopey smile.

He answers me with a hard kiss, his tongue immediately demanding entrance to my mouth, which I have no problem granting him. I can't be only a passive receiver of the kiss though. I give it back to him just as hard, digging my fingers in right below his shoulder blades to pull his body down closer on top of mine.

I never imagined I'd get to see this side of him—the confidently sexual side—but I love it. And even though I know it's only sex, nothing more, the knowledge that he *wants* me makes me feel like I've won some kind of prize.

Just like I intend on winning the May Games with him on Sunday.

I can't believe he agreed to participate with me. What's the town going to think? They won't believe it either when they see him out there. And he's doing it for *me*.

Wait, no. Not the time to get distracted. *Focus.*

Focus on the way Travis's hips are pressing mine into the mattress. Focus on how he's sucking on my bottom lip as he smoothly slides my underwear partway down my thighs, freeing my cock. Focus on getting him undressed too, so I'll be able to feel his skin on mine.

Yes. That.

I gracelessly shove his flannel off his shoulders, while he laughs gently and helps me by sliding his arms out of the sleeves. Then I work on tugging his T-shirt up over his chest and grunt when I can't get it any farther. He helps again, pulling it the rest of the way over his head and tossing both shirts to the floor beside the bed.

"Off," I demand, fumbling with the button on his jeans.

He laughs again but obliges, though he chooses to get off the bed, standing up to remove the offending article. As I quickly yank my underwear off my legs, I want to protest the loss of him, but then he's standing there in only his boxers, which do nothing to hide his erection. So really, no complaints here.

When he gets back on the bed, he lies down beside me and reaches for me, manhandling my body again until I'm the one on top. I'm straddling his thick thighs, and I can't help but roll my hips, making my hard cock slide against his.

I've all but forgotten the promise of a blowjob. At this point, I'm so far gone that I'll be satisfied with rutting against him until I get to come.

But then he scoots himself back so his head is propped up on the pillows. He pulls me toward him, forcing me to knee-walk my way up the bed and up his body until I'm straddling his chest. And then he says three words that almost undo me.

"Fuck my mouth."

"Um, er, what?" I sputter.

"You heard me," he says, voice low and sexy and doing things to my insides. "Do you want to?"

I laugh nervously. "What kind of question is that?" I mean, really. Has any gay man in the history of *ever* actually said no when another man asks if he wants to fuck his mouth? I don't think so.

Travis's lip quirks up. "Then what are you waiting for?"

Well, shit.

The way he's looking at me now, it almost feels like a challenge. And there's no way in hell I'm backing down. Wrapping my hand around my base, I inch my hips forward so I can swipe my cockhead across his lips. His tongue darts out to taste, and a full-body shiver runs through me. I can't wait any longer.

"Open," I command, my voice husky. And shit, who even was that? Surely, it couldn't be *me* talking like this.

When he drops his mouth open, eyes gazing at me with so much lust it scorches my skin, I lose all sense of decorum. I thrust forward, sliding my cock along his tongue and not stopping until I hit resistance at the back of his throat.

Even though he gags a bit, he makes no move to get away from the invasion. Not that he has anywhere to go, since I've pretty much got his head pinned to the pillows. But I remind myself that he wanted it this way, and I keep going, thrusting in and out of the wet heat of his mouth, building up a rhythm.

The heat of his stare urges me on. While my eyes are mostly focused on the sight of my cock disappearing between his lips, I'm pretty sure he hasn't taken his molten eyes off my face.

Good. I don't want him to forget whose cock is owning his mouth like this. I know I can't keep him, that this arrangement is only temporary, but that doesn't stop me from doing my best to lay a claim right now.

I'm thinking with the wrong head, the head that's nudging itself farther down Travis's throat. But so what? There's nothing wrong with wanting to paint my name in cum across his tongue. Or maybe across his face. Across his chest?

I can't decide. But if I don't slow down, the choice will be made for me, and I'll spill so far down his throat he won't even taste me. My toes are curling by his sides and *fuck.*

This is Travis fucking Reed underneath me. Hot, grumbly man of more complaints than smiles. The guy who swooped in to help me when I desperately needed it, like a knight in fucking flannel.

My fingers are threaded into his hair, holding him in place. *My* Travis. *Mine, mine, mine.*

I don't even realize I've shoved my cock all the way down his throat and kept it there too long, not letting him breathe, until his hands grasp my hips and squeeze tightly. I immediately pull out of his mouth, and he coughs and gasps for air.

Before I can apologize, his eyes spark with a challenge again and he says, "Is that all you've got?"

His voice is raspy from the way I was using his throat, and holy hell, I'm not sure either of us is going to survive this.

I slide into his mouth again, attacking it with punishing thrusts, but I make sure to pull back out after a few so he can catch his breath.

"That's it, baby," he says. "Make me choke on it."

Fuckfuckfuckfuuuuuck.

There's no way I'm going to last much longer. I continue to use his mouth, tugging on his hair as I barrel wildly toward my climax. My entire body tenses, and then I pull out right before I shoot, letting my cum land sloppily on his lips and cheek.

It's not quite my name, but I can almost see it there anyway.

His thumbs trace soothing circles over my hips as we both work to calm our breathing. My legs refuse to hold me up any longer, but I manage to fall over to the side of Travis, rather than sitting on his chest and crushing him. He reaches for me, tugging me back in closer, and we lie there in a tangle of limbs.

Then, slowly, I regain control of my brain and body. I look at Travis's face covered in my cum and realize, regretfully, that I should help clean him off.

"Hold on," I say, getting up and making my way to the ensuite. I grab a washcloth and dampen it with warm water before going back to him.

As I rest one knee on the bed and lean over him to wipe the mess from his cheek, I notice most of it is gone from his lips. I'm pretty sure he licked it off, and that thought sends another flare of possessiveness through me. Which, now that my mind isn't clouded with lust, I realize is crazy.

We may be having explosive hookups, but Travis isn't mine. And I need to remember that.

But damn, he makes it hard when he smiles lazily at me and encourages me to lie back down with him. I snuggle up against his side, throwing one leg over his and resting my head on his chest. His arm winds around my back, holding me to him.

We're both quiet for a couple minutes, and I could easily fall asleep like this, but then he speaks up.

"How do you really feel about May not doing the games with you? Are you okay?"

Ugh. Way to ruin the afterglow.

I should say yes, because how selfish would it be to admit I want my daughter all to myself? I want to remain her best friend forever, the most important person in her world. And I know that's unfair.

Sighing, I say, "It's fine. As long as she's happy, I'll be happy." Which is true enough. But my orgasm must have drained all of the pretense out of me, because I can't completely hide the sting of her decision. "It just sucks to feel like I'm being replaced."

"You're definitely not being replaced," Travis says.

"I know that rationally," I tell him. "But I've never really had to share May with anyone else before. I know it's a good thing though. She deserves to have her grandparents in her life. She deserves more family to love her."

I don't ever want her to feel as alone as I have after losing so many people close to me.

Travis runs his hand up my spine and cups the back of my head. "You deserve that too. Family. People to love you."

"I have May." My daughter loves me, and that should be enough. There's no need for me to be getting choked up here, but I am, and I hate it.

"You have other people too, you know," he says gently. "Family doesn't have to be blood. You have so many friends in this town, people who care about you."

I close my eyes, holding back tears. I might have a lot of friends, but it's not the same thing. I've never had another friend like April. And maybe it's my own fault. After everything I've been through, I have a tendency to not let people in all the way, not let anyone else get too close.

Because I don't think I could survive losing someone else I care about that much.

"And you have Elise and Grant just as much as May does," Travis adds, unintentionally twisting the knife deeper.

"No, I don't."

"I think you do," he argues. "Even if you don't realize it or can't accept it yet."

I want to ask him what he would know about it, but I need to put an end to this conversation. We're supposed to be basking in the post-orgasm bliss, not poking at old wounds.

Actually, I'm the only one who's gotten off. And I should remedy that.

Banishing all the sad thoughts from my brain, I prop myself up on my elbow. "The only thing I can't accept is the fact that you haven't covered me in your cum yet."

That gets me a small laugh. Then Travis studies me, and I do my best to project a happy image. Honestly, I'm a grown ass man, and May wanting to do something with her grandmother instead of me for the first time is *not* the end of the world. It's really not.

Especially not when I'm lying here with Travis in my bed after he made me feel so good that I saw stars. I want to make him feel that good too. I *need* to.

He must read this desire on my face, because he lets me maneuver my way out of the depressing conversation and onto my back. He strips off his boxers, tossing them aside, before crawling on top of me. We kiss, slowly at first, then eventually building back up to a frenzy.

He's hard again, his cock nudging into the crease between my groin and thigh, smearing precum along its path.

"Do you have lube?" he asks.

I stretch my arm out, and he lifts off me so I can roll onto my side to grab it from the drawer in my nightstand. He takes it from me, then finishes rolling me over until I'm lying on my stomach. I'm confused for a moment, but I let him do his thing, listening to the cap opening and the lube squirting out. I hear him slicking himself up, and then his big, capable hands part my ass cheeks before his hard, wet length slides up between them.

Oh.

Yeah, I can totally get on board with this.

I lie still, letting him take what he needs from my body. After a few moments of this, it starts to send me into a blissful haze. When he slides lower, his cockhead bumping gently behind my balls, a pleased sound escapes me.

His breathing has picked up, and he's letting out small grunts and moans, rutting against me now. "Cross your legs at the ankles," he orders.

And *yup, uh-huh, okay.* Anything he wants. I do as he says, then crane my neck to watch him as he slicks himself up again before pushing his cock between my thighs. I tighten them around him, making him groan.

"*Ngh.* Fuck yeah, just like that."

He keeps fucking my thighs, rubbing along my taint with each thrust. I'm growing hard again, but it doesn't matter. This isn't about me. This is all about Travis and the pleasure I can give him.

His rhythm eventually becomes erratic, signaling he's close. Then he moans, loud enough to make me remember the guests sleeping down the hall. But before I can urge him to be quiet, he releases, leaving a warm mess dripping between my thighs.

He collapses on top of me, draping his chest over my back, his breathing still harsh. I'm pretty sure some of his cum smears into my ass cheek.

It takes him a minute before he rolls off me. This time I think we're both too spent to clean up properly. He swipes at me half-heartedly with the dirty washcloth and then throws it to the floor. Then he positions us so we're spooning, him behind me with one strong arm wrapped around my waist.

Sleep threatens to overtake me. But before I succumb, I think about how Travis has already told me I can count on him whenever I need anything. Now he's reminding me that I have people in this town who care about me. And with the way he's holding me tightly against him . . . I don't think he's talking about Mitch or Mrs. Morris or Sal the mailman.

I can't read too much into this though. We can mix friendship and sex, but that doesn't mean we could ever have anything more. What I want from him is becoming increasingly confusing, but I know that he doesn't want more than this.

So I can't let myself want it either.

It's like that sad song Elphaba sings in *Wicked*. You shouldn't wish for something that's out of your reach, because that way, you can't be disappointed when you don't get it.

I mean, sure, she also sings about defying gravity, but I'm not about to try flying, okay? I need to keep my feet on the ground and my head in reality.

CHAPTER EIGHTEEN

TRAVIS

This is the first morning I've woken up with Brenden in the same positions we went to sleep in. It's also the first time we went to sleep cuddling. Last night, after I came my brains out between his thighs, holding him simply felt like the right thing to do. I'd been too sated and exhausted to wonder if it was weird.

Now, in the light of morning, one of my arms is sore from the way it's been awkwardly wedged between us all night, while my other arm is comfortably wrapped around his waist. It still feels right to have his warm body pressed tightly to mine, but everything is also confusing.

Because I know it's *not* right. He's not mine to hold. Not really.

Maybe he is for now, but it's only temporary. Only for fun. Once our charade is over, this will be over between us too. I have to be ready to handle that and move on.

And it's going to fucking suck, isn't it?

The smart thing to do would be to protect myself from falling for him as best as I can. I should get up and leave. Go about my day and try to forget how perfectly he fits in my arms.

But I never claimed to be the smartest guy, so instead I continue to lie here, letting myself revel in this physical closeness. His hair tickles my nose as I scoot my head even closer to his, but I don't care. The scent of his fruity shampoo has become a drug to me.

Slowly, he stirs, waking up while I'm breathing him in like some kind of psychopath.

I should probably back away, but I don't. I only loosen my arm around him so he can escape if he wants to.

Lifting my head, I catch his eyes opening, but it seems to take him a few moments to realize the position we're in. Then he lets out a soft, contented little hum and turns in my arms until we're face to face. "G'morning," he says sleepily.

"Morning," I say. I leave out the "good," but it really, really is.

As we lie here smiling at each other, I run my hand up and down his side, over the flowers that mean so much to him, and I'm hit with the oddest sensation. It's almost like a vision of the future. An impossibly happy future where we're actually together and this is how we wake up every morning.

I need to move before I let myself get lost in it.

But before I can extricate myself, his smile grows and he brings his hand up between us, placing it on my bare chest. This shouldn't prevent me from getting away, and yet I don't move an inch. His palm might as well be superglued to my pec.

"Do you have to get to the diner?" he asks, casually trailing his fingers through my chest hair like he's not even aware he's doing it.

I'm hyper-aware of it though, which makes it hard to focus on his question. "Benji's opening, but I told him I'd be there to help with breakfast," I finally manage to answer.

Business for me is a little unpredictable whenever Mayweather has a big festival going on. On the one hand, those things bring in lots of extra tourists, but on the other, people usually do most of their eating *at* the festival. Breakfast might get slammed, though, before things kick off over on the green.

"Hmm, too bad," Brenden muses. "If we had time for orgasms, I've got some good ideas."

As he trails his hand farther down my body, I use all my inner strength not to give in. Because while we could easily squeeze in a quickie, I'm guessing (or maybe just hoping) that none of his ideas would be quick. And more than that, I shouldn't give in to this fantasy with him any more than I already have.

The return to what we really are to each other when this is all over—nothing more than friends—will be enough of a slap in the face as it is.

When his fingertips graze along the waistband of my boxers, I trap his hand with mine, halting his exploration. A slight frown mars his perfect face, and I only barely manage to hold in a groan. He's killing me here.

"Save the ideas for later," I suggest. Because I'm only freaking human. And I did agree to friends with benefits, but hooking up with him at night somehow feels safer than doing it in the morning light.

There's a little twinkle in his eyes when he says, "Oh, I totally will."

I release his hand, and when he removes it from my body, I try hard not to regret my decision. Then he brings his hand to the back of my head, pulling me closer as he leans in to kiss me. And this is almost as dangerous as if I let him touch my dick. Because *fuck*.

It's lazy in the best way, slow and blissful and unhurried. It's not a kiss that's leading somewhere. He's simply kissing me because he wants to kiss me.

He wants to kiss me.

I let it go on until I start to get hard, and that's when I gently pull back. Definitely time for me to get out of this bed.

"I can whip something up quick for you guys before I leave," I offer.

Smiling, he shakes his head. "Don't worry about it. We'll survive."

"I don't mind," I tell him, getting up and heading to the dresser for some clothes.

He sits up and stretches his arms above his head, letting out a loud yawn. Then he says, "Really, it's fine. I don't wanna eat too much now anyway, since I plan on eating as much as possible later."

That sounds about right.

"Is it cool if I hop in the shower?" I ask.

"Yeah, I'll probably go downstairs and get coffee started."

"Or you'll fall back asleep," I say, because he hasn't gotten out of bed yet.

His smile is entirely unashamed. "That's also a possibility."

The way he looks right now in the morning light, lazy and happy and beautiful, has me tempted to crawl back into the bed and sleep for a bit longer too, just to be close to him. But I have to do the responsible adult thing and go run my business.

"I'll meet you guys on the green later," I remind him.

The idea of going to MayFest with him, May, and the Richardsons is pretty nerve-wracking. Not because I don't like going to the town festivals (although I don't), but because being out in public with them will be dangerous. But Brenden and I already talked about how we have to be careful, balance Elise's and Grant's expectations of our relationship with what we're letting the town see.

At least it isn't unheard of for Brenden to drag me around with him to do things I don't want to do. We just can't act too much like a couple while we do this.

"Everything's going to be fine," he assures me." Even though I know he's not entirely relaxed about this thing either.

"Right. Yeah. I'm gonna . . ." I gesture toward the bathroom.

"Right," he repeats. "Go ahead. I know you need to hurry."

I'm doing okay on time, but I do hurry in the shower, not wanting to give myself any extra time to stress. When I come out of the ensuite ready to leave, I'm not surprised to find Brenden back under the covers, eyes closed, breathing softly in sleep.

I allow myself a few moments to watch him, taking in every detail, then cross to the bed, unable to resist placing a featherlight kiss on his temple before I get out of here.

Don't get used to this, I warn myself as I close his bedroom door quietly behind me.

WALKING OUT OF THE DINER and heading over to the green, I feel like I might be walking to my own death. This fake dating arrangement was complicated enough when we only had to do it in the privacy of Brenden's house. Now it's gotten even more complicated, since we somehow need to pull it off in public without anyone else catching on.

But would it really be so bad if they did?

I remember Mrs. Morris the other day, her colorful way of suggesting I give dating men a try, and I almost laugh. Then I think of my dad and those words he shouted to the football players on the TV screen, and the urge to laugh disappears.

You can see the green from the diner's glass front. It's right across the road, and yet I manage to cycle through all too many emotions by the time I'm stepping onto the grass. But then I spot Brenden and his little group standing off to the side on the outskirts of the festival activities. May is pointing out one of the booths to her grandmother, Grant is frowning down at his phone as he types something, and Brenden is looking right at me. He's smiling, and the smile only grows as I walk his way.

And now suddenly, the only thing I feel is pretty damn happy.

I'm not sure what I ever did to deserve this man smiling at me like that. Like I'm the one person he most wants to see. But somehow amongst my questionable decisions and shitty attitude, I must have managed to do *something* right.

Brenden steps closer when I reach him, as if he might hug or kiss me. Then he stops, catching himself, and just says, "Hey."

May's grandparents both greet me simply as well, while May gives me a smile to rival her dad's. My face is doing something funny, almost unfamiliar, as I greet them all back. It takes me half a second to realize I'm smiling. I'm smiling, and it's not forced at all. I'm smiling, and I mean it.

Yes, I do smile on occasion. Especially when Brenden's around. But something about this moment feels different. Important. It feels like I'm a part of their group, like I belong here with these people. People whose company I actually enjoy, even Elise and Grant. And people who somehow, inexplicably, seem to enjoy my company in return.

Turns out I kind of like this feeling. Who knew.

Brenden's eyes are curious as he watches me, as if he can tell there's some weird inner workings going on in my mind. Rather than share anything I'm thinking though, I ask if everyone's ready to check out the festival, and Brenden tells May to lead the way.

She heads off, bypassing and weaving around booths like she knows exactly where she wants her first stop to be. When she comes to a halt in front of a plain looking booth, I glance up at the small wooden sign hanging over it that features nothing but a painted illustration of a cinnamon roll.

Colleen Barlow stands alone in the booth, ready to greet us. She's in her fifties, teaches second grade at the elementary school, and is known around town for these cinnamon rolls. She could probably put the bakery out of business if she wanted to, but she says she only bakes for the joy of it and that baking for a profit would ruin that joy.

Although I'm sure she makes a killing selling at the festivals. I always hear people complaining afterward about how she sold out before they could get to her. That's probably why May ran directly here.

Brenden looks equally as excited as May as the two of them peer at the display of obscenely enormous cinnamon rolls. They're practically drooling.

Elise, however, isn't impressed. "Shouldn't we have something substantial for lunch before you eat sweets?"

"Grandma, you have to get them before they sell out," May insists.

"It's true," Brenden says, backing her up. "Trust me, you guys don't wanna miss out on one of these."

Grant looks from the giant pastries to Brenden. "I think I'll pass."

"I'll just try a bite of yours," Elise says to May.

Brenden snorts a laugh. "Yeah, fat chance of that. She'll eat the whole thing before you can blink."

"That's not true," May claims. Then she turns to her grandmother. "I promise I'll share with you. But I get to pick the design."

"Design?" Elise and I ask at the same time.

Eyeing me like I'm some kind of alien, Brenden says, "Haven't you had one of these before?"

"Maybe." I think I remember having at least one when I was a kid, but definitely not since then. And I don't remember anything about designs.

"Colleen will draw you whatever you want on top in icing," May explains to me and her grandparents. "And the best part is, if you ask, she'll give you an extra cup of icing for dipping."

"Just what you need, more sugar," Elise comments. But her small smile suggests she's only teasing.

I catch Brenden stiffening up like he's about to get defensive, so I nudge his shoulder and ask, "What design are you going to get?"

"A coffee cup, duh," he says.

Duh.

"And what about you?" Elise asks May.

"A stack of books," May says proudly. Then she turns to me. "What design do you want?"

I immediately shake my head. "Oh, no, I'm not getting one of these things."

"But you have to!" she argues.

Even though I most certainly do *not* have to—because I'm an adult who doesn't take orders from teenagers—I find myself sighing in resignation. "Fine, I'll get one. But it seems like a waste, because there's no way I'm eating all that. And I don't need a design, just regular icing is fine."

I catch Brenden eyeing me again. But this time his expression is so soft it almost feels like a caress.

And then Colleen leans closer to us from inside her booth, interrupting the moment. "Of course you'll get a design. Everyone gets a design. That's how I do it."

"It's really not necessary."

She looks me up and down, then says, "Honey, nothing about eating a pound of cinnamon roll is necessary, so let me enjoy myself and give you a design. You don't even have to pick it out, I'll come up with something."

"He loves all things frilly and cute," Brenden chimes in, shooting me a teasing grin. "Hearts and flowers and puppies."

I grumble an unintelligible complaint and resist the urge to reach out and wrestle him into submission.

There's a line forming behind our group, so Colleen hurries to ring us up. Brenden reaches for his wallet, but I beat him to it, and he smiles his thanks. The look we share while we wait for Colleen to ice our pastries warms my insides more than any cinnamon roll possibly could.

May squeals in delight when Colleen passes hers over, along with a cup of icing. Somehow she manages to hold the giant thing in one hand while she takes a picture of it. Brenden looks just as pleased to be handed his, but he refrains from squealing. He holds it out toward May, letting her get a picture of the two of theirs side by side, before he brings it up to his mouth and takes a large, messy bite.

The tiniest moan escapes him, and my dick twitches in my pants.

When Colleen hands me my cinnamon roll with an oddly knowing smile, I glance down at it, finding that she drew a man's face. It's impressive, for icing art, but seems like a fairly uninspired choice. That's what I get for not having any hobbies or loving anything the way Brenden and May do, I guess.

Brenden thanks Colleen before ushering our group off to the side to make room for all the other sugar fiends behind us. As we're moving, May peeks at my cinnamon roll and laughs. "Oh that's cute! She drew you."

I glance at the design again, wondering if she actually thinks it looks like me, or just that it's *supposed* to be me. Then I notice something that wasn't obvious at first, because drawing in icing isn't exactly the most precise artform.

The icing man is wearing glasses.

Brenden leans in close to me to look at the cinnamon roll, but I'm looking at him. At his cheekbones, pink lips that are shining from the icing . . . and his glasses. She drew Brenden for me.

But why?

Is this elementary school teacher secretly some kind of witch who can look inside me and see what I want the most? Or is my desire for Brenden painted clearly across my face now? Have I lost the ability to hide it that I've perfected over the years?

It startles me when his eyes meet mine. His expression is unreadable, but I just know he spotted the glasses too. The chatter of May and her grandparents around us fades to background noise. His stare bores into me so hard I'm afraid I might combust.

So I do the first thing I can think of. I swipe my finger right through the icing, smearing the drawing, and then reach out quickly to wipe it across his cheek.

His eyes light up in surprise before he starts laughing. May whips out her phone to take a picture of him, and whatever intense things I was feeling a moment ago ease into something simpler. Something that feels an awful lot like contentment.

I go to offer him a napkin, but he uses his finger to wipe the frosting off his face, then brings it to his mouth to suck it clean. I quickly look away before my dick can get any ideas again.

We all stand around watching the festivities while we eat the pastries. As I predicted, I don't even come close to finishing mine. It's good, but way too sweet for my taste. Before I toss it, though, I give it one more glance and kind of wish I'd been like May and taken a picture before I destroyed the little icing Brenden.

Maybe I like sweet when it comes to him.

CHAPTER NINETEEN

BRENDEN

Walking around the festival with Travis yesterday was fantastic. Even Elise and Grant's presence couldn't dampen the fun of watching Travis relax and enjoy himself in an environment he usually avoids.

Sure, I caught him glancing around nervously sometimes. Probably scanning for potential gossipers who might be paying too much attention to us being here together. But that's understandable. I was nervous about it too. If he gets outed because of my crazy scheme, I'll never forgive myself.

We got some questioning looks, but everyone knows the two of us are friends. And that I occasionally make it my mission to get him to do things he doesn't want to—for both his own good and my own amusement. So I don't think anyone thought it was *too* weird.

I did manage to steer Elise and Grant clear of most conversations with the locals, so that helped. All it would take is one innocent mention about me and Travis being a couple, and both he and I would be screwed.

Let's just hope things go as smoothly today with the games. There will be many more eyes on us, since Travis and I are competing. I still can't believe he agreed to do it with me.

It's funny, because I was upset when May first said she wanted to compete with her grandmother instead of me. But now, slightly more than twenty-four hours later, here I am practically bouncing out of my seat at the idea of seeing Travis participate in all the craziness.

"Why are you smiling at nothing like a total weirdo?"

Ah, shit. I've been caught.

As I turn my head toward Addison, I school my face into a more neutral expression. Lately, I can't even think about Travis without grinning. Any time I see him, my brain immediately goes to, *I've sucked that man's dick.*

"I'm taking in all the excitement around us," I lie. I told her I'd help her out manning the booth early this afternoon before the games start. Not that she needs it. A few of the other employees have volunteered to do short shifts too. But being the owner, I should put in at least some time chatting with the tourists and locals.

Addison is working the booth for almost the entirety of the festival. I told her we could work out a different schedule so she could enjoy some of the activities too, but she insisted that she was fine doing this and didn't have any interest in wandering. She's definitely got a bit of Travis's antisocial tendencies in her.

Or maybe that's just a result of her divorce. Who knows what she was like before her ex cheated on her. I imagine that would mess anyone up.

"As much as I know you're enjoying this craziness, somehow I don't think that's why you were smiling like that."

"Well, you're wrong," I say, leaning into the lie, even though I'm sure she won't believe me. "I can't help that I love my town."

She gives me a skeptical look. "Uh huh, right. Are you sure it doesn't have something to do with a certain flannel-wearing man that you were prancing all around here with yesterday?"

"Wha-who? N-no," I stutter. "We're just . . . I had to drag him here. I thought it'd be good for him to get out and socialize every once in a while.

Wouldn't want him to turn into a scary hermit. Grow his beard too long, drive off in his truck and disappear into the mountains, never to be heard from again."

"Okayyy . . ." Addison's now looking at me like she's actually concerned for my sanity. Which is whatever. People look at me like that a lot. "I'm only saying I've seen you two when he's been around the inn. Lately, you get this moony-eyed look on your face when you're with him."

"I do *not* get moony eyes!" I argue. Because that can't be true. Maybe lust-drunk eyes, but that's all.

"You do," she says flatly. "It's annoying."

I laugh a little at that. "There's nothing wrong with liking someone, you know. What about you? Don't you think you'll ever want to date again?"

She scoffs. "Ew. No. I'm done with that nonsense. You can't trust anyone these days."

That sounds like a hard way to live, not trusting anyone. Though I can't judge her for it after what she went through. Not everyone has a Travis in their life, someone they know they can always trust.

"So you're okay with being alone forever?" Maybe that's a shitty thing to ask, but I'm honestly wondering. I hate the idea of being alone.

"Why not?" she says, shrugging. "I prefer my own company to most other people's."

"Hey!" I feel like I should be offended by that.

She rolls her eyes. "You're all right, I guess. In small doses."

That might not sound anything like a compliment, but believe me, coming from her, it's a big one. I wind up grinning ear to ear.

"Stop that," she says. Then she turns to fuss with the stack of brochures for the inn, and I assume I can consider this conversation over.

❀

IT'S TIME. LET THE GAMES begin. I am so ready.

I even remembered to put in a pair of contacts this morning, instead of wearing my glasses. Can't let anything get in the way of a victory. Not even my daughter.

May and I have been jokingly shit-talking each other for the last couple minutes while we're waiting on the field for things to get started. Although neither of us is particularly good at it.

While the rest of the festival takes place on the green, the games are held on the football field at the high school. It's just a quick walk from the green to here, and lots of people will wander over at some point to spectate.

Travis looks like he'd rather be getting a lobotomy than be standing here beside me right now. But I have a feeling he's going to make a pretty excellent partner, whether he likes it or not. He's good at basically everything. Let's hope his skills include silly field-day-type games.

Before I can start psyching him up, Mitch strolls over to us with Delilah strutting along in front of him on a leash. "Who's ready to watch some people fall on their asses?" he asks, much too loudly.

Elise immediately seems concerned, and Travis turns to give me an unamused look. "I will *not* be falling on my ass."

"Hopefully not," I tell him. "But there's no guarantees. The games have a way of making fools out of everyone."

He looks even more deeply unamused.

"Wait, you're doin' this shit?" Mitch says, whipping his head toward Travis. "I wouldn't think you'd be caught dead here."

Travis frowns. "I'm . . ."

"He's competing with me," I jump in. "Saving my ass since my own daughter ditched me."

May rolls her eyes as I lay on the dramatics, trying to take the focus off Travis.

"Okay, makes sense," Mitch says. Then he looks pointedly at Elise and

Grant before adding, "'Cause, you know, he's Brenden's *boyfriend* and all."

I barely hold back my groan, internally smacking myself on the forehead. Wish I could smack Mitch.

"Hey, Grandma, are you ready to play?" May asks, smoothly diverting her grandparents' attention.

Although I don't think Grant has even heard anything Mitch said, because he hasn't taken his wary eyes off Delilah. He's clearly not used to seeing a chicken walking on a leash, but that's a weekly occurrence in Mayweather.

But anyway, it's a relief when Roddy Harkins shouts into his megaphone that the games will begin in two minutes and asks all teams to get in place for the first event. I don't know how the bar owner got this gig, but he's been the announcer for the May Games ever since I moved to town. Pretty sure he gets a sick pleasure in narrating everyone's falls and misfortunes.

Grant hugs May and wishes her and Elise good luck, then wishes me and Travis the same. As the four of us go over to take our places, I watch him hastily distance himself from Mitch, which is definitely for the best.

The egg toss is the first event. (I have a sneaking suspicion this is to ensure a bunch of us get messy early on for the amusement of the spectators.) May and I are next to each other in one line, facing Elise and Travis a few feet away in the other line. Travis still looks a bit like he's being tortured.

"Come on," I tell him. "We've got this!"

His brow furrows and he gives me a skeptical look. "Can you even throw?"

"Well . . ."

May snorts, so I kick out at her ankle in retaliation.

"It's not my strong suit," I admit. "But surprisingly, I'm pretty good at catching."

Travis makes a choked, strangled sound. It takes me a moment to mentally replay what I said, and . . .

"Oh my god! Not like—I mean, well, yeah, I—That's not what I meant!"

He presses his lips together in what looks like an attempt to fight a smile. My face is flaming, but I'm also suppressing the urge to laugh. If Travis and I were alone, I'd probably think of something clever to say about how good I am at *that* kind of catching. But my daughter and her grandmother are within hearing distance, so nope. We will not be going there.

Luckily, one of the event volunteers is currently walking in between the two lines of partners, passing out eggs from a wicker basket. She reaches May first, then me, and I focus on not accidentally crushing the fragile egg in my hand before we even start. Because that's totally something I might do.

"We've got this," I assure Travis one more time.

I'm not a super competitive person normally. And even though she ditched me, I'd be perfectly happy if May won instead of me. But standing in front of Travis like this, I realize how much I really want to win with him. Something tells me we'll make a great team.

And something changes on his face, I think, when he catches the determined look on mine.

"We've got this." He repeats my words almost like he can force them to be true. Maybe my hunger to win is contagious.

Of course, when Roddy calls out, "One, two, three, toss!" I panic and fumble for a moment, before I realize that I can, in fact, throw an egg three feet. No big deal.

Travis opens his hand and catches it like he didn't even have to think about it. I give him a cheesy thumbs up, ignoring the way he rolls his eyes at me.

"This is kind of fun," Elise says, when it's their line's turn to toss the eggs back. I shift my gaze to her briefly, but only after I've safely caught my egg. I won't let her distract me into messing up. She and May could have planned to sabotage us. But she does look genuinely pleased to be standing in the grass in a T-shirt and jeans, in a line of excited towns-people and tourists.

I bet the novelty will wear off by the time she's covered in egg yolk or grass stains though.

"Brenden!" Travis calls my name impatiently, clueing me in to the fact that everyone but me has taken a step backward at Roddy's instruction. *Whoops.*

See? Sabotage.

The next toss is also easy enough and so is catching Travis's. But it only takes a couple more rounds before things start to get dicey. There's a delicate balance you need to hit in tossing your egg hard enough that it will make it all the way to your partner, while not tossing it so hard that it will break when they catch it.

We began with sixteen teams competing, and out of the corners of my eyes I notice a few teams already messing up and stepping out of the lines. I can hear the sounds of eggs cracking, but I keep my focus where it needs to be. Right on Travis.

He still doesn't look like this is taking him any effort. Until my next toss is probably a little too rough and doesn't go directly to his hand, so he has to reach out for it with panicked eyes. The look of relief that crosses his face when he catches the egg without it breaking does a funny thing to my insides.

It was like a chink in his armor, showing that he actually cares about the competition. And I know for a fact that winning the May Games has never even come close to being one of his ambitions, which means he cares about this *for me.* He cares about it because I do.

Shit. Focus.

I barely manage to catch his next toss. Taking a quick look around after I do, I see there's only five teams left. Us, May and Elise, and three others. Excellent.

Each team gets a ranking for each event, based on what place they finish in. And then at the end, the five rankings are added together, and the team with the highest overall ranking wins. So unless one team wins them all, you don't have to win every game in order to come in first place.

As we continue to move farther away from our teammates, the game gets harder, and I expect me and Travis to get knocked out, but we keep hanging in. He has great aim, so that makes it easier for me to catch. But what's most impressive is how, even with my wild tosses, he manages to keep catching the egg gently enough to keep it intact.

Who knew, under all the gruffness and muscles and flannel, that he was capable of handling things so gently? It makes me want to know what it would feel like if he handled *me* like that.

Okay, no, not the time for dirty thoughts. No distractions.

As I catch the next toss, I hear an egg crack right beside me, followed by a distressed sound from May. Turning to look, I find my daughter standing there with yellow egg yolk slowly dripping down her neck, and the laughter spills out of me before I can stop it.

"Mean!" she cries.

"Sweetie, I'm so sorry!" Elise yells, stepping out of her line and coming across to meet May.

But May's smiling now. "Don't worry about it, Grandma. We did good!"

Elise follows her as she heads off to get cleaned up, while I return my attention to the game. Apparently, the two of them weren't the only ones to get knocked out on that round, and I'm pleased to realize that it's just me and Travis and one other team left. But it's the damn O'Brien twins. They're too good.

The pressure's definitely on now as I get ready to make my next toss. But Travis just smiles at me encouragingly like he's not worried at all. And even though I know encouragement can't actually make me any better at this, when I toss the egg to him, it seems as if someone far more skilled than me did the tossing, and he catches it with no problem.

I exhale in relief and brace myself for my next catch. Right when Roddy calls for the toss, a bunch of things seem to happen at once. Jimmy O'Brien, from over on Travis's side, yells out some stupid taunt that's meant to distract me. Travis turns to him, and though it's hard to hear from this far away, I swear he growls, making Jimmy jump right as his egg soars out of his hand, which knocks his aim off. As Travis and I make eye contact again, he gives me a nod and tosses to me.

Tommy O'Brien lets out a loud curse just moments before I catch my egg, carefully curling my palm around it. Then Roddy shouts into his megaphone, "We have a winner!" And it takes me a few seconds to realize he means me and Travis.

I look over at Tommy, who's covered in egg yolk, and resist the urge to gloat. I can't believe we actually won this one. May's cheering as she runs over to give me a hug, and I don't even care that she's still got some egg on her.

I'm still cradling our egg in my hand when I glance over at Travis, who is coming my way with sure, steady strides. He's only smiling slightly, but it grows when he reaches me.

"Good job," he says.

"Thanks!" With a grin, I hand him the egg. "Turn this into an omelet for me, would ya?"

May laughs, while I fight to keep a straight face. But there's no hope for that when Travis takes the egg and smashes it against my chest. May laughs even harder, and I join her. After a few moments of this, I hear Travis laughing too, and *woah*.

I kind of feel like I already won this whole thing.

CHAPTER TWENTY

TRAVIS

After Brenden and I somehow win the stupid egg toss, his excitement reaches an all-new height. He's bouncing around so much, I'm not sure he'll have any energy left to complete the rest of the events. He's not even the tiniest bit bothered that I covered him in egg yolk, when he could've escaped totally clean.

"What's next?" I ask, in an effort to get him to focus and calm down a bit. Roddy announced that the second event would be starting in five minutes, and I don't see them dragging out anything crazy.

"Wheelbarrow race!" he shouts gleefully.

I look around again. "Where are the wheelbarrows?"

He grabs my wrist, giving me a disbelieving look. "Um. Do you really not know what a wheelbarrow race is?"

"Sounds like we push a wheelbarrow."

His snort of laughter concerns me. "No, Mr. Doesn't-Like-To-Have-Fun-So-He's-Never-Heard-Of-Classic-Picnic-Games. A wheelbarrow race is when one person holds the second person's legs up in the air and runs while the second person uses their hands on the ground."

Okay, I guess I have heard of that at some point in my life, but I must have tried to erase it from my memory.

"You actually think we can pull that off?" I ask warily.

"Yeah! I mean, normally I'm competing with May, so I've always been the one standing up. But you're obviously way stronger than me, so you should be the one to hold my legs. I even remembered to wear contacts so my glasses don't go flying off my face."

Using that last comment as an excuse to examine his face, I reach out and brush my thumb along his cheekbone. His eyes lock on mine. "I noticed you did that," I tell him. "And it was smart. But I've got to admit, I really like you in your glasses."

"You do?" he breathes out.

"Mmhmm."

I don't know what possessed me to say that, only that it's the truth. Sure, I like being able to look into his eyes without anything in the way, which is something I've learned by spending time with him at night after he's taken his glasses off. But glasses suit his face well.

Thankfully, before I fall under a trance and start confessing all the other things I really like about him, Roddy yells into his stupid megaphone for everyone to get into position. This also leaves me no time to consider how ridiculous the event is going to be and decide to bail out.

I don't want to bail on Brenden. But fucking hell, I don't want to do a damn wheelbarrow race either. I know so many people are probably already laughing at me for participating. It'll be a miracle if no one takes any pictures to send to my dad.

He'd believe that I got roped into doing this with Brenden without anything else sketchy going on, but he'd definitely give me shit for it. He knows I hate town stuff.

"Ready?" Brenden asks as he steps in front of me, facing the line that's been taped across the field.

"No."

He laughs and crouches down, placing his hands in the grass. "Come on, grab my ankles."

I swear under my breath for good measure, but do what he says, raising his legs up in the air behind him as he uses his arms for balance. This is going to end with someone breaking a limb.

Glancing over at Elise, who is two people away from me, I worry for a moment. But she's smiling as she holds up May's legs. At least May is light.

"Go as fast as you can and I'll try to keep up," Brenden tells me.

That sounds like a terrible strategy, but then Roddy yells, "On your marks, get set, go!" and I don't have time to argue. I just go.

It's awkward running like this, supporting most of Brenden's weight so he doesn't face plant in the grass, while also trying not to knock into him. But we find a rhythm pretty quickly, and I'm able to pick up the pace. It's hard to tell how anyone else is doing, because I'm afraid to let my eyes veer off course. In my periphery, though, I notice as we pull ahead of some people.

And maybe I get too confident. Because the next thing I know, I'm sort of toppling over Brenden as his legs swing in a wild arc through the air and he winds up on his back with me half on top of him. A whoosh of air leaves my lungs as I land.

"Shit! Are you okay?" I ask, rolling off him.

When he doesn't move, I panic, but then I realize he's actually shaking with silent laughter.

"I'm so sorry," I tell him.

"It was my fault, my hand slipped," he says. "But hurry up, get me back into position! We can still finish."

I eye him critically, but he quickly pushes himself onto all fours and insists, "Come on, come on!"

Ignoring the slight ache in my knees as I stand, I hoist his legs up in the air again. Those teams we've pulled ahead of have all passed us now, but Brenden's clearly not a quitter, and I guess I'm not either.

As we start moving again, I'm cautiously building up speed, and then

I see May with her hands on the ground, coming up beside Brenden. She and Elise must be going a little crooked, but at least they're still going. May sticks her tongue out at her dad when she's beside him, and Brenden laughs.

I keep pace with Elise, not fighting too hard to beat them. I don't want to fall again, plus I wouldn't mind watching May gloat to Brenden if they finish before us. But Brenden yells at me, "Go, go! Faster!" and my body just obeys him as we edge them out.

I'm winded when we cross the finish line, but relieved we're in one piece. While we don't come in last, and we're apparently not the only ones who fell, we've got to be in the bottom half of the rankings. And I immediately feel guilty for letting Brenden down. Even though he said it was his fault that his hand slipped, I feel like the blame is on me for going too fast for him to keep up.

That's why I'm determined to win the next event, even if I groan when I hear it's a three-legged race. Fuck these races. I enjoy running, but certainly not like this.

A volunteer comes over to us and ties my right leg to Brenden's left one, from knee to ankle. I feel ridiculous, and this seems even more dangerous than the wheelbarrow race. But I can't say I mind being tied to him like this.

He slips his arm around my waist and gazes up at me with his painfully lovely blue eyes. "Thank you again for doing this. I know you hate it."

It must be the eyes that get to me and have the words, "Anything for you," slipping out of my mouth without my permission.

He sucks in a small breath, and I want to kiss the surprise off his face. But I also kind of want to find a hole to bury myself in, because what the fuck. That was closer to confessing my feelings for him than I'm comfortable with.

Before I can do anything, though, Roddy shouts, "Places!" and we sort of hobble our way over to the starting line. I mirror Brenden by wrapping my arm tightly around his waist so we can support each other. Then the race begins, and I do my best to call out directions so we can move together, but it's confusing, and we stumble a bit too much.

It seems a lot of teams are struggling. Some fall behind, but no one really pulls ahead. Brenden and I manage to keep up with the top of the pack, despite our lack of coordination. The closer we get to the finish line, the more determined I become, squeezing him to me tighter as I propel us forward.

When I see the O'Brien twins pulling out in front of us, I know we can't afford to let them win after they came in second to us in the egg toss. So I push myself to go faster and end up practically carrying Brenden over the line, where we collapse together in a heap.

We're both huffing for breath, but we won.

"Oh my god!" Brenden pants. "That was awesome! You were awesome!"

"You deserve to win," I tell him plainly.

He stares at me for a moment. Then his eyes drift down toward my mouth, and he starts to lean in closer. I tense instinctually, which makes him freeze.

"Sorry," he whispers.

I don't know what to say. It seems like I'm the one who should be sorry.

Because I want to kiss him too, but I can't. Not in public. He knew from the start this is how things have to be. Yet that doesn't stop me from feeling guilty or wishing it could be different. Wishing I could give him everything.

Reaching between us for his hand, I give it a long squeeze. And I hope maybe that tells him some of the things I can't.

I THOUGHT THE FIRST three events were ridiculous, but I wasn't prepared for this. As someone ties a blindfold around my eyes, I question my sanity. I'm a grown ass man being blindfolded, and it's not for any kinky sex thing. Nope. I'm about to run through an obstacle course, relying on Brenden to call out directions and keep me from dying.

Okay, maybe *death* is dramatic. It's a simple course. But still. What the fuck.

I'd much rather be the one leading while Brenden makes a fool of himself, but he shot that down real fast. He told me I'm not the best communicator, and I couldn't argue with that.

"You can't just grunt and expect me to understand you," he said.

The thing is, I feel like he understands me better than anyone else, despite my shitty communication skills. But he's right. I know he'll do a better job at leading me through this than I would've done for him, but I'm still annoyed about it.

As our time starts and he instructs me to walk and turn and duck and climb, I do my best to follow what he says. It's not the easiest thing though, and after knocking into a few objects, I grow more and more frustrated. Though I still don't want to let him down. So I go faster, against my better judgement, and just sort of barrel my way through the course with no regard for my own safety.

I whack my head pretty good on something, but it seems like I finish fairly quickly. Since it's an individually timed event though, we won't find out our placement until every team has gone.

Brenden stands close to me while we wait, reaching up a couple times to rub softly at my sore temple. "You did good," he says.

I shrug. I'm not about to spout off another cheesy line about how much I'd be willing to do for him.

When the results are in, we come in fourth, which isn't bad. Then Roddy announces a ten-minute break before the final event, the popsicle contest.

Turning back to Brenden, I ask warily, "Popsicle contest?"

"We get a short amount of time to eat as many popsicles as possible and build a house with the sticks."

The only thing I can think to say is, "Please tell me you're joking."

He grins. "Nope. But don't worry. I'm an *excellent* popsicle sucker."

The absurd, suggestive look he gives me makes me laugh, despite myself.

"At least this is the last thing we have to do, and then this circus will be over," I say.

He pokes me in the side playfully. "You've complained all day, but I think you've had fun."

"I don't know what you're talking about."

"Right," he says. "I must be mistaken."

"Must be," I reply, the hint of a smile tugging at my lips.

When we take our seats at a plastic fold-out table, he sets his hand on my knee. "For the record, *I've* had a lot of fun with you today."

Those words hit me right in the chest, causing a warmth to spread through my body.

People like me well enough around town, I guess. But I'm not known as the fun guy. That's never been me.

Brenden pushes me to do things sometimes, but he accepts my personality for what it is. He's never really tried to change me. And it's nice to know he actually enjoys spending time with me. I kind of already figured that he did, but to hear him say it out loud . . .

It makes me wonder if maybe we *could* be more than a fake-boyfriends-with-benefits situation.

Because I'd rather spend time with him than anyone else. I'd rather do nothing but sit around with him—or even do something as crazy as this competition with him—than do any of my favorite activities with somebody else. Not that I have many favorite activities.

I'm struggling with how to respond to him without revealing all these truths, when I hear a squawk and spot Delilah. She's strutting over to us on her creepy, thin chicken legs, with Mitch right behind her.

He tugs a tiny bit on her leash so that she stops right in front of our table. With a chuckle, he says to me, "You're lucky you've got Brenden on your team for this one. He's got some practice at sucking down popsicles, am I right?"

Brenden laughs loudly, which is what stops me from jumping up and punching Mitch in the mouth. I also know he doesn't mean anything negative by his joke. He's not the slightest bit homophobic—just a pain in the ass. And yeah, Brenden made basically the same joke. But still, it's a harsh reminder of how comfortable people in this town are with getting up in other people's private business.

And no, I don't think I'm ready for that.

Mitch leaves us alone after our boxes of popsicles are brought over in a cooler full of ice and Roddy gives everyone a one-minute warning. I'm not a fan of popsicles, but building a house out of the sticks should be easy enough. So Brenden and I agree that we'll both eat a bunch at first, and then once we've got some sticks to work with, I'll focus on building, while he keeps eating as fast as he can.

When Roddy starts the timer, we dive in. Brenden rips open the first box, and we both take a popsicle and tear off the wrappers. Mine is purple and sickeningly sweet, but I keep sucking, ignoring the tiny pains in my teeth when I bite into it. Brenden's is green, and he finishes first, setting the stick aside and immediately tearing open a new one.

I try to keep up with him, but he's definitely contributing more sticks to our pile than I am. After a few minutes, he motions to the sticks for me to start building. He doesn't even pause his eating to use words.

Quickly, I build a base for our house, using the small bottle of instant-dry super glue they provided us with. I work as efficiently as possible, while being careful not to glue my skin to anything.

At one point Brenden opens a popsicle and holds it in front of my face. So I bite off as much as I can, and then he shoves the rest into his mouth beside the other one he's already working on. I would laugh at how ridiculous he looks with two popsicle sticks hanging out of his mouth and his cheeks bulging, but if I do, I'll choke on the frozen sugar I'm now sucking on.

I'm proud of the job I'm doing on building our house. Brenden must be feeling confident about it too, because he finally slows down to breathe a little more. Or maybe he has brain freeze.

I do my best to stay focused on my task, but I have a hard time tearing my eyes away from him as he places a new popsicle in his mouth. Holding my eye contact, he starts sensually sliding the treat in and out of his mouth, making sure I catch peeks at his tongue getting in on the action too. And then on one slide into his mouth, he just keeps going, taking it into his throat until his lips close around the base of it.

My eyes widen and I choke forcefully on air. The irony of me being the one to choke while he's the one with his throat stuffed isn't lost on me. He looks all too pleased with himself as he pats me on the back with one hand. Then he opens his mouth to show me all that's left of the popsicle is the stick.

I manage not to start choking again, but my jeans have tightened. Which is all sorts of wrong, considering there are kids around, as well as Brenden's family.

He grins at me for a moment before his face turns serious, and he tosses the stick on the table. "Okay, no more fooling around, keep going!" he demands.

I open my mouth to remind him that I'm not the one who was fooling around, but then snap it shut, deciding to just get back to work. My mind is distracted after that raunchy display, so it's a good thing I can basically do this job on autopilot. I just keep building as quickly as I can until Roddy calls time.

It takes a while for the judges to come around and look at everyone's structures. When they award me and Brenden first place for the event, he screams, leaping out of his seat. I stand too, only with less enthusiasm.

A handful of amused and disbelieving stares are pointed my way, which makes me slightly uneasy. But it's hard to care too much with Brenden beaming at me and bumping his hip into mine.

I'm freaking proud of us. We won three out of the five events and did really good in another. I think we actually have a good shot at winning this entire thing. I know how happy that would make him. And that, of course, would make me happy.

As everyone stands around waiting for the final rankings, Brenden and I chat with May and her grandparents. Most of the conversation is Brenden and May animatedly recounting how they did in each of the events, since most of the time, they weren't able to watch each other.

I notice Elise managed to do all of this and stay clean, which makes me wonder how much effort she put in. But regardless, I'm impressed with her for even participating. She doesn't seem as uptight as Brenden thinks she is. The jury's still out on Grant though.

Finally, Roddy says he's ready to announce the winner. He begins with announcing the team in last place and moving up from there. It seems mean to call out the worst placing teams like that, but it's clear by everyone's laughter and clapping that no one is too upset about losing.

May and Elise come in sixth place, so I guess Elise did give a good effort. Brenden high-fives his daughter, then spins toward Elise with his hand still raised. An awkward look crosses his face, and he starts to lower his arm, but she smiles and slaps him with a high-five too.

When he reaches third place, Roddy leads everyone in slapping their thighs for some sort of makeshift drumroll. I abstain from this, obviously. But despite myself, I'm getting amped up with excitement and nerves, because me and Brenden are somewhere in the top three.

Roddy announces a young local couple for third place, and then it's just between me and Brenden and the O'Brien twins.

Brenden and I turn to each other. "Holy shit," he whispers, reaching for my hand.

"In second place," Roddy calls out, after another corny drumroll, "we have Jimmy and Tommy O'Brien!"

I vaguely register one of the twins cursing as Brenden flings himself against me in a hug.

"And that means," Roddy yells over the crowd's cheering, "that our official winners of this year's Mayweather May Games are Brenden Sanderson and Travis Reed!"

"We did it!" Brenden squeals in my ear.

We've both got some grass and dirt on us, and his T-shirt is covered in egg yolk and streaks of popsicle juice, but I hug him tighter anyway.

"I'm so proud of you," I tell him.

"I'm proud of us! I knew we'd make a great team."

I'm aware all eyes are on us, but that doesn't stop me from cradling the back of his head and turning my face slightly to bury my nose in his hair. Even after all we've done, it still smells great. Like peaches and sunshine and happiness.

That smell is beginning to feel like home to me.

I finally force myself to pull away before people start getting the wrong idea. Or the right one. "So what did we win?"

Brenden laughs right as Roddy walks over to present us with an obnoxiously large blue ribbon. It says YOU'RE THE BEST. Like some freaking children's prize for winning the elementary school science fair.

I look from the ribbon to Brenden when he proudly accepts it, then raise my eyebrows. "Are you serious? We did all that for this cheap thing?"

His grin is almost blinding. "We did it because it's fun! Plus we get our picture framed on a plaque that they'll hang up in the grocery store."

Groaning, I recall that there are indeed pictures of the winners going back a bunch of years displayed on a wall at the store. I'm so used to ignoring them that I almost forgot. Although I'll admit, I have checked out each of Brenden and May's winning photos.

"I don't want my damn picture hanging up there," I grumble.

But Roddy points a camera at us anyway and yells, "Say cheese!"

Brenden tugs me closer, holding up the ribbon in front of us both, and it's clear I have no choice in the matter. So I sling my arm over his shoulders and do my best to smile, even though I hate this.

Then he presses himself more firmly against me, and that's all it takes for my smile to become a lot more genuine. My participation in this nonsense is going to be memorialized on a fucking plaque, but Brenden's pure joy and happiness in this moment might just make it worth it.

WHEN WE GET BACK to his house, Brenden's still beaming and bouncing around full of energy. His happiness is apparently contagious, because I'm still smiling too. I want to wrap him in my arms again, but I'd feel bad constraining him when he's this excited, so I just watch him appreciatively.

He's dirty and clutching that stupid ribbon, but his cheeks are flushed in a way that makes me think dirty thoughts. My mind flashes on the image of him fellating that fucking popsicle, and it's game over.

I reach for him and pull him in toward me, catching him by surprise. He gazes up at me with intrigue, lips slightly parted, and I want to devour him. "We should get cleaned up," I say. I'm aware of how rough my voice comes out, but hopefully no one else heard.

"Clean?" he asks. There's amusement mixed with desire dancing in his eyes now, so he's definitely caught on to my intentions.

"Clean," I repeat. Then, like a cave man, I practically drag him up the stairs, ignoring the keen look May gives us as we pass her. The last thing I want to consider right now is his daughter possibly knowing what we're about to do.

It's true that I want to clean him.

And then I want to get him dirty again.

We barely make it into the bedroom before my hands are all over him. Grabbing, feeling, groping, squeezing. He gasps into my mouth as I slam my lips to his. I tug at his messy hair, and he lets out a whine that goes straight to my dick.

"Shower," I say, pushing him backward toward the ensuite.

He nods frantically and helps me lead him there. We're still kissing, and I'm still groping, exploring his body like I'm on some kind of treasure hunt, leaving no inch unchecked. Once we step into the bathroom, I hurry to strip off his dirty clothes. I might combust if we're not naked and rubbing up against each other extremely soon.

"What's gotten into you?" he asks breathlessly, though he doesn't look upset about my urgency.

"Want you," is all I manage to say.

And it must be the right answer, because he becomes even more alive under my hands. He steps out of his briefs as he helps me undo my jeans. I yank my shirt over my head and toss it. Pretty sure it lands half in the toilet, but I couldn't care less.

When I step over to turn the shower on, I refuse to let go of him, holding him to me with my other arm. His cock is as hard as mine, poking the outside of my thigh. Turning back to him, I wrap my fingers around it while we wait for the water to warm up.

"Seriously, I'm not complaining," he tells me, in between sharp panting breaths, "but I've never seen you like this."

A growl escapes me, and I lean in to suck harshly on the side of his neck. Then I ease up, leaving a few gentle kisses over the same spot. With my nose still pressed to his skin, I inhale his scent and say, "You and those freaking popsicles."

He laughs, a beautiful, delightful sound, and then brings his hand down to cover mine where I'm still languidly stroking him. "Let's get in the shower. This will be even better when we're wet."

I couldn't agree more, so I practically push him in there, following right behind him. He goes for his body wash, but I wrap my arm around his torso, tugging his ass backward against my front. Then I reach around him and take the bottle off the shelf. As I wash him, I kiss his shoulders, his back, anywhere I can reach. And the way his body relaxes and leans into me even more fills me with a rush of pride.

It's obvious that he feels good and safe in my arms, and that's everything to me.

I'm reluctant to stop washing him, even though there's no place left on his body that I haven't cleaned. Then he turns and begins returning the favor. As he lathers his luxurious body wash over my abs, he tilts his chin up for a kiss. Somehow, despite how turned on I am—and can only assume that he is too—we manage to keep it soft, slow, and sweet.

Pulling back, he quirks his lip up. "So you like my popsicle skills, huh?" The smirk grows as my eyes glaze over with lust. "Can I show them to you again?"

My reactions are slow because of the spell he's cast over me, but I do stop him before he can lower to his knees. "Later. I have plans for you first."

"What kind of plans?" he asks in a flirty tone.

Eyeing him hungrily, I say, "Turn around and brace your hands on the wall, and you'll find out."

I swear I see him gulp before he spins around, slamming his palms against the shower tile. For a few moments, I just admire the view. Water droplets drip down his naked back and land on the round, perfect ass that's slightly pushed out toward me.

He grows impatient, whining high in his throat and blatantly pushing his ass out farther. But he doesn't take his hands off the wall.

I reach out, cupping his soft cheeks in each of my hands, and he goes quiet. Until I squeeze, which makes him exhale loudly. Unable to wait any longer to have him, I drop to my knees. Carefully, because, well, I am in my thirties. And then I spread his cheeks, holding them open to give me access to his hole.

He lets out a delighted little noise as he presses back some more. I give his cheeks another squeeze before moving in and licking a stripe from his taint up to his hole, getting my first taste of him.

And let me tell you, that one taste is enough to make me go feral.

I dive in, licking with the flat of my tongue, prodding at his hole with the tip of it, sucking on his rim. All the noises he's making above me are music to my ears, urging me to ramp up the intensity even more.

When I hear his hands slipping off the tile, I pull my face out of his cheeks long enough to order, "Hold yourself open for me."

He lets out a high squeak but follows my instruction. Now I'm free to use my hands for other things. I run one palm up his leg, from the back of his knee all the way to the bottom curve of his ass. Then my short nails scrape a light path as I travel back down. With my other hand, I reach between his legs and tug gently on his balls, wishing I could swallow the moan he gives me.

There's an ache building in my knees, but it's got nothing on my hard, aching cock. And I don't care about either of those problems as I continue feasting on him. His legs are starting to tremble violently though, and I still have enough sense to know I should let him come before he falls. With one hand firmly gripping the back of his thigh, I do my best to support him, then use my other hand to reach around his hip and grab his cock.

I stroke and twist him while keeping my mouth on his hole. He's loose and relaxed for me now, which allows me to slide my tongue in as deeply as it will go. I lick at him from the inside, and his weight falls against me a bit more until he's practically sitting on my face.

It only takes one more expert twist of my hand, my thumb brushing over his crown, before he lets out a guttural cry and shoots his release all over my hand and the shower wall.

His legs are still shaky, but he takes his weight off me, bracing himself against the wall as he turns to face me. He looks wrecked, which fans the fire of pride in my chest.

Slowly, I stand up, caging him in with one of my hands on the tile beside his head.

"That was . . ." he starts, trailing off into nothing.

He takes a deep breath, then all but collapses at my feet, batting my hands away when I attempt to keep him up. I rub his shoulder and run my fingers through his hair while he works to catch his breath. He nuzzles his head into my leg, and we stay like this for a few long moments.

My cock is a steel pipe, and I'm ready to hastily rub one out. But he seems to get some energy back as he turns his head, bringing his mouth only inches from my tip.

When he goes in for it, he doesn't hesitate, sliding most of me into his mouth in one shot. I brace my shoulders against the tiles and widen my stance for balance as I gaze down at him. I'm not going to last long, the need to come is building rapidly, burning me up like an inferno.

And then his fingers slowly roam behind my balls, edging toward my hole, and I become so desperate to have a part of him inside me.

He's watching me cautiously, as if waiting for me to tell him to stop. Expecting me to.

But I can't. I won't.

"Please," I beg, barely recognizing my own voice. "Please. I want to feel you."

He looks surprised for a moment, before his eyes light up like I've offered him a much greater gift than my ass. And then his finger is there. Teasing lightly around my hole before pushing in, ever so slowly.

We're both wet, which helps, and I'm also turned on beyond reason, so I bear down and let him slip in a little farther. Still, he keeps it shallow, simply exploring a bit as he sucks my cock down his throat like his life depends on it.

After only a minute of this delicious torture, he flicks his tongue over that hot spot under my head, at the same time hooking the tip of his finger around my rim and tugging lightly. I make some sort of animalistic noise as I shoot into his mouth.

I expect him to spit it out since we're in the shower, but no. He swallows it down and continues to suck me gently, with tiny licks over my head, until I become too sensitive and have to push him off.

He remains on his knees, smiling up at me like an angel of orgasms. And when I reach down, tracing my thumb across his lips, he chases it, biting down on the tip like a devil.

Releasing me, he says, "That was a much better prize than the ribbon."

I laugh loudly. "But they can't hang this picture of us in the grocery store."

He laughs too, and as we stay in the shower long enough for the water to turn chilly, I think about how I want nothing more than to hear the sound of his laughter every day for the rest of my damn life.

CHAPTER TWENTY-ONE

BRENDEN

"Thank you for visiting," I say, after the Pikes, a nice middle-aged couple, sign their bill. Danny's on break, but I enjoy handling checkouts so I can make sure the guests are leaving satisfied. "I hope you enjoyed your stay."

Mrs. Pike smiles at me. "Oh, we absolutely did. This town is one of our favorite places for a quick little getaway. We try to come for one of the seasonal festivals each year."

"It was fun to watch you and your boyfriend win," her husband says, pointing to the first-place ribbon, which I hung up on the wall behind the desk.

"Oh! Yeah, we . . ." I glance around to see if anyone overheard that. "It was mostly thanks to him, I think."

It feels weirdly good hearing someone call Travis my boyfriend—someone I didn't directly lie to about it. And I'm not even sure why. I know our relationship isn't real, and we can't let anyone else in town find out, but it's kind of cool how the Pikes assumed we were together just from watching us interact. Makes me wonder if maybe it would be possible for someone like Travis, who is smoking hot and completely has his shit together, to actually be into someone like me. Someone who's just faking his way through life.

"What are you daydreaming about?" Danny asks when he returns to take his position at the desk.

"Nothing," I lie. But the look he gives me tells me I'm so busted.

And fine. Maybe I was daydreaming about Travis. Maybe my mind was replaying our shower hookup a few days ago in vivid detail. That was so hot, I'm pretty sure it will still be playing in my mind on my deathbed.

Danny nudges me out of his chair and says, "Wish I was having sex good enough to put that look on my face."

I let out a very undignified squeak. "I didn't—I wasn't—"

"Come on, you totally have dick eyes."

That makes me snort. "What the fuck."

He shrugs. "I call it like I see it. And even if you haven't been getting some good dick, you were at least fantasizing about it."

Well, I guess looking hungry for dick is better than looking moony-eyed like Addison called me out on. Lusting is probably safer than . . . *feeling* when it comes to Travis.

Shuffling around the desk and avoiding eye contact, I mutter, "I shouldn't be discussing my sex life with my employees."

"Like that's ever stopped you before!" Danny calls out. But I'm already making a hasty retreat. He's not wrong, but I can't tell anyone about what I've been doing with Travis.

Honestly, since I moved Elise and Grant into a room here yesterday, I've been avoiding them in the common areas, because I'm afraid they'll say something about Travis in front of my employees. Maintaining this crazy fake dating scheme is like walking a tightrope.

But at least they're out of my house. That alone is a relief.

Although getting them out of there did come with a disappointment I never expected.

Travis didn't need to spend the night last night. He won't have to spend the night with me at all anymore. Which means our hookup arrangement is over, right? Which means I should probably stop daydreaming about his dick and his ass and his mouth, because we've taken that off the menu.

Sure, I might still get to kiss him if we need to be together in front of Elise and Grant again before they go home. But after what I've experienced with him, a kiss is not going to be enough to sustain me. And I don't even want to think about what happens when they leave and the entire ruse is over.

What am I saying? I mean, yes, of course I want them to leave. That will mean my life can finally go back to normal. It's just that after knowing how content I feel when Travis puts his arm around me, pretending to be my boyfriend, my normal life doesn't have the same appeal as it did before.

Oh fuck, I've really done a number on myself here, haven't I?

But how was I supposed to know that being with Travis Reed for a couple weeks—even if it was all for show—would shake up my foundation so much that I'm not sure things will settle properly in his absence?

The chatter of more guests filtering into the lobby behind me reminds me that I'm at work and this is no place for a breakdown. So I veer quickly toward the kitchen for some coffee and make sure to put on a smile, because Addison can sense weakness.

She's at one of the prep tables, and as soon as she sees me, she says, "The new help I hired start tomorrow."

It takes me a beat to process her words, due to just giving myself emotional whiplash a few seconds ago. "Okay."

"Is that a problem?" she snaps, making me freeze on my way to the coffee machine. "You said I have authority in hiring kitchen staff, didn't you?"

"Uh." I gape at her, desperately wishing I had coffee in my hand. "Yeah, you do. That's totally fine. Good. It's good, I mean. That you hired people. You need the help."

She levels me with a glare that almost sends me cowering into the corner. "Are you saying I can't handle running this kitchen myself? That I'm not talented enough to keep the guests happy?"

"What? No! It's just that you needed—Well, you shouldn't have to—"

Jesus, what kind of minefield did I step in here?

"People happen to like my cooking," she says, waving a pair of tongs at me. "People liked my menu for years, but then they go and let some traitor change it up. And now people are suddenly so much happier with something else, and they act like they forget how they used to love my food?"

I'm entirely lost now, so I hold my hands up in a gesture of surrender. After a couple moments of awkward silence, Addison sighs heavily, which sounds like her own surrender. Then I catch her eyes flick toward her phone on the table.

I risk approaching her. "Is something wrong?"

It's a dumb question. Something is obviously wrong. But unless it actually has to do with the inn, I don't expect her to share with me.

"You caught me at a really bad time. I just read this," she says, surprising me by sliding her phone my way. "And I'm sorry. That was super unprofessional of me."

"You know we're only professional here around the guests," I half-joke, offering her a tentative smile. Then I glance down at the phone. There's an article displayed on the screen, with a picture of a gorgeous, dark-haired woman wearing a white chef's coat. I look back up at Addison questioningly.

"Go ahead," she says.

So I pick up her phone and read the headline: "What Happens When a Rising Star in American Cuisine Takes Over an Already Well-Established Chicago Hot Spot?"

Trying not to grimace—because I'm already getting the picture—I keep reading.

CRAVE, a Chicago staple, has seen a rapid rise in popularity, brought about by the acquisition of its new head chef, famous social media influencer Raya Reynolds. Reynolds has taken the restaurant's menu in an entirely new direction, and the Chicago foodies are absolutely here for it.

That's as far as I get. I don't need to read the rest to understand what's going on here, so I slide back the phone.

"I don't know what to say other than I'm sorry you have to deal with this," I tell Addison sincerely. "I'm sure it feels shitty."

"Raya Reynolds is the woman my ex was having an affair with."

"Holy crap."

She stares forlornly at her phone like maybe somehow the device is to blame for what she's gone through. "Well, *one* of the women. Apparently, there were a bunch of others too, but she was with Raya for way longer than it should've taken me to catch on. Guess that's what happens when you're a workaholic."

With a sense of outrage, I say, "Wait a second. Don't you dare blame yourself for your wife cheating on you. That's all on her."

"No, I know that." She turns and heads for the coffee machine, and I follow her over there, because while I want to listen and be here for her, I could still really use another jolt of caffeine. She pours a mug and hands it to me before pouring another for herself.

I smile at the gesture. "Thanks."

"All I meant," she continues, "is that I was always so busy with the restaurant. We both were. But if we'd spent any more time together outside of work, I probably would've realized sooner that something wasn't right. And to be honest, I think I threw myself into my work as much as I did because when we were home together, I wasn't happy. I hadn't been for quite a while, and maybe I was trying to avoid admitting it."

Damn, that sucks. I can't imagine being married to someone for so many years and then just not being happy with them anymore. That must be a tough situation, especially when you own a business with your spouse.

"She's still a cheating cunt," I say, hoping to lighten the mood.

It seems to work, because Addison laughs and holds up her mug to clink it against mine. "Yes, she is."

"Just so you know . . . I'm sorry she did that to you, but I'm so happy and grateful to have you here. Seriously, you're amazing. If I could make you cook all my meals for me, I would."

Okay, maybe not *all* of them. Because that would be like cheating on Travis. And I could never give up the excuse to see him at the diner.

She takes her coffee back over to her workstation, knocking her phone to the side as she sets the mug down. "I appreciate you saying that. Coming from somebody who probably can't even cook a hotdog, I'm not sure if it's saying much, but . . ."

"Hey!"

"I'm kidding. Well, not about the cooking."

Rolling my eyes, I say, "Yeah, yeah. We all know I'm useless at a stove. I might as well let May store her books in there."

"That seems like a very dangerous recipe for a house fire."

"So our bonding moment is over, I take it?"

A hint of a smile forms on her lips. "No, really. Thanks for being here to talk me off that ledge. I'd really prefer to never give that woman another bit of my mental energy."

"I hear that."

As she gets back to prepping the lunch menu, she says, "Sorry I didn't clear the new hires with you first. I meant to, but I really needed to get them in here quickly so they can help me for the big Mother's Day brunch."

The words *Mother's Day* are like a slap in the face, ruining my good mood.

Taking a sip of my coffee, I manage to keep myself together and not trauma dump all over her. I'm so glad she opened up to me, but that would be way too much emotion in this kitchen for one day.

"It's really not a problem at all," I assure her. "I promised when I hired you that you'd have full control over kitchen staff. I trust you."

"Thanks." Picking up her tongs, she gestures to the door that connects to the dining room. "By the way, your family's having breakfast out there."

Ouch. Another word that shouldn't be painful, but is, in this context.

"They're not . . ." I start, then shake my head when she looks at me curiously. "Never mind. Guess I better go say good morning."

Fucking Mother's Day. This time of year is never great for me. It's awful that May doesn't have a mother to celebrate with. And to make things so much worse, April died shortly after the holiday, so that anniversary always brings up even more grief for me.

Usually, I'm good at preparing for the onslaught of emotions that I know are coming. I can let myself enjoy the spring festival with May, and then I spend the rest of the month compartmentalizing hard, only listening to depressing music and quietly falling apart when I'm alone in my bedroom.

This year, with Elise and Grant being here, they've kept me too busy and panicked to think ahead. So the fact that Sunday is Mother's Day has kind of snuck up on me.

We hold a brunch at the inn every year for mothers and daughters, and I'm thankful Addison is on top of the menu stuff. I'll do my part to organize, but as much as possible, I like to avoid being around during the actual event. I'll find myself other busywork to keep me occupied so I don't have to witness all the celebrating.

Hopefully Elise and Grant will be leaving by this weekend. Having them around for the holiday would make it so much harder for me to ignore my grief.

Because it should be April here. It should be April living a happy life with her daughter in Mayweather, and I should be fun Uncle Brenden who visits the two of them all the time.

But the world isn't fair at all, is it? And even though that's how things should've gone, I can't imagine a life for myself now where I'm *not* May's father. Maybe I'm horribly selfish, but I'd never want to give this up.

Walking into the dining room, I force a smile on my face. I'll need to find a polite way of asking Elise and Grant when they'll be checking out of here and getting back on a flight to Philadelphia so I can breathe again. The longer they've stayed, the more comfortable I've started to feel around them, but I can't expect Travis to keep up our charade much longer.

Shit, his dad could be coming home soon, and that would be a disaster.

Elise waves when she sees me. She and Grant both have glasses of orange juice and plates of eggs Florentine in front of them. I slide into one of the empty seats at their table, setting down my coffee as I say hi.

"This breakfast is delicious," Elise tells me. She slices her fork through a poached egg, letting the yolk flow out and over the spinach-topped English muffin. "And your chef is so sweet."

Sweet? Addison? She's an amazing cook, but I wouldn't dare describe her as sweet. Especially not to her face. She must be charming them for my benefit.

"I'm lucky to have her here," I say. Which is at least true.

We chat for a couple minutes, and then I tell them I should be getting back to work. I still haven't found a way to ask how long they're staying. Since they're using one of the rooms here, it's a valid question. I need to know when I can start booking the room again. But I'm afraid they'll see me asking as rude.

"So," I say as I push my seat back, getting ready to stand. "I imagine you'll need to get back to work soon, won't you?"

Grant sets down his fork. "Actually, I've arranged it so that I can stay as long as necessary."

"*Necessary?*" I almost squeak. What the heck is that supposed to mean?

I'd mostly stopped worrying that they came here to spy on my parenting and business skills, but those fears come rushing back quickly. Was it foolish to let my guard down?

Elise offers me what is probably meant to be a reassuring smile. "He only means that we're enjoying our time here with you and May, so we haven't exactly set an end date for our trip yet."

"Oh."

"Also, I heard about the brunch you hold here on Mother's Day, and I'd like the chance to share that with May. If you don't mind, of course."

"Oh," I repeat, the word sticking a bit in my throat this time. Yes, I think I do mind, but I can't say that. Because how messed up would it be for me to deny May the opportunity to celebrate Mother's Day for the first time? I'm not *that* selfish. But the idea of it fills my stomach with rocks.

"We're sorry we've imposed on you for so long though," Elise continues, when it becomes clear after a stretch of a silence that I'm not going to say anything else. "And we'd be more than happy to pay for our room here. We don't want you to lose business."

I shake my complicated thoughts aside to process at another time. "That's not necessary. You're welcome to stay here. I just thought you'd be eager to get home."

As Grant picks his fork back up and resumes eating, Elise says, "This town is a nice change of pace from the city. But if you won't let us reimburse you for the room, May gave us a great idea for how we could show our appreciation."

Wait, what? May shouldn't be giving them any ideas on anything involving me.

"We made a reservation for you and Travis this Friday night at a great restaurant we found in Stoneridge. The two of you can relax and enjoy a nice private dinner without us being in your way or Travis having to cook. It's all on us."

"Well, uh, that's very nice of you, but it's totally not necessary," I tell her. Because there's no reason for me and Travis to go on a private date. Since we're not really dating, obviously, though they don't know that. But also, I don't like the idea of them thinking they need to give me money for stuff.

I asked them for a loan to buy the inn so I wouldn't end up paying a bank out the ass in interest. That doesn't mean I need them to buy me dinner. I do like the idea of Travis not having to cook though. He deserves that.

"I've already left my credit card information with them," Grant says.

"We want to do something nice for you," Elise adds. "And May mentioned how she thought you and Travis would enjoy a night out together since you've been so busy lately."

"Oh, did she?" I try my best not to let my annoyance show as I glance around the dining room for an excuse to walk away. But there's only a few other guests in here at the moment, and they all look perfectly taken care of. Damn my staff for doing their jobs well.

"If you need to get back to work, that's fine, dear," Elise says. "We'll text you the name of the restaurant and reservation time later. And we'd be happy to go over to the house that evening and stay with May so she's not alone."

My thirteen-year-old is perfectly capable of staying at home alone for an evening. She's apparently also capable of meddling in my life for reasons I can't figure out. But I understand that Elise wants to spend as much time with her as possible.

Fuck, she wants to spend Mother's Day with her.

"Sounds good, thank you," I say dutifully. "But yes, I should get back to work."

I'll have to find somewhere else to go waste a couple hours Friday evening. I can't ask Travis to go on a date with me. He'll think I've lost my mind.

I get back to work, but there's not much going on today, so I'm not really needed. And my mind is spinning in all different directions—about me and Travis, about Elise and Grant, about Mother's Day, about everything. Whenever I try to concentrate on a task, I can't, so I might as well get out of here.

I don't intend to end up at the diner, yet somehow after parking my car in an open spot on the side of the road, I realize I'm staring up at the Reed's sign. My stomach growls, like a Pavlovian response. Guess grabbing some food wouldn't hurt.

The place is pretty full when I walk inside. The counter is empty though, so I slide onto a stool, not wanting to take up the only free table. Travis is behind the counter, his back to me, loading his arms up with plates from the passthrough window. As he turns with them, he sees me and smiles.

Giving him an awkward little wave, I say, "Hey."

"Hey, I didn't expect to see you. I thought you were working."

"I'm playing hooky for a bit." I motion to the plates. "Go deliver your food."

"Right," he says, swiftly moving around the counter and over to a table of four by the window. His balancing act is impressive. After he passes out all the plates, he heads back over here, grabs an empty pitcher, and starts filling it with iced tea from the large metal urn. "Sorry," he says, glancing at me over his shoulder as the tea pours. "I'll get you a coffee in a minute."

"I'm not in a rush," I tell him. "Don't worry about me."

He gives me a grateful smile before heading back to that table to refill people's glasses. Then, dangling the empty pitcher off one finger, he does a quick sweep of the room, clearing plates from other tables and grabbing a credit card as soon as someone slaps it down on top of their check.

It only takes a few minutes before things settle down and he returns to me. Still, when he pours my coffee and asks what I want to eat, I just order a basket of fries, not wanting to be too much trouble.

He keeps working, stopping over to chat with me whenever he has a free minute. And watching him turns out to be a pretty good distraction. Then a bunch of tables leave at once, so suddenly the place is a lot quieter. Travis ducks below the counter and stands back up with an empty bus tub.

Glancing around at the dirty tables, I ask, "Can I help?"

"You don't work here," he says.

"So? You don't work at the inn either, but you've helped me a lot."

He reaches across the table with his free hand and takes one of mine, giving it a quick squeeze before letting go. My heart speeds up. There are still customers in here, but he doesn't seem concerned. "You're sweet, but I'm good. Eat your fries."

My cheeks flush, and I duck my head to grab a fry. *Did he really just call me sweet?*

When he's done with the cleanup, he returns to me and steals a fry off my plate.

"You know, I've bitten people's hands for that before," I warn teasingly.

He smirks. "I think I can handle you biting me."

And just like that, I'm feeling flushed again.

"So you must be happy that Elise and Grant are at the inn now," he says, moving on like it's absolutely normal for him to make flirty comments to me.

I heave out a big sigh, not really wanting to talk about them and how they're planning to stay even longer. Or how Elise wants to take May to the Mother's Day brunch, and while I know she has every right to do so, the idea is killing me for some reason.

"What's going on?" he asks, frowning in concern. "Did they do something to upset you?"

"They did some . . . things," I say lamely. Where do I even begin with trying to explain the mess I've got going on in my head?

He needs to know about how they expect us to go on a dinner date, though. So I tell him, making sure to keep my voice down even though the place has mostly cleared out now.

"But we obviously don't have to go," I add, before he thinks I'm getting confused about what this thing with us really is. "I'll just leave the house that night and hide out somewhere for a while. Maybe plot how to murder my daughter."

He levels me with a stern sort of look.

"I was kidding about the murder."

"Brenden," he says, voice soft now. "We should go."

"On the *date?*" I whisper, shocked.

"Grant gave the restaurant his credit card to pay for it. He'll notice if there's never any charge."

"Oh, right," I say dumbly. "I didn't think of that." Of course he doesn't *want* to go on a date with me.

"Plus, it sounds nice," he says, leaning in closer over the counter until I can smell his cologne. "You know I don't get out much."

"Pretty sure that's by choice."

"True, but if it's with you . . . I wouldn't mind."

He shifts his gaze slightly away from me after that admission.

My heart is now beating out a bouncy, happy song. "You want to go on a date with me?"

His eyes fly back to mine. He looks unsure, and for a second, I think he's going to grunt something at me to play it off. But then he says, "Yeah. I do."

Oh my god.

I want to climb over the counter and kiss him. But I hold myself back, because I know I can't do that. I can't stop grinning though. "Then it sounds like we've got a date Friday night."

CHAPTER TWENTY-TWO

TRAVIS

After leaving Benji in charge of the diner Friday evening, I picked up Brenden, drove us the twenty-five minutes to Stoneridge, and now here we are in the parking lot of Lozano's Steakhouse. It's fancier than anywhere I'd normally go. I can tell just by the building's architecture and the looping cursive of the sign. But at least it's steak.

From the way Brenden describes the Richardsons' tastes, I kind of expected something like a French restaurant, where I wouldn't even be able to read the menu and would wind up eating snails.

"I've heard this place is really good," he says, turning to face me after unbuckling his seatbelt.

"For the prices I'm going to assume they charge, it'd better be," I gripe.

He laughs. "But we're not paying, remember?"

Yeah, I remember. The idea of Grant treating us makes me a little uncomfortable though. But I'm the one who told Brenden we should go on the date, so. "Let's get inside. Seems like the kind of place that would cancel your reservation if you're one minute late."

Again, he laughs at me. But he accompanies the gentle laughter with a squeeze of my thigh and says, "Come on, Grumptopus," in a way that makes me feel appreciated. If that even makes sense. Like he actually enjoys my company, despite the sour attitude that I'm unable to rein in sometimes.

He's the only person I really *try* to rein it in around. He's also the only person who can transform my mood just by smiling at me.

And this is a date, right? Even if we were basically coerced into it, I need to get my act together and make it a good one. Brenden deserves to be treated right.

So I tell him, "Hold on, stay there a sec." Then I hop out of the truck and quickly come around to his side to open the door for him.

His eyes light up as he smiles at me, taking the hand I offer to help him get out. "Oh, are you being a gentleman now?" he teases.

Placing a hand on his lower back, I guide him toward the restaurant, silently marveling at how natural the gesture feels. "I haven't been on a date in a very long time," I admit when I grab the heavy front door and usher him inside in front of me. "But I do remember how they work. I'm not a total jerk."

That was essentially a joke, but he stops right before we reach the host station and turns to face me, placing his hand on my chest. "I've *never* thought you were a jerk. You're the best guy I know."

My mouth goes suddenly dry, and I have no idea how to respond to his sincerity. Luckily, he doesn't seem to expect a response, because he simply graces me with one more magical smile, then turns to the hostess to give her our names.

She studies her tablet a moment before looking back up at us with an even wider customer service smile. "Yes, Mr. Sanderson and Mr. Reed. We're so glad you've chosen to join us tonight. If you'll follow me, we've reserved one of our most requested tables for you. It has a wonderful view overlooking the river."

I glance around the restaurant as we weave our way through. There's a soft lighting that gives the place a nice ambiance, rather than making it look dim. The booths are very high-backed, offering people privacy. And there are a couple of tiny tealights shining on each tabletop. It all creates a romantic atmosphere.

We're seated in the back beside a large window that does provide a nice view. There's a deck outside, extending over the water, with string lights woven around the railings. I'm betting they hold small functions out there.

Brenden is smiling at me when I turn back to him. "Not your kind of place, right?" he says, running his finger along the stem of an empty wine glass.

"Maybe not. But I can see the appeal. And I can handle trying new things."

"It's not really my kind of place either," he offers. "But it's pretty. I imagine it would be nice coming here if . . ."

"If what?" I ask when he trails off.

He gives me a look that seems almost sad. "Just, you know. If you were with someone you loved or whatever, like for a special occasion."

"Being on a date with me isn't a special enough occasion for you?" I tease, reaching for his hand across the table.

He exhales sharply, and I go to pull away, worried I did something wrong. But then he flips his hand and holds on tightly to mine. "It's enough. This is great. Even if it's not exactly real."

Ouch.

That shouldn't hurt, because technically it's true, I guess. This is all a part of keeping up the fake relationship ruse for Elise and Grant. Yet it was starting to feel like maybe . . . I don't know. Like maybe it was turning into something more.

It's on the tip of my tongue to say, *It could be real,* but I don't. Because what if I'm wrong?

Brenden made himself clear when he said "friends with benefits." And if I tell him I've been starting to see this as more, will he think I took advantage of the situation—of *him*—somehow?

Our waiter appears at the table, filling our water glasses and saving me from my budding internal crisis. "Hello, gentlemen. My name is James, and I'll be happy to serve you tonight. I've been told to make sure you order one of our finest bottles of wine, so let me know if you'd like any help with the selection."

I give Brenden an imploring look, letting him take the lead here. I'm not sure if it was Grant who insisted we get an expensive bottle, or the restaurant's management when they heard there was a credit card with no limit on file.

"You don't like wine," he says to me. Quietly, as if he doesn't want to offend the waiter. Or maybe he doesn't want to embarrass me. "You can order a beer, and I'll just get a glass of something."

I might not like wine, but fuck, I like him. So I say, "I'll share a bottle with you. I have no clue what's good though."

He looks surprised for a second, then he smiles and turns to the waiter. "We'll take a bottle of red please. Whatever you choose."

The waiter grins, probably already anticipating his fat tip, which I can't fault him for. "Excellent! And here are your menus." He slides the large, laminated sheets at the edge of the table closer to us. "Take your time perusing, and then let me know if you have any questions. I'll be right back with that wine."

I pick up the menu, appreciating that it's not one of those giant books with a million options. But when I catch some of the prices, I blanch. This dinner could cost as much as a lease payment on the diner.

"Wow," Brenden says, reading his menu too. "Leave it to Elise and Grant to find the most expensive restaurant in this whole area."

"Uh, yeah. Are we sure . . ."

"What?" he asks.

"I guess I'm not too eager to spend so much of someone else's money," I explain.

He frowns at the menu, then looks back up at me. "It's fine. I hate taking money from them, and it's hard for me to accept that they would want to do something nice for me, but they wouldn't have done this for us if they didn't want to. So just for tonight, I'm going to swallow my pride along with a juicy filet mignon."

I chuckle before returning my attention to the menu. They're his family, so it's his call. And man, I could destroy a porterhouse right now.

When the waiter comes back to uncork the wine and pour our first glasses, we let him know we're ready to order. After he leaves and it's just us again, with no menus for distraction, we fall into a stretch of silence.

Talking to Brenden has always been easy. But this is new for us. *A date.* Hell, I can't even remember the last person I've been on a date with. Although he obviously doesn't consider it a real date, so there shouldn't be any pressure.

My body doesn't get that memo though. I feel stiff, and I'm sure I look out of place here, even though I wore a navy blue button-down instead of my usual flannel. I'm worried I'm going to do something wrong and look stupid.

Something kicks my leg lightly under the table, and I jolt before locking eyes with Brenden. This lighting makes his appear an even brighter, brilliant blue. And he's smiling at me. He's always smiling at me, isn't he?

And what have I done to deserve that?

"You're thinking too hard over there," he says. "Pretend we're at the diner and yell at me to eat a vegetable or something."

Just like that, I'm back with him. The imposing details of the restaurant fade away into the background as the familiarity of our friendship settles in.

"You're going to eat the vegetables that come with your steak," I tell him, making sure to sound stern.

He shoots me a troublemaking look and says, "We'll see." Then effortlessly changing the subject, he asks, "So how's your dad doing? His hip must be almost healed by now."

"Yeah, he's doing better. I don't want him to come home until his doctor has fully cleared him to go back to work though. Because knowing him, if he's told he can do some stuff but to take it easy, he'll push too hard and set himself back. He's stubborn like that."

Brenden chuckles. "Sounds like someone else I know."

"I'm not stubborn."

"Who said I was talking about you?" he asks, eyes sparkling playfully.

"I'm *not*," I argue. Even though, sure, I know I can be. But I'm not like my dad.

He doesn't respond, just raises his wine glass to take a sip, hiding his smile behind it.

And okay, I'm probably making his point, but whatever. "If I'm so stubborn, then how come you can convince me to do just about anything you ask?"

His teasing expression fades into something much softer. "I don't know. You tell me."

"I . . ."

I have no idea what to say. Because I'm afraid the truth of it isn't something either of us is ready for.

Once again, I'm saved by the waiter when he comes over to deliver Brenden's lobster bisque and my side salad, along with a basket of hot rolls that smell amazing. We thank him, and as soon as he's gone, I stab my fork into my salad and shove a large bite in my mouth like a coward.

Brenden idly stirs his spoon through the soup for a minute. Then he says, "I like that you always give in to me. But I hope you know I don't take it for granted. I don't . . . I would never take *you* for granted."

My heart does something odd then. Skips a beat, or flutters, or whatever dumb cliché you want to call it. He can't say stuff like that and expect me not to fall even harder for him.

Is this still not supposed to be real?

"You make my days better whenever you're around," I say, the words escaping me before I can stop them. But he deserves to hear the truth.

He gasps softly and asks, "I do?"

God, how has he not already realized this?

I suppose I make it hard, since I don't exactly offer my emotions too freely. Not the positive ones anyway. But shit, he makes me want to try.

So I reach for his free hand again. "You do. And you don't even have to do anything. When I see you walking into the diner, I—" I break off, shaking my head. "You just make me happy. There's something about you, like you make everyone happy. I'm sure you know that."

He shrugs nonchalantly. "I try to make people happy. I remember things about them, compliment them, because I know it'll make them feel good. I'm not saying it's not genuine, but it *is* something I'm consciously doing. I don't do all that with you though. Because for starters, I don't think it would work on you. But it's mostly because I can simply exist with you. I don't always have to be on and sunny if I'm not really feeling it." He adjusts our hands so our fingers intertwine. "When I'm around you, I'm comfortable just being me, like that's enough for you. And that makes *me* happy."

I'm struck speechless again, and this time the waiter doesn't come over to save me. I'm trying to be open with him, letting him in when it's never something I've been good at. But I'm afraid of being *too* open, of revealing too much and scaring him away.

He said this wasn't a real date. But he's still holding my hand.

Apparently, I wait too long to respond, because he gives me a small smile and slowly slips his hand from mine. Then he takes his first taste of his soup, completely unaware that my heart is now practically beating itself out of my chest.

The soup must be delicious, because he moans softly around his spoon. Which does things to me that aren't appropriate in a fancy, crowded restaurant. When he glances up and catches me staring, he blushes.

"This is really good. You need to try some," he says, nudging the cup carefully toward me.

I try a spoonful. It's creamy and perfectly seasoned, but I'm happy to slide the cup back to him so I can watch him enjoy it.

By the time our entrees arrive, we're keeping up a normal, friendly conversation like we would in any other setting. Somehow the topic veers back to my dad, and I find myself sharing memories from my childhood and teen years that I haven't thought about in forever.

It was just me and him for most of the time I was growing up. And while we're not super close now, I idolized him when I was much younger. He taught me how to throw a baseball, how to drive, how to tie a tie (though I hated occasions when I had to wear them). When something went wrong, he knew how to fix it. It seemed like he was capable of anything.

But neither of us were the best communicators, which is likely partly to blame for the invisible wall that exists between us now. And that's how I grew closer to my grandfather as I got older. He was a talker. Standing side by side in the diner's kitchen, we talked as he taught me how to cook.

Cooking was one of the few things my dad didn't have much skill for, and he had no interest in it. But I ended up loving it. And the more time I spent at the diner with my grandfather, the less time I spent with my dad.

Brenden gives me a contemplative look when I pause my stories to eat. "So one time, years ago," he says, "May was walking home from a friend's house, and she tripped on the sidewalk and skinned her knee. Your dad saw her crying as he drove by in his work van. So he stopped, used his first aid kit to clean and patch her up, then drove her home."

"He did?" I ask, my gaze trained on him while I cut at my steak.

He nods, then chuckles. "In any town besides Mayweather, a guy ushering a child into his large white van would probably be considered kidnapping. And I did teach my daughter stranger danger. But she knew him, of course, and she felt safe with him." When he smiles, his face is highlighted beautifully by the soft glow of the tealights. "Anyway, it was really kind of him to do that for her."

"I never heard about that."

While my dad isn't bad with kids, it's still kind of surprising to learn he'd go out of his way to help someone else's kid when it wasn't anything serious. The story makes me wonder what else I may have missed about him, but I'm glad Brenden told me.

Then he starts talking more about May, and his face lights up in an extra special way that it doesn't for anything else. He gets so animated in telling me all the details of this fantasy series she's been reading—a series he hasn't even read himself—that he almost knocks over his wine glass.

"Oops," he says, giggling as I reach out to steady it. Maybe it's not only his excitement for the topic that made him clumsy. It could also be the fact that our bottle of wine is almost gone, and I'm still on my first glass.

"You're cute when you're tipsy," I say without thinking.

"*Pfft.* I'm cute all the time," he says, then smiles brightly.

I roll my eyes. I'm not about to confirm that, but I can't bring myself to deny it either.

"Did you know this date was actually May's idea?" he asks, looking down at his plate now as he scoops up a forkful of risotto.

"Really?"

"I have no idea why. I think she just likes to watch me stress out."

"I'm sure that's not why. Maybe she honestly thought you deserved something nice." I slowly chew my steak, pondering something I want to ask. Then I decide to go for it. "Is being out with me really that stressful?"

"What? No!" He frowns deeply. "That's not what I meant. But May knows we're faking this. And she knows my relationship with her grandparents is pretty strained, so this puts me in an awkward position, right?"

I'm not sure why it's hard for him to accept that people love him and might want to do nice things for him. Though I am wondering a bit about

May's motive too. I haven't forgotten the gleeful way she pushed me into competing in the games with Brenden.

"I'm still afraid Elise and Grant are secretly here because they're planning to take May away from me," he continues, pushing his steak around his plate now, rather than eating it.

"*No one* is going to take May from you," I assure him. "Legally, there's no way any judge would do that after all this time. And I promise you, if anyone ever tries to take her, they'll have to get through me to do it. It's not happening."

He hums what sounds like a meek agreement. "I'm probably silly for worrying about this. I know they can't take her. But the idea that they still might not think I'm a good enough father for her breaks my heart."

Seeing Brenden like this breaks *my* heart, so I get up and move around to his side of the booth. I urge him to scoot over so I can slide in, then place my hand firmly on top of his thigh. "I've already told you how great of a father you are, how you've done an incredible job raising May. But if you need me to keep repeating it to you every single day until you believe it, I will."

When he looks at me, his grateful, awestruck expression makes me want to wrap him in my arms and kiss him until he's breathless. Maybe even tell him how much I want him. How my desire goes beyond the fucking phenomenal hookups we've been having. How I'm starting to imagine a life where those blue eyes are the first thing I see when I wake up in the morning and the last thing I see before I fall asleep.

"You'd really fight them for me?" he asks softly.

"I'd fight anyone who tries to hurt you."

He leans his head against my shoulder, and we sit like that for a few moments. Then he says, "Sometimes I think they *are* just trying to be nice, but I get weird about it anyway, and then I end up feeling like a jerk. But I don't know how to stop being anxious around them."

"You could try talking to them," I suggest as gently as possible.

Lifting his head, he eyes me critically. And I know what he's thinking without him having to say it. What would I know about having a real conversation with family?

"Yes, that's hypocritical coming from me," I admit. "You're a better person than me, though."

"Well, that's simply not true," he replies, laying his head back on my shoulder.

Giving in to my instincts this time, I wrap an arm around him.

He scoots the tiniest bit closer, and I revel in his warmth. "I know they care about May. But it seems like . . . I don't know. Like they want to see her more, yet they've made no effort to do it until now. I've never told them not to visit, but they hardly ever do. And I can only assume that's because they disapprove of me as her parent so much that they don't want to be around me any more than they have to be."

Okay, that's it. It may not be my place to get involved in their family stuff, but I can't let him keep thinking the distance between them is because they dislike him.

As I card my fingers through his hair, I tell him, "I think they don't come here more often because of April, not because of you."

He lifts his head to look at me again, his hair slipping from my grasp. "What do you mean?"

"This was their vacation spot with her, right? I'm sure it's hard for them to be here in this place that constantly reminds them of their daughter."

"I . . ." Understanding slowly dawns in his eyes as he stares at me. "I've never even thought about that." He lets out a small, humorless laugh. "Wow. How self-absorbed am I?"

"You're *not* self-absorbed."

The face he makes says he doesn't agree with me. "I've spent so much time being sad for May losing her mom and for me losing my best friend. And then I've spent even more time and energy trying not to show how sad I am. In the midst of that, I've almost forgotten about the fact that they lost their *daughter*. They don't talk about her with me."

"Do you talk about her with them?"

"Oh," he says so softly that I see the word form on his lips more than I actually hear it. "I don't really talk about her with anyone."

"I know," I tell him, guiding his head back down to my shoulder. "And you have the right to deal with your grief in whatever way works best for you. I'm not trying to make you feel bad. I only wanted you to consider their perspective, because that might help your relationship with them."

"No, I appreciate it. Really." He turns slightly so he can bury his forehead in my shirt. "But I don't want to bring down the date night mood. So let's change the subject now, and I can process all this later when I'm alone."

I subtly sniff his hair. "Deal. Just so you know though, you don't *need* to do it alone."

He sighs and burrows into me a little more.

I hope he understands the part I didn't say. That I'll always be here for him if he needs me.

The waiter comes back a few moments later to box up our leftovers and ask about dessert. Regretfully, this prompts Brenden to move away from me. But I get it. No server likes standing awkwardly at a table while a couple is being all cuddly.

"You pick what you want for dessert," I tell him. "I'll only have a bite of whatever you get."

"Like hell you will," he says. Then to the waiter, "I'll have the crème brûlée, and he'll have the raspberry cheesecake."

I laugh softly at that. Why do I have a sneaking suspicion that he plans to eat both?

Once we're alone again, I return my arm to where I want it. I don't know when I became this person, feeling the need to hold someone, even in public, but he doesn't seem to mind. He leans easily into me, running a finger over the line of buttons on my shirt. "You look really good in this."

"Had to dig through my closet to find something appropriate to wear," I confess.

"Believe me, I appreciate the lumberjack look a whole lot, but this just proves you'd look good in anything."

"You look amazing," I say. But he always does.

He leans in to kiss me, taking me by surprise. It's only a brief press before he pulls away, but I chase him, capturing his lips again for a few more sweet moments. He has a smile on his face as the kiss ends, but it fades as he glances nervously past me.

"I'm sorry," I say. "Did I do something wrong?"

He shakes his head. "No, no, you didn't. That was really nice. Um. I just thought you might be worried about doing it here. I'm sure it already looked like we're on a date, but that makes it kind of impossible to deny."

Oh. Maybe I should be worried about that. But I'm not.

"I wouldn't have kissed you back if I cared," I assure him. Then I remind him how I was living my life as essentially out for years while I was in Boston. "I don't really care what strangers think of me."

Only my father.

So yeah, if we were at a restaurant in Mayweather, it would be a different story. And the more time I spend with Brenden, the more I'm ashamed of that.

"Do you ever regret moving back?" he asks.

I take a moment to consider it. Sometimes I'm resentful of being stuck in Mayweather, of the way I escaped for a while, only to eventually wind up back in the town's crazy clutches. And I stuffed myself back in the closet when I returned, but that's not exactly the town's fault.

And maybe it's not exactly my dad's either.

Maybe the only person I can really blame is myself.

And as I'm looking at Brenden now, I realize that if I hadn't moved back, I never would've met him. And *that*, well . . .

That's just unacceptable.

So I run my thumb along his cheekbone and tell him the honest truth. "No. I really don't."

CHAPTER TWENTY-THREE

BRENDEN

This date has done something to me. Altered my brain chemistry somehow so that it's become impossible for me *not* to be touching Travis. I've spent the entire drive back to my house with my hand on his thigh or the back of his neck, my fingertips trailing over the short hairs at his nape like that's their only purpose in life.

And this isn't lust. Or maybe it is, but it's something else too.

It's Travis.

It's this thing that's been building between us. Slowly at first, and now rapidly, out of control and impossible to ignore.

Or am I crazy? Am I letting myself get carried away in a silly fantasy where a dream man like this actually wants me? Wants me for more than sex, that is. The way Travis looked at me tonight—the way he touched me and talked to me—made it feel like there's something real going on here. But I can't afford to be wrong about this.

My life is great. I have May, I have a career I'm passionate about, I have the town. What happens if I fall for Travis and then find out I'm the only one falling? That would probably destroy me.

Going into this fake relationship, we agreed we wouldn't let it affect our real friendship.

And Travis doesn't date. He hooks up. That's not just town gossip. He told me this himself. So how can I expect him to suddenly change who he is for me?

I can't.

I need to break myself out of whatever magic spell this fancy date night put over me and remember that Travis is only mine for now. He's not mine to keep.

As we pull into my driveway, we see Elise and Grant's rental car there, and Travis unsnaps his seatbelt. "I'd better go in with you."

"Right," I mutter. "Keeping up the act."

He frowns, but before I can puzzle out why, he's out of the truck and coming around to my side. I let him open my door for me and help me out again, because Elise might be watching us out the window. Not because it feels nice.

When we get inside, we find May and her grandparents in the process of cleaning up after a board game. They ask how our dinner was, and I tell them the food was amazing, while Travis brings our leftovers into the kitchen to put away. He comes back and stands close to me, placing his hand over my hip like it's the most natural thing in the world. Then he thanks Elise and Grant for their generosity.

Grants waves him off. "It was the least we could do."

"We wanted you two to enjoy yourselves," Elise adds.

May grins devilishly, her eyes darting between me and Travis. "Yeah. It must have been nice for you guys to get some alone time, right?"

"So nice," I reply, with a minimal amount of sarcasm that hopefully only she can detect. I still don't understand why she keeps pushing us together beyond what's necessary for the lie.

"Well, we'd better get going back to the inn," Elise says, motioning for Grant to follow her toward the door. "We'll leave you all to the rest of your night."

After the goodbyes, May turns to me and Travis and announces that she's going to her room to read. "I'll be playing music too," she adds. "Loudly."

Next thing I know, she's run up the stairs, leaving us standing here alone. She must be happy to have her room back.

Travis's hand is still on my hip, and he keeps his hold of it as he turns to face me. With his other hand, he cards his fingers through the hair at my temple. "I really did enjoy going out with you tonight."

"Same," I tell him, barely resisting the urge to nuzzle my head into his hand like a cat.

"And you know, the night doesn't have to end here."

"What do you mean?"

He gives me a small smile. "I mean I could give Grant and Elise a few minutes to get out of here, then I could head back to my place. Or . . ."

"Or?" I whisper, like he's about to tell me a secret.

His brown eyes study me as he cradles my face in his warm palm. Then he says, "Or I could stay, and we could go up to your room."

Oh my god.

I've hooked up with him a handful of times now, and he's said some surprisingly filthy things to me. So why does that simple sentence sound like the goddamn sexiest thing I've ever heard?

I worried our hooking up was over now that he doesn't need to share a bedroom with me anymore. But here he is, looking at me like he wants this to continue as much as I do.

He tilts his head, waiting for my answer.

"Stay," I tell him.

And then I throw myself at him.

My hands land on his chest, and he wraps both arms around me as we kiss, his fingers curling into the material of my shirt. I run my palms up his pecs, then wrap one hand around the back of his neck so he can't get away. His mouth is hot and insistent against mine. When he urges me to open up for him, I do it eagerly, letting his tongue explore.

We kiss our way up the stairs, doing our best not to make too much noise, but unwilling to let each other go. By the time we make it to my room, my lips are almost swollen, yet still, I'm insatiable.

Travis guides me to the bed, where he pushes me down on my back, commanding and gentle at the same time. He kneels on the floor to take off my shoes, then kicks off his own before climbing on top of me.

His hands travel my body, lighting everywhere he touches on fire, even through my clothes. I'm burning up for him. My need to touch him during the drive here has nothing on the intense need I feel now. If we're not naked together in the next minute, I'll go out of my mind.

I try to make that happen by yanking at his shirt until it comes untucked from his jeans. Who knew this man would look as hot in a button-down as he does in flannel and a black T-shirt?

Unfortunately, this shirt is more difficult to get him out of. I only get one button undone before I get frustrated and attempt to rip the whole thing off him.

I'm entirely ineffectual at that, of course, and his hand covers mine to stop me. He sits up, straddling my hips, and finishes undoing the buttons with long, skillful fingers. And while I appreciate the striptease, I don't have time for this. It's essential for my survival that we get naked and he gets back to touching me.

"Hurry up," I urge, working hastily on my own clothes now.

He chuckles. "Someone's impatient."

"Someone's horny," I fire back. "Now do you want to keep teasing me or do you want to let me get my hands on your dick?"

His eyes flash with lust, then he smirks. "Sorry, I wasn't aware I was teasing you."

This entire night has felt like a tease. Not only a tease for orgasms, but a tease of something more. I don't tell him that though.

I whine in protest when he rolls off me, but then I realize he's taking off his jeans, which is fantastic. He removes his boxers too, tossing them to the floor. Then he laughs at me, watching me try to wriggle my way out of my pants before he moves in to help.

Finally—fucking *finally*—we're both naked. Getting on top of me again, he lines up our cocks so that they slide gloriously against each other as he rolls his hips. He's got one arm braced beside my head to hold himself up, and when he grips both of our cocks in his other hand and starts stroking slowly, I turn my head to the side and bite him, because I don't know what else to do with how good this feels.

He growls, making my dick jerk in his hand. And this wild kingdom thing we've got going on is great, but I need him to make me come, and then I need to make him come. Or the other way around. It doesn't matter, as long as we're both coming our brains out very, very soon.

Apparently, he has other ideas about dragging this out though. Because he lets go of our cocks and slides himself down my body until he's settled between my legs, which he spreads open by wrapping a strong hand around each of my thighs.

He gives me a feral look, right before he leans down and sucks at the crease of my thigh and groin.

"*Unnngh*," I moan.

That only seems to encourage him to continue on with the perfect torture. He's kneading my inner thighs with his hands and using his mouth to suck and bite and lick at the sensitive skin. The rough scrape of his facial hair there is almost enough to send me over the edge. But it's not quite enough, and he's ignoring my cock, even though it's leaking shamelessly now.

"I thought you weren't going to tease," I whine, fisting the sheets to resist grabbing his hair and forcing his mouth where I want it the most.

He glances up at me with a dangerous smile. "I didn't say that. I just said I wasn't aware I was doing it before."

The noise I make is something between a frustrated growl and a pitiful whine. But I don't care if that was embarrassing, because he sits up to get the lube bottle out of my bedside drawer, then returns to his spot between my legs. A spot I wish he'd never leave.

I brace myself up on my forearms to watch as he rubs some lube between his fingers, warming it. And then, with his eyes locked on mine, he reaches down, rubbing two fingers around my hole before he slowly slides them both inside. I gasp, but my body welcomes the intrusion.

He fingers my ass like he's on a mission, alternating between shallow strokes and going deeper. Then he gently scissors his fingers to spread me open, and I wait eagerly for him to add a third finger. But he gives me a wink and lowers his head to lick at my rim instead, while his fingers continue to drive me wild.

As soon as he curls them and taps on my prostate, I almost shoot off the mattress. Unable to control myself, I begin thrusting down on him, riding his fingers, silently demanding more. My head falls back onto the pillow as my arms give out, and I reach down to wrap my hand around my cock, but he grips my wrist, stopping me. That's when I start pleading.

"Oh god, oh fuck, please, please, please. Make me come. I need to, please, I can't take it anymore."

Suddenly, his fingers slide all the way out of my ass.

I sit up quickly, ready to fight him. "*Nooo.* Why did you do that? I was so close!"

"Do you have condoms?" he asks huskily.

And I'm pretty sure my brain short circuits for a second. Is this really happening? Blowjobs and fingering are one thing, but fucking is another. I've wanted to fuck Travis probably since our first kiss, if I'm being honest. But I don't think I ever expected it to be an option. I don't believe that sex needs to be reserved for love or anything like that, but with Travis— someone I'm already so close to—this feels like crossing a line that might change me forever.

His brow furrows. "Or do you not want to?"

"No!" I shout. Maybe too loudly. "I mean, yes. Yes! I very much want to, yes. Let's do that. Right now."

When he smiles at me, it warms my skin like a physical touch. "So, condoms?"

"Bathroom, under the sink." I haven't used any in a while, but I always keep a box with a safe expiration date, just in case.

He gets off the bed and goes to get them, and I use the few seconds to try to calm my racing heart. I want this so badly. Badly enough that I'm willing to leave behind any sense of self-preservation and risk the future heartache when we go back to being just friends.

When he steps out of the bathroom holding a condom, I spread my legs in anticipation. Climbing on top of me, he runs a hand up my ribs. It feels possessive. So does the look he gives me while he's rolling the condom over his hard cock.

It's possessive the way he pushes at the backs of my thighs to get me to pull my legs up. Like he owns me, when he hasn't even been properly inside me yet.

I hook my arms around my knees, leaving my hole on full, slutty display for him. Begging him with my eyes to take me, own me.

It's hard to remember what I told myself in the truck—that I can't fall for him, that he doesn't date. Because in this moment, it feels like I'm entirely his. And when his cock pushes inside me, inch by inch until he's filling me completely, filling me in ways I didn't even know I needed to be filled, it feels like I've *always* been his.

He kisses me, pressing my legs back even farther, then turns his head to breathe roughly in my ear. "You feel so good. Perfect. Fuck, you're perfect."

I moan back at him, words failing me. And apparently our roles have reversed, because for once, he's the one who doesn't stop talking. He keeps telling me how good I feel, keeps praising me, though I'm not even doing much besides taking his thrusts.

When I wrap my legs around him and scratch my nails down his back, he groans and slams his mouth over mine.

Possession. This is possession. The way he's taking me, the way he's looking at me, the way he's claiming my lips, then only releasing them so he can duck his head down and claim my neck as well.

In between sucking and biting at me, he mumbles, "Wanted you for so long."

I'm struck dumb by the words, by the bruising pressure of his mouth, by everything. I try to process what he said, because there's no way that can be true. But my brain is pretty useless right now. The only things running through it are *want, need, yes, more.*

"Come on baby," he says, eyes on me again. "Are you gonna come with me?"

I can't look away from him. I can't do much except nod and breathe heavily. He changes his angle and starts nailing my prostate on every thrust, sending stars shooting up my spine. I could probably come just like this, but I'm certainly not complaining when he reaches between us and grips my cock, stroking at a fast pace that matches the new pace of his hips.

"Oh god!" I cry out. A wave of pleasure washes over me, my cock swells in his fist, and then I'm coming hard, making a mess between us.

He groans and his hips stutter, and I feel the warmth of his cum filling the condom inside me. He collapses on top of me, and we both lie there, breathing like we finished a race.

Eventually, he shifts his weight off me, but he doesn't go far. "That was . . ."

"Mmhmm," I agree.

Fantastic, mind-blowing, hot as all fucking hell.

Everything. That was everything.

And I know I'm so screwed, but in this moment, I feel too good to care.

CHAPTER TWENTY-FOUR

TRAVIS

I wake up to the sensation of something rubbing my chest. No, not something. Someone.

Brenden.

I don't need to open my eyes to know it's him, and not just because I remember what happened last night and whose bed I slept in. It's also because somehow, in such a short time, his touch has become that familiar to me.

He lightly drags his fingers through my chest hair, charting his way across my muscles and gently sweeping a thumb over my nipple, coaxing it to harden for him. His touch is soft, likely not meant to wake me. But for how aware I am of him, he might as well be branding his fingerprints into my skin.

I don't think I'd mind that. In fact, I think maybe he branded himself on me a long time ago.

All those small touches, all those smiles. They stay with me after he leaves. And over the years, he's managed to become a part of me. Maybe it's okay that I'm grumpy on the outside, because I'm carrying his happiness inside of me.

Oh, for fuck's sake. That's some sappy shit.

I can't do this. My feelings for him have been manageable all these years. I was able to suppress them enough in order to be his friend. Now suddenly, all those suppressed feelings have broken free, rushed to the surface with an intensity that's impossible to ignore any longer.

But how can I be the man that he needs me to be for him?

I'm not boyfriend material. I'm not that guy.

Faking it is one thing, because I'm able to play a role, to be someone else. What if he expects me to be that person all the time? What if I disappoint him?

"Your heart is racing," a soft voice says.

When I open my eyes, his face is right above mine, and his calm blue eyes immediately soothe my doubts. This connection between us is so strong it makes me feel like I can do anything. Like I can love him, and take care of him, and make him happy every day from now until forever.

Shit, did I say love?

He presses his palm over my heart, branding himself on me once more.

And yeah. I think I fucking love him.

So I lean up to kiss him, because what else can I do?

He kisses me back, but keeps his mouth closed, and when I lick at the seam of his lips to coax him to open for me, he pulls back. "I have morning breath," he mumbles.

"I don't care."

"Oh," he says softly, like that's something to marvel at. But really, who the fuck cares about a little morning breath when you've got someone's warm naked body against your side? When you've already been inside them?

Then he smiles and presses his mouth to mine, lips parting, tongue licking into my mouth. I wrap my arms around him, pulling him down until he's half on top of me. One of his legs finds its way between mine, and the weight of his thigh is a steady reminder that this is really happening.

It's just like my fantasies, except even better. Because it's real.

He's really here with me, in my arms, tangled up, turning my fantasies into something more. Into something that looks an awful lot like a future.

"Thank you for last night," he says when we come up for air. And I'm not sure what he's thanking me for, since I didn't pay for the dinner. All I did was show up.

So I kiss him again. Because I can. Because I want to. I always want to.

We kiss until he grows hard against me. But when I reach down to take him in my hand, he rolls himself off me.

"I should get to work." He sounds regretful, but also like something else I don't understand.

I won't push him though. I let him slip out of bed and watch him tug a pair of pajama pants over his legs, skipping underwear. He tells me he's going to take a shower, and I'm tempted to get up and join him, but it didn't sound like an invitation.

Then he says, "You've got to get to the diner, right?"

I nod, although I really don't need to go yet. I made sure Benji would open this morning, because I knew I was going out with Brenden last night. Even if I never expected the night to end the way it did, I figured I'd be tired.

Before I can work up the nerve to ask if something is wrong, he comes back over to the bed, leans down, and kisses me confidently. Pulling away, he says, "Last night was wonderful. I'll see you later."

All I can do is nod again and watch as he disappears into the bathroom. Then I get up and find a T-shirt and a pair of basketball shorts in his drawer where I've still got some of my clothes. A long run might help clear my head so I can figure out what's going on here.

Because I woke up thinking I'd just gotten what I've always wanted, and now I'm questioning if I misread the whole thing. If Brenden doesn't want this the same way I do.

He did say it wasn't real. But that was before we . . .

There's no way he would have slept with me only as some messed up form of repayment for me playing his fake boyfriend. Right?

Leaving my truck at his house, I run down the street. Then I take a left and keep going. I run my way through town until my legs ache and my lungs burn. Running is my preferred form of exercise, but I've been slacking lately, and my body is making me regret that now. But I keep going.

I only stop when I realize I've run all the way to Shaw Family Farm. Connor is there, crouched down in one of the orchards. Leaning against the short white fence to rest, I call out, "Hey!"

His head whips around, and he smiles when he sees me. He stands up, wiping his palms on his jeans as he heads over my way. "Hey, man. What are you doing out here?"

"Just went for a run," I tell him, still catching my breath.

He raises his eyebrows as he sets one boot on the lowest rung of the fence. "All this way?"

"Kinda got lost in my head."

"Oh yeah?" he says. And I realize I shouldn't have said that. He knows I'm not the sharing type, but now I probably piqued his interest.

"It's nothing," I say quickly.

"Well, that nothing has got you dripping sweat, which means maybe it's something."

Stepping away from the fence, I mutter, "I guess."

"You feel like telling me about it?" he asks.

"Don't you have work to do?"

He grins. "There's always work to do, but the beauty of owning your own farm is you can take a break whenever you want. No harm in pausing to enjoy this nice weather."

I should come up with an excuse to leave—tell him I need to get to the diner, which is not that far off from being the truth. But as I scuff the toe of my sneaker into the grass and he continues smiling at me, waiting me out, I make a decision.

A couple weeks ago, he told me about his sexuality. If there's anyone besides Brenden who I can talk with about this, it's him. So I take a deep breath, and then I say it.

"I'm . . . gay."

It seems to take him a moment to process my words. When he does, his eyes grow wide. "Wait, what? You are? But how?"

"*How?*" I say irritably. Because what the fuck.

"Oh, shit! Damn, no." He shakes his head. "I'm sorry. Fuck! I did to you exactly what I don't want people doing to me. You caught me off guard, that's all. I'm sorry."

"It's fine," I tell him.

"No, it's not. I hate how everyone has always just assumed things about me, but I did the same with you."

I shrug, because whatever. I told him. I told somebody. And if I have to come out to the whole damn town, I need to expect this kind of shock and disbelief, at the very least. There are worse reactions, aren't there?

But am I really thinking about coming out?

"How long have you known?" he asks after a minute.

"A long time."

"Does anyone else know?"

"Only . . . someone," I say.

He studies me carefully, and I'd sort of prefer if he just buried me in the dirt like his crops so I could hide. "Uh, huh," he says. "And I take it this someone is who's got you distracted enough to run all the way out here?"

"Maybe," I admit. Then I realize what's really been nagging at my brain this whole time. The reason I just came out to him. "I'm worried that me being in the closet is going to ruin what I've started with this guy. Who wants to be in their thirties and having to hide a relationship? We're fucking adults. I should be able to take him out in public. I want to show him off, I want everyone to know he's mine and they can't touch him. We should be able to move in together when the time comes. But it'll never come if I can't even do something as simple as introduce him to my dad."

"Woah," Connor says when I'm finally finished.

I think that might be the most I've ever spoken to him at one time. And I didn't entirely mean to say all of it. It just came out. Because it's the damn truth, and if I don't want to lose Brenden, I need to face it.

It's very possible that this is what caused him to pull away from me this morning. And I refuse to lose him. So maybe . . .

"Have you come out to your family yet?" I ask.

"My parents," Connor says. "I haven't figured out how to explain it to Mason yet, and I don't plan to make a big declaration to the town or anything. But I'm not going to worry too much about hiding it either. My parents were super chill about it. They were surprised, but they said it could never change how much they love me."

I try to imagine myself getting that reaction from my dad, but I can't. Because even if I'm wrong, and he's not homophobic at all, he and I don't really talk about how much we love each other like that. Neither one of us is good at that stuff.

"Are you worried about coming out to your dad?" Connor asks, reading my mind.

Reluctantly, I nod.

He frowns. "That's tough. I don't think your dad's a bad guy at all. But obviously I don't know him like you do, so I don't want to give you the wrong advice here."

"It's complicated. I don't think he's a bad guy either. I just also wouldn't call him progressive or anything."

"People can change. That's what progress is. Maybe he'll learn to see things differently if he finds out about you."

"Maybe," I agree. *Maybe.*

I've spent too long with these *what ifs* taking up space in my head. Maybe I was wrong in assuming that not knowing was better than knowing something terrible. Maybe it's time I find out what my dad really thinks, and then I can go from there.

Because I want to be with Brenden. I'm so fucking lucky to get the privilege of him looking at me the way he does. Sometimes he looks at me like I'm the greatest thing he's ever seen.

I need to live up to that.

And when it comes down to it, if my own dad can't be happy for me when I've found someone I care about this much, then that's his problem.

"I should start running back. I've got to be at the diner soon."

"Let me give you a ride," Connor says.

Shaking my head, I tell him, "I've got a lot more thinking to do. But this helped. Thanks, man."

I'm about to head off when I turn back to him, not wanting to be a shitty friend. "Hey, I'm sorry, I didn't even ask how you and Mason are doing."

Tomorrow is Mother's Day, and with Emma recently leaving the two of them, I'm guessing this is going to be hard for them.

I know Brenden's having conflicted feelings about May celebrating with her grandmother. And I know I've hated the holiday since my mom left when I was a kid. It sucks how a day that's supposed to be nice and make people happy can make some people feel like shit.

"We're good," he says. "Not looking forward to tomorrow, but I'm gonna try to keep Mason busy with some fun stuff, so hopefully he won't have to think about it too much. I don't want him to feel like he's missing out on anything because he's only got me now."

"Well, this might not mean much," I offer, "but coming from someone whose mom left him around the same age . . . it does get easier. You eventually learn that what you've got with the people who stay is worth more than what you're missing with the people who choose to leave."

He gives me a small, sad smile. "I'm hoping I can be everything he needs."

"You already are," I tell him. Because I know Connor, and I know what kind of guy he is. And because I know firsthand that one good parent is enough. My dad proved that. Brenden's proving that every day.

Of course, all of this is what makes my decision to come out to my dad harder. One parent is enough, but I'm not ready to have none.

Still, I need to figure out a way to tell him. Because Brenden is worth it.

❁

MOTHER'S DAY IS the busiest day of the year for the diner. The spike in profits is great, but by two o'clock, I'm beat, and I've reached my limit on being polite to people. Luckily, the place has mostly cleared out and probably won't get busy again for a couple hours. Benji's already cashed out the last two tables, although the families are still lingering, and now he's going through the credit card receipts to calculate his tips while I wipe down the counter.

The bell on the door makes me flinch. I swear, one day, I'm going to rip that stupid thing off.

But when I glance up, I get a fluttery sensation in my chest. I didn't expect Brenden to come in this early today, if at all, since he was hosting that big brunch at the inn. So this is a nice surprise. After the morning I had, I couldn't be happier to see his face.

My happiness quickly fades, though, when I realize something's off about him. He's not smiling, which is probably why he doesn't quite look like himself. In fact, he sort of looks like he got hit by a train. Not physically—his work outfit is perfectly coordinated and clean. He looks like he got hit by an emotional train.

Shit.

"What's wrong?" I ask, moving around the counter and rushing toward him.

He's just standing there, two steps inside the door, glancing around like he's never been in here before. Like he's lost. Blankly, he says, "Hi."

I grasp him firmly by his upper arms and search his face for clues. "Brenden. Are you okay?"

He shakes his head as if coming out of a daze. "Oh. Yeah. I'm fine. I just . . ."

When it becomes clear he's not going to finish that sentence, I lead him over to a stool at the end of the counter and encourage him to sit. Then I run behind it to pour a cup of coffee. I slide it in front of him, but he shakes his head again, eyes downcast, and doesn't touch it. And that's when I really worry.

I'm aware Benji's watching us, and the last few customers probably are too, but that's the least of my concerns. Bracing my forearms on the countertop, I lean all the way into his space so that he's pretty much forced to either look at me or deliberately turn away. He doesn't turn away.

"Baby," I say quietly. "Please tell me what happened so I can fix it."

There's a sharp intake of breath from my right. Benji.

But Brenden still doesn't speak.

I don't know how to make him talk to me, because I'm not good at this shit. All I know is that seeing him obviously distressed is making me crazy. I want to grab coffee mugs off the tray and smash them on the floor just to *do* something, but I can't look away from him.

Then his chin starts to tremble and his eyes well up with tears. He whips his head around the room like he's panicked, and I immediately understand that he doesn't want to cry in front of these people. Probably not in front of me either, but I'm the one his desperate eyes lock back on to.

It's a silent cry for help. And even though I still don't know what's going on, my protective instincts for him kick in. In a flash, I'm back on his side of the counter. I wrap one arm around him, and when he tucks his face into my chest, I bring my other hand up to the back of his head, shielding him from the world the best I can.

As I lead him toward the back area of the diner, I shoot a glance at Benji. "Can you please stay for a bit?"

He's staring at me like he's rapidly figuring out some stuff about me, but he says, "Of course. Take as long as you need."

I nod. Although really, I'll take as long as Brenden needs. I don't care if I have to close the diner.

We walk through the back, past the kitchen on one side and the stockroom on the other. Brenden has wound up here in the employee space a few times for various reasons over the course of our friendship. But he's never been beyond the closed door that leads upstairs to my apartment. The soft, "*Oh*," he lets out as I gesture for him to head up the narrow stairwell reminds me of this.

Even before the fake dating scheme, I spent time at his house, but he's never seen my apartment. That goes to show how much of a private person I am. How I keep to myself as much as possible. And after spending so much time these last couple weeks with Brenden and May and May's grandparents—sharing dinners and movie nights, sharing a *home*—I'm realizing that surrounding yourself with good people you care about might just be a better way to live.

By the time I step inside the apartment with him, his cheeks are wet. Holding his face in both hands, I use my thumbs to gently wipe them dry. Then I lean in and kiss him, softer than I knew I was capable of. I hope the barely there press of lips is enough to let him know that I'm here for him. That I'd do probably anything for him.

But first I need him to tell me what it is I can do.

He still doesn't say anything, just sags into me. And when I wrap my arms around him to hold him up, I can feel the relief in his body. Standing in the middle of my small apartment, I rub his back, run my fingers through his hair, and whisper to him assurances that everything will be okay.

Finally, he pulls away. He gives me one long look, then sighs. "Honestly, it's nothing. I'm overreacting, and I know it. It was just the brunch, Mother's Day . . ."

As he trails off, I lead him over to the couch to sit. "I know it's hard for you."

"It's always hard," he agrees. "That's why it's crazy that I've made it through so many years of this perfectly fine, and now this time, I decide to have a breakdown. But seeing May at the brunch with Elise, having someone to celebrate with for the first time . . . I'm happy for her. I swear I am. I'm so happy that my daughter's happy. And that's what makes everything *else* I'm feeling so confusing."

He scoots a bit closer, and I open my arm to him as the well-worn couch cushions cause him to fall against my side. "My head's all jumbled up in dealing with stuff. I know May isn't trying to replace me with her grandparents, but it kind of feels like that's what's happening anyway."

"That's *not* what's happening," I insist.

"I know!" he yells, though I'm pretty sure he didn't mean to. A remorseful look crosses his face, followed by one of defeat. "I'm sorry. Like I said, I know I'm not being rational. And I'm so sorry I bothered you at work."

I tighten my arm around him and pull him in closer so I can kiss the top of his head. He still smells like sunshine and happiness even when he's sad. But I fucking hate that he's sad. "You aren't bothering me. I want you to come to me if you're upset, and I'll do anything I can to make it better."

His hand lands on my thigh, and when he looks up at me, something shifts in his eyes. He squeezes, then runs his fingers up the inseam of my jeans, higher, higher. I hold still, not sure if I want to stop him or spur him on.

I know what I *should* do, obviously. But I did just tell him I'll do anything to make him feel better.

It becomes clear that he doesn't want to talk anymore when he kisses me roughly, like he's trying to swallow my mouth. The next thing I know, he's climbing onto my lap, hands grabbing at me aggressively, teeth biting down on whatever skin they can reach. This is really not what I imagined happening when I brought him up here, though I do nothing to stop him.

If this is what he wants, he can have it.

"Please, please, please," he chants in between kisses and bites.

Getting a good grip under his ass, I manage to stand, hefting him up with me. He wraps his legs around my waist and works on sucking a mark on my neck while I carry him to my bed. But after I lay him on it and crawl on top of him, he seems suddenly uncomfortable, whining and trying to squirm away.

I panic, rolling off him to give him some space. Did I read him wrong? Did he not want to go this far?

"I'm sorry," I say.

"No, wait." He rolls onto his side and reaches for me. "Don't stop. I just need . . ."

"What do you need?" *Please tell me.*

He lets out a frustrated groan as he gets on top of me, straddling my thighs. He drags his nails down my chest and stomach over the material of my shirt, then slides his hands under it to travel back up. "I don't even know. But I don't want to be passive right now. I need to *do* something, have control. Because it feels like my life has been spinning so far out of control lately."

Before I can come up with a solution for him, he pops open the button on my jeans and yanks down the zipper. "Let me ride you. Or can I—" He cuts himself off. "Let me ride you. I just wanna be on top. I need to get out this frantic energy, and I don't know what else to do with it."

Having him ride my cock sounds like a fucking dream. And the fact that I'm lucky enough to have him begging me for it is insane. But there was something else he wanted to ask for.

I sit up enough to get my hands around his nape, then pull him back down with me. We kiss some more. He turns it hard and aggressive again, stroking his tongue into my mouth, biting my lip. He's grinding his hips as he does this, and my cock hardens in no time. He must feel it, because he goes back to tugging at my jeans.

"Please," he says again.

"Whatever you want," I tell him. "If you wanna ride me, baby, I promise I'll love every second of that. But you were going to ask for something else. What was it?"

Shaking his head, he says, "No, it's not—It doesn't matter."

"Anything that would make you happy matters to me."

His eyes search mine like he's trying to make sense of that, but fuck, I thought it was obvious by now.

I grab his waist gently. "Tell me what you want."

A blush blooms on his cheeks, spreading rapidly down his neck. But he doesn't sound shy at all when he says, "Can I fuck you?"

Oh, hell yes.

I almost laugh at something as simple as this being the thing he was hesitant to ask for. If he didn't, I would have asked for it eventually.

When he starts to look nervous again, I realize I didn't give him an answer out loud, so I hurry to correct that. "Yes. Fuck yes, baby. I want that."

"You do? But have you ever . . .?"

"Yeah, I have. I'm vers. I'm sorry if I should've told you that right away. I just thought we'd figure things out as we go."

A grin slowly spreads across his face. And while I haven't forgotten that he came to me upset, and I still want him to talk to me about it more, I'm taking this as a small victory. Putting that look on his face makes me feel like I did something right. Even if all I did was offer him something that I want just as much as him.

"Wow," he says around a tiny, pleased laugh. "I can't believe this."

"Why not?" I ask, rubbing a circle over his hip. "I know bottoming isn't for everyone, but what made you think I wouldn't do it?"

He cringes. "I don't know. I guess I suck for stereotyping. But most guys I've dated who look like you usually scoff or laugh at me when I ask to top them."

The thought of him with other men makes the feral beast hiding inside me rise up. I resist the urge to take him and claim him right now—only because *he* wants to do the taking.

"Well, I'm not them, am I?" I tell him. "It sounds like you've been with the wrong guys."

And hopefully you won't be with anyone but me from now on, I add silently.

The look he gives me is filled with awe and want and need. He leans down and our mouths come together again. This time, rather than yanking at my clothes, he works me out of them purposefully while I do the same to him. He said he needed to get his frantic energy out, but it doesn't seem frantic anymore. It feels laser-focused on me now.

Once we're both naked, he slides down my body and takes me in his mouth without using his hands. His nails dig into my hips as he sucks and licks. Then he pulls off my cock and uses one hand to hold it up and out of the way as he moves his attention down to my balls.

It's all I can to do to keep my hips on the mattress, to not wrestle to get him under me. I want this, and I'm more than happy to let him have me however he wants me. But the anticipation is killing me.

"Come on, more," I urge him, bordering on demanding it.

His head pops up to shoot me a look that's clearly meant to remind me he's the one in charge this time. So I lie back and enjoy the torture. Thankfully, he doesn't make me wait any longer before he starts massaging my hole. He pushes at the back of one of my thighs, and I bend my leg for him, giving him better access.

"Lube," he says.

I jerk my head toward the nightstand, and when he opens the drawer, he lets out a surprised gasp. It takes me a moment to realize what he must have found.

He holds it up, eyes darting gleefully between me and the thin prostate massager. "Oh my god."

Unabashed, I tell him, "Hope that proves I like things in my ass."

With a sexy little growl, he drops the toy onto the mattress and lunges for me, kissing me like his life depends on it. "You're perfect," he mutters between kisses. "Fucking perfect."

The praise lights me up inside. That's never been my thing before. But then again, I've never had Brenden Sanderson telling me I'm perfect before, have I?

"Can I?" he asks, grabbing the massager again.

I spread my legs wider for him in answer. He gets the lube and a condom out of the drawer, then shimmies down the bed again, resituating himself between my thighs. He starts with one finger, which I take easily, so he soon adds a second one.

Then he asks, "More?" And he barely waits for my nod before he's got three fingers buried inside me, fucking me roughly with them.

My aching cock is begging for some relief, so I reach down and wrap a hand around it, stroking myself slowly. I almost expect him to stop me, but all he does is fix my cock and hand with an intense stare.

"God, you're so hot."

I groan in response and squeeze the base of my cock to hold off my orgasm.

Probably realizing I need him to hurry this along, he lubes up the massager and carefully slides it inside me until the curved head hits just the right spot. A jolt of pleasure shoots through me, making me arch off the bed. He grins and slides the toy almost all the way out before pushing it back in again. In and out. In and out.

I'm practically panting by the time he settles it against my prostate and presses the button on the base to turn on the vibrations. He ducks his head between my legs to suck on my inner thigh as he pushes the toy into me a fraction more. The pressure has my toes curling, and I resume stroking myself, faster this time, hurtling my way toward an explosion.

"Don't come," he warns. "Not until it's me inside you."

"Then you need to stop," I tell him huskily. "So I can come on your cock."

He moans in what sounds like approval and turns off the toy, pulling it swiftly from my hole. I work to catch my breath as I watch him jack himself a few times before rolling on the condom. Then he says, "Turn over," and the breath rushes out of me again as I hurry to comply.

He tugs at my hips, and I let him pull me onto my hands and knees. And then his cock is there, nudging at my hole. I relax and bear down as he slides in steadily inch by glorious inch until his hips are flush against my ass.

"*Fuuuck*," he whispers.

I could say the same. I thrust backward against him, silently urging him to fuck me. And he does. He starts out slowly, but it doesn't take long for him to grab my hips for leverage and begin slamming into me at a punishing pace.

I love it. I fucking love it. I love the shape of him behind me, of him filling me. I love taking him. I love that I can give him something he so desperately wants. I love . . .

Draping himself over my back, he keeps one hand possessively on my hip and brings the other to the top of my shoulder. Then he bites down on my upper back, and I cry out, and he licks over the spot. I shouldn't be surprised by anything he does at this point, but it's still amazing to experience him like this. So in control but also wild, possessive, almost feral.

"I'm not gonna last," I tell him.

"Me neither. Fuck. Me neither."

When he wraps one arm around my body and grips my cock, I know I'm done for. It takes barely three strokes before I'm shooting ropes of cum across the sheets.

"Yes!" he shouts, fucking into me a couple more times. Then he stills, giving in to his release.

A moment later, my arms give out. I collapse to the mattress, managing to move sideways enough to avoid landing in my own mess.

Brenden clings to me, falling on top of me with a quiet grunt. "Am I crushing you?" he asks.

"Not at all."

"Good."

He seems either too lazy or too content to move, and while I'm not ready to be separated from him, I do want to see him. So as soon as I regain strength, I roll over underneath him and adjust us both until I'm on my back and he's only half on top of me, his face close to mine.

I run my thumb along the shell of his ear and gently ask, "Did that help?"

He beams. "That was fucking fantastic. And I feel much calmer now, not like I'm going to crawl out of my skin."

"Are you ready to talk more?"

"I don't need it," he says, shaking his head. "Not right now. Maybe I'll want to talk about stuff later, but I don't want to ruin this feeling."

I guide him in for a short kiss, glad to know I helped him in some way. But I'm aware that talking about the things that are bothering him is a healthier method than trying to fuck the feelings away. "Promise you'll talk to me later when you're ready. I don't want you to keep holding everything in."

He pulls back, eying me uncertainly. "Since when do you want to talk about feelings?"

Since you.

"Since now, I guess."

Reaching for my hand, he threads our fingers together, then rests our joined hands between us. "I promise."

CHAPTER TWENTY-FIVE

BRENDEN

After my meltdown the other day, I can see the concern in Travis's eyes every time he looks at me. Like now, at the diner. He's trying to be subtle, but I know he's watching me as I sit here with May, picking at my Reuben. We still haven't talked more about why I was so upset. But what's the point? I can't explain it.

All I know is I haven't felt normal ever since Elise and Grant showed up. I'm lying to them, and my guilt about it keeps growing the longer they stay. I'm forcing May and Travis to lie to them too, which also sucks. But at the same time, they're making me feel like I'm not a good enough father or business owner. And whether intentionally or not, they're digging up feelings about losing April that I painstakingly buried long ago.

I can't go on like this much longer. If it weren't for having Travis around, to calm me with his thoughtful gestures and distract me with the incredible orgasms, I would've already lost it completely.

Though I won't say May's grandparents have been entirely awful. Sometimes my brain tries to convince me they're being that way, but actually, for the most part, they've been kind of great. Much less uptight than I expected. They're clearly happy to be here, spending time with

May. And me too, I guess, by proximity. But that's also what makes it hard.

Because this thing—the four of us, and even Travis—is almost starting to feel like a real family. But it's *not* real. It can't last. There has to be an end date, right? They have to go home sometime.

And then Travis will stop pretending to be with me, and May and I will be all on our own again.

I look at my daughter, watch her ripping apart pieces of a buffalo chicken tender, and I smile despite the painful thoughts going through my head. It's been just me and her since she was two. She's always been more than enough for me. But it's not fair to assume I'm enough for her.

Maybe Elise was on to something when she said she wished May had two parents. I'd be blind not to notice how easily May's bonded with Travis, how she enjoys having him around as much as I do.

Travis.

What are we doing?

He's at a table nearby, using a pitcher to refill someone's water. As if he can sense my stare, he glances over mid-pour, and we exchange brief smiles. But then he cuts his eyes back to his task just in time to not over-flow the glass.

We've fucked twice now. I know what he tastes like, know what noises he makes when he comes. I know the intimate way he watches me as we move together.

And I just don't know how I'm ever supposed to give that up. I don't want to go back to the way things were between us, where all I know are his grunts and occasional smiles and his skill at changing a flat tire.

It's dangerous to hope, but I can't help it. I'm hoping that there's some way I can keep him.

"I need to ask you something," May says, disrupting my thoughts. "And I think it's going to upset you, but please just listen."

"I'll always listen to you," I assure her, a bit hurt that she'd ever think I wouldn't.

She picks more of the breading off her chicken, her fingers covered in dark orange sauce now. "Grandma and I were talking when we had brunch . . ." she starts ominously. And while I have no idea what she could possibly be gearing up to ask me, I'm guessing she's right in that it's going to upset me. "It's just kind of weird that we never talk about my mom. You and me, I mean."

My heart sinks like a stone to the pit of my stomach. Of course we don't talk about April. Because for one thing, I don't think I'm capable of talking about her without breaking down. And for another, I always thought it would hurt May to hear about what she lost. In a way, I thought she was better off than I was by not being able to remember.

Swallowing the lump in my throat, I tell her, "I thought I was doing what's best for you."

"I know," she says quickly, attempting to clean her hands with a napkin, but they're too messy. Travis appears out of nowhere with extra napkins, and after he walks away, she turns back to me. "I'm not blaming you, Dad. I love you."

"I love you too, kid."

She smiles. "I know you do. And I'm sure you don't talk about her because you don't want me to be sad. But I think *you're* sad. You try to hide it, but I think maybe letting yourself talk about her will help. And I . . . I think I deserve to hear about my mom."

"You do," I choke out. Because she does. Maybe it was selfish of me to hold my memories back from her.

"Grandma talked about her a tiny bit at brunch the other day. And we were thinking maybe it would be nice to have a sort of memorial where we could all talk about her."

"A memorial?"

No. My gut reaction is to say no. Because I don't want that.

But May pushes her plate aside and gives me a gentle yet imploring look. "Dad. We both lost her, but I didn't even know her. I think it's harder for you than it is for me, and I think you're holding in a lot of stuff that you might need to let out. I can handle it. I don't want you to be sad, but I can handle it if you are."

"I'm not . . . I don't . . ."

It feels like I'm drowning. Like my lungs are filling up with water, not air.

Then as if by magic, as if he could sense my growing distress, Travis appears beside me and places his hand on my shoulder, his long fingers applying just the right amount of pressure to make things inside me settle. I don't think he was eavesdropping on our conversation, because all he says is, "Hey. You good?"

Glancing up at him, I force myself to nod. "Yeah. I'm fine."

That's not one hundred percent the truth, but under his touch, I do feel much closer to fine. Like he threw me a life preserver when I was drowning. Although really, I'm sure that if I was drowning, Travis wouldn't hesitate to jump in himself to save me.

He gives me a long, searching look, then squeezes my shoulder. "Okay."

After he returns to helping other customers, I turn back to face May. My daughter never asks for much, but she's asking me for this. And as much as the idea of talking about April and being forced to dredge up all my pain fills me with dread, I would give my daughter anything she wants. So I'll have to give her this.

"Travis can be there," she says.

"What?"

"If you want him to. I know he didn't know my mom, but if it would make you feel better having him there with you, I think he should be."

"Why do you think he would make me feel better?" I ask, averting my eyes down to my half-eaten sandwich.

She doesn't say anything for a few moments, and when I risk a glance up at her, I find her smiling at me knowingly. "Because he always makes you feel better."

It seems like I should argue that, but I can't. Because it's true. There's a reason I ran to Travis on Mother's Day when I couldn't handle all my emotions. And while he can't fix any of this stuff for me, he *did* make me feel better. And maybe I didn't recognize it so much before, but I'm realizing now that he's been doing that for me for years.

TRAVIS HAS ALWAYS shown up for me whenever I've asked him to. But this time he's done it in such a big way that I honestly don't know what to say to him. At some point, *thank you* stops cutting it. When I sneak into the back area of the diner—where I'm not supposed to be, and yes, he's going to yell at me—to find him at the grill cooking pancakes, I'm overwhelmed with everything I feel for him.

He not only agreed to be at this freaking memorial, but he offered to close the diner early so we could have it here. Because apparently, Elise and Grant told him that April loved coming here for pancakes on their vacations.

When he asked Elise if she liked the idea, her eyes watered. Then she thanked him, and hugged him, and looked at him in a way I'm not even sure she's ever looked at me. *Almost like family.*

Turning around now, Travis spots me standing in the small kitchen. "Get out of here!"

I chuckle at how right I was. "I just want to help."

"That's nice, but according to my insurance company, you aren't allowed to help, so get your sexy ass out."

"The restaurant's not even open," I argue, enjoying our typical banter even more now that there's an element of flirting to it. Up until a few weeks ago, I thought this man was as straight as an arrow, and I've never been so happy to find out I was wrong.

"It doesn't matter. Out!"

"But—"

He gives me a stern look and repeats, "Out!"

Huffing, I tell him, "Fine, but at least let me help bring things to the table."

This time the look he gives me is much softer. "Go stand on the other side of the passthrough."

Good enough for me. That's still behind the counter, which still makes me feel kind of special. And really, I was only looking for a task so I wouldn't be sitting out there miserably with May and her grandparents. It seems like we're waiting for Travis before we start this thing, so they're being weirdly quiet. They look sad already though.

Who thought this would be a good idea? I don't understand the point of talking about the most painful thing we could possibly talk about. We all went through it once. Why do we have to do it again?

I remind myself I'm doing this for May. It sounds horrible to me, but if she wants me to rip myself open for her, I will.

"Can you carry this stack without dropping it?" Travis asks me from the kitchen, as he sets a giant platter of pancakes on the passthrough ledge.

I want to be insulted, but it does look heavy, and I'm not the most coordinated person. "How about I bring out the toppings and leave this to you?"

The way he smiles at me makes me want to get him naked, cover him with some of his homemade whipped cream, and then lick it off him. But I try to wipe that fantasy from my mind as he passes me bowls of blue-berries and sliced strawberries. The last thing I need is to pop a boner while everyone else is crying.

Once we have the food set out on the largest round table and everyone's served themselves, I have nothing left to distract me from the building panic. What are we supposed to do now? Do we just start saying shit about April? Who goes first? And is there any chance I can get away with not speaking at all?

Travis pulled the blinds down over the diner's big glass windows to give us privacy. I appreciated it when he did it—because lord knows, I don't want the whole town to witness this sobfest. But now it's getting claustrophobic in here.

"I know this is a little unorthodox," Elise starts, glancing around the table at each of us. "We had a memorial service after April passed away, of course. But May was only a baby, and after she and I discussed it, I realized that she'd appreciate the opportunity to hear more about her mom. So we don't need to be formal here. We can all share whatever we're comfortable with." She turns to May and places a hand over her wrist. "And if there's anything you'd like to ask us, please do."

May sets down her fork, a huge chunk of pancake speared on the end of it. "I wouldn't even know what to ask."

"That's okay," Grant assures her. "You can just jump in if you think of anything."

"Would you like to go first, Brenden?" Elise asks.

As everyone's eyes focus on me, I avert mine down to my plate where I've drowned my pancakes in a lake of syrup. "No," I say meekly.

Thankfully, no one pushes me. Elise begins talking about April as a child, her favorite games and books and movies. I swirl my fork through the syrup lake while I pretend to listen. When Grant joins in with Elise, I force myself to eat just so I'll have something to do.

They keep the conversation flowing for a while, and May chimes in with comments and questions. Beside me, Travis is quiet, but I can tell he's listening.

Once they move on to talking about April in high school and college, it gets harder for me to let their words float in one ear and out the other. I have things to say. This was when April was my favorite person in the world, and I want to talk about how awesome she was. I want to tell May how much of her mom I see in her. But I'm afraid of what will happen if I open my mouth.

I'll either start sobbing instead of talking, or I'll start talking and never be able to stop. Neither of which is productive.

It keeps itching at me though, the desire to talk about those years with April. But is it appropriate to tell her parents and daughter about how often April snuck out of her house to spend the night at mine? Do they need to hear how much Elise and Grant drove her crazy?

They definitely don't need to know that she gave her first blowjob before I did, and then I made her demonstrate for me with a hairbrush handle because I was worried I'd do it wrong.

Although I'm avoiding eye contact with anyone, I can sense May watching me. Without looking at her, I can't tell if she's concerned at how silent I'm being, or if she's disappointed in me for not participating. Either will make me feel like a failure.

Travis's chair scrapes across the floor as he scoots closer to me, but the conversation continues. He puts his hand on my leg, right above my knee. The form of comfort doesn't magically work like it has every other time he's touched me like this. But I'd give anything for him to keep his hand there anyway.

Actually, I'd give anything for him to pick me up and carry me right out the door, but I know that's not going to happen.

"Dad?"

My eyes instinctually look up to find my daughter's, and I can see she's been crying. I feel awful. It's my job to shield her from things that would make her cry.

I'm failing. I'm failing. I'm failing.

I need to get her out of here.

"Can you please try to talk about her? For me?"

Oh.

She doesn't want to leave. She wants to keep sitting here and talking about these things that are making her cry. How is she so strong? She certainly didn't get it from me, because I'm not sure how I'm going to make it through this. She must have gotten it from her mother.

But didn't April tell me I was strong, and that I'd teach May how to be too?

My lungs start to fill with something other than air until Travis squeezes my leg.

I glance down at my soggy pancakes, then back up at May. My brilliant, wonderful daughter. I agreed to do this for her, but I'm not really doing it, am I?

I'm supposed to teach her how to be strong.

And it's becoming impossibly harder for me to hold back my memories. Because here we are, having pancakes for dinner, which April would've loved. And suddenly, something that April said to me when she asked me to adopt May comes to mind, along with another memory. But this one's not of April.

"I don't know if this counts . . ." I start slowly, letting my voice adjust after the disuse. "But do you remember your seventh birthday? We had a party on the weekend, but I asked what you wanted for dinner on your actual birthday, and you said cookies. It made me remember the talk I had with your mom when she asked me to adopt you. One of the things she said was that she wanted you to grow up healthy, but she also wanted you to know that sometimes it's okay to have cookies for dinner."

Elise makes a small noise, but I keep my focus on May.

"So I made the cookies, and we ate them together right at the kitchen table, and we talked about the silliest things. And . . . maybe it didn't mean anything to you. You just thought it was cool I was letting you have cookies for dinner. You probably don't even remember it now. But it felt like your mom was there with us, and it was one of the best nights of my life."

There's an excruciatingly long moment of silence after I stop talking. Then May says, "Of course, I remember."

She gets out of her seat and comes around to me, bending down and throwing her arms over my shoulders. I hug her back like she's a lifeline.

And as soon as she steps away, I break. A wretched sound rips from my throat, and she spins back around, looking concerned. I quickly insist I'm okay, but the tears have escaped now.

"Dad?"

Waving my hand frantically, I say, "It's fine. I'm fine. All good. Please ignore me."

"Dad."

"No, no. Don't let me ruin the party. Everyone can keep talking."

I have no idea what I'm saying. Words are just spilling from my mouth, anything to trick them all into looking away from me as I fall apart. Because I'm supposed to be strong for my daughter, *damn it*. And how can I do this to her? How can I let her see me so weak?

As May reluctantly takes her seat again, she gives me the saddest smile. "Thanks for telling me that. I didn't know the part about my mom, but I do remember how much I loved that night with you."

It takes everything I have not to sob out loud. It's like I finally wrenched open a rusty valve, and now that the tears are flowing freely, they may never stop.

Elise offers me the slightest saving grace by continuing the conversation, drawing eyes to her. And as much as I want to be ignored, I can't help adding some more of my own anecdotes about April to the mix. But I'm crying silently the entire time.

Stop it, stop it, stop it, I beg myself. *This is not me. This isn't what I do. I smile and laugh and make people feel good. I don't drag down the mood.*

Right when I'm about to get up and flee, because I can't stand to let everyone witness this any longer, Travis scoots his chair even closer so that it's jammed up against mine. He puts his arm around my shoulders, tugging me to his side. I go willingly until there's no space left between us.

It feels like that's exactly how it's supposed to be. And with him supporting me, rubbing my back, kissing my hair, I make it through this.

BY THE TIME EVERYONE'S ready to go, I'm so emotionally wrung out, I'm not sure I can move. There are a lot of pancakes left on the table. There's a big mess left on the table, actually. I want to help clean it up, but all I do is sit in my chair as if I've been permanently fused to it. I live here now. At least I know I'll always be well-fed.

I'm aware of Elise and Grant saying goodbye. Aware of Travis telling me and May to wait for him to take care of the mess and then he'll drive us home. I'm aware that May gets up and helps him, the two of them talking quietly while they clear the table.

The dried tear tracks on my cheeks make my skin feel tight. I need a warm shower. Or maybe an exorcism.

When it's time to go, May comes over and gives my hand a squeeze. I'm afraid to look at her, but then she says, "Thank you for being so strong for me," and my eyes shoot up to hers. The words don't make sense, but she looks so sincere. "I love you."

"I love you too," I say, my voice raw and scratchy.

It's not until Travis grips my side and urges me up that I realize I'm supposed to stand. I follow him outside like a puppy and climb into his truck after May. The drive to my house only takes a couple minutes, but I spend each of them silently bemoaning the fact that my daughter is sitting between me and him.

I need to be closer to him again. Feel the press of his body against mine and just know that he's there.

And because he's Travis, he doesn't even make me ask for that. After pulling into the driveway, he leads me into my own house with an arm around my waist. May disappears, and he takes me up to my room.

At least I've finally stopped crying. He's not a fan of emotions, so dealing with me like this must be hard for him. "I'm sorry," I tell him as he helps me get undressed.

"What in the world for?" he asks.

I gesture uselessly at myself. "For me. This. You didn't sign up for taking care of me."

He gives me an odd look and steps closer, one hand curling around the back of my neck and gently bringing my forehead to his. "I think I did. In case you haven't realized it yet, there's not a single part of you I don't like. You bring so much sunshine into my life, but don't think I can't handle the rain too. I'll be here no matter what."

"I . . . um . . ."

What could he possibly mean by that? I was saying that him having to take care of me wasn't part of the fake dating or fun hookups deal. But it sounds like he's talking about something more than that.

Not a single part of me he doesn't like?

There's no way he means that the way I want him to, right? I've tried to pretend I haven't been falling for him these last few weeks, because I never imagined he could fall for me too. Except now we're alone, no one to put on a show for, and I'm a terribly unsexy, tear-stained mess. And he's looking at me like he'd move mountains just to be in this room with me.

So I don't question it. I watch him take off his own clothes, then I get into bed when he pulls down the covers for me. Instead of going around to the other side, he gets in right behind me, nudging me forward enough to make room for himself.

But he doesn't let me go far. He's the perfect big spoon, molding his slightly larger body around me, one arm slung over my waist and securing me tightly against him.

"You've been holding all that stuff in for a long time, haven't you?" he asks, his lips tickling the back of my neck.

"What stuff?"

"About April."

My body tenses. He's not wrong though. And with the way I completely fell apart, trying to deny it would be stupid. "I don't talk about her, but I think about her every day. I just never wanted May to find out how sad I am inside. I mean, I'm happy too, don't get me wrong. I love my life, but I'll always miss the people I've lost."

The arm around my waist squeezes me comfortingly. "It's okay to be sad sometimes, you know. Do you want your daughter to think she has to hold in any negative emotions? Or do you want her to be able to talk to you when she's sad?"

"Of course I want her to be able to talk to me," I say, as his words sink in and I realize he's right. I want May to have healthy coping mechanisms.

He places a kiss at my nape. "So you should be able to talk to her too. Being a dad doesn't make you any less human."

I hum in agreement, feeling foolish that it took me this long to understand that. And maybe it's weird that someone who's not a parent, and claims not to even like children, is the one who helped me get here. But maybe not.

Travis might not talk a lot, but that doesn't mean he isn't listening, that he doesn't understand. I'm beginning to think he understands me better than anyone else could, because he pays attention so well.

As we lie here naked together, warm skin to warm skin, the idea of initiating something sexual occurs to me, but I let it pass. Sex with Travis is fantastic. But somehow this form of intimacy is even better. It's friendship and understanding and contentment and stability and fulfillment. It's everything all at once.

He holds me as my eyelids grow heavy, as his breathing slows. He holds me like he never intends to let me go.

The two of us may have started out faking this, but as we drift off to sleep together, I'm certain that nothing has ever felt quite so real to me.

CHAPTER TWENTY-SIX

TRAVIS

Last night was a lot. I hated seeing Brenden so upset and not being able to do anything about it. But I think it ended up being good for him. Hopefully he realizes now that he doesn't need to act like everything's fine and wonderful all the time when it's not. That he's allowed to hurt.

And I meant it when I said I'll be here for every version of him.

He knows I'm not the best with words, but if this is going to work, I'm willing to try for him. I want him to know how I feel.

Right now, as he begins to stir in my arms, it feels like I'm living in a dream. Neither of us moved away from the other while we slept. Not like he could've if he wanted to with the way I wrapped myself around him. I've even got my leg hooked over his.

I'm not normally this cuddly, this possessive with someone I'm dating. Granted, I have minimal experience with actually dating, and it's been a long time. But even with Christian when I lived in Boston, I never felt this aching need to keep him as close to me as possible.

Brenden's different, of course. He has been since the day I met him, even if it took longer for my feelings to develop into this.

"G'morning," he mumbles sleepily. It's so cute that I have to bury my nose in his hair and kiss the back of his head. His hair tickled my nose all night, but it was worth it for the privilege of being surrounded by his scent.

"Morning," I tell him, twirling my fingers aimlessly over his stomach. "How do you feel?"

"Wrung out. And not in the fun way."

I laugh, squeezing him to me a little tighter.

"But I'm glad we did that," he continues. "I think it was good for everyone."

"Mmhmmm," I murmur, pressing my lips to the nape of his neck as my fingers resume trailing over his soft skin.

"This feels nice," he says, and I can hear the smile in his voice.

It feels more than nice, but I'm not sure I'm capable of finding the right words for how perfect this is, so I kiss him again. And again, and again, marking a path down his spine. I don't get too far though, because I'm not willing to move away from him that much.

When he lets out the tiniest, sweetest moan, I can't help myself. I remove my arm from around his waist and bring it down between our bodies. My hand almost covers his entire ass cheek. I squeeze, making him moan again, and then I use one finger to rub over his hole.

"More," he says softly. "Please."

Hearing him beg for me makes me feel like a king, but I'm incapable of making him ask twice for anything. So I roll away to grab the lube and a condom out of the nightstand drawer, then come back to him. Even though I revel in being able to give him what he wants, I still take my time. I start by pressing only the tip of one slick finger inside him, crooking it to tug gently at his rim. I fuck him shallowly with it, waiting until it feels like he's sucking me in, his body requesting more before I go deeper.

Eventually I add a second finger and work to loosen him up. He pushes back against me, matching my slow pace and whimpering when I suck on the juncture between his neck and shoulder.

"Ready?" I ask him, though I know he is.

"Yeah. Can we stay like this?"

That's music to my ears. "Yeah," I tell him. "Just like this."

I wedge my bottom arm underneath him and wrap it around so I can splay my hand across his chest and press his upper body against mine. Then I use my other arm to adjust his top leg, pulling it back just a bit and setting it over my thigh to keep him spread open for me.

He shivers as I push the head of my cock past his rim. His body grips me so tightly, even after I loosened him up, and I have to fight the urge to force myself in and slam all the way home. Instead I only give him a couple inches before pulling back so just my cockhead is inside him again. Then I repeat the motion, giving him a bit more each time, until I can slide in fully with no resistance.

With my hips flush against his ass, I rock us back and forth, only pushing into him a tiny bit each time. Pretty soon he's whining, making it clear that he wants more, so I give it to him. I start pulling out and thrusting into him for real, but I keep the rest of our bodies as close as possible.

We create a slow but steady rhythm together. I slide my hand up to grip his throat lightly, and he brings both of his hands up to cover mine. He presses down, urging me to hold on tighter. I growl my approval in his ear, then bring my mouth back to the same spot I was sucking on before, determined to leave my mark on his skin.

My brain is screaming at me, telling me he's mine. That I need to keep him, and protect him, and love him, and fuck him. And fuck him, and fuck him, and fuck him. I can tell he's getting closer when his hands fall away from mine and his fingers scrabble in the sheets. He could easily reach down and touch himself, but for some reason he doesn't. I like that he's leaving it up to me to take care of him.

So I do. I wrap my hand around his hard, leaking cock and give him a few strokes. He whimpers and whines, his hole clenching around me as I continue to fuck him.

"That's it, baby," I murmur in his ear before tugging at his earlobe with my teeth. "Love being inside you. We fit together perfectly, don't we? Are you ready to come for me?"

"Yes, *yesss*," he moans. "Want to. Please. Need you."

"I need you too, baby."

He gasps, and whether it's at my words or the way I twist my hand over his cockhead, I don't know. But what I just said surprises even me, because it was more than the standard dirty talk. I'm pretty sure I *do* need him. In ways I never realized I needed anyone until right now.

The need to come overtakes me before I can worry too much about that, though. I pick up the pace of my thrusts and my strokes, working us both steadily toward a climax. Right before he comes, Brenden twists his neck, his mouth seeking mine. I kiss him as best as I can from the odd angle, swallowing his moan as he shoots over my hand and onto the sheets.

The way his ass tightens around my cock as he comes sends me over the edge right after him. He's still trembling in my arms, making me reluctant to let him go even though one of my hands is messy with his cum. I don't want to pull out of him either, but eventually I have to.

When he rolls over to look at me, he's got a beautiful, blissed out smile on his face. And I'm pretty sure if I looked in a mirror, I'd see the same thing reflected on mine.

"Shower with me?" he asks quietly, as if talking too loudly will ruin this perfect connection between us.

"Anything you want," I tell him. Because it's true. And because it's easier than saying the other thoughts going through my mind. *I love you. We should live together. I'll shower with you every day. Let me keep you forever.*

❀

YOU'LL HOPEFULLY never catch me participating in a yoga class on the town green. Or any yoga class. I'm all for exercise, but I'm not flexible, and yoga isn't my thing. It's not Brenden's thing either. I can say from recent experiences that he's pretty flexible, but he's also clumsy. Plus he hates exercise in general.

But Andrew Rowland—who lives over the yoga studio and takes classes regularly—convinced him to try it this morning. The weather's perfect for it, and May loved the idea. She even got her grandparents to do it with them. It didn't surprise me that Elise was willing to participate, but seeing Grant in workout clothes was interesting.

Thankfully, it's Saturday, and Brenden knew I needed to be at the diner for the breakfast shift, otherwise he might have asked me to join. And my dumb ass is so gone for him that if he asked, I probably would've agreed.

Can't say I minded watching the show through the windows though. Brenden twisting himself into poses and sticking his ass in the air, while wearing a pair of thin, tight, gray sweatpants, was a sight to see.

The class just finished, and my breakfast rush has died down, so I have time to run outside. As I jog across the street, it strikes me how Brenden and I haven't really been faking anything for Elise and Grant lately. This has all begun to feel natural. I'm going over there because I can't pass up the opportunity to see him, even if it's only for a few minutes, but I'd like to say hi to them too.

Brenden mentioned to me that it's weird how they're still here, but after the memorial for April last week, he's seemed much less on edge about having them around. Maybe bawling his eyes out released some of his anxiety.

"Hey!" he calls out, smiling big when he spots me approaching their little group. Although they all have a light sheen of sweat on their faces, they seem happy.

"Hi," I say. Ever since the memorial, too—or really, since that next morning of slow, intimate sex—I get the urge to tell him I love him every time I see him. But obviously, this isn't the right moment. I'll find it soon. "It looked like you guys didn't do too bad out here."

Standing behind May, Elise puts her hand on her granddaughter's shoulder. "This one had no trouble at all. I had to skip a couple poses, but it was fun."

I eye Brenden's body appreciatively and ask, "Think you're gonna be a yoga convert?" I don't want to be dragged to any classes, but I wouldn't object to seeing him in these pants more often.

He pulls a face. "Doubtful."

"Oh my gosh, did you see Dad fall over?" May asks gleefully.

"Hey! I did not fall over!" he counters indignantly. "I very gracefully decided to lie down for a moment, that's all."

Sarcastically, I tell him, "Yeah, that's exactly what it looked like." Because I *was* lucky enough to catch it.

His huff is cute, and I can't help but reach for him, tugging him in against my side. He glances around us before relaxing. There are still some people lingering with yoga mats, and others milling around the green, but it doesn't matter. I've let my guard down a lot when it comes to being with him.

I don't plan on engaging in any major PDA, obviously. But I find myself always wanting to touch him now, and since he seems to love it when I do, I'm not going to worry too much about what the nosy towns-people might think.

It feels natural to let my hand rest on his hip. Natural to chat with Elise and Grant while Brenden tips his head onto my shoulder.

And maybe it's crazy that it only took us a few weeks to get here. Or maybe this has been ten years in the making.

All I know is my life is suddenly looking much different than I ever expected it to, and I'm realizing I might not be such a loner after all. Turns out that having people around you isn't so bad, as long as they're the right people.

While May is saying something to her grandparents, I rub my thumb over the thin material of Brenden's sweatpants and tilt my head down to whisper in his ear. "I really like these pants on you."

"Oh yeah?" he whispers back, beaming.

"Mmhmm. Almost as much as I'll like you out of them."

He sucks in a breath, but before he can respond, Elise says, "What are you two whispering about over there?"

"Nothing," Brenden squeaks, managing to make the one word sound entirely guilty. I shake my head fondly.

"Secrets are no fun, Dad," May says with a teasing glint in her eyes.

He turns red, further giving us away, but I just laugh. Flirting with him is fun when he gets flustered so easily.

"We were just discussing the possibility of you guys all coming over to the diner to grab an early lunch," I say in an attempt to save him. Plus I wouldn't mind that.

"Yup, that's *totally* what we were saying," Brenden says, nodding like a bobblehead doll. I give his hip a squeeze and try to hold in my laughter this time.

There's a hint of a smile on Elise's face when she says, "We believe you, dear."

"We did have breakfast before we left the inn, though," Grant says, "so I'm not sure I could eat again so soon. But I'd be happy to sit and have a cup of coffee."

"Well, it sounds good to me," May chimes in. "I'm starving."

Brenden makes a face at her. "Hey, I made you breakfast! Don't act like I don't feed you."

"You 'made' cereal," she says with air quotes.

"But I cut up a banana in it!"

I can't resist giving him shit. "A *whole* banana?"

He sends me a sheepish look. "Well, I put half in each of our bowls."

"Okay, come on," I tell him, using my grip on his hip to turn him with me. "I'm going to make you eat something with vegetables."

"I want a burger," he says petulantly, dragging his feet. "And that comes with lettuce and tomato."

May snorts. "Which you usually pick out."

"And toss off your plate so they don't touch your fries," I add.

He gasps, then shouts, "Vicious lies! This is a deliberate character assassination. I could sue you both."

"How about a veggie omelet with bacon?" I offer.

"And ham," he barters.

"And ham," I relent.

With a one-shoulder shrug, he says, "I suppose I could eat that."

As we all head toward the diner, I squeeze him again, and he jumps away squealing and laughing.

"You're lucky to have a boyfriend who's such a good cook, aren't you?" Elise asks him.

"Sure am," he says easily, coming back to me and grasping my wrist between his fingers. The adoring smile he gives me has me tempted to break out into some kind of happy dance. But I don't, of course. I just smile back at him.

Then from behind me, I hear—"*Boyfriend?*"

My good mood instantly drains out of me and my stomach plummets into my ass. *Oh no. Fuck, no.* This can't be happening right now.

Yanking my hand away from Brenden, I turn around to face my dad. My no-longer-on-crutches-and-looking-very-horrified dad.

"Dad. What are you . . ." I shift my weight from one leg to the other as I fumble for what to say. "You didn't tell me you were coming home."

He looks good. Healthy. And I should be happy to see that, but instead I feel like the walls are closing in on me. And we're fucking outside. *Shit.*

The last time the sight of my dad scared me this much was when I was twelve and accidentally threw a baseball through our front window.

"I didn't want you to give me any crap," he says. "Like trying to check with my doctor to make sure he cleared me or something. Because he did."

"Great," I mutter. "Glad you're back on your feet."

For a minute that feels like an eternity, no one says anything. It's possible that my dad didn't actually hear what I think he heard, right? What I'm truly hoping he didn't fucking hear, because that would be very, very bad.

Then his eyebrows slowly creep up, and my hopes are shattered. "Looks like I missed a lot while I was gone." He cocks his head toward where Brenden is standing, slightly behind me. "Boyfriend, huh?"

"What? No!" I practically shout.

A loud buzzing fills my head, drowning out any rational thoughts. I still hear the tiny, wounded noise Brenden lets out, but I ignore the way it makes my heart hurt.

My mouth just keeps moving, nonsense words tumbling out in my attempt to salvage this situation and not have my dad looking at me in disgust. "We're not—He's not—This isn't what it looks like."

"No?" he questions.

"No. It's fake. It was all fake. We're not anything."

This time the noise Brenden makes is louder and even more pained, and someone else sucks in a sharp breath. And oh no. *No. Fuck! What did I just do?*

The look my dad's giving me now isn't disgust—but it's something strange I can't decipher. That buzzing has gotten louder in my head, still making it hard to think. The only thing I know is that I fucked up. I fucked up in so many ways.

How do I fix it? Tell my dad the truth? What is the truth? How did this get so complicated?

Before I can figure out what to do, Brenden takes off running across the green. And I continue to stand here like the world's biggest asshole.

I stand here, rooted to the spot, slowly realizing that I may have just made the biggest mistake of my life.

May steps in front of me, between me and my dad. She doesn't say anything, but her face screams of betrayal. It makes me feel like such a piece of shit that if lightning struck me down right now, I would think I deserved it. With a slow shake of her head, she turns and jogs off to catch up with her dad.

Then Elise and Grant are in front of me, looking confused and disappointed at the same time. When they walk away too, the full weight of what happened sinks in.

I ruined everything. I ruined me and Brenden, and I let May's grandparents know we've been lying this whole time, which could ruin his relationship with them. I was supposed to help him, not make things worse.

And my dad. How am I supposed to explain this to him? I have no clue if he believes the crap I said about everything being fake, but I don't think I have it in me to keep lying to him if he questions me.

I was going to tell him.

I was going to come out to him so I could be with Brenden. But I didn't expect him to show up like this. I panicked. And now . . .

This is all too much for me to handle.

Avoiding my dad's stare, I mumble, "I need to get back to work." And then I leave, like a coward, tail between my legs.

A few minutes ago, I was thinking about how right everything felt. How things were turning out better for me than I ever expected. But I messed it up so quickly. I should have known I'm not meant for that kind of happiness.

It's like I always thought. I'm the type of guy who's meant to be alone.

CHAPTER TWENTY-SEVEN

BRENDEN

I'm an idiot.

I'm such a pathetic fucking idiot.

I knew better. Knew Travis and I were only faking a relationship. And still, I let myself fall for him, let myself believe he actually had feelings for me too. But shit, can you blame me? He's so damn hot and wonderful and kind. I guess I already knew all that, but when he showed me his secret soft side . . . I was a fucking goner.

It truly felt like we were developing a real connection, something deeper than friendship. I didn't think we were just faking it anymore. But I'm an idiot.

No matter what, I never thought Travis would hurt me. And that's what he did.

He panicked. I get that. But even if his dad caught him off guard, and he didn't mean to hurt me, the end result is the same. It feels like he punched me right in the heart.

I can't breathe.

Although the fact that I just ran my ass all the way home is probably the culprit for that. Running is *not* something I do. Not physically, at least.

Fuck, I should have run away at the first hint of me catching feelings for him. I should've never gotten in this deep. The night that I cried, the night he held me until I fell asleep, and then held me in the morning while he fucked me so slowly . . .

I should've known I'd never be the same after that.

Foolishly, I let myself start picturing us together years from now. I pictured a life with him after May went off to college. A life where I wouldn't be alone.

And of course it was too good to be true. Everyone leaves me. How could I forget that?

I'm leaning against the wall in the foyer, still desperately trying to catch my breath, when May bursts through the door.

"Dad! What the heck?" She bends over, putting her hands on her knees and panting for a few moments before she straightens back up. "I didn't know you could run like that."

"Me neither." But when an animal is wounded, it will do anything necessary to get away.

She steps forward and wraps her arms around my waist, hugging me as she pulls me away from the wall. "I'm so sorry," she says softly, her cheek pressed to my chest.

"Nothing to be sorry for. I'm fine. Everything's all good."

I'm sure she doesn't buy my fake bravado, but she just squeezes me tighter and says, "I love you."

There's a framed picture hanging on the wall behind her. It's of the two of us, laughing and covered in paint after we bailed on a class at the art supply store because we were both so terrible at it.

I focus on how happy we look there as I fight to keep the tears at bay. "I know you do, kid. And I love you more than anything."

"I know," she says, releasing me after one more squeeze. "And Travis—"

"No."

"Dad."

"I don't wanna talk about it."

She frowns as she steps back. "I'm sure you don't. But Grandma and Grandpa were in the car right behind me, so you need to figure out what to say to them."

Fuckity fuck fuck fuck.

They know I've been lying to them about Travis this whole time.

Oh god, this is so humiliating. But this is what I get for coming up with the insane idea of pretending to have a boyfriend instead of telling them the truth in the first place.

All the insecurities I had when they first got here come rushing back at me. That they won't think I'm a good enough father to take care of May. That I'm a failure at everything.

I've almost worked myself up into a full-blown panic attack by the time Elise and Grant walk in. Rather than acknowledge them, I spin on my heels and hightail it to the kitchen. Mostly to delay facing them, but also because I really need some fucking coffee right now.

Naturally, they don't let me get away with this. They just follow me in there, with May a few steps behind them. Elise takes a seat at the table, but Grant remains standing in the middle of the room. I can sense his eyes on my back as I shake out the coffee grounds into a filter. After hitting the button on the machine, I stand there staring at the pot, waiting for it to brew.

No one says anything. The only sounds in the room are made by the drips of coffee hitting the glass pot. I don't even last a minute of this weird torture before I can't take it anymore and turn around to face the inquisition.

Grant crosses his arms over his chest and starts it off. "I'd like to know what's going on here, if you don't mind."

"Right." I nod. "Well. You see . . ." I trail off, my eyes flicking over to May as if she can save me. But she only gives me a sympathetic look from the seat she's taken beside her grandmother. Because I need to do this myself.

"We'd just like to understand, dear," Elise says kindly. Too kindly. I don't deserve kindness when I've screwed up so badly.

"Does anyone want coffee?" I blurt out. I grab my mug and fill it, then glance around at everyone watching me like I'm an act at the circus. A tightrope walker who fell off the tightrope.

Looking tired (of me, not physically), Grant says he'll have a cup. We both take a few moments adding cream and sugar before we sit down, and then I'm out of ways to stall this conversation. I can only hope that all the time we've spent together over the last few weeks, getting to know one another better, will have meant something, and keeps them from hating me too much.

"So I didn't intend to lie to you guys," I say to preface my confession. "But I lied. About Travis. Well, about me having a boyfriend." I look at Elise. "It just sort of came out when you called and were talking about how you wished I wasn't raising May alone. It was stupid, but then I didn't want to admit that I made it up, because that would've made me look bad. So I roped Travis into pretending to be in a relationship with me. It's not his fault, and I'm so sorry."

For a minute, nobody says anything. May nudges me with her foot under the table, and when I glance at her, she smiles at me encouragingly.

Then Grant says, "That's outrageous."

I wince. "Yes. I know. I'm sorry."

Elise reaches out, lightly tapping my arm. Though with how hard I have to fight not to wince again, you'd think she smacked me. "We just don't understand why you thought you needed to make up something like that."

"Because you said . . . I thought . . ." I wrap my hand firmly around my mug, letting the heat almost burn me. "I didn't want you to think I wasn't enough for May on my own."

"Oh, honey, no," she says, shaking her head. "That's not what I meant. Not at all." She shoots her husband a meaningful look, then turns her gaze back to me. "When I said I wish you didn't have to raise May alone, I

actually meant . . . Well, Grant and I mostly missed out on May's childhood, and we don't want to miss any more time with her. With the both
of you. So we've been discussing a move."

"A move?" May asks.

She nods. "We planned to use this trip to look for a house somewhere
near the two of you. I don't think this town is the best fit for us, but one of
the surrounding towns would be nice. So we'd only be a short drive away."

Holy shit.

"You want to move here?" I say dumbly.

"We do," Grant confirms.

"So you don't think I'm a bad father?"

May leans over to pull me into a side hug. "Are you kidding? How
could anyone think that? You're the best freaking dad."

"We think you've done a wonderful job here," Elise says. "Really. I
didn't mean to imply that you *couldn't* do it alone, only that you don't need
to, because you have us. And we want to be a real part of your lives from
now on."

"I don't understand."

"Dad."

"Sorry. No. I mean . . ." I take a giant gulp of my coffee to buy myself a
few seconds. I'm having a hard time processing what they're saying. This
past hour has been a lot. First Travis, and now whatever this is.

They want to *move* here?

Elise reaches out to touch my arm again, this time her fingers lingering
a bit longer. "We hope you won't mind. We're not trying to get in your way
or take over anything. But the two of you are pretty much the only family
we have left."

"Family?" I repeat like it's a foreign word.

"Well, yes," she says as if it's obvious.

"I didn't know."

She tilts her head, giving me a puzzled look. "Didn't know what?"

Okayyy. This is awkward.

I bite the inside of my cheek. How do I tell her that I never considered them my family because I didn't think they thought of me that way?

But they do. It sounds like maybe they've thought of me that way all this time.

Woah. Travis was right. He told me I wasn't giving them a chance. That it was only my anxiety making me think they hated me.

For a second, a warm feeling rises inside of me. But it crashes back down when I think about Travis again.

Elise and Grant are right here, sitting in front of me and telling me we're family. Letting me know they care. That they want to be here. Permanently. They want to stay and spend time with May *and* me. And I should be happy about this. I think I *am* happy.

Yet it still feels like there's a giant, gaping hole in my heart. A place Travis methodically carved out of me to make room for himself in there. And I let him do it. Because I believed he was going to stay and fill it.

But now he's gone.

It was all fake. We're not anything.

It only took seven words to destroy the relationship it took us over ten years to build.

After he gave me a perfect glimpse of what it's like to have everything with him, I don't know if I can go back to only a friendship. And I don't even know if he wants that. He didn't say we were friends. He said *we're not anything.*

"Brenden, are you okay?" Elise asks gently.

No, I am totally not okay. Rather than say that, though, I take a moment to look at her. Really look at her. I've known her and Grant for over thirty years. They've been in my life now longer than my own parents were—which is a terribly painful fact I can't bear to think about right now.

When I was young, they were just my best friend's parents. April didn't get along with them too well, and since I only really saw them through her eyes, I figured that was their fault. And maybe it was or maybe it wasn't, but that doesn't really matter anymore, does it?

We all lost April. But they're still here, and I'm still here. And I'm a grown ass adult. It's time for me to stop being intimidated by them. To stop feeling like I'm going to get in trouble. They haven't done anything to hurt me. May and I don't see them often, but they've still been there for us. They loaned me money when I needed it, and they check in on us. Just because we don't have a lot in common doesn't mean we can't have a good relationship.

Elise, who wears cashmere sweaters that are probably more expensive than my electric bill, is sitting here in yoga pants and a baggy T-shirt, because she was more than happy to try yoga in the middle of the town green when May asked her to. And while Grant looks slightly more uncomfortable in his workout clothes, he did it too.

They've been trying, and I'm the only one who hasn't been. If I want to be closer to them, maybe all I need to do is put in the effort.

And it sounds like I'm going to get the chance, if they'll be living here soon. It's strange how I don't actually hate that thought. Guess we've already made some progress.

When I glance at May, she's watching me closely, her eyes cautious but hopeful. She wants this. She must be thrilled at the idea of her grandparents moving here, but I suspect she's holding back her reaction for my benefit. Because she's worried about how *I* feel.

I give her a reassuring smile before I turn back to Elise and Grant. "I think having the two of you closer would be great."

For once, I'm not lying to them.

At my words, May squeals and jumps out of her seat, a huge grin taking over her face. First, she hugs me, whispering in my ear how much she loves me, then she hugs each of her grandparents. Everyone's smiling now.

And damn, I wish Travis were here to see this. I think he'd be happy for me. Probably even proud of me. But he's not here, which again puts a huge damper on my mood. A sad sigh slips out before I can stop it.

Elise catches it and frowns. "I'm so glad you won't mind us being here," she tells me. "But honestly, Brenden, I'm still confused about what happened with Travis."

I turn my gaze out the window. The flowers on the magnolia tree have wilted. "I told you," I say, unable to look at her. "It was all fake."

Grant clears his throat, forcing my attention. "So you mean the two of you were never dating? At all?"

"Nope." Despite what I thought was happening, none of it was real.

Both Grant and Elise still look like they don't get it, and I don't know what's so confusing here. I mean, sure, it's confusing for *me*. But it shouldn't be for them.

"But we thought . . ." Grant says.

"I realize how messed up it was to lie to you," I offer, desperately wishing we could stop going over this. It doesn't matter what they thought. It doesn't matter what *I* thought.

All I want to do right now is hide in my room under the covers. And maybe learn sorcery, so I can cast a spell that makes me forget how phenomenal it felt kissing Travis fucking Reed.

Damn it. Every time I get in my bed at night, I'm going to be reminded of what we did there. Maybe tomorrow I should go shopping for a new bed. That's completely rational, right?

"We're not mad," Elise says. And the look she gives me is full of pity, which almost makes me wish they *were* mad instead. "What he's trying to say is that we don't understand how that could have all been fake, because . . ." As she trails off, she averts her eyes down to the table. "Well, because we saw you on the couch that day. And also, we, um, *heard* you two. You know. At night."

Oh, god.

I'm not sure which of us turns more red. "Oh. Okay. Yeah, I'm sorry about that. We just, uh . . ."

While I struggle to come up with a polite way to explain that Travis and I were only hooking up because it was fun and convenient or whatever, May's got her lips pressed tightly together and she's shaking, obviously holding in her laughter. I can't believe she's hearing this. My sex life isn't something I discuss with her. Though she's clearly not too shocked by it.

I shoot her what I hope comes across as a stern parental look. A look that says, *This is none of your business, and don't you dare laugh at me.* Unfortunately, this doesn't work, and in fact, it seems to have the opposite effect. The barely contained laughter escapes her in a short, loud burst that makes Elise jump.

"Oh no, I'm so sorry," Elise says. "We shouldn't have said anything. But I could see how hurt you were at what Travis said today, and it just seems clear to me that he must not have meant it."

"He said it," I reiterate with more than a tinge of bitterness. "I can only assume he meant it."

"No," Grant says firmly. He curls his hand over the top of his coffee mug and shakes his head. "I know we only recently met that man, but I could see it plain as day from the beginning."

"See what?" I ask.

"How strong his feelings are. I'm pretty damn sure he loves you."

I open my mouth to disagree, then close it. My desire to believe he's right overrides my rational thinking for a moment. But no. That can't be true. If Travis loved me, he would've told me. He wouldn't have disregarded me so easily. Like I was nothing. Just leftover food on a plate to be scaped into the diner's garbage.

"If you guys don't mind," I say, avoiding eye contact with everyone as I stand, "I'd prefer not to talk about this anymore. I appreciate you not being upset with me. But whatever Travis and I were doing, it's done now."

Without waiting for any responses, I walk out of the kitchen and head up to my room. I'll let myself wallow today. Listen to Adele, maybe eat a gallon of ice cream. But tomorrow, I need to start finding a way to move on.

CHAPTER TWENTY-EIGHT

TRAVIS

E xcuse me, could I please have some extra napkins?"

I fight not to roll my eyes as I stalk over to the counter to grab a stack for the woman who asked. When I toss them on her table, a couple flutter to the floor, but I don't pick them up.

People are being extra annoying today. They've been extra annoying all week, actually.

Mina and Arnold, a retired couple, are sitting at a corner table and can't make up their mind on what to order. They've already been there for fifteen fucking minutes with the menus open in front of them. When I glance over yet again to see if they're ready, the old man points at his coffee mug in a silent request for a refill. *Jesus Christ.*

Some coffee splashes over the edge of the mug when I pour it. "Know what you want yet?"

"Oh, I'm sorry, no," Mina says. "We're not quite ready."

This time I do roll my eyes. "You've been coming here for years. The menu hasn't changed."

She looks taken aback, but I turn and walk off. I slam the coffee pot onto the burner a little harder than necessary, then survey the diner. I hate everyone here.

Okay, maybe that's not true.

Maybe I'm just really fucking sick of this life.

I could sell the diner and go back to Boston, get a job behind a computer so I wouldn't have to talk to anyone. Even as I think this, though, I know it's not what I want.

I almost had what I wanted, but then I lost it.

That's the truth of why I'm in such a shitty mood. I'm being a miserable asshole to everyone because I fucking miss Brenden. It hasn't even been a week, and all I want to do is go crawling to him on my knees and beg him to forgive me. But I can't. He deserves so much better than someone who refuses to claim him in public.

What makes things worse is that I don't know if my lame attempt to save face in front of my dad even worked. We haven't really talked much since he's been back—mostly because I'm avoiding him—but it feels like he didn't believe me when I told him that me and Brenden were nothing.

Fuck. I can't believe I said that. What is wrong with me? I'm a grown ass man, and I acted like a scared teenager.

Yeah, Brenden definitely deserves better.

After a busy lunch rush where I snap at so many people that I almost start to feel bad, I'm behind the counter restocking, when the bell on the door chimes. Looking up, I see May's unmistakable purple hair, and an immense wave of guilt crashes over me. I grip the counter, resisting the urge to bolt into the back.

Because I broke my promise to her. I hurt her dad.

She has her backpack over her shoulders and a frighteningly determined look on her face as she marches over to me.

"I'm sorry," I blurt out nervously. "I know how badly I messed up, and I understand if the two of you never want to see me again. I'll leave Brenden alone. I'll—"

"How *dare* you," she cuts me off sharply. "You think I want you to leave him *alone*?"

Now I'm confused. "Well, don't you?"

She gives me a look like I'm being dense. "I want my dad to be happy, you dumbass."

I'm taken aback, because I don't think I've ever heard her swear. Certainly never at me. "I want him to be happy too. That's why I'll stay away. He probably hates me."

"Are you serious? He doesn't hate you."

"But I—"

Rolling her eyes, she cuts me off again. "You acted like a jackass. Yes, I know. But that didn't change how he feels about you."

I glance around the diner at the remaining customers, cataloguing who's here to witness me getting told off by a thirteen-year-old. The old couple I was a dick to earlier is still here, no surprise. They're staring into their empty coffee mugs, pretending not to listen, but I'm sure they've caught every word.

Returning my focus to May, I tell her truthfully, "I don't understand what you want me to do. Your dad and I didn't exactly discuss what was going on with us. I thought I'd made it clear how I felt about him, but . . ."

"But you're not the best at communicating," she fills in for me. "And Dad can be a ball of anxiety. I think he doubts his own worth sometimes." Her face softens as she tucks a strand of hair behind her ear. "You make him happy though. He's always smiling, even if he's not always happy. But when he's around you, his smiles are different. It's like he lights up inside whenever you look at him."

A little ball of hope begins forming in my chest. That's what happens to me whenever Brenden looks at me. And I want to be that for him too. I want to be the one who makes him the happiest, who gets to see his most genuine smiles.

But I still think he could do better than me.

"Okay, so here's what we're gonna do." May slaps both hands on the counter and fixes me with a very intense stare. "Remember that fake story I told my grandparents about how you and my dad got together?"

How could I forget? She said she basically tricked me into asking him out by telling me she was going to find someone else to do it.

"Well, consider this another version of that, only for real this time," she says. "I know you love him. I'm pretty sure you've loved him for years, even if you didn't realize it."

"I—"

She holds up a small hand to silence me. Which is more intimidating than it has any right to be, but probably also for the best, since I have no idea what I was going to say. "It's time for you to pull your head out of your ass. Excuse my language."

That almost makes me laugh, because she's been swearing since she walked in here.

"If you can be brave enough to really be what he needs, then I'll help you get him back."

"What?" I ask dumbly.

The look she gives me has me thinking I should keep any sharp objects out of her reach. "But if you're not ready, if you can't do it . . . then I promise I'm going to make sure he gets over you. I'll find him someone else who will love him like he deserves."

Just like that, the tiny ball of hope she gave me evaporates. The thought of Brenden with someone else makes me sick. I might not think I'm good enough for him, but apparently, I'm selfish enough not to want him with anyone else.

"I . . . I don't know," I tell her, though I'm not even sure what I mean by that. Because I *do* know what I want.

I want Brenden. I want me and him, together, every day. I want to love him, and take care of him, and listen to him babble about drag queen competitions on TV, and fuck him so well that he whimpers and trembles for me.

But I don't know if I should go for it. Don't know if he'll forgive me. I don't know how to make the right choice.

"Hurry up and decide," May says. "I won't wait much longer."

With that, she spins around and walks out, leaving me standing here dumbfounded. And *shit.* I might not know what the correct choice is, but she's right. I need to do *something.*

I START WITH my dad. Because regardless of what I decide about Brenden, my dad should know the truth about me. It's way past time.

I think he knows I've been avoiding him, because when I show up on his front step and knock on his door, he looks surprised as he opens it. It might be strange that I knock on the door of my childhood home instead of using my key to let myself in, but we don't have that kind of relationship. And I'm not sure who's fault that is anymore. Probably mine.

"Hey," I say. "Are you busy?"

He shakes his head. "Nah, just double-checking the books from when I was gone. Marty isn't the most organized, but it looks like he did a good job."

"Can I come in?"

When he steps aside for me, I walk past him and into the living room. It's cleaner than it usually is, probably because he wasn't living here for the last month. But there is a thick ledger spread open on the coffee table with a bottle of beer and bag of chips beside it.

I take a seat on the couch, and he plops down in his recliner. The silence stretches between us while I figure out how to start. Maybe I should have figured that out before I came, but honestly, once I got up the nerve to do this, I just needed to get over here before I lost it.

"I need to tell you something," I say uneasily, scratching my jaw.

"Uh huh," he says, already sounding unhappy. "And I'm guessing this has something to do with whatever shit was going on with you and Brenden and his family the other day, right?"

That catches me off guard, even if it shouldn't, and anything else I might have said next flies out of my head.

Grabbing his beer off the table, he takes a long pull from the bottle, eyeing me critically the entire time. My skin feels clammy, like I'm coming down with something. Except I know that's not what it is. It's just me being a chicken, cowering under my dad's stare.

This man raised me. Practically on his own. I know he loves me, just like I love him. Even if neither of us says it too often. There's no good reason I should be so afraid of telling him I'm gay. I may have my reasons, yeah, but they're not good enough. Not anymore.

Do I really think he'll stop loving me when he finds out?

I'm honestly not sure. But I do know that if he does, then that's on him, not me. I can't let how *he* feels stop me from living my life the way I want to.

All these years, I wasn't interested in dating, so I didn't think it mattered if I was out. Now things are different though. Because now there's Brenden. Now there's someone I want to be with. Not just in private, but in public too, without having to hide. And if there's any chance that he might still want to be with me too after I screwed everything up so badly, then I need to do this.

So I sit up straighter and meet my dad's stare head-on. "It does have something to do with Brenden. But it's also about me."

"Okay."

I take a deep breath. Here goes . . . something. "I'm gay."

"Right," he says shortly.

That makes me pause, because what the hell? Was that supposed to be sarcasm? Does he think I'm playing a freaking joke on him?

"Uh." I quickly gather myself again. I don't want to back out of this. I need to make him understand me. "So when I told you there was nothing going on with me and Brenden, that was a lie. The truth is, there *was* something going on. It's kind of complicated, because at first, I was only doing him a favor. We were pretending to be in a relationship for May's grandparents because he thought . . ." Shaking my head, I try to keep this simple. "Well, it doesn't matter why he wanted to do that. The thing I need you to know is that it turned into something more."

"Okay," he says again, taking another sip of his beer.

"I have feelings for him," I admit. And as soon as I say those words out loud, I feel lighter. So I keep going, putting it all out there, ignoring the inscrutable way my dad's looking at me. "I want to be with him. If he wants that too. Honestly, I don't know if he does anymore, because I really fucked up."

I pause for a second, realizing I don't actually know if Brenden ever wanted to be with me at all. I thought we were on the same page, but . . .

"But either way, you should know this about me," I continue, dealing with one issue at a time. "I'm gay, and I want to be with a man. With Brenden."

"Okay," my dad says yet again.

Growing frustrated, I ask sharply, "Is that all you're going to say to me?"

He frowns, setting his bottle between his thighs. "Well, no. I was waiting for you to finish what you wanted to tell me."

"I'm gay!" I practically shout at him. I shouldn't have to keep repeating myself. "That's what I'm telling you. It's a simple concept to understand."

"Okay . . ." he says, and when I open my mouth to shout again, he holds up his hands. "But I thought you were going to tell me more about you and Brenden."

My anger deflates, replaced by confusion. "Don't you understand what I'm saying? We were . . . with each other."

He snorts out a laugh. "Yup, got that. I know I haven't been in a relationship in just short of forever, but I remember how they work. So I'm not sure why you keep trying to explain it to me like I'm a kindergartener."

I'm all jumbled up now. It's like we're speaking two different languages and something's gotten lost in translation. "Uh. I thought you'd . . . have questions." At the very least.

"Look, what kind of questions do you expect me to have?" He grimaces. "I don't need to know about who sticks what where."

I grip the edge of the couch cushion, grounding myself. That was crude, but he doesn't sound as disgusted as I feared he might be. "You're not upset?"

"That you didn't tell me you were dating Brenden before I came home? We don't talk about feelings much, so whatever. If you wanted to wait to do it in person, that's fine. I'm just confused why you acted so strange the other day and lied about it."

This conversation isn't making any sense. I should be relieved that he's not going on some kind of gross, homophobic rant. And I am. But how does he not understand why I lied? How is he not more shocked about this?

He squints his eyes, scrutinizing me, then shakes his head. "Wait a minute. Did you just come out to me?"

"Well." *What the fuck?* "Yeah."

Is he so in shock that it's taken him this long to process that?

Suddenly, he starts laughing. Deep, belly laughs. I flinch at the outburst, and my legs itch to stand up and bolt. *Here it comes.* I don't need to take this.

As his laughter dies down, he looks at me and frowns. "Ah, crap. I'm sorry. Didn't mean to laugh. But was I not supposed to know you were gay?"

What. The. Fuck.

"Um. No?"

"You lived with your boyfriend in Boston, didn't you?"

Okay, I don't know which way is up anymore. He *knew* Christian was my boyfriend? I never told him, and I assumed he was clueless about it. I assumed that *he* assumed I was straight.

With a long sigh, he gets out of his chair, sets his beer on the coffee table, and comes over to sit beside me, looking serious now. "I think I ruined your big coming out moment, huh? But I swear, I didn't know that's what this was. I only thought you were trying to tell me that you finally got your head out of your ass and realized you were tired of being alone."

"That's . . . Yeah, that's part of what I was saying, I guess. But how did you know I was gay?"

Slapping me roughly on the back, he says, "I'm your fucking dad, aren't I? Jeez." Like it's that fucking simple.

I just sit here stunned.

He knew this whole time?

And he's acting like it's not a big deal to him.

I didn't entirely expect him to react awfully, but the fear was still there. So for him to have no problem with me being gay, but to also not even be surprised by it . . . I wasn't at all prepared for this.

Now I'm mentally recalibrating everything I thought I knew about my dad and my relationship with him.

"I don't understand," I finally say. Because I really fucking don't. "You've always hounded me about when I'm gonna settle down and get married."

"Yeah. So?" He gives me a few more quick pats on the back before he gets up and goes back to his chair. "Forgive me if I didn't want you to spend most of your life alone like me. You're a good guy. You'd do anything for people you care about, and you'd make a great husband. I think you deserve to have someone who'd do anything for you too. I never said it had to be a woman."

Well, fucking hell. I guess he didn't. I just assumed that was what he pictured for me when he mentioned marriage. Have I been under-estimating this man my whole damn life?

As I stare at him, I try to come to grips with this reality. One where my dad is completely accepting, just wants me to be happy, and doesn't care if I marry a guy. I want to believe it, but something is still nagging at me, making me doubt it.

And while I never intended to bring this up with him, I think I have to. Averting my gaze, I scratch at some gunk on my jeans, probably a bit of food I dropped on myself at the diner. "But uh, when I was younger, you used to say things. Pretty shitty things."

"What the heck are you talking about?"

I still can't look at him when I explain. "I used to watch sports with you. I only stopped because when you got mad, you'd yell slurs at the TV. Homophobic slurs. So I assumed you didn't like queer people. Or at least, you wouldn't want your son to be one."

The silence that follows my words feels as loud as a million people screaming in my ears. The couch becomes fascinating to me as I stare at it. It's old as hell, the cushions marred with stains and rips from my childhood. Why hasn't he ever gotten a new one?

My stomach ties itself in knots while I wait for him to say something. But he doesn't. Finally, I risk looking up at him.

His eyes are pained and—*Is he tearing up?*

He rakes his fingers through the graying hair at his temples before dropping his head into his hands. And all I can do is watch as his body shakes and I hear him choke back a sob. When he looks up again, he swipes harshly at his wet eyes, then holds my stare.

"Fuck, Travis, I'm so goddamn sorry. If that's how you thought of me . . . that's what you assumed I thought of *you*, my own kid . . ."

He shakes his head. "I had no idea. I don't even remember that. But it kills me that my words affected you that way. I don't wanna make excuses for myself. I just need you to know that whatever stupid shit I said was just that. Stupid shit. Guys like me talked that way all the time back then. And that doesn't make it okay, but I'd like to think I've changed with the times, and I swear I'd never use any slurs like that now."

"I mean, yeah, I haven't heard you say anything like that in a very long time," I tell him. "Maybe I should've brought it up so much sooner and not held on to it for all these years."

"No, don't blame yourself," he says, leaning forward in his chair. "I'm just sorry I ever made you question how I felt about you. You're my fucking son, and I love you. I don't give a crap if you're straight, gay, bi, or any other letters of the goddamn rainbow. People should be able to love whoever they love without being judged for it. I've never felt any differently, but I regret that my actions didn't make that clear."

His eyes are watering again, and I'm pretty sure I've never seen my dad cry. He hasn't seen me cry since I was a little kid either. Hell, I don't even know the last time I cried. But alarmingly, I'm starting to do it now.

Because my dad just told me he loved me.

While it's not the first time, it *is* the first time I've heard him say it after knowing that he fully understands who I am. Maybe if either of us were any better at communicating, it wouldn't have taken us this much time to get here.

I swipe at my eyes the same way he did, as if the tears offend me.

It kills me to think my relationship with him could've been different all this time if only we'd been more open with each other sooner. We still have more time though. This conversation doesn't have to be the last time we're honest with each other.

But as long as we're being honest right now—

"I love you too, Dad."

"You want a beer?" he asks, standing abruptly.

I laugh. "Sure."

When he comes back with a bottle for me and a new one for himself, he turns on the TV, but we don't really watch it. We just talk. About random stuff, nothing important.

It occurs to me that this could be a good time to address his habit of using gender stereotypical language, and how that can also be harmful, even if he doesn't realize it. But honestly, I'd rather deal with that issue another day. Right now, I'm enjoying that the two of us can still be like this, how we've always been with each other.

Only it's even better somehow, now that everything's out in the open.

He surprises me when he smirks and says, "So Brenden, huh?"

My face heats. "Yeah, but I fucked it up."

"But you love him?" he questions.

"Yeah. I do."

He takes a pull from his beer, then asks, "Did you tell him?" And I don't even have to answer. After a few seconds of my silence, he huffs. "Dumbass."

For a moment, I gape at him, but then I can't help chuckling. Because he's not wrong. And also, it's so strange that I'm sitting here talking to my dad about a guy I love. Strange, but not bad.

It feels like there's so much more I could tell him. About me. About me and Brenden and how I could see myself spending the rest of my life with him. I might not be great at talking about this kind of stuff, but being with Brenden has helped me become better at it.

Truthfully, I think just *knowing* him has made me better in a bunch of different ways. And damn. That's one of the many reasons I need him back in my life, isn't it?

As I sit here, drinking a beer with my dad, I realize I have my answer for May.

I'm ready to be the man Brenden Sanderson deserves.

And I'll do whatever it takes to prove it to him.

CHAPTER TWENTY-NINE

BRENDEN

L ook, I know you sign my paychecks, but could you please take your sad, pathetic face out of my kitchen? You're distracting me and scaring the new guys."

It takes me a second to realize Addison is talking to me. And another second to process what she just said. I glance around to find her staring at me, while her new hires are standing at one of the prep tables, awkwardly *not* looking at me as they're chopping or mixing or seasoning, or whatever it is they're supposed to be doing.

Oh.

I'm not sure how long I've been sitting on this metal stool in the corner, but the coffee in my mug is cold. This is what I've been like for the past week. Sad and pathetic. Missing Travis.

Not only missing what I thought we could have, but also missing the decade-long friendship that came first. That might be what hurts the worst. The fact that I can't even talk to him, see him. And in a town this small, avoiding someone is also pretty freaking difficult.

So maybe I've been spending more time at the inn than I need to. I didn't think anyone had noticed though.

"I'm just taking a break," I tell Addison lamely.

"Sure you are." Crossing the kitchen, she studies me critically, like she's trying to find what's wrong with me. But all the wounds are internal. "You want something to eat?" she asks finally.

"No," I respond reflexively. Then I realize that I'm actually hungry, so I amend that to, "Wait, yeah. Thanks."

She gives me one more searching look before going to the large fridge and pulling out a few things. She sets them down on the end of the table where the prep guys are working, then says to them, "Hey, why don't you two go get some air."

They both give her quizzical looks, and she scowls.

"Take a hint. Scram."

I almost laugh as they drop their knives and make a hasty escape out the swinging door.

If I had it in me, I'd suggest being nicer to the employees, but whatever.

Addison carefully sweeps some stuff aside and begins whipping something together for me. I don't bother asking what it is.

"All right, what's going on with you and Travis?" she asks, not looking up at me.

"Nothing," I lie. Or maybe it's not a lie. There *is* nothing going on with us. Not anymore.

This time she does look at me, and her face makes it clear she doesn't believe me. "There must be something going on, because I'm pretty sure I've fed you every one of your meals this week."

"Not *every* one," I hedge.

She gives me a flat look. "Pretty damn close. So tell me why you haven't been eating at the diner, and why Travis hasn't been showing up here to fix things without being asked, and why you're moping around like there's a storm cloud hanging over your head."

Wow. I'm surprised she's even paid that much attention to me. It almost sounds like she cares.

Does this make us officially friends? The thought cheers me up, but only momentarily.

I gaze into my mug, wishing my coffee was still hot, but too lazy to get up and pour myself another one. "It's complicated."

Snorting a laugh, Addison says, "Honey, your whole life seems complicated."

"No, it's not!" I argue. But when I consider how things have been lately, I guess that's fair. "Fine. If you really want to know, the short version is that Travis and I had started . . . something. Something I thought meant the same thing to him as it did to me. But then he basically said it meant nothing to him."

"Somehow I don't believe that." Walking over to me, she holds out a fancy looking sandwich. "I've seen the way that man looks at you."

My heart does a little flutter. "How does he look at me?"

"Like you personally put the damn sunshine in his sky. It's a bit nauseating."

Well. That makes my stomach flutter some more, but even if it were true, it doesn't change the fact that he still doesn't want his dad to know he's queer. Or the fact that he was so quick to cast me aside, throw me under the bus with Elise and Grant. Luckily, I was able to work things out with them, but that was shitty.

Maybe he did feel something for me too.

But it wasn't enough, was it?

I pick at the sandwich while I try to think of something to say. I'm pretty sure whatever bread she used here is homemade, and it's probably delicious. But honestly, I could be eating cardboard for all I care. I can't enjoy anything.

I might have put the sun in Travis's sky, but then he let it burn out.

Addison leaves me be, dropping the conversation as she gets back to work. I can still feel her watching me though, so I make sure to take a few big bites of food so she can stop worrying about me.

Then my phone vibrates on the table, making me jump. Which is dumb, because I get work calls on my personal line all the time. I'm really off my game.

It's not a work call though. And when I see May's name on the screen, I hurry to accept it. She normally sticks with text messaging when I'm at work.

"Hello? Are you okay?"

"Yes, I'm fine," she replies quickly. "But Dad, it's Grandpa. We're on the green, and I need you to come."

That immediately activates my panic mode. I spring off my stool, sandwich forgotten as I rush to my office for my keys. "What happened? Did you call 911?"

"No, yeah, it's okay. Just come."

Running outside, I tell her, "I'm coming!"

"Thank you," she says. And then she freaking hangs up on me.

Oh my god, why would she do that? I still don't know what's going on, and I want to call her back, but I also just want to get to her as quickly as possible, so I focus on driving. I debate if I should be heading straight to the hospital, but I'll have to pass through the center of town to get to the highway anyway.

Fuck. Things were finally good between me and her grandparents. They said we were a family.

I don't want to lose Grant now.

I'm scared.

I'm scared, and my mind is screaming at me to call Travis. Because Travis will help. He's good in a crisis, and he's good at calming me down. He'll make sure everything's okay, I know he will.

So I call him as I drive. I don't care if it's weird or pathetic. I don't have time to feel awkward about it. This is an emergency.

Except.

He doesn't pick up.

It rings and rings, and then it goes to his very brief, surly voicemail.

I hang up, tossing my phone aside. It lands on the passenger seat, then slides to the floor. I can't believe he didn't answer for me.

That fucking hurts. But I push the pain down and keep driving. I'm going way over the speed limit, but there's only like three cops in this town.

When I get near the green, I park on the side of the road and hop out of the car, not caring that my bumper is sticking out too far. As I run, my eyes are scanning the area for May and her grandparents. Damn it, there are so many people out here. Does nobody have anything better to do today?

I see Andrew. He kind of stands out with all his tattoos and his gauged ears. He's with his friend Toby, but I don't have time to wave to them.

"Dad!" May calls out, and I spot her right in front of the gazebo with Elise and Grant.

"What is it? What's wrong?" I ask as I reach them. I visually scan Grant, but he seems perfectly fine.

"Nothing," May says.

I turn to her, my eyes narrowing. "*Nothing?* What the hell?"

She bites her lip, looking sheepish, then says, "Well, actually, there is something wrong."

"What is it?"

"You've been sad," she states matter-of-factly. And before I can argue, she holds up her hands. "You're allowed to be sad, but I'd rather see you happy. And I'm not the only one. I think everyone in town would rather see you happy, so . . ."

"So?" I prompt, my fear slowly morphing into annoyance. Yes, I haven't been doing a very good job at hiding how I'm feeling. But does she really need to bring this up in public?

"So just stand here," she says.

"What? Why?"

Grabbing me by the shoulders, she turns me so I'm facing away from the gazebo. "Please, you'll see. Stay there."

As she walks backward a few steps, joining a handful of people standing off to the side of the pathway, I do what she instructs and stay where I am. Only because I'm too confused to move. I give Grant and Elise a questioning look, hoping they'll explain what's going on. But they only smile and walk away to sit on one of the benches.

I'm really getting frustrated now. Just last Saturday, I was standing out here when I got my heart broken, so believe me, I'd rather be anywhere else.

All of a sudden, loud music starts playing from somewhere.

It only takes a few seconds for me to recognize "This Is What Love Is." My favorite Skyler James song off his newest album.

Then something weird happens.

It starts with May and the people she's standing with. They're dancing to the music. And that wouldn't be entirely weird, except they're all moving in sync with each other. Like they choreographed it.

That's when Andrew and Toby cross from the other side of the grass to join them. Now a group of people are coming up the pathway toward me, all of them grinning as they move to the beat of the music.

And oh. My. God. It's a freaking flash mob.

Before I know it, I'm surrounded by people dancing as Skyler James sings the opening lines.

Spent too long waiting for the right time
Thinking we needed permission
For a love that's just yours and mine

Holy shit, I can't believe this is happening. Did May do this for me?

It's impossible not to smile as I watch everyone. There's Roddy from the bar. And Sal the mailman, whose dancing skills are unexpectedly good. There's a bunch of my employees from the inn who weren't working this afternoon. The sheriff, out of uniform. All of May's friends. Cheryl and Mark, the owners of the art supply store. A couple yoga instructors. Colleen. Angy, who owns the bakery. And so many more people.

It looks like half the town is here. For me.

Or maybe they're only doing this because so many people in town love a spectacle. But it feels like it's for me.

The only way this could be better is if Colleen were holding a cinnamon roll.

Suddenly, the crowd breaks into two, each group moving past me now, still dancing. As I turn around to keep watching them, I see something even more unbelievable than this flash mob.

Travis.

There he is, walking up the steps on the other side of the gazebo. He's holding a speaker in one hand and a microphone in the other. And as I gaze up at him, he raises the microphone and sings, his voice ringing out over Skyler's.

This is what love is
So baby, embrace it
This is what love is
We won't let them take it away

Wow. He's a really bad singer.

And this is fucking amazing.

It doesn't seem real. It's like I'm having an out-of-body experience. Or maybe I crashed on the way here and hit my head, and none of this is actually happening at all.

But no. If I were imagining it, Travis wouldn't sound like a frog with laryngitis.

My heart is racing, and I'm smiling so hard my cheeks hurt. Travis keeps singing to me as everyone else dances all around the gazebo. I'm not paying attention to the dancers anymore though. I can't take my eyes off the man I fucking love.

Oh shit.

I *love* him. I really do.

He looks so out of place up there, in the center of all this chaos. But he's smiling back at me as he sings, and kind of laughing at himself too. And even though he's wearing his typical flannel and jeans outfit, like I've seen him in a million times, I swear he's never looked so fucking hot.

The dancers slow to a stop as the song ends.

Then without all the music and singing and dancing, the awkwardness quickly sets in. Everyone's staring at me now. I mean, they were staring before, but they were the ones making fools of themselves, so I wasn't embarrassed.

I'm not sure what's supposed to happen now. All those videos of flash mobs you see on social media cut off right when the song ends.

Travis is still standing in the middle of the gazebo, so I focus on him. He smiles and gives me a tiny shrug. Like he didn't just blow my mind. Then he raises the microphone again and speaks into it, his eyes locked on me. "Brenden, I know I messed up. So this is me saying I'm sorry. And I miss you. And I hope I can make things right."

Oh my god, oh my god, ohmygod.

"I have a lot more I'd like to say," he goes on, while I struggle with remembering how to breathe. "Though I hope you'll come up here and talk to me without this microphone, because I feel ridiculous. But if you want me to keep going for everyone to hear, I will."

He raises his eyebrows in question, holding out a hand toward me. I want to go to him, but my feet won't work. I might be a little bit in shock from everything that just happened.

Then May is behind me, shoving me. I turn my head to give her a dirty look as I stumble forward. But once my feet are moving, it's like there's nowhere else they can go except right to Travis.

Right where I belong.

My heart is beating wildly in my chest as I make my way up the gazebo steps. *Is this real life?*

Travis sets down the speaker and microphone and takes my hand. Now we're standing up here together, with half the town watching us. Some people start murmuring quietly, but I can't make out what anyone's saying. And I don't care.

In this moment, no one exists to me but this incredible man. This man who hates participating in crazy town things, yet organized the most ridiculous, crazy town thing for me as an apology. I would have taken a simple, *I'm sorry*, but this was way better.

This showed me how much he cares about me. I think he's always shown me that, actually, in his small, everyday gestures.

But damn. Today he showed *everyone.*

He lifts our joined hands and presses them to my chest. "So I know you weren't entirely serious when you said you wanted a flash mob, but I hope you liked it."

"Are you kidding?" I can't stop grinning. "This was awesome! I loved it!"

For a second, he simply gazes at me with a fond expression that makes me feel all warm and gooey inside. Like a chocolate chip cookie fresh out of the oven. A *homemade* chocolate chip cookie.

Then he squeezes my hand tightly and says, "I love *you.*"

I very quickly stop thinking about cookies. "You . . . you do?"

"Were you not listening to the song?"

Unable to resist a chance to tease him, I say, "I mean, I was kind of distracted by your terrible voice."

He frowns in classic Grumptopus style, and I laugh, reaching out to grip his shirt and tug him in even closer to me, our hands still clasped between us.

"I'm just kidding! Well, kind of. You really won't be winning any Grammys, but it was the most amazing thing I've ever heard. That's one of my favorite Skyler James songs. How did you know?"

His free hand comes around to my waist. "May picked it out. And helped recruit people and organize everything."

Of course. God, I love my fucking daughter. I totally forgive her for scaring the crap out of me with that bogus phone call.

He lets go of my hand, and I almost whine at the loss, but then he reaches up to cradle my face. "I really am sorry. I was an idiot. But I need you to know that I want to be with you. You make my life better. You always have. And if you feel the same about me, then I promise I'll do everything I can to keep that gorgeous smile on your face every day. I'll always be there for you, for whatever you need. And May too, obviously. I love you."

I open my mouth to tell him that I love him too. Because boy, I fucking do. But then I remember.

"What about your dad?" I ask cautiously, not wanting to ruin this but needing to know how it's going to work.

Then it hits me that this wonderful grand gesture he just did for me was extremely public, and there's absolutely no way his dad won't find out about it. I glance around us, panicking, but he gently takes me by the chin and guides my eyes back to his.

"He was out there somewhere," he says.

"Wait, your dad was *dancing*?" I ask incredulously. "I didn't see him."

He snorts. "Oh hell, no. He was just watching. And I already came out to him two days ago."

I gasp. "You did? For me?"

"Well, yeah. But it was also something I needed to do for me." He chuckles. "Turns out, he already knew. Apparently, I was the clueless one, not him."

I'm trying to wrap my brain around what he's saying, but at this point,

I'm so overwhelmed. Did the town really just do a flash mob? Did Travis really sing like a frog? He came out to his dad after spending half his life hiding who he was? Or thinking he was hiding it, I guess.

Did Travis Reed actually tell me he loves me?

Oh, shit. I didn't say it back.

"I love you!" I blurt out frantically. Probably too loudly. Because I don't want him to take it back.

"Thank god," he says, much quieter. And then he kisses me.

It's not brief, not chaste.

He kisses me like he's missed me as much as I've missed him. Like maybe he wants to meld us into one person. He kisses me like half the town isn't watching us, but they definitely are. The clapping and cheering that starts up makes that abundantly clear. And still, he keeps kissing me.

I kiss him back with everything I have.

When we finally break for air, we're both smiling like fools. He goes in for one more quick kiss, then says, "So what do we do now, and how do we make these people go away?"

As if on cue, my stomach lets out a loud, long rumble, and we both laugh.

"Can you make me a burger?" I ask, using my sweetest voice. The one I know he can't say no to.

He smiles at me, looking honestly happier than I've ever seen him. And he says, "Baby, anything you want, it's yours."

I grin, taking his hand and leading him down from the gazebo. Then together, we walk away from the crowd, ignoring everything our friends and neighbors are calling out to us. When I gesture for my family, May, Elise, and Grant follow us across the street and over to the diner.

Travis pulls out a chair for me at an empty table, and I sit. But I can't take my eyes off him as he goes behind the counter to pour a cup of coffee. Setting it down in front of me, he presses a kiss to the top of my head. And damn, I could get used to this.

As he turns to walk away again, I reach out and grab his ass. Because I can do that now. Even if he'd probably still prefer I don't do it in public.

He jumps and slaps at my hand, but he's laughing. It's a beautiful sound.

Taking a sip of coffee, I smile in contentment. Perfect, like always. The truth is though, I don't need Travis to make me coffee or burgers or pancakes, as much as I crave those things. Even if he was as terrible of a cook as I am, I'd still want him.

I'll wait until we're alone to tell him that when he gave me his heart, he gave me the only thing I really need from him. The rest is just a bonus.

EPILOGUE

BRENDEN

SIX WEEKS LATER

R ight there, yes, yes, *yes!*"
"You like that, baby?" Travis rasps as he nails my prostate repeatedly.

I'm bent over the desk in my office, trying to be quiet, but *fuck*, it's hard. My forearms are braced on the desk, and he's using my hips for leverage, so I really don't need to do anything but take it. But I'm greedy, so I keep doing my best to push back and meet his thrusts. I want him as deep inside me as he can go. I want all of him, everything, always.

I moan wantonly when he reaches around for my achingly hard cock and starts stroking.

"*Shhh*, I've got you," he soothes. "But you can't be too loud."

He's right, though at this point, I'm so far gone that I'm not sure I care if anyone hears us. I just need to come.

We haven't made it a habit to fuck in my office, but I'd be lying if I said this was the first time I've gotten so intimately acquainted with my desk. One of my favorite times was when he laid me across it, pushed my knees up toward my shoulders, and ate me out like I was his last meal.

As he trails kisses up my spine while continuing to stroke me—the sweetness in total contrast to the harsh way he's driving into me—my legs begin to tremble.

"I'm close, I'm so close," I tell him desperately.

"Me too." His voice is right by my ear now, the huskiness making me shiver. "Your ass feels amazing squeezing my cock. Gonna fill you up as soon as you come for me."

Those dirty words and one flick of his wrist over my cockhead are my undoing. I bite my lip to keep from screaming as I shoot off into his hand.

He tries to catch it all so we don't make a mess of the desk, but I think he's distracted by his own orgasm. He bites my shoulder in a primal way as he fills my ass with his warm release, and then he drapes himself over my back, breathing heavily.

Less than a minute later, when I'm only barely regaining the use of my legs, there's a knock on the office door. Travis and I jerk away from each other as May's voice calls out, "Dad, are you in there?"

It's like I've been doused with a bucket of cold water. Thank fucking god we were already finished, because hearing my daughter's voice during sex . . . *Eww*, no, I can't.

When Travis elbows me in the side, I call back, "Yes, I'm here, but I'll be out in a minute! No need to come in."

"Um, okay," May says through the door. "Is Travis in there with you? I thought he'd get here before me and Grandma and Grandpa."

"What? No! I mean, yes, he's here, but we weren't doing anything," I ramble compulsively. "There's absolutely no sex happening in here."

"Oh god, Dad, please shut up," May says. And the look Travis gives me says the same thing.

I cringe. "Right. Well . . . we'll be right out. Go to the dining room and grab a table for us."

"Got it," she says. "And then we'll never speak of this again."

My thoughts exactly. This is mortifying for both of us. Once it's clear that she's left, though, awkward laughter spills out of me.

Travis shakes his head, and I realize he's standing there with a hand covered in my cum.

"Oh, shoot," I say, grabbing his hand and doing my best to clean him up with my tongue.

His eyes glaze over before he pulls his hand away and tells me, "Okay, I'll leave first and go wash my hands. And then you, uh . . ."

He glances down at my naked body, and *yeah*. I can already feel the cum starting to drip out of my ass. We really didn't think this one through. A condom would have been helpful. I'll just have to go to the bathroom to clean myself up as much as I can, and then I'll hope I don't wind up walking around with damp underwear.

"Yeah, you go," I say once he's dressed. "I'll be right behind you."

As he turns to leave, I grab his wrist, and he turns back to me.

"Kiss?" I request.

His smile as he closes the distance between us tells me he's more than happy to oblige.

By the time I get to the dining room, Travis, May, Elise, and Grant are already seated and drinking iced tea. I'm sure May's glass is the only one that's sweetened, because these other three are healthy weirdos.

There's a basket of rolls on the table, and the smell lures me over. When I take the empty seat between Travis and May, Travis squeezes my side gently, then rests his hand on my leg. Sunday lunches here have become a regular thing. Sometimes Travis's dad even joins us.

I never thought I'd have a family tradition like this, but it's pretty cool.

Elise and Grant don't make me anxious anymore. They just moved into their new house, and May's been going over to decorate her room there. They made it clear that she's welcome to spend the night any time she wants to, but they respectfully checked with me before telling her that.

And surprisingly, I love this. It doesn't make me jealous like it would have a few months ago. I can probably thank the therapist I've recently been seeing for that. (Turns out therapy actually works. Who knew?)

I'm already planning on encouraging her to go over there sometimes, so me and Travis can have the house to ourselves. Because as I recently and embarrassingly learned, the walls of my house aren't particularly thick. It'd be nice to let Travis fuck me so hard I scream the roof off. Or the other way around, I'm not picky.

"Dad," May whispers, leaning closer to me and abruptly banishing my dirty thoughts. "*Riley Rowland is here.*" The excitement in her voice is evident, even though she's keeping it down.

"Don't stare," I warn her.

"I'm not, but it's so cool. She's so pretty."

I nod in agreement. I already let May know we had a celebrity staying here so that she wouldn't freak out about it. Riley grew up in Mayweather, and apparently most of the town just treats the country star like a regular person.

I didn't live here back then, so I was admittedly pretty starstruck when I first met her. But I was still professional, and I instructed all my staff to be the same way.

May doesn't even listen to Riley's music much, but I knew she'd be excited because of the connection to Skyler James. Riley dated Skyler when they were younger. Supposedly, at least. A lot of stuff about Skyler's dating history is unclear now since he came out.

Though I do know Riley's been facing backlash because of their very public relationship, which people now believe was only for PR. I'm pretty sure that's part of the reason she left Nashville and came to rent a room here indefinitely.

Sneaking a peek over at her table, I notice she's sitting there with only a glass of water. And while I trust Addison and the servers to do their jobs, I figure it couldn't hurt for me to pop into the kitchen and check that she's being well taken care of. So I excuse myself from the table.

I don't expect her to post on social media about the inn—I don't think she wants the public to know where she is—but I still want to make sure we keep her exceptionally happy.

In the kitchen, everything appears to be going smoothly. Addison is at the counter, cutting up chunks of fruit and tossing them into a blender.

"Hey," I say. "Do you know Riley's in the dining room? Someone's waiting on her, right?"

"Of course," she snipes at me. "Everyone's taking care of the famous princess. Don't worry."

I frown. "She's not being demanding, is she? She's been nothing but sweet to me."

Addison sighs and goes to the fridge, coming back with two different juice cartons. "No, she's not. She's just *there*. All the time. With her red hair and her flimsy little sundresses."

As understanding dawns on me, I have to fight back a grin. "Oh my god, you think she's hot," I whisper gleefully.

With a glare, she says, "No, I don't." Then she huffs as she pours juice into the blender. "Fine, yes. I'm a lesbian and I have eyes. But who cares? She's famous and too young for me. And let's not forget that she's straight. Little America's country sweetheart, right?"

"You do know why she came back here to lay low, don't you?" I ask, glancing around the kitchen to check that none of the other staff is listening.

"How the heck would I know that?"

"There were like twenty gossip articles about it."

She looks intrigued for a second, but she tries to hide it with a shake of her head. "I don't have time for gossip. I have a kitchen to run, and you're in my way." With that, she pops the lid on the blender and turns it on, the noise drowning out any response I might have had.

Well, fine. If this is how she wants to be, then I'll let her find out on her own that someone recently posted a video online of Riley in a dive bar, drunk and making out with another woman.

"Here," Addison says, thrusting a glass of freshly poured smoothie at me. "You can bring this to her."

"You made her a smoothie?" I question, eyeing it. They're definitely not on the menu. "I thought you said she wasn't being difficult."

"She's not." Addison hesitates, then says, "I offered."

I snort a laugh. "Oh yeah?"

"Shut up," she demands, but that only makes me laugh harder.

"Tell me again how you feel about her flimsy little sundresses," I tease.

She fixes me with a look that's clearly meant to be intimidating. And while she's my employee and we're sort of friends now, it still works. "Look," she says sharply. "I'm happy for you that you got your man and now you're all domestic. But not all of us are looking for that shit, so back off."

I hold up my hands in surrender, one clutching the glass, and literally start backing away. This could get interesting.

After delivering the smoothie to Riley and ensuring she doesn't need anything else, I head back to my table to find that they all ordered lunch without me.

When I pout, Travis kisses my cheek and says, "I ordered you the French dip with fries." Which is exactly what I was in the mood for.

I take his hand, sighing happily. What a wonderful, wonderful man.

ALSO BY TAMMY SUBIA

Heartbreak Honey (MM)
It Always Leads to You (MF)

ABOUT THE AUTHOR

Tammy Subia writes romances that are both sweet and spicy. While most of her stories are M/M, she sometimes spreads the love to other pairings too. If she's not writing or listening to filthy audiobooks, you can find her in New England spoiling her cat, drinking iced matchas, and watching *Gilmore Girls*.

Connect with Tammy: 🅾 tammysubiabooks